THE ROARING

THE ROARING

T. KATARINA TAYLER

STØRMY
HOUSE PRESS

STORMY HOUSE PRESS

The Roaring

This is a book of fiction. Names, characters, places, and
incidents are either drawn from the author's imagination or
are used fictitiously. Any resemblance or reference to actual
persons, living or dead, business establishments, events,
organizations, or locals are used fictitiously or are entirely
coincidental.

Printed in the United States

First Edition, April 2021

Library of Congress Control Number: 2020926034
ISBN 978-1-7359005-3-7

Cover design concept by Tasi Tayler
Cover illustration by Jorden Salzmann
Copy edit by Sara Magness

www.stormyhousepress.com

I dedicate this book to my Nana, who I know is dancing the Charleston up in heaven. This one's for you Nana.

Now, let's take it back to

The Roaring, shall we?

PROLOGUE

There was never an era so full of glamour yet so burdened by misfortune at the same time. An era where alcohol was illegal, yet the entire country drank its way into a roaring oblivion.

It was the twenties, *the 1920s*. Things were different. The time had its own rules and its own rule breakers—different from any other era. It seemed that the scandals were more scandalous, and good people participated in breaking the law while bad ones helped them. People cared less and let loose, girls cut their hair boy-short, and along with shorter hair came shorter dresses. The 1920s invented a new woman. Necklines became lower and hemlines higher. Heels were taller and makeup was bolder. In 1920 women gained the long-awaited and well-deserved right to vote, and with that came a new generation of women.

History gave these 1920s women a name: flappers. They wore beaded headpieces accented with a feather, long strings of pearls, red over-lined lips, and the scent of floral perfume. We call it the Roaring Twenties, and why exactly is that? It's because it was nothing less than an absolute roar. These stories showcase the twenties in its finest and not-so-finest moments. The good and the bad. Many stories intertwined. Many memories. Many lessons. Read and you will find out why exactly the 1920s was not only an era to remember, but one to relive. The music set the tone and the people set the scene. The events set the plot and New York City set the stage.

This isn't your average story with a beginning, middle, and end ... but rather one of many beginnings, middles, and ends. Many stories that make up *The Roaring*

These stories are all over the place—as were lives during the ever so *Roaring* Twenties. Stick with me and in the end, I promise you, you'll grow fond of our special six and their motion-picture-like lives.

Their **Roaring** lives.

WHERE IT ALL BEGAN

The *roaring* music, the *glitzy* fashion, the *glamorous* life. Living in the 1920s was eccentric. From the flapper dresses to the speakeasies, the parties to the cars. The Roaring Twenties was quite the time to live in. A dramatically *alluring* time, if you may. It was the jazz age; the era of *romance* and *excitement.* A time where bathtub gin was all the rage and bootlegged alcohol ran wild. An era that made its mark for eternity, especially when it was spent in the electric city of **New York.**

Scarlett Roxy Elliott, who was known as Roxy, was a 17-year-old girl living on Manhattan's Upper West Side. She was the single most intriguing person you'd ever meet. The most popular, most admired girl in school. The cat's meow, and the center of all attention. Her mother Caroline up and left her and her father a year before our story begins. Roxy lived with her father in **The Dakota**, an elite residential building located on Central Park West. She was an only child and spoiled by her dad (the don of the Elliott crime family). With golden brown hair and copper brown eyes, she was absolutely gorgeous. Known for her beauty. The girl *all* girls wished to be and *all* boys wished to be with. Roxy was a wild one; she was lively, always fearless, and *quite* entertaining. Ambitious and rather intelligent, Roxy Elliott was one of a kind. Miss Elliott got the most out of the era—she lived it with absolute allure and charm. A dame who was kind to everybody, everyone's friend, but had her *best* friends. Her two best girlfriends were Marie and Virginia.

Marie Romano came from a very well-off family, and a father of Italian descent. She was bold, honest, charming, and rather friendly. Marie lived only a few blocks from Roxy with both of her parents and her two siblings, in a townhouse much too big for them. Miss Romano and Roxy had known each other since they were just four years old. Almost like sisters, their bond was extremely strong. They were almost always with each other, as was the whole group. Roxy and Marie shared everything. The two girls were the best of friends.

Then there was **Virginia Williams**, the sweet girl who lived across the park on the Upper East Side. Miss Williams was a soft soul with a kind heart, and one of two children. It was Virginia, her mother, and her brother who lived in a penthouse in one of the tallest residential buildings at the time. Virginia came from a long line of wealth, and when her mother divorced her father, they only grew in riches. She moved to the city in

1917 with her mother and brother. Her father, still back in Chicago with his third wife, whom Virginia was not fond of, was shy when it came to calling only daughter. There was always something or someone more important than Virginia. Needless to say, it didn't bring any sliver of sadness to her exceptionally glamorous life. Virginia lived her life with no worries and always had her friends to help her through the hard times. Roxy, Marie, and Virginia had been the closest of friends for as long as they could remember.

As for the other best friends, the boys of the group, there was Johnny, Dalton, and Frankie. **Johnny Davis** was not your average American 1920s high-school boy. He had dated almost all the girls in school—he was popular, handsome, *and* rich. Admired by all, Johnny was the first in school to own his own automobile, the 1924 Rolls-Royce Silver Ghost. It was quite the car, if I do say so myself. He'd often make weekend trips with different girls to his mansion in The Hamptons, an invitation any girl would go wild for, and Frankie and some other new dame would often join him. He was Johnny Davis, the boy who could do anything he wished. With his absentee parents Lillie and Allen who cared only for themselves, him and his older sister Beverly had the privilege that every adolescent so longed for, the ability of *complete freedom.*

Dalton James, however, was *very* disciplined. With a curfew of eight pm, he was not exactly fortunate enough to have the free-spirited life of Johnny. That being said, it didn't hold him back from partying with the rest. He just had the wonderful added stress of worrying about his parents finding out. Dalton

5

James was a smart boy, a preppy kid. One who would attend an Ivy League school. He was on the path to success, with his parents being big-shot criminal lawyers. Dalton was the nice guy, the one you could count on for everything. With that being said, he was also Mr. Tough Guy and would do anything to protect one of the girls. The type of guy who stood up for what was right, but also loved everybody and gave everyone a chance, even the bad ones. Dalton loved all of his friends very much and considered them family. The gang wouldn't have been the same without Mr. James.

Last but certainly not least, there was Frankie. **Frankie Matthews** was the intelligent bad boy of the 1920s. He, like Johnny, could get any girl he desired, and he sure did. Frankie unfortunately suffered from very strict parents similar to Dalton's, with his father being semi-abusive to him (but not to his mother). However, unlike Dalton, it made Frankie all the more rebellious. He was not only the most handsome boy in the whole high school, but also the most well liked. Everyone wanted to be his friend—he and Roxy had that in common. Nevertheless, Frankie was the boy always getting into trouble. Roxy and Frankie often got into trouble together. The young lovers were inseparable. The two carried out the most pranks, threw the biggest most exhilarating parties, and got into the most unfortunate of events with every stunt they pulled. Frankie and Roxy had known each other since kindergarten. They were extremely close and extremely in love, yet they somehow didn't know it. You could say they were cluelessly in love; they were Roxy and Frankie, loved by all and in love with each other.

Regardless of that pair's oblivious romance, all six of them loved each other like family. A very close-knit clique. The best of friends, the most popular, and the most well loved.

This is a story of The Roaring. The Roaring Twenties. Our stories take place in 1925 New York City. The story of Roxy Elliott, Marie Romano, Virginia Williams, Johnny Davis, Dalton James and Frankie Matthews. I invite you back into the jazz age and into the events that follow the group of six extremely fascinating friends, into their rather complicated lives, through the pages of the now not-so-secret diary of Roxy Elliott, and the narration of an outsider who witnessed it all go down in each and every moment. Welcome to the stories that made the 1920s as famous and as eccentric as we know today. How memorable and brilliant they truly were—the reason the decade is described and known the way it is. The famous name it was awarded: the _Roaring_ Twenties.

CHAPTER 1

THE FIRST ROARING NIGHT OF 1925

"I'm not going to say it again, Johnny—get in here, we have to go, if we don't leave soon it's all gonna be over! We are going to arrive at an empty house …"

"My God, I'm coming Roxy. I'm on the telephone, can you not yell at me?"

The friends were waiting in Johnny's car for him to say goodbye to all of his "girlfriends" before they were off on their little trip, driving upstate for a party thrown by Marie's cousins.

"I am not going to say it again, Johnny—"

"I'm coming Roxy, calm down!"

"It's not going to matter anyway, he's got a flat," Marie sighed.

"He's got a flat?" Frankie questioned.

"I do not have a flat. The right tire upfront is just a little deflated, that's all."

Frankie and Dalton shared a look and a laugh.

"No Johnny, it's a flat—"

"That's impossible, this car is the cat's meow! It doesn't get *flat tires*, it's barely but five months old. I'm telling you … it's fine! Let's go."

It turned out Johnny's "deflated" tire was in fact a true flat, and by the time they figured that out it was too late in the day to make it in time, as they had an over four-hour drive—and though "fashionably late" was their style, "obnoxiously late" was not. So no, they didn't make it upstate to the party that cold January evening, but in the end, it had maybe been for the best.

Roxy was more than upset that Johnny had been the cause of what now looked like a dull night, though she didn't know how dull the party itself would *actually* be this year (in comparison to the party she usually attended or the one she threw herself). When she realized they wouldn't make it to the long-awaited Romano upstate mansion party, her thoughts shifted in a different direction. Roxy would throw her own party that night, her own *exhilarating* party.

In great thanks to her father and family owning and operating speakeasies all over New York City, she had a very fortunate unlimited source of alcohol, which then of course came in handy for the *many* parties she threw. Not to mention it being almost the same weekend as her annual affair she had held for the past decade. Within only but a few hours, Roxy planned the glamourus affair and held it just a week before she had usually in the past. It was as if the Romano party hadn't even existed in the first place. The vain grief over not making it upstate had vanished from the six.

She was now in tunnel vision, determined to turn her next week's party into one happening just hours later. Roxy and the gang put together the annual night at the eleventh hour, with the help of her many maids and butlers. As the extravagant affair was coming together, the six worked together to change the date of the party to that very night, then had men accessorized by white gloves hand deliver them to the high society guests.

Roxy had a divine sense of style, in everything she wore *and* did. Her invitations were held individually in small but heavy glass boxes, tied with deep-red silk ribbon to ensure the top was held on tight. The box alone was something to keep forever, yet the surprise inside was much more exciting. A white piece of perfect card stock with dark-red shiny words was the key to one of the most fabulous nights of the year. When you opened up your door to see this mesmerizing box delivered to your doorstep, your eyes lit up with excitement and joy. The invitation was perfumed with Roxy's ever so iconic scent of Chanel No. 5, and on the back, red lips smack in the middle showcased Roxy's special style and charm. She spritzed every letter she wrote and every invitation she gave with her perfume and kissed the back of them. *All of them.* Her red lips were a sign of how much she cared for and loved everyone she associated with. Roxy was kind to everyone, but she had her crowd, her special large circle whom she socialized with most. She was of a certain class, a class that required work and specific standards. Not everyone was invited to her soirées, especially her annual party. You see, there were certain social classes back then, and you stayed well within yours. The elites with the elites, keeping wealth surrounding you every which way.

January 9th, 1925

Dear Diary,

Tonight I have my annual soirée, only it's a week earlier than usual due to the unfortunate flat tire Johnny had that prevented us from the party at the Romano's upstate mansion. Boy how that would have been a night, but I'll make sure mine's better. This is, after all, my biggest party of the year, my most anticipated. The party that gets wilder every year, the night of exhilaration that I started back when I was just seven years old. This will be the tenth one. Oh how I remember the very first party—we were so young and innocent. Us girls played music and dressed up in our mother's clothes, dancing around in my bedroom.

I miss the days where I wished to be a teenager and almost all grown up. The days where I put on my mother's red lipstick and shiny pearls, wore her perfume and fancy dresses, and stole her heeled shoes.

It's hard to believe that's how the first iconic party started. The party used to be all girls up until we were fourteen. We would stay up all night and do the most crazy things.

This year will be the first year Marie, Virginia and I will begin the excitement at midnight and keep it going till the sun rises, in honor of the ten-year anniversary of the very first time I held this special night. It'll be at my father's speakeasy below our building, since there will be a bar full of champagne and crystal glasses for us to take advantage of.

Earlier today the girls and I went to that new department store, Barneys, to find ourselves the most amazing of dresses. My dress, beaded from the top till the fringe at the bottom, is the cat's meow and I know once it's on me it will be admired by all the boys.

Though, I'm hoping to catch a certain someone's attention tonight. Marie and Virginia's dresses are nothing but the bee's knees, and paired with the handbags they choose, we are all going to be dressed to the nines.

This party, of course, consists of a certain dress code: boys must wear a proper suit and tie while girls are fully dressed up. There are only forty-five guests invited and twenty on a waiting list in case some can't make it—and if they're not dressed in proper attire, Johnny will be escorting my guests out. Dalton will be the doorman till everyone has arrived, and the password is top secret and passed on only by ear. If anyone spreads it to the wrong fella, they are not only off the list but the password must be changed.

It can sure as hell be a lot of work, but I know it's all

worth it when Monday comes around and the entire school is
thanking me and my friends.

    Roxy and the gang held this party every year up until they
were ninety years old—it was an honor to be on the wait-list
and an even bigger honor to be invited. This was the night
everyone wished they could be a part of. It wasn't like her other
parties, it was the *annual affair.*

    The clock struck twelve and the wealthy, well-picked
adolescents flocked to The Dakota, to the secret underground
speakeasy owned by the Elliott name. With the girls all dressed
up and the boys looking on point, this was the event of the year.
The exclusive *first* party of 1925. A *true* Manhattan gathering.
Her party was such a roar that the friends had forgotten about
their original night's plan at the Romanos', which the talk of the
town said had been a drag this year anyway.

    "Well you look rather dapper, Frankie baby," Roxy yelled
over the roaring live jazz.

    "Why thank you love, might I say you're glowing with
charm yourself?" Frankie wasn't shy with complements.

    "Oh Frankie, don't you just know how to make a girl blush,"
she teased. "But I have to say, who's the broad you decided to
bring … I'm most positive she wasn't on the—"

    "You see, I understand she wasn't invited, but since she's
with me I— I figured she could enjoy all the dance and music
and the glitz and glamour that follows you, Roxy." He batted his
long eyelashes and gave her a smirk, then a kiss on the cheek.

    "I see," Roxy smiled. "Alright then, how 'bout we show her

some dance and some glitz and glamour—the music is right and you know the Charleston, don't you?" Her eyes lit up as she grabbed his large hand, to which Frankie found it hard to refuse. "You don't mind, Elle, do you?" she said in a tone that was not meant to be taken as a question.

"I'll be right back, sweetheart," Frankie told his date.

The two couldn't keep their hands off each other, dancing all night long. Frankie's "girl" was ignored by him till dawn, when he was too drunk to remember her name but knew he was responsible for taking someone home. Although that didn't matter much, because by two in the morning she had left with the boy Roxy was set out to impress—the *irony*. As for the party itself, the music was loud and the champagne was crisp, the air was filled with laughter and the scene was straight out of a movie. The sun eventually rose and her many guests cleared out, leaving only the saucy six.

January 10th, 1925

Dear Diary,

Matthews and I danced all night—which was wonderful yet quite bothersome. I asked him for one dance, only to make his mystery date envious, but we somehow managed to never stop. He and I danced ALL night, and I'm not quite sure how to feel about it.

Anyways, enough talk about Frankie and his devilishly charming ways—the party will be the talk of the town. Marie had an interesting time with a new boy she found, and as for Virginia, she partied hard with just about everyone. Johnny was a flirt all night, as usual, and ended up sleeping with some broad in a private room. Dalton tried to make sure we all didn't drink too much of the good stuff, but failed miserably as he somehow ended up more than tipsy on gin and bubbly.

Frankie and I ended up asleep together on the bar counter, Marie and Virginia on a table, and Dalton and Johnny—well, they said we were to never speak again about the two snuggled up on the same small couch fast asleep. Of course, I had to write this down, just in case I forget or someone someday reads this. I would want them to giggle at the thought of it. Virginia and I woke up first and had a laugh when we found them on one of the red velvet sofas at opposite ends, dreaming about the night before. However, I am still confused as to how and why Frankie and I fell asleep on a bar counter together ... with his arm well around me. Although he did look rather dapper, I feel like I wasted my entire night dancing with him instead of the boy I've had my eye on since the beginning of the school year. The back aches I have today, my God! But we had a roaring time, so all in all I'm not one to complain. I am sure not going to worry about anything like that—we have bigger problems on our horizon. The kitchen maid situation is a real doozy, did that god-awful thirty-something-year-old woman think she could steal from the Elliotts? My God! And now how *am I supposed to have breakfast in the morning with the gang, especially on a Sunday before church?*

The weekend was filled with lots of excitement from Roxy's annual affair, but it soon came to an end with the gloomy approach of Monday, an eventful weekend's coming.

Saturday night, the night after the speakeasy party, Roxy's father Dennis discovered their kitchen maid in an attempt to steal a string of pearls from a hidden jewelry box in the master bedroom closet. Pearls that belonged to Caroline, Roxy's mother, who had left her family without a goodbye in March of 1924. *Or should I say abandoned?* Dennis fired the maid and was in search of a new one. For now, however, they had no cook, and he was *more* than clueless in the kitchen. When Sunday morning came around, Johnny and Dalton encountered an unusual side of Miss Elliott.

"Cooking like a housewife, Roxy? I'm not sure I've seen this side of you," Johnny said as he and Dalton walked into her grand kitchen.

"I agree with Johnny here, Scarlett Roxy—I didn't know you were the stay at home and cook kind of dame," Dalton laughed. The boys always gave the girls trouble, and they would especially throw Roxy a good tease. They knew she hated the idea of a woman in the kitchen, contrary to the times.

"Oh boys, don't you ever say that. I will never be a housewife—not *ever.* And I'm baking, *not* cooking. I'm making brownies. One of our maids, *the one who cooks*, stole from us and now we're in search of a new one," she said with a sigh. "I decided to make all of us a batch of brownies before church, since there's no one else to. So be grateful, you fools."

"Well I don't mind that at all, but last time I checked— brownies didn't qualify as a breakfast food …" Dalton told Roxy.

The gang always got together at Roxy's for breakfast before church. They usually sat down in one of the grand dining rooms looking out to Central Park, with a table full of breakfast laid out for them by the kitchen maid. The Elliotts had multiple maids and butlers in their residences. Each one had their own tasks and parts of the residence they took care of.

"Like I said, I don't cook—it's either brownies or we sit through two hours of preaching hungry."

"Alright then, brownies'll do!" Dalton said calmly; there was no point in arguing with Roxy, she won *every* fight.

"Attagirl, bake us brownies!" Johnny said as he winked at Dalton, before taking a sip of Roxy's tea.

"Oh shut your mouth Johnny, or you're getting nothing," she laughed.

Roxy handed each boy a brownie as Frankie walked in.

"Mr. Davis, Mr. James …" She looked at Frankie with a glare, still mad at him for distracting her from the boy she wanted to talk to at the party. "Matthews, don't you just stand there with your hand out like a puppy waiting for a treat. If you want one, then get one yourself," she sassed.

"Excuse me darling, are you upset with *moi*?"

"Oh Frankie, you are really a smart one, you know that?"

"Oh *Roxy*, would you like to tell me why you're extra sassy this morning? I mean, it is … church day and all. Shouldn't we try to be extra kind and thankful on this fine morning?" He gave her a wink.

"You danced with me all Friday night when you damn well knew I was going to ask Dean to dance. I had told you about him as we were all planning the party and delivering invitations."

"Dean? Who's Dean? I don't think I know a Dean. Boys, do you know of this Dean?" He took a sip of her tea.

"Frankie, Dean is the boy I've had my eye on all of junior year. You distracted me from him and—"

"I distracted you from him?"

"Yes, yes you did."

"I'm sorry—you see, I thought dancing went both ways. Oh darling, you know the 'it takes two to tango' saying, don't you? A new song began and we continued to dance. If anything, it was you who distracted me from Ellis!"

"Ellis," Roxy glared.

"Yes, *Ellis*, the girl I brought with me. The girl who you took away from me when you brought me to the dance floor to do the Charleston."

"Ellis …"

"Yes Roxy, Ellis!"

"Frankie, her name is Elle," she said as Johnny and Dalton shared a laugh.

"Oh cut it out, you two," he answered back to the boys.

"Alright alright, how 'bout no one distracted anyone. Roxy, you missed your chance with Dean; and Frankie, you abandoned your girl—*Elle*—but not because one distracted the other. Okay? My God, you two are like an old married couple."

18

Johnny made an attempt at ending the elementary argument the two had been dragging on.

"Yeah, you were two friends who danced all night. That's all. Nothing to fight about," Dalton added while smiling at Johnny. Anytime the two fought (which was often), they knew it was only and purely because they were meant to jump into each other's beds, though that wouldn't happen for a *very* long time. The sexual tension between the two was strong, as was their refusal to give into it.

Marie walked in and heard part of the conversation. "Frankie and Roxy fighting again? Like an old married couple? Oh for heaven's sake, can it." She hugged the boys.

Roxy and Frankie shared a look.

"Just take a brownie, Frankie. I need to change my clothes for church. Marie, where's Virginia?"

"She's not coming today. I rang her earlier this morning and she said her and her mother were off to Connecticut to visit her grandma."

Roxy went upstairs, slipped into a new dress, changed her shoes, put on a white crochet hat, and grabbed her handbag as she walked out of her bedroom.

While exiting The Dakota, Roxy and Frankie continued to argue the point of who had distracted who that Friday night, finally to be broken up by the sound of church bells as they all sat down together along the wooden benches. Ever since they were young kids, the six had chosen to sit on the left side of the aisle and in the seventh-to-last row. Despite their wild nights and roaring parties, they would attend a church service every

Sunday morning. Kind of funny if you ask me. All Catholic and all dressed nicely, the group of friends sat through the service and parted ways after.

When Dalton was walking home later in the day from a bakery just three blocks from the Williams penthouse, he noticed a nervous Virginia pacing back and forth in front of her building's double doors, smoking up a storm as he passed by her residence.

"Virginia!" Dalton cupped his hands around his mouth and yelled while waving from across the street, as he made his way over to her.

Startled, she looked his way and answered, "Dalton! Oh, oh I sure did not expect you here. Why are you on the East Side? I know for a fact you live in the Village."

"I was picking up a pie from a family friend's bakery. Virginia, I was told you were in Connecticut to visit your grandmother?"

"Oh yes, it … it was a lie, okay? Sometimes we lie, we *are* human after all." She pulled out another cigarette for herself and offered one to her friend.

"No, we don't lie. Especially not to each other. When you spoke to Marie on the telephone this morning you made up some silly story?" he said as he lit his smoke.

"I know, I know, we don't lie. But …" She took a pause, debating how to say what she was about to tell him. "Well you see, well, alright so—"

"Virginia."

"My father is in town. He's in town and he's brought his

new wife. Only, this 'new' wife is not the new wife I met in 1923 at their wedding. No no, he has remarried *again* to a fourth woman and didn't tell me. I saw him this morning before Marie rang me. He was coming out of a taxicab with a woman, a woman I know. This woman is *not* the woman who was married to him last, that's not how I know her. I panicked as I heard the telephone ring, so I made up the Connecticut grandma story. She doesn't even live in Connecticut, actually, she lives down south in one of the Carolinas, I always forget which one," she raced through without a breath.

"Honey, continue about your father—"

"Yes! Right, alright." Virginia had the tendency to get off track; she suffered from attention deficit disorder, but didn't know it. "He's in New York to introduce me to my new stepmother, only she is *not* a woman I would ever consider a mother."

"What's so wrong with her? And Virginia, can we please go inside, it's very cold out here," Dalton said to her as he shivered and finished off his cigarette. The cold was not something that bothered Virginia Williams. She remained unfazed by the chill in the air, probably a result of the distracting situation.

"Not inside the building! Are you mad? My dad is in there waiting for me. I escaped through the back door this morning and haven't been back since. Let's go here," she told him as they walked into the corner diner.

"So, what *is* so wrong with this woman? You said you knew her, but not from being with your father. How exactly *do* you know her?"

"I know her from pictures, I've seen photographs of her and heard stories from my cousins in Chicago."

"Alright, what kind of stories?"

"Bad ones. She's bad news."

CHAPTER 2

THE DECKER FAMILY

"I don't think I understand—you have a *new* stepmother?" Roxy said to Virginia as she tried to explain her rather dire situation to the others.

After Virginia and Dalton's rather anxious 5th Avenue run-in, they went over to Johnny's and rang Marie and Frankie.

Johnny lived in the building right across from Roxy, The Majestic. His bedroom window looked out to Roxy's and when Virginia and Dalton arrived, he yelled for Roxy from across the street.

She then went over to his apartment, as did the rest of them that night.

"Yes, *Roxy*. My goodness, aren't you following along?" Frankie said sarcastically, following with a smirk.

"Oh shut your mouth Frankie, let her explain," she scoffed.

"You absolute children, would you *both* shut it?" Marie told the babbling duo.

"I'm not quite sure when they got married, but yes. They're married and I have a new stepmother."

"Wow, your father sure knows how to get the ladies," Johnny said as he and Frankie laughed.

Dalton looked over; he was the only one who knew the whole story. "Let her speak, dammit."

"It gets worse. She's not just some 'nice young lady' my dad fell in love with. She's really no *lady* at all. People like to call her a choice bit of calico, but I can tell you she is *not*."

"I don't know, Virginia—from what I can see in this photograph of her, she sure looks rather desirable." Frankie turned to Johnny and Dalton. "Am I wrong?" he winked.

"Frankie, Johnny, shut it. Would you like to leave? 'Cause I can walk you two out if you can't take this seriously," Dalton gruffly told them.

"What's with you, Dalton? You need a little giggle water to calm you down?" Johnny answered.

"Boys, please, I'm going to slap the both of you across the face if you don't shut your damn mouths," Roxy declared. The boys sank back into the couch, looked over to Virginia and smiled on command.

It was quite funny actually, and quite cute.

"My cousins back in Chicago told me about this woman last year when I visited them over the Fourth of July. They told me about stories they had heard of her. How she's been married now *five* times. She's only out for money. And I won't sit around and watch my father be with a woman like that. Even if he and I aren't always on the best of terms."

Frankie looked up. "Okay, so she's a gold digger? Big deal. Your father can handle that."

"Oh that's not all, Frankie. Every one of her husbands has 'died of a natural or unknown cause'."

"What?" they all asked, suddenly intrigued.

"Leaving her with almost their entire fortune."

"DID SHE KILL THEM?" Marie yelled as she stood up.

"Quiet down, Marie! My goodness. As for their deaths, I can almost assure you she was involved. I mean, wouldn't *you* think so?"

"I can't imagine she wouldn't have been. Coincidences like that just don't happen. But then, if this is true, she's already got all the money she would ever need. Why then work her way into the Williams family?" Dalton added.

"She has also been involved with organized crime," Virginia said with worry. They all looked over to Roxy, as she was looking down, examining her fresh manicure.

As the room fell silent and the attention shifted to her, Roxy looked up. "What, with the Elliotts? No no, my family only does bootlegging and gambling crimes, along with a coupla other things ... *but that's not the point*. We don't get involved with—useless—murder, or whatever the hell this woman has done. Only if someone is a threat to us, owes us something large, or is in harm's way. Gold digging, husband killing, isn't our way of acquiring money ... you all know that," she assured, trying to make her mafia background sound like less of a terror.

The Elliotts were a mob family, one of the biggest mafia families in the country—did I mention this yet? I'll explain a little later in this chapter. I'll enlighten you with who they really were and what exactly the Elliotts were involved with. However, I may hold off on some of the "mafia related details" for another time, specifically when it comes to this special family.

"I'm telling you, she wasn't involved with my family. I know I have a big family and all, but I know everyone we're associated with and she's not one of them." She handed Virginia the photo.

"Alright alright, that's not the point."

"Virginia, you need to talk to your cousins in Chicago."

"Dalton, have I had the time? I suppose I could phone them now," she said as she went over to Johnny's telephone.

The gang was sitting in one of his great rooms. Virginia gave her cousins a call and found out this mystery woman had married her father no more than six weeks ago. They all ended up asleep as time went on and night fell over them. The next day, they decided to investigate this new wife of Mr. Williams.

Virginia's new stepmother's name was Helen Bessler. She had never worked a day in her life, grew up with money, and married into even more. Helen seemed to have no criminal record, and they couldn't find any dirt on this so-far-perfect Mrs. Bessler. Or should I say, *formerly Bessler.*

January 12th, 1925

Dear Diary,

We are in a real doozy with Helen. I've tried as hard as I can to find out any information on Virginia's stepmother. I rang cousin Vita in Chicago and she's never heard of a Helen Bessler. My aunts and uncles know nothing of that name either. I rang just about everybody I knew in Chicago and didn't get one answer on who she is or who she's involved with. That is, until my grandfather came by to drop something off for Daddy.

At school today, all I could think of was one thing. One name: Helen Bessler. It seemed as if she didn't even exist. Virginia's cousins only knew of this woman by picture, and everybody I know has never heard of the name. And I know everybody. When my grandfather came over, however, he noticed the photograph on the table. He told me he had seen this woman before. I told him her name was Helen Bessler, or now technically Helen Williams. My grandfather had never heard of the name either but told me he's seen the girl in the picture. As I walked home today, I wondered to myself why it seemed that people only knew this woman by her face and not her name. Then it hit me.

Roxy, Marie, Virginia, Johnny, Dalton, and Frankie continued to use all of their failed resources to find information on this twenty-three-year-old Helen Bessler. Though, a group of seventeen-year-olds at an attempt to play detective doesn't always pan out.

"Your father is forty-two years old, Virginia! She's … *not*. That girl's too young for him—everything about her seems rather off," Roxy criticized.

"She's a grown woman, Roxy."

"No, she's *not*. She's a girl."

"She is in her twenties."

"She's twenty-three, Virginia!"

"I suppose a nineteen-year age gap is a bit much," Virginia admitted as Roxy glared at her, annoyed. Roxy then went over to Dalton.

"Don't you believe she's too young?"

"Oh for sure, and Virginia, why are you taking up for her? I thought she was 'bad news'."

"She is, Helen is real bad news, but I need to keep an open mind. Maybe I *am* mistaken. Maybe I'm making this a bigger deal than it is, just because she's my dad's new wife. My new stepmother. My new stepmother who is seven years older than me." Virginia fell into the couch.

Roxy and Dalton shared a look.

"Darling, you are not," Roxy said as she went back over to her. "What twenty-three-year-old marries an old forty-two-year-old?"

"Are you trying to get at something here, Roxy? Because if you are, I'm not picking up on it."

"You said yourself she only marries for money."

"Yes, and?"

"Men in their late twenties and thirties have money, Virginia."

"And?"

"Well, you see, I believe there's another motive here. Helen didn't need to marry *your* father, a forty-two-year-old man. She did not *need* to marry a Williams. There are plenty of other rich men in the sea."

"I guess you're right."

Dalton pondered, thinking about what Roxy had just said. "I'm with Roxy on this one. If she only marries for money, then supposedly 'gets rid' of her husband to inherit their fortune, why your father?"

I have to say, there *are* truly women out there like this. I like to call them the criminally insane. Though at least they are a very, *very* wealthy criminally insane.

"He's not even good-looking," Roxy said bluntly.

"Roxy!"

"What? He *is* sort of a combination between a dewdropper and a bimbo." Roxy and Dalton laughed.

"This is not funny, and my father is—very handsome," she assured.

"Handsome? I really wouldn't go that far. I mean come on, it's Mr. Williams for heaven's sake," Dalton muttered to Roxy as they laughed.

"Okay, guys come on. Stop being such children. You are right, Roxy, she's not only after his money. It must be something else. But why us then? What does he have to offer her? Sure he's a Williams, but it's not like he's an Elliott. And it's not like the Williams family has made any *real* enemies."

"I'm going to ask my grandfather about Helen. He told me before I left for school that he had seen her before. He didn't know the name Helen Bessler, however."

Roxy walked over to her grandparents' brownstone. They lived on West 85th Street between Columbus and Amsterdam Avenues, not far from Roxy's residence on West 72nd and Central Park West. She brought the picture of Helen to her grandfather and asked him where he had seen her. Mr. Elliott couldn't remember exactly where he had come into acquaintance with this woman, but only that he had seen her before. Her grandparents' chefs made them dinner, which Roxy stayed for, but left quickly after to go home. When Roxy arrived back in her penthouse at The Dakota, she rang Marie to gossip about Helen. She told her the details on her theory and that her grandfather had met her. Frankie phoned Johnny that night as well. The boys came to a conclusion that they should meet this Helen Bessler herself, and dig up any information they could find on this assumed criminal bearcat.

At school the next morning, the six devised a plan to meet her along with Mr. Williams. Frankie had the grand idea for a dinner party at Keens Steakhouse, *his personal favorite*. The girls told Frankie he only liked the plan because he got a steak dinner at his favorite place out of it, but he assured them this wasn't the reason behind the idea (though I'm not quite sure that's true). A dinner with the Williams family, the Elliotts, the Romanos, the Davises, and the James family would sure give an easy, non-suspicious way to find out about Helen. It would be a situation where their personal interrogation would seem nothing far from getting to know her in a casual dinner scene. Merely high-school adolescents edging to know more about their friend's new stepmother. That's not a weird situation, right? This dinner idea was pitched by each of them to each of their parents. Starting with Virginia and her father. He was staying at the Plaza Hotel on 59th and 5th Avenue. She knocked on his hotel door.

"Father, I'm so happy you came to visit me!"

"Oh, my sweet daughter, I have truly missed you," he said.

Was that really true? We may never know.

"Virginia, I would like you to meet someone," her father said, shifting to his left to reveal the woman herself.

"Well, hello Virginia!" She appeared at the door. "Your father has told me so much about you. Might I say you are even more beautiful in person! The photographs he has shown me don't do justice."

Virginia gave her a quick fake smile and a little half-nervous, half-annoyed laugh.

"I'm Helen Bessler."

As if she didn't already know.

"Hi, Helen," she answered sweetly.

"Virginia, this woman makes the best pumpkin pie! Even better than that bakery you love by your apartment," her father added.

"Oh, does she?" She gave Helen another fake smile. One that faded quickly.

"Your father is too kind! Why don't you come inside …"

Virginia entered the suite with no fear—she was there on a mission. A mission she knew she would accomplish.

"It was Helen's idea to come and visit you so soon. I was going to come for your seventeenth birthday in July, but she insisted on meeting you now!"

"Oh, did she?" Again with that fake smile.

"Oh, I did! I was eager to meet you, Virginia! I told your father I couldn't wait so long," Helen said, with such excitement that Virginia cringed on the inside, thinking about what an absolute twenty-something bimbo she was.

"So how long exactly did you know each other before tying the knot?" She went right in for it.

"Virginia!"

"What? I'm only curious," she said with innocence and a raised voice.

"Oh no, it's okay! We met just under a year ago and we have been married just shy of six weeks!"

Virginia raised her eyebrows. "Isn't that soon?" she grinned.

"Not one bit, I knew she was the one from the moment I laid eyes on her."

Must have been true—her father couldn't take his eyes off his young new bride.

"And how exactly did you meet?"

"My brother had met her in one of the Elliott speakeasies. He told me she was an Oliver Twist, the best dancer he had ever seen. He gave me her telephone number and since then we have been in love!"

"Oh, how sweet," Virginia said in a low, monotone voice.

"It sure was. When your uncle told me about your father, I knew I had to go out with him! He rang me that night and the next day we saw a show at the Chicago Theater. A wonderful jazz band," Helen added in.

Helen and Mr. Williams had been gazing into each other's eyes as Virginia was rolling hers. What a scene.

"That sounds delightful," Virginia said, getting ready to dive into the invitation for Keens. "I wanted to ask you if you would like to meet my friends and their families. They're quite the catch, I'm sure you'll love them. We have all planned a gathering at Keens Steakhouse for next Friday night. Would you and Dad be interested in joining us for a dinner party?"

She couldn't stand to watch them fawn over each other anymore.

"Oh honey, we leave Wednesday night."

"Daddy, I wanted to introduce Helen to everybody though. To the Romanos, the Davis family, the Matthews family, the James family, and of course, the Elliotts."

"Oh Charles, why don't we leave the Saturday after, instead of this Wednesday? It would be nice to extend our trip."

"Well, alright, if you're okay with that, Helen."

"I'd be more than happy to stay in New York for another week and a half."

"Then it's settled, we will join you and everyone for a dinner party on January 23rd." He sounded so formal.

"I will see you then, Father."

As Virginia started for the door, Helen jumped up toward her. "Wait!" she said anxiously. "Virginia, I would like to take you to tea this weekend. Would you like to have afternoon tea on Saturday? Next Friday is so far away!"

Virginia thought about Helen's offer. "I will have to see if I have plans or not."

Helen handed Virginia a piece of paper with their hotel room telephone number on it.

"Alright then, give me a ring if you can!"

"I will." There was that sweet, innocent, fake grin again. This time, however, it came from both sides.

When Virginia left the Plaza, she went over to Roxy's. Marie was already there. The two girls had been doing homework and smoking high-end cigarettes. Virginia lit one and started talking about everything that had happened after school when she met her father and Helen. She told them what Helen looked like, how she acted, and how she was toward her and her father.

"It seems like it's all an act!"

"Oh Marie! Maybe Virginia was wrong. Maybe Helen really *is* a genuine dame," Roxy laughed.

"Girls please, she was overly nice. Too nice. Way way *way* too nice. She wants to have tea with me, isn't that a bit strange?"

"If Helen wasn't a criminal, it wouldn't be."

Roxy and Marie shared a laugh at that one.

"Roxy's right. She *is* your stepmother now."

"What is that supposed to mean?" Virginia raised her voice.

"Maybe you should go ..." Roxy said with an idea in her mind. "You could go and dig up information about her. It would give us a head start for our dinner next Friday. We need as much information as we can get. We don't want to make fools of ourselves at a nice dinner." Virginia thought about what Roxy had come up with. Going *only* for an extra, pre-interrogation.

"You are absolutely right!"

The girls continued to talk about Virginia's tea date with her new stepmother. She then made a call to the Plaza and spoke to Helen, telling her she would love to have tea on Saturday. At school that next Wednesday, the girls talked to Johnny, Dalton, and Frankie about everything. Frankie made a reservation at Keens Steakhouse for their private dining room. *The one only given to the wealthy, elite New Yorkers.* The night was planned out and each of them had their own set of questions. Each that fit into the perfect puzzle that was, "Who is Helen Bessler?"

January 23rd, 1925

Dear Diary,

We walked into Keens Steakhouse with tunnel vision. Virginia was already there along with Marie and Johnny. Dalton came soon after me, and Frankie was the last to arrive. A dinner between the Williams family, the Romanos, the Davis family, the James family, the Matthews family, and the Elliotts. Let's just say ... it did not go as planned. Virginia was sitting next to her father with Johnny and his family on her other side. The table was long, fit for all of us specifically. We sat in the private dining room. On my right was Marie with her family, and on my left was my dad and then Uncle Clyde and Aunt

Eliza. Beside Charles Williams were Frankie and his parents, and next to Helen was the James family. It was as if we had her surrounded, this woman that had so easily infiltrated our lives.

If it was Virginia's issue, it was all of our issue. We stick together, always and for eternity. Helen wore bright-red lipstick, but not the classy kind, the tacky kind, and black satin gloves that went past her elbows. A dress that dropped down to the floor, and shoes that had little bows on the sides. Helen was quite put together, if I do say so myself. Besides the tacky choice in lip color, of course.

As the night began, I prepared myself to know who this woman really was, why she married Mr. Williams, and what exactly she had planned. Or if we had all been overacting and she truly had fallen for a forty-two-year-old. Although, I did have an idea on why she inserted herself into this specific family. We all did. All six of us were hungry for answers. I did not, however, expect everyone to take such a liking to her. My father and uncle, in particular. By the end of the night the room was filled with laughter. The laughter of everyone except the six people who planned the damn dinner. Not one question. All of us there, and all for the wrong reasons. Even Johnny couldn't get a word in. And Frankie—he usually knows how to insert himself well into conversations, he's real convincing. When it came to last night's dinner, however, he sat there staring at me with anger painted across his face. That boy was utterly useless.

Helen charmed her way through all of our families. It almost seemed as if SHE was the one performing the interrogation. An interrogation on OUR families. She took a particular interest in my family. No surprise there. The conversations that took place between her, my father, and my uncle were long and personal. This want—to—be flapper seemed to get all the answers she desired. Who knew the night would end with my father and uncle inviting Charles Williams and his new lady to a gathering in the ballroom at the St. Regis Hotel? The St. Regis is not meant for a woman like Helen Bessler. That little snake. I do not want her entering those doors next Saturday night. We are in the same position we were two weeks ago, especially since Virginia was not able to make her tea date due to an essay she didn't know she would have to write. All I can say is I get a bad feeling when she is in the room, and that's not good.

The dinner was a disaster in the minds of our now irate friends.

Keens Steakhouse will be remembered to them as the place they felt abandoned. A restaurant where only good things used to happen. Marie's first date took place at Keens Steakhouse. Johnny's cousin proposed to his now wife at Keens. Virginia's mother used to take her to Keens when she was young for a mouthwatering steak dinner on the eve of every birthday. Dalton's parents took him and the team to Keens after he won the baseball championship game in freshman year. As for Roxy and Frankie, they went for dinner together at Keens when their parents first gave them the freedom to leave the house alone at age ten, something young ten-year-old New York City kids found very exciting, so they had to mark the occasion with a special, memory-filled dinner.

At this point in time, where they are right now, they will soon resent Keens in an even greater passion than when they left.

Roxy is near to finding the *real* reason this so-called Helen Bessler snagged Mr. Williams and headed to town. This is the first event that leads to an ending with quite an unhappily ever after. I said to expect some ups and downs, didn't I? A shock and a sadness ... and then a happy ending. I said the joyful ending wouldn't last forever, however. I warned you that a happily ever after came before the grief and heartbreak that would come much later. Then to conclude in a recovered ending, though you may not know it. Does that make any sense? Oh, it won't matter, you'll get it in the end.

This is the *first* event, the *first* appearance of the Elliott–Decker feud. An occasion that reset the bad blood to boil. The Elliott gathering at the St. Regis Hotel was now taking place. Johnny and his family attended, as did the Romanos and Mr. and Mrs. Williams. The families entered the doors to the St. Regis, were greeted by men dressed in hats and white gloves, and were escorted to the grand ballroom. Many of Manhattan's best came to enjoy the Elliott carnival. That is, however, until the soirée seemed as if it was going up in flames, when Roxy discovered the answer to the inquisition we're all now curious about: Helen Bessler, if that is her name of course.

"Do I know you?"

"No, I don't believe we have ever met."

"I'm sure I do," Roxy said with certainty.

"I *think* I would remember a girl like you, Roxy Elliott."

"Well, I *think* you do." Roxy didn't mask her feelings as she greeted this girl who looked more than familiar.

"I can be sure we have never met."

She walked away. Roxy went over to Johnny.

"I've met her before. I know I have, and she's denying it."

"What?" Johnny said with confusion, enjoying his warm dinner roll.

"That girl, over there." Roxy pointed to a tall 18-year-old blonde.

Johnny raised his eyebrows, as Roxy had determination in her eyes.

"I'm certain of it."

All night long, Roxy thought long and hard about who the girl was and where she had met her. That was when a specific day came into her mind and her heart sank deep into her chest. Her eyes were wide with worry. She dashed back to Johnny.

"March 18th, 1922. Around three years ago, that's when I met her."

"Excuse me?"

"I knew I had. She *is* a liar!"

"Roxy, calm down—why are you so angry? She must have just forgotten. No big deal." He sipped his champagne.

"We need to talk to Virginia."

"Slow down babe, what's this all about?"

"That girl, she's not who she says she is. And—neither is Virginia's stepmother."

"I thought we were giving up on Helen?"

Roxy glared with displeasure at Johnny.

"What? We know she marries for money, we know she may or may not have killed her husbands, but she's too fast for us to follow. We cannot live our lives as private detectives for Mr. Williams."

"Johnny."

"Roxy—yes, she's bad. There is nothing we can do about it though. The organized crime stuff we can't do much about either."

"Johnny, that organized crime was with the Deckers."

He put down his glass. "What?" he said, now interested.

"Julia Decker, that girl who claims she has never met me. Her name is Julia Decker, and her sister is Virginia's stepmother," Roxy said.

"They're DECKERS?" His eyes widened with worry.

"March 17th was a day that stuck with me. It was the first time the Deckers had tried, *attempted*, to take away our power, and of course failed."

You couldn't touch an Elliott, even if you tried. However, the Deckers thought otherwise.

"It was the first time Thomas Decker, Julia and Helen's grandfather, broke into my grandfather's study to collect information on our speakeasies and who we import our alcohol from. He and his son also tried to uncover any family scandal he could find on the Elliott name. Thomas Decker found none, of course. My uncle caught him during the invasion and in the act of his failure, and to no surprise, guns were pulled. However, no one was hurt and my uncle let them leave, *under threat of course*. On March 18th I ran into Julia after church. I saw she was curious and staring at my mother while we were taking Communion, so I went over to confront her on why she was acting somewhat out of the ordinary. 'Cause I didn't like it. She told me her name was Julia Decker and that my family *ruined* hers. Now, we have been in a feud with the Deckers for generations; however, for a few years we had no interaction with them—whatsoever. The Elliotts and the Deckers had finally gone their separate ways, but when the prohibition hit, they felt differently, and the 'somewhat' understanding we had with them disappeared right into thin air. The Deckers blame us for their loss of the small power they once held. Funny isn't it. Anyways, Julia is nothing but a dumb dora who has been caught up in the lies of the Decker name. When she told me our family had ruined theirs, I laughed in her ignorant face and told her the Deckers ruined themselves, which is nothing but the truth. The Elliotts always held more power and we knew how to use it. The Deckers did not. I haven't seen her since, but I did remember the face she was sitting next to at church, and that face was Virginia's stepmother. Also known as Helen Decker, not whatever the hell made-up last name she gave herself. They were sisters, I remember that from a conversation I overheard."

"You mean eavesdropped?"

"No *Johnny*, overheard. You see, that's it—this goes deeper than we thought. It has nothing to do with gold digging or taking Mr. Williams's fortune. She married a Williams to get closer to us, the Elliotts. I had my assumptions but now I know for sure. It was a smart move, attempting to snag an in on the circle, but her little sister may have ruined it for her three years in advance." She took a breath. The Elliott family and the Williams family were very close with each other, as they were with Johnny, Frankie, Marie, and Dalton's families. "Mr. Williams just happened to be divorced, available, and the easiest to get to. The Deckers did their homework and devised a plan they assumed would be lethal to us. Miss dumb dora Julia over there is going to be very sorry, as everyone who shares the Decker name will be."

"I don't know if I'd call her a dumb dora—she *is* the reason that what they have planned will fail. If anything, we should be thanking her." He gave a subtle grin.

The two laughed. "I guess you are right, Davis. I need to tell Virginia, but first I need to let my family know."

"Why not tell Virginia now, she is right over—"

"Because my father and Uncle Clyde have planned a poker night with Mr. and Mrs. Williams. It was her idea … THAT MUST BE IT!"

"Huh?"

"Oh no Johnny, that *is* it. The Deckers are going to get my family out of the house to try and get a hold of something they could take us down with."

"You said they had tried before, and failed. What makes you

think they could get something this time?"

"They will have more time. This is what it's all about."

He stood still.

"Johnny, we need to go, now. I'll phone my father and then we can tell Virginia. After, I'll need you to get your car and we can race over to The Dakota. My uncle is there now, we need to warn him so we can all get what we need out of the penthouse. When the Deckers arrive tonight, my grandfather will be there to greet them. They will have lost this game once again. The Deckers have dug their own grave this time."

"Go ring your father and I'll get my car."

Not long ago, I told you I would soon explain the Elliott family in greater detail. Well, congratulations, the time has come, and I'll now happily enlighten you with who they really were and what exactly they were involved with. Why they are who they are, and why they have had an immense rivalry with a fellow crime family known as the Deckers.

To fully illustrate the Elliotts and the Elliott–Decker feud, I am going to have to first tell you who the Brooks were. The Brooks were Roxy's "other side of the family". Her mother was Caroline Brooks and her aunt was Daisy Brooks. Their mother and father, also known as Roxy's grandparents on her mother's side, were Ruth and Walter Brooks. The Brooks were into making alcohol. You could say moonshine was their specialty. Anything from rum to bathtub gin, vodka to brewing beer. It only became a hidden secret after 1920's ever so delightful gift of prohibition. Before then, everyone knew them as their own local supplier of booze. An expensive supplier, however.

The Elliotts in New York acquired a substantial amount of alcohol from them. The Brooks were one of two families they bootlegged alcohol from.

The Elliotts also had alcohol imported from a family they were close to in France. The Levees (pronounced *leh-vee*). Their relationship with each other went back generations. It was Dennis Elliott's great-grandfather who had his first encounter with the Levees in Paris in 1836. The two families instantly clicked and began a generations-long friendship, and the Elliotts visited them throughout the year on their trips to Paris.

The Levees had imported alcohol to them for decades for their restaurants and bars, which then became speakeasies in 1920. The Elliotts were the only family the Levees would send alcohol to, and they had among the best on the planet. The French family had their own speakeasies in Paris as well, but provided for themselves and the Elliotts *only*. The Deckers were not fond of the Levees' overseas bootlegging for the Elliotts, how they had their own private family sending them the highest quality of alcohol on the market, next to that of the Brooks. Jealousy is never a good look, but one they knew well. The Levees also sold their alcohol for the lowest price to the Elliotts, because of the relationship they had. The two families *were* family.

The original feud between the Elliotts and the Deckers began in 1852 when they wouldn't sell their alcohol to the Deckers for their own businesses. The Deckers figured the Elliotts got their booze so cheap, they could ask the Levees to send more over and offer to pay the Elliotts an extra small fee. The Elliott family said no due to their loyalty to the Levees—they would never have put them into a situation like that. Overseas alcohol trading was strictly only from the Levees to the Elliotts and no one else. The Deckers had many restaurants and bars in Manhattan during this time as well, but when prohibition hit in 1920, they were not as easily converted into speakeasies as the Elliotts' were.

The Deckers had two speakeasies in Manhattan and one in Brooklyn during prohibition. The Elliotts had seven in Manhattan, four in Brooklyn, one in Queens, five in Chicago, and three in LA. They also had a few in Boston and Philadelphia. The family was fortunate with their many secret spots of illegal alcohol consumption, and they were able to spread throughout many cities across America because of their resources, and because they were able to bootleg so much alcohol. There were also so many of them, as a family alone, and then add on all of their associates.

The Elliotts were no small crime family, and that was another reason they were who they were. Roxy's grandfather, Griffin Elliott, had six siblings who all married and had kids—leaving Dennis Elliott with four uncles and two aunts, and many, many cousins who all ran speakeasies and participated in the family business of crime.

Like I said before, part of the Elliott family's power remaining so high was due to their ability to have such a great quantity of alcohol in all of their speakeasies, making them the most well-known and the best in America's speakeasy scene. Everybody wanted to get into an Elliott speakeasy. Not to mention the whole mafia deal, which directly connects to why they own them—which we can dive deeper into a little bit later.

With the Elliotts refusing to help the Deckers in the importing alcohol deal, the Deckers could never be as successful as the Elliott family. Their restaurants and bars did not compare to any with the Elliott name behind them. That's when the heavy resentment began. When 1920 hit and they all converted quickly into speakeasies, the Elliott–Decker feud developed into rage. The Deckers were highly jealous of the Elliott name and the title it held—who wouldn't be? Though the Decker name was powerful in New York, it came in *no* comparison to Elliott. No name could.

So, as I've said, jealousy only grew on the side of the Deckers: a family who couldn't see themselves in the wrong. When a family member of each name would intertwine, they often got into fights in the streets. You could say it had a Capulet–Montague feeling to it.

The Deckers had wanted to take over the speakeasy scene for five years now, and they had been struggling with a way to do so. That brings us here, to the end of January 1925 on the Upper West Side. Virginia's stepmother was not who she said she was, and her poor bastard father was *far* from knowing. Virginia only had suspicions of this Helen because of her cousins in Chicago, thank God for them. To think of what would have happened if they had been clueless in this silent battle is to be filled with worry. Let's not go there, let us get back to where we really are. Things have unraveled quite quickly, and the end is all but a mystery. Well, for you at least.

Now, before we get to our unhappily ever after, then to a

somewhat joyous one, as I said before (oh how confusing), I'll let you read what you think is a conclusion to the Decker–Elliott feud. A feud between none other than two crime-committing, mafia-participating, wealthy-as-hell families. As of this very moment, the trouble stirred up by Helen Decker and the Decker family is a priority.

Our other ending, however, will take place *much* later. After I get through telling you the many other stories that took place in this era between the six families, primarily Roxy-related. It may seem endless and assuming, but stick with me, let me tell you these many stories, because I can guarantee you there will be an ending to all endings you will not expect.

But maybe it won't be an ending at all?

Oh, just read and see, why won't you …

CHAPTER 3

THE FALL OF THE DECKER FAMILY

Roxy raced to the telephone and rang her father. She told him everything she knew about Helen and warned him about what the Deckers could potentially be planning against the family. He knew it all. She was beyond confused, wondering how he already knew, but then of course quickly remembered that he's an Elliott, of course he would have known. Even I knew there was no way he was oblivious to Helen's secret agenda.

Dennis assured his daughter she shouldn't worry, that everything was under complete control. All Roxy could think about was why her father didn't tell her sooner. He explained to Roxy how dangerous all of this was. As rival mafia family dealings usually were. Anyways, the "poker game" he had agreed to with Helen and Mr. Williams was an idea sent from an angel, he told her. It was *his* way of getting to the Deckers, *not* the other way around. He knew every single face that belonged to the Decker family. Dennis had recognized her from the moment he saw her at Keens Steakhouse. That's when he knew she was only with Virginia's father for one reason, to get to the Elliott family.

Dennis Elliott and his brother Clyde had talked about a potential plan to use this unfortunate marriage as a way to secretly hinder the Deckers. The night of the dinner, the two brothers devised their own plot against the family. Before the dinner was close to being over, Clyde had the idea that led to them both inviting Helen and Mr. Williams to their soirée with the rest of Manhattan's roaring elites. They knew exactly what would come after: phase two of the Decker plan to take down the Elliotts. Helen deciding to throw her own poker game was almost a surrender to the Elliotts. If only she had known what *they* had planned for her.

Roxy's grandparents, Dennis and Clyde's parents, were already set up in the penthouse at The Dakota. It seemed as if half of the family arrived for the showdown with their ever so loved Decker family. Griffin Elliott, Roxy's grandfather, and his wife Margret phoned in the Elliotts who were available. Five of Griffin's six siblings came, along with some of Griffin's nieces and nephews. The ones who came were Chester and Elsie, who were Griffin's brother Peter's kids. Then Jeanette and Douglas, Griffin's brother Bruce's kids who flew in from Chicago as well. Bruce left New York for college when he was eighteen and began his life there. Bruce and Griffin were very close as kids.

Griffin visited him in Chicago regularly, and when they both had kids of their own, they made trips out to each other often. Dennis and Clyde were closest to Jeanette and Douglas out of all their cousins. Roxy was also very close to Jeanette's kids Vita and Jennie. Vita and Jennie flew in with their mother, father, and uncle as well. Griffin's other nieces and nephews could not attend. Some were in LA and some in Paris. The other ones who were in Manhattan had obligations they could not get out of that night. Figures.

As for everyone else, Clyde and his wife Elizabeth brought their twenty-two-year-old son and his fiancée. He thought it would be a good idea for her to see the reality of the family she was soon to marry into. When Dennis uncovered all of this to Roxy, she immediately wanted to be there for it all. He told her it wasn't safe and that she was to stay next door at Johnny's. He didn't want her participating in the family business until she was eighteen.

"No, Roxy, you are not staying," Dennis said to the young Elliott with his stern, parental voice.

"Daddy, I'll be fine!"

"I said no!" Dennis said with growing anger.

"Vita and Jennie are coming."

"Vita and Jennie are older, darling."

"Only by a few years!"

"Roxy, I am your father and you are staying at Johnny's," he said to her as she glared angrily back at him.

Helen and the rest of the Deckers were unaware of what awaited them. It was now midnight and the party was over. It was one that ended rather early, as it was on the fancier soirée side of things, and Dennis was on his way to the Williams residence for the poker game. Everything was set in place. The Deckers had their plan, and the Elliotts had theirs.

"Dennis just rang me, he's telling Charles Williams I felt ill and came home to rest. That I won't be able to make it to the table," Clyde said to his father, Griffin.

"Get your guns, we need to be ready. I expect Thomas Decker to arrive within the hour."

The family was ready for a battle. They knew how to take action. Griffin decided to leave the lights off; he wanted Thomas to be in complete shock when he saw the Elliott family had known all along what was about to go down. Half of the family was at Griffin and Margret's residence in case they decided to check it out as well. It was highly unlikely, however.

Five years ago, when prohibition hit and he knew the Deckers would once again be after the Elliott power and fortune, he had moved everything over to Dennis. Every important document, every bill. The tabs they had on which people, the places their money was hidden. Everything from medical and dental records to which bank in Switzerland held their grand fortune. Information on the Levees, information on the Brooks. Information on every crime they committed and every speakeasy they owned, not to mention other dirt that they may need handy on the other mob families in New York City, just in case. This was when Griffin stepped down as Don, or head of the family, and gave the title to his son Dennis. Thomas Decker and his brother planned to uncover it all that night. He thought he had finally succeeded in distracting the Elliotts so deep into utter cluelessness in their current situation, but he was *far* from the right path. He took a road which he did not know had a fork in the middle. A fork where one side led to him giving up, and the other to him pursuing his plan. *He took the wrong one.* Thomas took the road which ended with a cliff. A cliff with a fall that went on indefinitely.

"Johnny, let's turn this couch around," Roxy said after she walked across 72nd Street to Johnny's. Her father was not going to let her stay, and she knew not to fight him on this one.

They both turned around the sofa in the living room next to his bedroom. His bedroom window looked out to Roxy's, and his living room looked out to Mr. Elliott's study. Johnny's building, The Majestic was many stories taller than The Dakota; however, Johnny's flat was on the same level as the penthouse suite at The Dakota. So the two friends would often talk through their bedroom windows across the street in a very movie-like scene.

That night, however, Roxy was at Johnny's and she was set to be involved in this dangerous rendezvous. Whether it was in person or from across the way. So they turned the couch to face the window for a perfect viewing of what was about to go down. Johnny and Roxy sat and watched the Elliott penthouse, soon to be at war. After Roxy was settled in, a fear came upon her. Not the fear of her family losing this battle—she knew the Elliotts would always win and come out ahead—but instead a fear of the triggers that would be pulled during this turmoil, and where exactly the bullets would go. One of Johnny's maids came around with a pot of Earl Grey tea. He knew it was her favorite, so he had a special box of the loose-leaf Earl Grey imported from England. Every time she was over at his place, she loved to drink it.

"You know me so well, Johnny darling," she said as she sipped her tea. "But if you thought this was the answer to calm me down, you're mistaken. Not even gin could solve this problem. What if my uncle is hurt? My aunts, my grandparents, my great aunts and great uncles, my cousins and—"

"Baby, baby—it will all be alright. Isn't that what you like to say? It will all be alright?"

"If you think you're helping, you aren't," she sassed him back.

"Well then, sugar. I guess I'll just go—"

"GO? You aren't going anywhere, Johnny—sit down right now or I'll slap you across the face!"

Roxy was always strong and fierce. She said what needed to be said, and she usually got what she wanted. She wasn't kidding, either.

"Alright, alright," he said as he sat back down and grinned.

Roxy and Johnny sat there on his expensive couch looking out to the Elliott residence, in wonder of what was going to happen. It was an hour later. An hour of impatience and waiting for the fall of the family who messed with the most powerful name in all of New York City. Roxy heard a car door slam shut, immediately looked down and out the window to see who was arriving next door at The Dakota, and there they were. Thomas Decker, his son, and two and only two of his "guys".

How pathetic. Two, really?

Roxy's heart sank deep into her chest; she had butterflies in her stomach, but not the good kind. She was watching Thomas enter the building, knowing he was making his way up with his son Kenneth. Roxy knew they were soon to approach her uncle and grandfather, along with the rest of her family. She gave Uncle Clyde a ring, warning him they were only a few seconds away. The only thing keeping Roxy somewhat calm throughout this war was knowing her father was across the park at the Williams residence. Even if it meant he was playing poker with Helen.

Coming back to the building across the street, the Deckers were standing confident at the tall double doors, about to break into Dennis Elliott's residence at The Dakota. Thomas and his son were holding guns in their hands, along with the two of their guys behind them. If only it was enough. The Elliotts had them so far outgunned, they wouldn't have a chance if they tried.

Thomas didn't bring the rest of the Decker family with him on this night because he thought the place would be empty. Idiot move. Absolute idiot. However, when he would walk in, it would appear empty. Thomas shot off the doorknobs and walked into the penthouse at The Dakota. A crystal chandelier imported from France hung high above their heads, and a marble double staircase sat twenty feet in front of them, along with two other staircases beside each of them. Behind the staircase directly in front of them was one of the many living rooms. Elegant white couches imported from Italy faced each other, with a large rug in between them. With two frosted glass tables on each side of the couches and a fireplace in the center, all surrounded by large and intimidating windows that looked out to the park. The vibe of the grand room was the epitome of art deco.

Thomas halted his motions as he heard a sound, almost the sound of people talking. The men got their guns ready, wondering if someone *had* really been there.

It was the radio.

Griffin Elliott had put the radio on to greet his favorite guests as they broke into his son's home. The four of them walked into the living room and found it on sitting proudly on an end table. Thomas was quick to turn it off—he didn't want any distractions. On the right was the room they had come for: Dennis Elliott's study in the center of a grand and long hallway. Thomas poured himself a drink out of their crystal and took it with him as he walked over to the doors. The place was dead silent—no one talking, no radio, not even the sound of a single breath. So silent you could hear your thoughts.

That was until the first gunshot went off.

"WHAT WAS THAT?"

"CALM DOWN, I'M SURE IT'S ALRIGHT!" Johnny yelled back to Roxy as her mind freaked to the sound of a gun gone off, with only the thought of one of her many loved ones lying dead in her father's study with a bullet in the chest.

"I'm a strong girl, Johnny—"

"Trust me, I know—"

"But this? I cannot deal with this!" She stood up and grabbed a bottle of gin sitting tall on a table against the window, pouring some into a glass for herself.

She was being a tad bit dramatic if I do say so myself, but this *was* a dramatic situation. Roxy had never had a front-seat view of anything like this before. She may have grown up in a mafia family and knew that every now and then the Deckers would come screwing around, but she never saw it happen in person, with her own eyes.

"Nothing's wrong, look at me, look into my eyes Scarlett Roxy—"

"I can't live without my family, Johnny, I just can't. I'm a strong and independent girl and can sure as hell take care of myself alone, but I love them all with such great passion and could *not* handle them being gone in such an instant. My mother already left me and my father and no one else can," she said as she held the glass in her right hand, up against her cheek, standing in the window of Johnny's living room and looking out anxiously to The Dakota.

Roxy loved deeply and of course wanted her family to come across no harm or foul in any way; she was not only worried for her own well-being with the thought of that gunshot gone into her uncle or grandfather. She thought of her father and how he was truly the one who would not be able to handle losing a family member. Roxy was a strong girl, so strong she could endure anything. **She herself could take a bullet to the chest and live with it.** She lived her life as if her mother had never walked out of The Dakota doors and not come back. She could certainly handle anything, though she did not want to have to. Her father, however, had gone through so much with the absence of Caroline, and Roxy worried much too greatly for him and how he would cope with any extra unfortunate hiccups in his life. Johnny knew this—he knew the worry in Roxy's heart was not for herself, but for her father. Her compassion was one of her many strengths. The way she cared for people; it was like no other.

"Roxy please, calm down. It was only a gunshot."

She looked into his eyes, and he was able to calm her down. And there it was, a sudden rainbow of assurance that everything was going to be alright.

That was until the next gunshot went off.

Cue the triggers being pulled and the bullets flying, and slient screams from Roxy's heart. They both looked to the window and into the Dakota penthouse, where these sounds of grief went off like firecrackers. This time Johnny *was* worried— he didn't know what to say anymore. It was *truly* a war between the two families. It had begun, the battle between the Deckers and the Elliotts.

A sudden ring of the telephone, and a calm and relaxed voice on the other end would accompany the anxious, older Elliott receiving the call.

The ringing stopped. "It's over, they shot first and we shot back," were the first words said as the phone was picked up.

"And Thomas Decker?"

"Dennis, I'll tell you everything when you get here. Tell Helen it was nice doing business with her."

"Brother, is everyone alright?"

"Just get over here."

The conversation between Clyde and Dennis Elliott was brief. After Clyde phoned him over to The Dakota, Dennis was on his way across the park to see the bloody outcome of this war. Roxy and Johnny raced across the street after the gunshots came to an end. They were brief, but there were many bullets flying through the penthouse.

When she arrived, Roxy's cousin Vita ran over and hugged her. Roxy and Johnny had finally been relieved of the unknown and where the bullets went as they saw Thomas Decker lying on the ground of her father's study with a gun in one hand and a file in the other. The file was something vitally important to the Elliotts; however, Roxy never found out what the mystery folder contained, and I'm sure not going to tell. Only Griffin, Margret, Dennis, and Caroline knew.

Thomas's son, Kenneth Decker, was tied to a chair, ready to be delivered back to his family. It was Tommy Elliott, Roxy's twenty-two-year-old first cousin, who pulled the trigger that led the bullet steadily into Thomas Decker's chest, resulting in his death.

Thomas was the one who first pulled his gun, only to blow the lock off the door to the study. When he entered the study, he and his son Kenneth began to sort through files and documents as Griffin Elliott and the rest of the Elliotts so kindly joined him. Thomas turned around in fear and pulled his gun; he shot at Griffin, almost killing him, as his grandson Tommy pulled the trigger aimed at Thomas. Clyde got a hold of Kenneth and tied him up. During all of this were many other gunshots firing from the Deckers' two men and the rest of the Elliott family.

With the two men having escaped with multible wounds, and Thomas lying on the floor of the penthouse where he dared to enter, it left only Kenneth alive and *mostly* intact to return to his family. By this time, everyone was at The Dakota. When Roxy saw her father she ran to him and gave him a tight hug. The family was dealing with the sorrow-filled vibe that permeated the first floor of the penthouse. Helen and Mr. Williams had no knowledge of the events that had been going down during their friendly game with Dennis Elliott. They were on their way to bed as the phone rang loud.

"This is the Williams residence, who am I speaking to?" a butler said into the telephone.

"This is Griffin Elliott, please put Helen on the phone."

"This is Helen, who am I speaking to?"

"Helen Decker," he said slowly. "What a true pleasure it is to hear your voice."

"Excuse me?" She was in shock. Who was this and how did he know she was a Decker?

"I'm sorry, did your butler not give you my name?"

"I am about to hang up this telephone if you don't explain to me right now—"

"This is Griffin," he said with a calm strength. Her eyes opened wide and her heart sank deeper into her chest. Helen began to feel ill. They sat in silence for a solid minute. Sixty seconds of listening to only the sounds of their deep, quick breaths. "If you are wondering, your father is here, alive."

"Mr. Elliott—" A panic joined her voice.

"And your grandfather, he's here too. I'm surprised he

didn't bring more men. Then again, he was not expecting an Elliott to be home."

"Put them on the phone, now."

"That is not going to happen, Helen. If you want your father you can come here and pick him up yourself. As for your grandfather, you have my—deepest—condolences," he said with a smile.

The winter night grew cold and long as the maids cleaned up the rather messy Elliott residence. Helen waited until Mr. Williams was asleep, then left the Upper East Side with rage.

It was over, *truly over*.

She left the Elliotts with her father at her side. They informed the family on all that had happened. Everyone was in shock. The Decker family had finally thought they would win. They imagined an easy takedown on the Elliott family. Of course, however, *that would never happen*. It was time to move on from the endless battle they had started. It was getting to the point of embarrassment for the Deckers. Two elite families, staring each other down for decades, all to come to this point where we stand at today. The death of dear old, don of the family, Thomas Decker.

This ... was the fall of the Deckers.

Well, here we are. The Helen Decker story has been told and we have had the first of our many endings.

I guess that means we are set to move on. Another story to add to the roaring life of the 1920s Manhattan adolescent.

It's on to the next chapter of their lives: Caroline Elliott and the mystery she left behind in New York, all when she disappeared off the glittering island of Manhattan.

Where did she go?

What happened to her?

Was this a product of scandal?

Was she even alive.

CHAPTER 4

CAROLINE'S CITY AND VALENTINE'S BLUES

Three girls—dressed to the hilt—walking the streets of New York. It was now February, almost Valentine's Day. A day with special meaning to our dear Elliott. Roxy, Marie, and Virginia were giggling about the boys who had recently caught their eye just in time for the romantic holiday.

A frigid wind took them by surprise as they stood at the Flatiron Building, gazing into its wonder and beauty.

"My goodness, this must be just my favorite building in all of Manhattan!" Roxy said.

"Darling, I think it's everyone's favorite," Virginia added as she stood in awe of the iconic structure.

They walked into a diner and sat down at the best table, took off their coats, their hats, and their gloves and all asked for a hot chocolate with extra marshmallows. Roxy asked for a cherry on top of her hot chocolate, something her mom used to do for her.

"Do you miss her?" Marie said to Roxy with sympathy.

"Every day I wake up thinking she will one moment just walk through those double doors and into the foyer, yelling through the penthouse how she's home," she said slowly. "So that would be a yes."

"Do you have any idea where she is? I still can't believe your mother left, even though it's been this long," said Virginia.

"Not one little clue."

They sipped their hot chocolate as it arrived and moved on to a new topic: Valentine's Day. The three girls gossiped for an hour about who would ask them to the dance and what they would wear. *Typical teenage girls.* Marie and Virginia's minds were only on the simple topic of the holiday, while Roxy's was spinning mad with the topic of Caroline, her mother. Valentine's Day was Caroline's favorite, and this was the first one without her. As the other two were rambling on about every boy in the junior class, Roxy sat in silence, staring into her hot chocolate, pondering about where her mother was. Roxy's driver took the girls back home and when Roxy walked into her bedroom, she was startled by a serene Frankie lying on her bed reading a book.

"Well hello darling, can I help you?" she said to him with extra sass.

"This book is wonderful: *The Beautiful and Damned,*" Frankie said, knowing it was her favorite and how she let *no one* touch it. Not even him.

"Put it down now, Frankie, it's signed by Fitzgerald himself!"

"I'm not even halfway through!" he said as she darted at him, ready to take the book out of his hands.

"Frankie Matthews!" she yelled as he jumped up. Then she began to chase him.

"It looks like it's in perfect condition, not more than a day old, let alone a coupla years—"

"Frankie!" she yelled again.

At this point they were chasing each other through the entire penthouse, before he landed on a couch and continued reading. She stood over him with a red face.

"Frankie, have I ever told you how much I love you?"

"No, I don't believe so."

"Well good then, I try my hardest not to be a liar!" were the words that came out of her mouth as she snatched the book from his hands. He gave her a smirk as she sat down next to him, out of breath. His eyes wide with love.

"You seem upset, what is it?"

"You, Matthews. You and the way you bring no delight— whatsoever. The way you bother me."

He smiled, looking straight into her golden eyes as the mood changed from playful to serious. "Oh, it can't be that … Roxy—"

"My mother, her favorite holiday was Valentine's Day."

"Ah, I remember. She even decorated the house," he said as he pictured Caroline telling every maid and butler in the house where each pink and red decoration belonged.

"I want to find her," she said, straightforward. Roxy almost *always* spoke her true feelings.

Frankie turned to look at her soft face and clear complexion, all with an aching heartbreak in her eyes. He didn't take a moment's breath before he said, "Then let's find her."

She turned to him, eyes big and in shock. "Really?"

"Yes, Roxy, really," Frankie exclaimed. "I want to help you find her, *darling.* I'd do anything to help you get her back."

Roxy smiled at Frankie as he grinned back. She had this sort of contagious smile that lit up any room. Frankie would truly do anything for his Roxy, and she knew that. However, she was taken back by the sudden taking of action to find her mother, whom she assumed was lost forever. It had been almost a year since she departed. March of 1924 was when she left without a goodbye. Caroline Elliott, the woman everyone loved. The dame from whom Roxy got her beauty, and she had the most perfect of hair. It was short and curled from the roots till the ends in perfect swirls of harmony. Not to mention the beautiful face that accompanied it.

One eerie night of March 23rd, she told her husband and daughter she was on her way to the barber shop to have that beautiful hair of hers done. No one questioned her motives when she said this, but they wondered why she left in such a rush. She had packed a small Louis Vuitton bag that morning when everyone had left The Dakota, knowing her plans for the night to come.

After her quick departure from the penthouse suite, Caroline left The Dakota and entered the car that would take her to the station to board a train to a city far, far away. A few hours after her departure, Roxy had begun to wonder where her mother was. Dennis took Roxy to Caroline's regular salon, though there was no sign of her. Dennis couldn't imagine his lovely wife abandoning him and their sixteen-year-old daughter.

The two searched the city all night for her as the skies darkened and rain poured down into New York. Roxy rang everyone she knew, as did Dennis. The police were involved by the next day, though they were no help. Roxy assumed it was the Deckers who took her, or even *killed* her. Dennis, Clyde, and Griffin paid a visit to Thomas Decker on March 25th of 1924. He and the rest of the family swore they had no business in Caroline's disappearance—and they didn't.

Roxy was preparing for the worst, thinking her mother had been killed in some horrific event. She would rather stomach the thought of her dear mother Caroline Elliott loving her till her death, than thinking she didn't love her at all and had left the two people she pretended to care about most. She couldn't bear the thought of all those "I love you"s being a lie. Thinking her own mother could leave without a simple hug was heart-wrenching.

It *was* in fact the second circumstance, however.

The hard one.

It *was* that Caroline left her husband and young daughter without as little as a goodbye kiss. She had escaped to a place she loved and to people she desired more than her own family. Not even Caroline's mother, Ruth Brooks, knew of her whereabouts. Her own sister Daisy hadn't received a call or a visit either.

It was as if she had left the planet for good and ended up on Saturn, with her whereabouts in the absolute unknown. That was until February of 1925, of course. When her daughter and her best friends took it upon themselves to search for the ever so missed Caroline Elliott.

"Do you have any idea, at all, where she could have gone?"

"Frankie, if I knew I would have checked a long time ago." Roxy rolled her eyes.

"Roxy, answer the question."

"I'm sorry," she said, staring at the ground, then looked up with annoyance. "No," she said with an attitude.

"No?"

"No, I don't know!" She became irritable. Talking about her mother was a hard subject.

"Alright, then let's figure it out."

"You make everything seem as if it was just as simple as figuring it out."

"That's because it is."

"Darling, it's not. The only one who is going to be able to help us is God. We can't figure it out."

"Then I suggest we start praying," he said as she looked at him with her eyebrows raised.

Frankie and Roxy went through all the possible cities she could have gone to. They started with the East Coast cities and worked their way over to the West. Then they began to broaden their ideas outside of the country and to Europe. After they had gone through every possible city in the world, they narrowed it down to three. She *was* in one of these cities, and Roxy knew it.

"That leaves us with three, we have too many reasons against the others," Roxy said to Frankie.

Paris, Chicago, and San Francisco were the three cities. One of which would bring some so-desired answers to everyone.

The two spent all night to get this far, though it seemed as if it was still as hopeless as it was a year ago when she left. The next morning as the sun came up on the New York City skyline, the rest of the gang joined in and helped with the search for Caroline Elliott—or was it now Brooks?

Virginia had many addresses in Chicago where her current residence could possibly be, Johnny had a few ideas in Paris, and Dalton knew a few people in San Francisco who could help. Roxy's hopelessness slowly began to fade as memories rushed back into her mind.

"It's San Francisco. She, my mother, is in San Francisco."

"How are you so sure?" Dalton added.

"My mother loves the city, she had been many times when she was a child. She always talked about it and said she had a good friend who lived there. Of course she adores Paris and Chicago too, but she's not there. I am certain."

"Who's the friend?"

"His name is Nick Terry."

"Nick Terry? I know Nick Terry!" Dalton said with enthusiasm and a cute smile.

Frankie looked up at him. "How would you *possibly* know this Nick Terry ..."

"Caroline and my mom knew each other as kids, and they went to school with him. He moved to San Francisco after college. My mom told me about him, they used to date. She had visited him a few times, and they are still good friends. She also told me how all three of them were close. Caroline, Nick, and my mom."

"Wow, I was *not* expecting that," Virginia said.

"Well damn, I didn't either!" Marie said, thrilled and pleased by the new information.

"I bet he knows where she's at!" Dalton exclaimed.

"Could be, do you know his address?"

"Not off the top of my head, but I bet I could find it."

"Oh Dalton, I LOVE you!" Roxy squealed as she hugged him tight, and Frankie rolled his eyes.

The day went on as Roxy's mind was flooded with the idea of being reunited with her dear mother. She had missed her so deeply, and only imagined the day where she would finally see her beautiful curly locks dancing in the air as she turned her head to her daughter, saying the words "I've missed you my darling!"

Dalton went home and searched for a letter his mother, Frances James, had received from Nick a while back when he had first moved to California. He rang Roxy the minute he found the address. She got up out of her bed and walked slowly over to her desk, picked up the telephone, and answered half asleep.

"Hello?"

"I FOUND IT!" Dalton exclaimed. He had a tad too much caffeine in him that night.

Roxy looked over to her clock on her golden-and-glass nightstand. Her eyes closed. "James, it's three o'clock in the morning! I'M COMING OVER THERE AND I'M GOING

TO KILL YOU—"

"I FOUND NICK'S ADDRESS!"

Suddenly she was awake. "You what?"

"Roxy, I found his address—Nick Terry."

She barely got out the words, "I'M COMING OVER!" before she jumped out of bed and hung up the phone.

Roxy snuck out of the house and hailed a taxi that flew down Central Park West at just the right time. She was still in her nightgown, with only a coat and hat on over. Her father didn't know of her plan to bring Caroline home, and she intended to keep it that way until she had returned with her mother on her right arm. Dalton heard a knock on his townhouse door; he looked through the peephole and opened the door quietly.

"DALTON!" she smiled.

"SHHHHHH."

"SORRY, sorry—" She was a little overexcited.

"My goodness, Roxy, calm down! If my parents wake up, they'll kill me … and then you!"

"I know, I know, I'll be quiet," she said as they sat down on the couch, anxious about the whole situation.

"712 Steiner Street," Dalton said as he handed the address, written down on a piece of paper, to Roxy.

"Wow, I can't thank you enough," she said as they both turned their heads to the door at a sudden loud knock.

"Who could that be at this time of night?"

"HEY LET ME IN, IT'S FRANKIE—"

Dalton ran to the door before he got any louder. "Frankie, be quiet—you'll wake my parents up," he said as he knocked him upside the head. Frankie raised his hands up in surrender and laughed it off.

"What's with you?" Frankie said as he hit him back.

"His parents are asleep, Frankie—we can't be loud, my God," Roxy specified.

"Oh like you're quiet—"

"Would you both shut it?" Dalton said as he sat back down. "And why are you here anyways?"

"Roxy rang me as soon as she heard the good news," Frankie said as he helped himself to the kitchen. "Oh, and Roxy, what's up with your hair?" he laughed and smiled.

"Shut it Frankie, I just got out of bed." She gave him an agitated smirk.

"You called him?" Dalton smiled and raised his eyebrows.

"Well it was only fair, he's helping me too," she said, making it seem like no big deal.

"Okay, I guess," Dalton responded before turning to Frankie. "My God can we please get on with this? Frankie, get back here."

"Hold on!"

"So this is his address, for sure?"

"Well, it was his address back when he first moved, but there was a photograph with the letter. A photograph of the house, and it's a nice one. I doubt he'd leave it."

"But there's a chance he doesn't live there anymore?" she agonized.

"You couldn't have found a current address, Dalton?" Frankie came back into the living room with a slice of pie.

"You should be happy I remembered my mom had told me about Nick Terry and that I was able to give you some sort of anything," he said, ticked off they didn't seem to appreciate his hard work of searching through his mother's old letters. "It's more than the two of you came up with."

Roxy and Frankie shared a look. "Sorry, you're right. Thank you, Dalton, I love you." She smiled and gave him a kiss on the cheek.

"I'd like to go to sleep now, goodnight you two. Love you."

"Goodnight."

"Goodnight."

And then there were two.

"I'll take you home, Roxy," Frankie said as he grabbed Roxy's coat and put it on her. He always treated her like royalty, and that's exactly what she was. *Mafia royalty.*

She slipped on her leather gloves and put on her hat as she said, "Not just yet, I'm in the mood for a bite to eat."

The two went to Katz's Delicatessen, a deli on Houston Street open all hours of the night. *What a place.* Dalton lived in the village, not *too* far from the Lower East Side where Katz's was located. Frankie and Roxy and the rest of the gang grew up going to the well-known deli. Frankie knew he could always count on it for a middle-of-the-night sandwich. They sat down in a booth, talking about their plan of action to find and bring home Caroline. Roxy decided to book a flight for February 21st, two weeks from that night. She wanted to stay for the Valentine's Dance at school in hope of going with the boy she liked at the moment. Roxy spent the next week focusing solely on Valentine's Day, forgetting about her mother for the time being, knowing there was nothing she could do until she boarded the flight to San Francisco.

February 7th, 1925

Dear Diary,

Last night was one of the greatest nights of my life! I, Roxy Elliott, am going to find my mother.

She is in San Francisco, I just know it. Dalton's mother Frances was good friends with my mom and their mutual friend Nick Terry, who lives in San Francisco. Dalton was able to get me his address. 712 Steiner Street. To tell you the truth, I'm nervous. I am not the nervous type—I usually go into things with the trust I will be fine, then rely on God. However, I am terrified. I didn't act like it when I was with the gang or when Frankie and I talked over our plan at Katz's, but I am. The whole situation is a major doozy and I wish it hadn't even happened, but it did and now I have to fix it.

I'm not worried that my mom won't be happy to see me, I know she will. I am, however, worried that she'll not want to come back to New York with Frankie and me. I have prayed to God every night for her to return, and now I have the resources to make it happen. God handed over the address, all I have to do is show up at the doorstep.

Thankfully I'm fortunate enough for air travel. If I had been born any earlier or born without the wealth that accompanied the Elliott name, I wouldn't be able to fly all the way to San Francisco to find my mother. Not many can do what we do, as air travel is usually not for just anyone. Trains are the way to get around, but I'm not just anyone. I'm an Elliott, and I'll bring back my mom.

I'm not sure what's in San Francisco for her and why she would have left. I believe that's the reason why I'm so nervous. How could anyone leave New York City? She had a perfect, extravagant, big, and beautiful life and threw it all away to move to a California city. Sure, San Francisco's great and all but it's no New York! Frankie and I will fly there on Saturday the 21st and stay in a nice hotel not too far from this Nick Terry's residence on Steiner Street. As of now, I'm choosing to forget about the matter until I leave. My focus is going to be on a different name: Dean Andrews. One of the cutest boys in the class of 1926, behind Frankie, Johnny, and Dalton of course.

His family is of old money and he is just the PERFECT gentleman. I've been eyeing him in history class all year. He came to my party last month but I didn't get the chance to talk to him. I want Johnny to talk to him for me, tell him how he should date me and all, but Johnny refuses. He said it would be weird because he's into Claire, Dean's ex-girlfriend. I think it would be perfectly fine! I asked Dalton but he said no because he doesn't know Dean all that well. So then I went to Frankie and he just gave me a flat-out no, without any explanation. Figures. But I want him and I want him before Valentine's Day. I refuse the topic of Caroline and San Francisco until Dean has asked me to be his girlfriend and to go to the dance with him.

It was now Monday, February 9th, only days away from the romantic holiday that had been keeping all the girls in school from getting any work done. Every girl had been worrying about this Valentine's Dance on Saturday. Virginia was a part of the council in her junior and senior year and planned all the dances. This year's Valentine's Dance was going to be one of the best, thanks to the love Virginia shared for the school dances of Manhattan West High School. Roxy and Marie were walking down the hallway as Virginia was putting up the dance signs.

"Well would you look at that, our own Virginia, designing and putting up the Valentine's Dance posters," Marie said with a smile.

"I betcha this'll be the best one West High has ever had." Roxy walked up to Virginia.

"It'll be awful when we graduate next year, they won't have me to plan any more dances!" she laughed.

"And to think you didn't plan any freshman or sophomore year, how atrocious!" Roxy kissed Virginia and Marie's cheeks, as she spotted the boy she was set out to have. "Gotta go! See ya in ma—" she began to say as she rushed over to Dean Andrews.

She fixed her hair, applied a second coat of red lipstick and tapped Dean on the shoulder.

"Roxy Elliott! What a pleasant surprise," he said.

"You know my name, I'm absolutely flattered!"

"Oh honey, you know everyone in town knows your name."

"Oh you're so sweet." She batted her eyelashes and began to blush. "So, Saturday—" Roxy began to lean into the holiday's events as the intercom cut her off.

A British voice glared over the speaker, "This is your principal speaking. I would like to inform all students that our Valentine's Dance will be held this Saturday from seven till eleven. Girls should come in proper dresses, none above the bottom of the knee, and boys in a suit and tie. If one shows up not dressed accordingly, they will *not* be allowed to enter the dance. Also, there will be no smoking and absolutely no tolerance for any alcohol. If alcohol is found, the New York Police Department will receive a call and the students responsible will face suspension for three days, and it will go on your permanent record, along with the chance of being condemned by the authorities. With that being said, I hope you all have a wonderful time this Saturday, and tickets will be sold by Virginia Williams and Hazel Flynn this week during your lunch period. Thank you and have a wonderful rest of your day, students."

"She makes prohibition sound all the more fun, you know," Dean said to Roxy as the intercom shut off and the school rolled their eyes at the *lovely* principal's voice.

"You are absolutely right! So, what I was going to say before—"

"Yes, Saturday. Valentine's Day ..."

"Why yes, it is."

"Was there something you were going to ask me, Roxy?"

"Actually, I was going to suggest you ask me, but if you'll make a girl do the deed," she began to walk away as she twirled her hair with her fingers, "then I guess—"

"Would you like to go with me to the dance, Roxy?" Dean said, leaving Roxy with a smirk on her face as she turned back around.

"Well, IF YOU INSIST!" she said as she ran through the halls back to her best friends. He smiled and walked off to his class. It wasn't exactly easy to get Roxy Elliott, so he had really accomplished something.

"You're not going to believe it, girls! I'm going to the dance with Dean!"

"Well we figured, Roxy," Virginia said to her as she shared a laugh with Marie.

"Oh, and what is that supposed to mean?"

"Roxy, you always get the boy you want. We didn't think this time would be any different," Marie said.

"Well, darlings, I guess you're right!" Roxy laughed and shared her contagious smile.

The bell rang and the girls were off to math, where they met up with the boys.

"Johnny, you won't believe who asked me to the dance ..." Roxy said to Johnny as he sat down at his desk next to her.

Marie came up behind them. "Oh no, you won't believe it at all …" she said with sarcasm. "Hmmmm, it couldn't be …" She tapped her chin with her index finger and laughed as she sat down.

"Dean Jack Andrews! What a shocker, right?" Virginia blurted out as she entered the classroom and sat behind Roxy.

Roxy smiled. "I am so excited, Johnny. God, he's SO cute!"

"That's great sugar, but I didn't doubt you would get him."

Virginia whispered into Roxy's ear, "See, I told ya!" and Roxy laughed.

The girls were whispering about Dean Andrews all throughout class while Frankie and Dalton listened in from across the room, as they *were* quite loud. I guess "whisper" isn't *really* the correct term to use.

"So, how do you feel about Roxy and Dean becoming an item?" Dalton nodded to Frankie.

"Oh it's, uh, great!"

"Lies."

"Lies?"

"Oh come on, you know you're not happy about it."

"And why would you say that?"

Dalton rolled his eyes. "Never mind, Frankie, you'll never admit it anyways."

As math ended and the morning turned into afternoon, Marie and Virginia were asked to the Valentine's Dance by two of the most desired boys in school, and Johnny decided to go out and get the girl *he* desired.

"Claire! Wait up!" he said, running to her as she walked

down the steps leaving school, just as the frigid wind ran through her perfect blonde locks.

"Johnny Davis, well how do you do?"

"I'm wonderful, and you?" He gave her his irresistible smile.

Claire giggled. "Oh, I'm fine."

"Do you have a date to the dance this Saturday?" He jumped right into the question he had been dying to ask for weeks.

"As a matter of fact, I do not."

"Well then, look how that worked out!"

"What is *that* exactly?" she said as she got closer to him.

"Well, if you must know, I just happen to not have a date either. If I were to say so myself, I'd think it was fate!" he told her as he gave her that dashing smile once more.

"Oh is it?"

"Oh yes, indeed. So, Claire, would you like to be my Valentine?" were the words he said as he pulled out a single red rose and gave it to Claire. How poetic.

He went home and rang Frankie.

"Frankie here—"

"Claire said yes!" he said with the same excitement Roxy had over Dean. In other words, he sounded like a girl who had just been asked by the guy she had been crushing on for months. (Not that there's anything wrong with that.)

"Johnny?"

"She said yes! I'm going to the Valentine's Dance with the school's cutest blonde."

"Way to go Davis, she's gorgeous, I almost asked her. Good

thing you did before I got to her," he laughed.

"She's not your type, Frankie," he angrily said.

"I was kidding! Jeez."

"I really like this one, Frankie. She's kind, beautiful, *and* she makes good grades."

"She seems nice, but won't it be weird when you show up with her and Roxy's with Dean, her ex-boyfriend?"

"Yeah, I thought of that, but they broke up over three months ago—it should all be jake, right?"

"I don't know, maybe, but I doubt it."

"Frankie, what are you saying."

"Well, maybe we should pay Dean a visit, tell him how he's gonna to be forced to spend the night with his ex."

"Why, to scare him off?"

"Yeah, so he and Roxy don't go together and you don't have to worry about upsetting Claire."

"I guess we could think about that, I mean it would be kinda weird—"

"Great, let's go—"

"Hold on, are you just saying this because you don't want Roxy with him?"

"Why would you think that?" he said nonchalantly.

"Oh, come on Frankie—"

"You know what, Dalton said the same thing and I don't know where you guys are coming up with this from. If you're jake with Dean being there, close to you and this sheba Claire, then don't talk to him. It's fine, I was just tryna help you—"

"No, I didn't say that—"

"No no, I'm sure Claire will *love* Dean being so close to her on such a romantic holiday—"

"Frankie—"

"I mean maybe she's not over him, maybe this will be a good way for—"

"Okay fine! Let's go!" Johnny yelled through the telephone and Frankie grinned as he hung up.

The two boys went over to Dean's in an attempt to persuade him not to go with Roxy. However, they were *highly* unsuccessful. Dean had always liked Roxy and never asked her out only because he didn't know if she would be into him or not. He sure as hell wasn't going to give up a chance with the Elliott princess.

Frankie put on a good show, but inside he was *not* the happiest about their budding love.

Johnny wasn't too happy about it either, but for very different reasons.

Frankie and Johnny decided to go over to Roxy's in an attempt to convince *her* that Dean wasn't the best choice, but by the time they had arrived at The Dakota, she had already spoken to Dean and was furious with the boys for what they had done. Roxy didn't let them in and they were forced to give up, knowing there wasn't any chance at changing Roxy's mind anyways.

Tuesday quickly approached and Frankie asked one of the *many* girls who fawned over him to the dance, as did Dalton. School dances were the only event Dalton's parents let him stay out past eight for. Of all the other times he had been dancing out late, his parents knew nothing. Wednesday came and went, and Thursday arrived with a rainstorm. By Friday, the girls were searching for dresses for the dance and slept over at Roxy's in preparation for Saturday's big day. Roxy had kept Caroline off her mind all week—that was until her father gave her a pair of Caroline's ruby earrings for the dance.

"Your mom would want you to have them, Scarlett Roxy," Dennis said to Roxy as she and the girls were doing their hair for the dance.

"Oh wow, I remember when she used to wear those. Gold and rubies were *always* her favorite."

"They were, and I know they're yours, too."

"Daddy, I can't take these," she said as she handed them back to her father, shedding a tear she quickly wiped away.

"And why not?" he said as she sat in silence for twenty seconds, putting a feather in her hair.

Roxy turned back to her father. "Because she cherished those so deeply and if anything were to happen to them she'd kill me and—"

"Honey, I want you to have them. She's not here to say otherwise, and I know they will look absolutely gorgeous on you, sweetheart." He gave her a hug. She still hadn't told him about her plans for next weekend and how she intended to bring her mother back home.

"Alright Daddy, I guess I'll wear them!" She smiled as she put on the perfect chandelier earrings.

"Beautiful, just like your mother," he said to his daughter as he made his way downstairs.

"Wow darling, those are divine!" Virginia said as she

admired the way the earrings shined and twinkled in the light.

"Absolutely gorgeous, darling," Frankie said as he entered her bedroom.

"Frankie!" She got up and gave him a hug and a kiss on the cheek. "Look at you, handsome."

"And it's all for you, Roxy."

"Funny," she smiled and he laughed.

"Marie, baby you look gorgeous."

"Why thank you Frankie," she winked.

"And Virginia, might I say you are a true Williams woman." He gave her a hug.

"Oh stop it, you're going to make me blush!"

Frankie sat on Roxy's bed as the girls finished putting on their bold lipstick and perfecting their cupid's bow. Roxy slipped on long silk gloves to match her dress and Marie added a string of pearls. Virginia put one of Roxy's diamond bracelets on and they all walked down one of the grand marble staircases of the Elliott penthouse. Dean, Marie's date Stephen Thomas, and Virginia's date Michael Howards rang the doorbell and were greeted by one of the Elliott butlers. The boys took the girls' hands and escorted them out the door to a car downstairs. Frankie's driver drove him to his date's townhome and met the rest of the gang at the school, along with Johnny and Claire. As they all entered the well decorated gym, the band was playing loud and the red and pink aesthetic gave the perfect Valentine's Day feel. Really, it was all picture perfect, all until Johnny and Dean decided it was a grand idea to get into a fight.

CHAPTER 5

DEAN ANDREWS AND CAROLINE ELLIOTT

Valentine's Day has always been a day of romance, love, and *hopeful in perfection* lousy school dances. However, that was not the case for our special gang on the cold February 14th of 1925.

As the dance began, everyone and everything seemed to be as perfect as it could be. Johnny tried hard at an attempt to keep Claire away from Dean, and Roxy kept Dean clear of Claire. That was until the very end of the dance, around 10:30pm, as things began to slow down and couples shared the floor slow-dancing. Roxy and Marie ran to the ladies' room as Dean waited for his girl to return. Johnny went over to get Claire a glass full of bright-red punch as *she* decided to say hello to her ex.

"You look nice," she smiled and said to Dean as she walked up to him, with nothing but sinister intentions.

"Thank you, Claire, but I'm here with Roxy, and you're here with Johnny. Please, don't make any trouble."

"Dean, I'm not making trouble—we're friends, aren't we?"

"I suppose so. However, I know for a fact that both Roxy *and* Johnny wouldn't appreciate this, so why don't—"

"Oh come on, a girl can't be friends with a guy?"

"Claire, please—"

"At least dance with me," she said as she attempted to grab his hand.

"Excuse me?"

"Dance with me, a quick dance!"

"I'm here with Roxy, Claire. What part of that do you not understand—"

"Only as friends Dean, only friends!"

Dean thought about it, and he knew it would be the only way to shut her up, so he took her hand and led her to the dance floor for a short dance. He also figured there was nothing wrong with two friends sharing a dance—this was the 1920s after all ...

"Well, this isn't all that bad," she grinned with sparkles in her eyes, "Dean Andrews."

"Only for one song, until Roxy and Johnny get back. And don't get any ideas, this is *only* as friends," Dean made clear to the blonde. Johnny, however, did not quite understand the circumstances.

"What the hell are you doing with her? Get off my girl!" Johnny said as he raced over to a rather calm Dean, dancing with *his* date. He pulled him away and threw him off the dance floor and against the wall of the gymnasium.

Roxy and Marie were walking back from the ladies' room as Johnny began to pick a fight with Dean.

"Johnny, you don't understand. It was only an innocent dance as friends. You and the girls dance all the time—"

"Yeah, well they aren't my ex-girlfriends!" he said angrily as he turned back around and threw a rough punch that broke Dean's nose.

By this time, everybody at the dance had noticed what was going on and the gym quickly fell into silence. Dean made an attempt to explain himself but Johnny wouldn't listen, so Dean did the only thing he figured he could do and he fought back.

Within seconds the fight had escalated to another level, and Frankie and Dalton tried to break it up, but Dalton got hit in the middle of the forehead and Frankie in the eye in an attempt to end what never should have even started. Roxy and Marie heard the fight echoing from the hallway and ran back to the dance as teachers made their way over to the well-dressed boys. The fight was finally broken up by Mr. Colton, their history teacher, who took the four boys outside, even though Frankie and Dalton had no part in the fight, as they were merely trying to end it.

The girls also followed them as things began to take a turn for the worse. Mr. Colton decided to check the boys for alcohol, and as a matter of fact, they had been dumb enough to bring the forbidden substance to a school function. Dean, Johnny, Dalton, and Frankie *all* had booze hidden on them. *Idiots*. The police were called and the boys were taken down to the station. The girls followed behind, driven by Roxy's driver.

Thankfully, Virginia had witnessed the entire "innocent dance" and explained the event to the girls.

Claire remained back at the dance, for her own sake. When Roxy and Marie found out how the bitch Claire had seduced Dean into slow-dancing with her, they were filled with rage. Roxy had a bad feeling about this Claire all along, but never thought much of it because Johnny had liked her for so long. Roxy already had enough on her plate with her trip to San Francisco in a week, and she didn't need to have to deal with the Claire–Johnny–Dean and herself love square that had arisen. As the girls arrived at the station, the boys were put behind bars for possession of the illegal liquid. Frankie's father came and bailed the four boys out of jail, and when they got out, Virginia told Johnny what had happened and how Dean had only danced with Claire to get her to shut up. *What a way to ruin a holiday.* Johnny apologized to Dean, as did Dean to Johnny and Roxy for agreeing to give Claire the simple affection of a dance. If you ask me, the whole thing was blown out of proportion.

Meanwhile, the dance came to an end and Claire had gone back home, where she anxiously awaited a telephone call from her date. Johnny was ready to end things with her, but she managed to talk herself out of the deep hole she had dug. By Monday morning, tensions were high between Claire and the others. Roxy, Marie, Virginia, Frankie, and Dalton were also angered by Johnny's poor decision to stay with Claire after what she had pulled. They were certain she was trying to make a move on Dean, but Johnny was blinded by her blonde-haired, blue-eyed all-American beauty.

As the week went by, Roxy decided not to think or care about Claire, Dean or Johnny. She was only steering her focus to the road of Caroline and everything that was about to happen. By Friday, Claire had been forgiven by them all (with the exception of Roxy) and she was back to being known as the sweet blonde girl who used to date Dean Andrews.

Was that true? Far from it—however, that story will come much later, far after we continue with the Caroline dilemma. Claire and Johnny's relationship wouldn't be one to last, and certainly wouldn't end on the best of terms. As for Dean and Roxy? They weren't bound to be together forever either, as fate had a different boy in mind for Roxy Elliott. The problems Claire Reed would soon, or not so soon, stir up come after I tell you what the weekend of February 21st would bring. For now, we will return to the topic of Caroline Elliott and the mystery that follows.

Answers will be brought to Roxy tomorrow, Saturday the 21st of February, 1925, as she boards a flight with Frankie to the beautiful West Coast city of San Francisco. Dennis Elliott was told by Roxy that she and Marie were staying at the Romanos' upstate mansion over the weekend for a "girls' trip" with Marie's cousins. However, that was quite a long distance from the truth.

CHAPTER 6

THE FLIGHT THAT CHANGED HER LIFE

Suitcases filled with bright beaded and lace dresses, hats galore, designer gloves handmade in Italy, and every other necessity an Elliott princess could possibly need were being transferred by men in hats and white gloves to the lobby of The Dakota.

The sky was a light, powdery blue, with few of its white fluffy friends corrupting the beauty of looking up into the wonderful beyond.

Roxy looked into the mirror of her ever so shiny, cherry-red vanity as she outlined her lips in a liner of the same color. She grabbed a hat from her grand closet and ran to the window facing The Majestic, Johnny's apartment building where Frankie had spent the night. As she opened up the window, a chilly breeze flew into her room, blowing her canopy drapes delicately into the excitement-filled air. She yelled out to Johnny's window across the street.

"HEY FRANKIE!" There was no response." FRANKIE—
DARLING," she said again, this time with a touch of attitude. "HELLO MATTHEWS, ARE YOU ALIVE IN THERE?"

This time he ran to the window, opening it to speak to his anxious friend.

"ROXY, I'M COMING! DON'T HAVE A COW!" he yelled back as she smiled and shut the window tight.

Roxy left her room with a wide grin of excitement. She took a blueberry muffin with her from the kitchen as her dad came in.

"Honey, have a great time with the Romanos, I love you," he said as one of the butlers handed him a cup of black coffee while he read the newspaper. He gave her a hug and kiss goodbye. "Ring me when you get upstate."

She hated lying to him, but she knew it was for the greater good. "I will, Daddy. I love you!"

An anxious girl left The Dakota with a million thoughts spinning round and round through her mind. She was almost utterly consumed by the thought of rejection from her own mother; however, Frankie worked his magic to calm her down.

The seatbelts were buckled and the pilot began to move them off. Air travel was still relatively new in 1925, a luxury only the wealthy could afford, *the extremely wealthy*, and it didn't look like it would in years to come. It would still be quite a few years before it became something common. Roxy and Frankie had been on many planes; however, the people in front of them hadn't and began to freak out. Roxy was listening to them bicker about how the plane wasn't safe and the pilot was too young to fly.

"Do you hear them?" she giggled. "They're a wreck!"

"It's funny because they aren't even going all the way to San Francisco, they are getting off when we land in Chicago."

"My goodness, what sissies."

The bickering couple helped to ease Roxy's mind. She looked out the window as the plane began to rise into the still blue sky. The couple's rambling dulled into a dead silence, and Frankie dozed off into a sleep before Roxy made sure to wake him up. She made it clear he was *not* allowed to sleep, that he was supposed to entertain her for the hours to come spent flying across the United States.

"Roxy, *darling*, I need my sleep thank you very much," he said as he put on a silk eye mask, before Roxy was quick to notice something out of the ordinary.

"Is that mine?"

"Is what yours?" he said with a calm, soft voice as he slipped further into his seat and tilted his head closer to Roxy.

"The eye mask, you fool."

"This old thing? No no, I picked this up in Paris last December," he smiled as he continued to relax deeper into his seat.

"It's pink, *Frankie*."

"It is most certainly, *not* yours." His cute and juvenile smile widened as he giggled.

"It most certainly *is* mine!"

"Most certainly not."

She took it off him as he let out an "OW!"

"It's monogrammed 'RE', it most CERTAINLY *is*. Picked it up in Paris, oh sure."

"Well your bedroom is—sort of like Paris," he smirked.

"Oh how so?"

"Goodnight love," he whispered as he shut his ocean blue eyes.

"Frankie!" She slapped him.

"Okay, okay! I won't sleep. What would you like me to do?"

"Entertain me, distract me," she said with a humorous grin.

"Oh what, am I supposed to sing for you?"

"Alright then, do you take requests?" she laughed.

"Break out into song? Right here? On an airplane. Oh sure."

"I'm bored." She twirled her soft, shiny hair through her fingers and bit her lip as she raised her eyebrows.

"I bet you are, it's not like you should be thinking about your mother or anythi—"

"I'm trying to get my mind OFF of her, Frankie. Thank you very much."

"Right," he said as he grabbed the eye mask back out of her hands and put it on. "Why don't *you* sing for me instead?" he said and she slapped him again.

The skies darkened as they were entering the state of California. Ten minutes out from landing, the two were fast asleep on each other's shoulders. They were woken up by the sudden motion of landing fast on the ground. As they got their luggage and found a taxi, the thoughts began to once again flourish in Roxy's mind. "What if she doesn't love me? What if she doesn't want me? What if she doesn't care?" were racing through her special mind as fast as they could go. Frankie knew of a nice hotel near Nick Terry's house and they stayed in a large room on the seventh floor.

"One bed."

"One bed …"

"Well I guess that means you're sleeping on the floor! Have fun *darling*," Roxy said as she threw her coat onto Frankie, and went into the bathroom to change into a nightgown and get ready for bed. They had just checked into their room after having dinner at one of the best restaurants in the city. Roxy slept on the bed and Frankie on the floor but, somehow … someway … like always, when they woke up they were *both* on the bed in a deep slumber.

"I just don't understand how this happens, WAKE UP YOU LOLLYGAGGER!" were the first words to come out of Roxy's mouth, on the morning of the day that was to end in a much different tone.

"Huh?" He was groggy. "Oh, ha ha," he laughed and smiled, then closed his eyes as he attempted to fall back asleep. Frankie, like Roxy, had a great smile. He smiled from his beautiful blue eyes. "I guess fate wants us together!" he laughed and pulled the covers over to his side.

"Real funny, you dimwit," she said as she pulled the covers to herself and pushed him off the bed and onto the floor.

Roxy got up and telephoned her father, telling him she was

ready to have a fun day with Marie and her cousins, then rang Marie to make sure everything was smooth back in New York. As they got ready for the day, Roxy managed to change her outfit not once, not twice, but a grand Elliott-style ... seven times.

"Is this alright? Does this say ... 'Mom, come back home, you can't abandon your family'?"

"Like I said the other *six* times, yes it's absolutely marvelous," he hinted sarcastically, "and nothing says *that*."

"Alright alright, let's go to breakfast. Then to Nick's."

Roxy and Frankie stepped outside onto the San Francisco streets, searching for a café to have breakfast at. Roxy ordered French toast and eggs, and Frankie decided on pancakes and bacon, their usuals. Frankie was a gentleman and picked up the tab, something he most always did—and *always* did if he was with a girl. They left the restaurant full, yet unfulfilled. There was only one thing that could satisfy them that morning: Caroline Elliott opening her arms to her daughter, agreeing to board the flight back to New York. 712 Steiner Street. They were headed in the direction of her mother and Nick Terry.

"702."

"704."

"706."

"708."

"710 ..."

"Seven twelve."

712 Steiner Street—they were there.

"It's beautiful," she said with a glimmer of hope.

"Truly."

"You can wait here."

"That I'll do," he said with a bit of disappointed shock, having hoped he would accompany her to the front door. Yet he understood; it was Roxy, and she needed to do this alone.

He said a prayer as she walked up the many steps to Nick's front door, as did she while she climbed them. In both of their minds, "Everything is going to be perfect" was read three times, and she gave the door a knock after looking back at Frankie. With butterflies in her stomach and a hopeful heart, she got no response. She knocked again, this time with an aggressive force. She stood there, at the top of the staircase, right there in front of Nick Terry's large and beautiful home for a solid minute before she turned to Frankie again with a look of fear and grief. A look he was hoping he wouldn't have to see. She almost began to walk down the glorious stairs back to him as the door began to open …

CHAPTER 7

DAISY WHO?

There it was, the creeping of a door being slowly opened by the person standing on the other side. That daring *other side*, someone—there—breathing deeply only a few inches away.

Frankie's eyes widened, as he was the first to see the face behind the red door. Roxy's face relaxed, though not the calming kind of relaxed, but the fearful "in shock" kind instead. She waited a moment before she slowly yet anxiously turned her body around; chills came over her, goose bumps captivated her smooth skin, and she almost began to feel a wave of nausea in the mere two seconds it took to get from looking out to a park to looking into the eyes of the person on that almost *too* daring, other side. There she was, standing with confidence in what would happen. Roxy, that was. On the other side of the door was a woman: a woman with shiny, copper eyes. Eyes just like her daughter's, only hers were filled with shock and a touch of sheer happiness.

There was a long pause before the only word Roxy could think of blurted out of her mouth and off her red lips. "Mother," she said, in the most straightforward tone she had.

It was her, the real, authentic, curly-haired, tall and thin, *Caroline Elliott*. The woman who, for a reason that remained unknown, had abandoned her family a year ago.

"Why," Roxy stated in that same tone, as another long pause took place.

Clouds came in, thunder was approaching, and before Caroline could say a word, Frankie was standing at the bottom of the stairs in the pouring rain, with no porch cover over his head like Roxy. She spoke, Caroline Elliott *finally* spoke. She told Roxy everything. Right then and there, with no hesitation. She felt the need and went for it. The reason she left? The answer to everyone's questions? She was pregnant, and it wasn't Dennis's child. Didn't see that one coming, did you? *I sure didn't.*

So there you have it, the reason. But not the *only* reason. Caroline Elliott had gone to lunch with Nick Terry a year ago when he visited New York for a meeting. Nick Terry was Caroline's first love. He visited a couple of months before Caroline left. When she found out she was pregnant, she knew it wasn't her husband's. The lunch they had gone on wasn't your average hour-and-a-half "nice to see you, glad we got to talk" catching-up-with-an-old-friend lunch. This was a lunch that took place between two old loves.

"But that wasn't the only reason I left." The words of Caroline Elliot, spoken with a sincere heartbreak in her voice.

They took a long pause once again, Roxy with confusion and her mother afraid to say what she had always kept hidden from her. Roxy looked away as Caroline began to speak again.

"Oh baby girl, you know I love you."

"Why?" she said, staring angrily at the wet ground, ready to run back down the steps to Frankie.

"Come inside sweetheart, it's—pouring out there!"

"No thank you." She turned her head the other way, looking at the pretty homes lined up down Steiner Street.

"Please, honey—"

"I said no thank you." Roxy's voice was stern and filled with anger. "Say what you need to say out here."

Roxy's heart was, yet again, ripped out of her chest with vigorous force. Only a year ago she had lost the mother she loved so dearly, desperately, and had optimistically waited for her return. A return she would never get. Then she decides to go out alone and search for her, and is told, on the spot, of her mother's indiscretions. She was filled with emotions she had never felt before. It wasn't just heartbreak and worry this time— it was anger, fury, and confusion. It was an emptiness in her heart and a hole in her stomach. She felt sick, and her mind was running rampant with thoughts she couldn't control. She was tempted to leave and never return, but she knew she couldn't do that. After all, Caroline was still her dear old mother. *For now.*

"I really think you should come inside, dear—"

"I said no!"

Another long and uneasy pause took place before Caroline finally spoke the words she thought she would never tell her daughter. It happened so fast; they flew off her tongue like a bird taking flight for the first time. It was fast yet clumsy and filled with hesitation. "I'm—"

"You're?"

"Aunt."

And there it was, she had said it. Caroline had finally spoken the forbidden truth to her daughter, after seventeen years of living a lie. Seventeen years of scandal buried under wealth and a "perfect" life.

Roxy turned her head ever so quickly, glaring at her so-called mom with big, broken eyes. "What?" she said with a sarcastic laugh, then yelled out with no time to think. "That's funny—*Mother*! What a grand joke!" Roxy said, almost too quickly to understand.

"Baby girl, your father and I have wanted to tell you all your life, but Daisy wouldn't let us. She didn't want you to be upset."

"Daisy … Daisy Daisy Daisy—" Roxy said repetitively before Caroline cut her off. Her red eyes were locked onto Caroline's; she was furious.

"Oh Roxy, stop it! Stop it right now, I said. I know you are in shock and upset—"

"No no, not shocked. Not upset. Well, you see, I just don't believe you!" she said while laughing nervously. She never could have calculated this into the equation, this was never something that had *ever* crossed her mind. Ever. She was in utter denial. "This can't be true, you wouldn't do that to me and neither would Daddy." Tears ran down her face as she continued to speak with a saddened grin. "Mom, Caroline, whoever you are, you need to stop this silliness night now. It's almost funny. Isn't it funny? Oh, I believe it to be just *marvelously* funny." She kept her eyes fixated on her mother's, as the tears began to run down her face like a tsunami of betrayal.

"Roxy …"

"I came here to bring you home. Daddy is still distraught, and I've missed you just every day. The whole town wants you back, *Mother*."

"Honey, it's just not that simple."

"You outright left us! You left your sixteen-year-old daughter. Mother, you said you were going to the 'barber' to have your hair done and you never returned. Before we decided that you had abandoned us, we thought something had happened to you. That you had been killed or taken or something! That the Deckers had done some awful thing. I thought you were dead!"

Caroline's beautiful eyes soon became puddles of tears, running down her soft face. "I didn't mean to hurt you, but I wasn't strong, I'm not strong like you are, baby girl! I knew you were and I knew you would be able to go on. I found out I was carrying a child who wasn't your father's and I panicked. I walked out the doors of The Dakota and went straight for San Francisco, and knocked on Nick's door. I told him how I was carrying his child and we decided on raising it together. He couldn't move out to New York, so I stayed here. I thought about you every single day! Don't think I didn't. I had a very hard decision to make but I made it. But you have to understand, it's an adult matter and—"

"You sound like an absolute crazy person. Someone who belongs in an insane asylum. This is the most ridiculous thing I've ever heard. You're right, you're not strong. You are nothing but *weak*, Mother."

"I'm sorry." She took a pause. "When I rang you on Christmas, I was going to tell you everything. I heard you crying over the telephone and I hung up because I couldn't bear to say it. I thought it was better to leave it as is and let you move on without me, Scarlett Roxy."

Roxy knew in her heart all of this was true. She looked deeply into her—*aunt's*—eyes with anger and grief. "So ... you were never going to ever come back? *Aunt*—Caroline?"

"Oh sweetheart, please continue to call me Mother. Honey, I may not have birthed you but I am your mother."

That was true.

"My mother? A mother wouldn't leave her daughter. I'd like to think you would still care about me, but it wouldn't be true—"

That wasn't true. Caroline did in fact still love and care deeply for her daughter, it was just a ... *complicated situation.*

"Oh Scarlett, of course I care. I love you more than words can describe. I knew when I took you in as my daughter, I would be your mother. Maybe an aunt by blood, but a mother by heart."

"Pathetic."

Roxy gazed into Caroline's eyes, confused and afraid— and this was a girl who didn't fear. The thought of the woman whom she called Mom never gave birth to her frightened Roxy. Everything she knew was suddenly a lie. Can you imagine?

"Would you like me to tell you about your mother—my sister—Daisy? Would you like me to tell you how this all went down?"

"I only met Aunt Daisy but a few times. I only remember her face from the photograph of us when I was just born. The picture that now truly says a thousand words. It all makes sense why Daisy was crying in the photograph, because she gave me to you. So no, I don't wanna hear it. She clearly couldn't give a damn about me, she didn't even keep me!"

"Scarlett, come inside please."

Roxy looked to her right, debating the choice of staying or walking down the steps to Frankie, only to get in a car and leave, returning back to her sparkling city of New York.

Roxy turned away from Caroline as her eyes became waterfalls. "Scarlett Roxy, don't go!" her mother yelled.

Roxy turned around with heavy tears in her eyes and wet cheeks from crying; heartbroken, she decided to go into the house—only to find out about Daisy, as she was starting to become curious. Wouldn't you be?

Frankie was still standing at the bottom of the steps. "I guess I'll wait here then," he said to himself quietly, "in the pouring rain." He sat down on the concrete.

A straighter-faced Roxy took her right foot and stepped into the beautifully decorated home. "Tell me everything."

"I'll put on the kettle for tea."

"Aunt Caroline, please," she said with a stern voice.

Caroline was upset by Roxy using *aunt* instead of *mother*. She didn't want Roxy to think of her as an aunt. Caroline put on the kettle and grabbed two porcelain teacups from the cabinet. She put two Earl Grey tea bags into the cups and walked to her bedroom where she searched under her bed. A box of old pictures was centered, hidden by the other miscellaneous items she owned and crowded under her wrought-iron bed. Many photographs of Daisy, pregnant. The photos were the key to this untold story; they would reveal the truth to Roxy.

As Caroline walked back into the living room, she turned off the radio and handed the mysterious box to her now known niece. "These are photographs—of Daisy."

"I can see that," Roxy said, refusing to make eye contact with Caroline.

"She was only eighteen. An unmarried young girl."

"Not much older than me."

"Not at all. It's a very long story, Roxy—why don't you spend the night and I'll explain everything in the morning."

"I don't care to stay here."

Nick Terry was out of town, in Los Angeles for work.

"Honey, it would be great. You would get a chance to be with Ruth."

"Ruth?"

"Your sister."

"Don't you mean cousin?"

"Oh Roxy."

They took a silent pause.

"You named her after Grandma?"

"Roxy, please stay—"

She put her coat back on. "No, Caroline, I will not. Frankie is outside in the rain and if I leave him out there much longer he'll turn into a fish. I have to go—"

"He can stay too!"

"We have a hotel room. I'll be back in the morning."

Roxy left the house and slammed the door quicker than Caroline could get out the three words "I love you".

Roxy raced down the steps with an umbrella she had taken from the house. "You look—"

"Wet? Yes, that's because I'VE BEEN STANDING IN THE RAIN FOR THE PAST—"

"Go fly a kite, Frankie."

He rolled his eyes and clenched his perfect jaw, but knew he couldn't argue this one. He had no right to be mad and he was okay with that.

"I'm sorry love, was it … worth it?"

"I'm not sure yet."

She was walking in front of him on the sidewalk. He took her hand and gently pulled her around.

"What happened, Roxy doll?" he said as they peered into each other's eyes.

He could tell she was an utter wreck; her cheeks were still puffy and wet and her eyes glassy. He grabbed her and hugged her tight. She wrapped her arms around his neck and they stood there in the pouring rain, holding each other. He loved the way she felt in his arms, and she loved the way he held her so tight, the way they *both* held each other so tight.

She told him everything that went down as they got into a taxi back to the hotel. Frankie wanted to get her mind off of everything, so he took her to a park. The weather was still dark and rainy. They danced in puddles and had their own unique fun while everyone else was attempting to escape the angry wetness falling swiftly from the sky. Roxy went back to the house the next morning, ready to hear everything from the woman whom she felt had betrayed her.

In order to explain this to the best of an understanding, I am going to have to take you back in time to the early 1900s, many events and many years before … *The Roaring.*

CHAPTER 8

THE YEAR OF 1907

It was 1907, Daisy Brooks was just eighteen years of age and Caroline was twenty-two. Dennis Elliott was twenty-three and engaged to the young Caroline. They loved each other deeply, and he wanted to spend the rest of his life with her; however, he was not at all *in* love with her. There is a difference, you know. He was *in* love with the younger Brooks girl, Daisy. He and Daisy, however, both knew they could never be together—that it would destroy Caroline.

"Darling, you are engaged to my sister—"

"But I don't have to be! I want to be with *you*, Daisy darling," the young Elliott boy said with passion to his true love.

"Ruth won't have it. You know my mother and her *ways*—if you were to break off your engagement to my sister and run away with me, it would cause a scandal too grand," Daisy said with the most distraught agony.

Daisy spoke nothing but truth when she dreaded the scandal that would come, that would be hidden by two rather powerful American families. However, the young Dennis could not have cared less as he proceeded to fall in love with the beautiful Daisy Brooks. The air that day was thin, as February in New York was cold and lonely. The pair brought heat and warmth, however, to the near-freezing temperatures of the city. Dennis was over at the Brooks family townhome on 5th Avenue at the time, planning the grand and costly wedding Caroline had pictured since she was a child.

He had taken a break from her and gone up to Daisy's room. "I cannot keep living this lie—"

"Lie? There is no lie, Dennis, only scandal, and our families cannot be known as such—"

"New York is filled with scandal and lies! What's one more to add—"

They couldn't keep from cutting each other off as they fought the idea of loving each other.

"Brooks, Elliott, Decker, Romano, Matthews—" Daisy began to name off some of the highest of society names in New York, but Dennis cut her off.

"And?"

"The New York names of prestige! Of wealth, and yours happening to be one of the five families. We are pictured as perfect, and cannot fall from that with a 'Young Elliott boy ditches his fiancée Caroline Brooks to run away with the younger sister' scandal. It's simply not allowed!"

"You act as if we don't already have popularized scandals—"

"This is different, my darling—"

"Then let's break the rules! I want to be with YOU, *not Caroline*. God knows I love her, but not like I love you, not at all. And though the Elliotts are seen as 'perfect', we are also a mob family nonetheless and a scandal like this won't change New York's view on us. We are perfect because we are powerful, wealthy, and, dare I say, *very* attractive. A scandal doesn't change that. We'll still have our wealth, we'll still have our power, and we will still be known as the glamorous family that gets away with crime."

He wasn't wrong.

"Dennis …"

"I would only be hurting her—"

"You would be hurting both your family and mine!"

They took a moment of silence, Dennis with his hand holding up his head and Daisy looking out her window to the park. The two let out a simultaneous sigh.

"Dennis!" Caroline called from downstairs.

"Yes my love," he said with a lack of enthusiasm while giving Daisy one last look, then left her bedroom.

She rushed to him, grabbed his right arm and turned him around. She gave him one last look and kissed him with passion. A kiss that lasted but seven seconds before it was interrupted by an aggravated Caroline yelling from the dining room downstairs. Dennis took his hands and held Daisy's soft face as tears ran down their cheeks.

"I love you."

He made his way downstairs back to Caroline as they finished up their guest list. Daisy decided the best choice for her to make was to leave. She thought she'd go to Paris, maybe Vienna, or possibly London. She knew she had to leave in order for Dennis to learn to love his Caroline. Hurting her sister was never Daisy's intention, but love got in the way, as it always seems to do. She had always known there was a thin line between love and hate, and if she stayed, she would experience what was once love turn into a loathing hatred against Daisy from Caroline. Experiencing her sister crossing that daring line. She knew she would lose her dear sister and she couldn't bear the thought.

Daisy had locked herself in the room for the rest of the day, packing what she would need for her journey to begin a new life in Europe. She had friends in many cities whom she knew would help her start a life over there. The last thing she took was her diary as a tear dropped onto the red leather cover, then she dropped it into her Louis Vuitton Steamer bag. She looked out her once beautiful window and turned off the lamp next to her bed. Daisy gathered her things as a knock came from her door. She dropped them with fright and a chill came across her entire body. Night had fallen and she had figured no one would hear or see her leave.

"Daisy, darling, open up. It's me."

A voice so familiar, so loving—yet it was only panic that greeted her as she listened. The plan to leave without a goodbye was now far from inevitable. Her face tense and her heart near shattered, she stood still in terror.

"Please, Daisy, I need to speak to you," Dennis said before he took a long pause, finishing with, "I am planning on telling her in the morning—Caroline. I don't care what happens, but I owe it to her, to you, and to myself. We deserve this and she deserves to find her own happiness, her own true love. Oh come on, I know you're in there."

Daisy fell onto her bed, now in a full-blown cry, waiting for the right decision to enter her mind. But it never came. It was gone, along with her perfect idea to disappear.

"No." She couldn't come up with anything better to say. "No, Dennis."

"Oh, open the door," he said, and she opened the door to the confused and frightened Elliott boy.

"What is this? What—" he said as his eyes went straight to the luggage.

"Dennis—"

"Are those—?" He looked away from the luggage and met her eyes once more.

"I'm leaving, and there is nothing you can say. I am leaving to go to Paris tonight."

Roxy got her love of Paris from her mother; she swore it was where the other half of her heart was, and she felt this way until her death met her at age ninety-seven.

"No!" he said, exasperated, making his way into her bedroom.

"Please, just leave already! I've … made up my mind."

"You can't be serious, Daisy—" His voice cracked; he knew she *was* serious and there would be no convincing her otherwise.

He was filled with emotions he couldn't comprehend. All saddened ones.

"I am, and there is nothing you can do about it!"

"Will I ever see you again?" he said, as his eyes began to water with tears from a torn-apart love.

"I don't know, maybe someday, years after you have started a family with my sister—"

"No."

"Dennis."

"DAISY!"

"PLEASE! I'M BEGGING YOU!" She wanted to avoid this. "Stop or I will cry too ..."

"How am I supposed to go on without you in my life?" His voice grew soft.

I guess he figured out how, because after that night, he *would* in fact go on without his dear beloved Daisy Brooks, and would live on with Caroline. That is until she decided to leave, of course. Though, he did see Daisy regularly for nine months, but not in the way he would have ever preferred.

"Oh Dennis, please, just let me leave—" she began to beg as he grabbed her by the waist with his left hand, then her neck with his right, and kissed her.

The two lovers stood there in the dark, kissing passionately. They felt no shame in that moment.

Their conversation ended and the tears began to dry as minutes went on and clothes came off. Dennis ran his hand down Daisy's back and back up again as he began to unbutton her silk dress. It fell to the floor, and she stepped out of it and closer to him. She kicked off her shoes while taking the first part of his suit off, throwing it onto her luggage. The room was filled with steam as pieces of clothing were slowly falling off onto the floor. Daisy stopped kissing him, locked the door, took his hand, and led him to her bed. This was February 17th, 1907, nine months before Miss Roxy Elliott was born. This was the first time they had ever slept together, and it was electric. They truly "made love", as one would say. He was soon on top of her as he slid his hand up her thigh, unclipped and removed her stockings—then eventually made his way to her silk and lace knickers. She removed his underwear and pulled him close by his tie, before taking it off of him and tossing it to the floor. They were meant to be together, and this would remain the best night of each of their lives. They held each other all night before the sun woke them up.

"Dennis—" she whispered.

"How 'bout we both leave?"

"What?"

"We can both leave and we won't have to face the Elliotts or the Brooks. We can write a note and start a family in Paris. We can find a place in the fifth or the second arrondissement, those are your favorites, aren't they? Or by the Eiffel Tower in the seventh—"

He was so ambitious, ready to leave everything behind for her. She wanted the same, but knew this wasn't how it could be. Not for them.

"No."

"No?"

"Oh, Dennis, God last night was incredible, and I will cherish it for the rest of my life, but I still stand with my plan to leave. I'll leave today."

He lay there in shock and confusion. "But, I don't understand, last night—"

"Was a wonderful way to say goodbye." She shed a single tear.

They both lay there for another few fleeting minutes, in each other's arms, heartbroken and silently crying. This was *true* love. The kind of love Roxy and Frankie would someday have. *Not yet though, of course.*

That was the last they saw of each other, until she arrived back from Paris, two months later, *two months pregnant*. She had come back to a married Dennis and Caroline Elliott; she was now her true love's sister-in-law. She met with him in a private room at Keens Steakhouse, and he felt yet another feeling beyond description. He was now married to Caroline, and yet, having a baby with Daisy. Her sister, his love. This was the scandal she wanted to avoid. A scandal that called for the help of her mother, Ruth. He took her back to their new place, the penthouse of The Dakota, where he rang Ruth. When she found out about the pregnancy she was mortified, though Ruth knew she would figure out a way to keep it under wraps, without all of New York City finding out what had happened between the two families.

The Elliotts and the Brooks were in unison with this new plan, to send Daisy back to Paris while she was pregnant, where she would eventually give birth to Roxy. They would have

113

Caroline fake a pregnancy and have the two newlyweds raise the child as their own, and keep the secret between the two families for eternity.

Guess that didn't happen.

Caroline and Dennis both agreed to *never* tell Roxy the truth, and Ruth banished Daisy from New York. On the day Roxy was born, November 17th, 1907, a photograph of Daisy and her baby was taken.

Only a few times did Daisy see Roxy: her first birthday, her third Christmas, and one time at the park when she was five, though Dennis secretly kept her in the know about every big thing that happened with her. Roxy barely remembered the three encounters she had with her biological mother, but she knew she loved her.

Daisy was just as beautiful as Caroline, if not more so. She was glamorous like Roxy and loved to laugh, and Roxy always felt that when she thought of her, though she couldn't remember her soft voice. She kept the picture taken at her birth on her nightstand her whole life, never knowing what it *truly* meant. Never knowing what the *real* story behind the photograph was. Dennis wanted to tell her the truth, always, but Caroline refused to let him—always worried Roxy would never forgive them. Roxy had always wondered where her mother's sister was. Why wasn't she at any family events or holidays? Little did she know she was banished from the city she once called home. Daisy lived in Paris for years before living in Chicago. She then eventually moved to Los Angeles, where she was known to the world as aunt to Roxy Elliott.

CHAPTER 9

THE LIES NO LONGER BELIEVED

The flight was bumpy and the turbulence caused Roxy to feel even more sick than she had been from the recent events that had taken place, and the new information that she now held. After that morning, the morning Caroline Elliott revealed her *biggest* secret, her *largest* lie, and the *saddest* scandal she had ever kept hidden, Roxy took the box of photos and ran back to the hotel. Frankie packed all of Roxy's belongings up as she sat on the edge of the bed in the hotel room trying to put the pieces together, sorting through the photographs of her mother. *Daisy, that is.*

After everything was packed up and ready to go, she looked at Frankie with tears in her eyes while remaining the strong girl she was. He went over to her and hugged her tightly, then whispered into her ear and made her laugh, that contagious laugh she had. Frankie *always* knew how to make her feel better and how to make her stubborn self see things in a brighter way.

They complemented each other, they *completed* each other.

You could say it was thanks to the fact that they were in love with each other. Cluelessly, of course. Well, at least for a few more months that is.

They held each other firmly for a moment of bliss before he kissed her on the cheek and grabbed their bags. They walked out the hotel door to a cab ready to take them back to the airport, ready to leave for New York.

On the airplane, Roxy slept most of the way, as she hadn't got much shut-eye during their short yet eventful San Francisco trip. When she returned to New York, she entered the Elliott residence with a new perspective and a different mindset than when she had left. Her father greeted her with a hug and a kiss on the forehead and their chef made her a cup of coffee. Grandfather Griffin was there as well, and so was Uncle Clyde and Aunt Elizabeth. They knew the truth, *the whole family did*, as did the Brooks. Though, the rest of Manhattan was kept cautiously in the dark.

"Roxy, how was your trip with Marie?" Aunt Elizabeth said to her as she sipped her warm coffee.

"I'm just curious … did you all know?"

They all gave Dennis a look as Uncle Clyde sank onto the couch and took a sip from his glass. They were all gathered in the main living room, the grand one in the center of the penthouse with the fireplace, grand furniture, and the chandelier hanging tall above their heads of course.

"Roxy—" Dennis began to say as he was cut off.

"Oh, you have your damn nerve—"

"Roxy!" Griffin chimed in, sternly.

"What? It's not like you weren't in on it—"

They all knew what exactly was about to go down. They had never seen Roxy so furious, all led by what she thought was betrayal.

"Honey, let your father explain—" Aunt Elizabeth added, trying to sympathize. However, she wasn't helping the least bit.

"No, I love you but this doesn't include you. I'm angry at you all for keeping this from me but it's my father who's to blame."

"Let me explain."

"No!"

"How did you find out?"

"I wasn't with Marie, Daddy." She took a pause before adding, angrily, "I went to San Francisco with Frankie—"

"San Francisco?" he said, too in shock to have heard the "with Frankie".

"Yes, San Francisco," she said with the utmost anger she could have pulled forth. She took a pause before continuing, "She's alive, just to let you know—Nick Terry, you know him?"

The whole family took another pause and looked back at Dennis, as Grandma Margret walked through the door.

Dennis took notice of his mom. "Mother?"

"I brought a pie! Dahlia, my cook, made it. She is just absolutely incredible!"

"Mom, this isn't the time—" He was cut off as she walked

toward her fury-filled granddaughter.

"Roxy! Darling, I brought you a new lipstick, thought this was a beautiful color—"

"Thank you, Grandma," she said softly, before returning her glare toward her father.

Margret went over to Griffin and sat next to him while the pie was being dished up for the family.

"What's going on here? Why is everyone so tense?"

"She ... she knows, Mom," Clyde said, almost with a touch of embarrassment, though he was laughing on the inside. He knew this day was to come and had wanted Dennis to stand up to Caroline and tell Roxy, but he wouldn't. This was almost an "I told you so" moment for Clyde.

Margret looked up at Roxy. "Oh, baby—"

"I'm only angry with my father."

"She found her, she found Caroline," Aunt Elizabeth told Margret.

"You found your mother?"

"Is that the only thing you have to say?" Roxy raised her voice.

"I think we all need to take a break," Griffin said as the room fell silent and the butlers brought everyone a slice of pie on a small porcelain plate accompanied by a silver fork.

Clyde and Dennis simultaneously took a sip of their scotch as Grandma Margret went into the kitchen and made herself a martini. *A strong one.*

"I don't want to take a *break*, I want to know why you never told me."

"Honey, I love you, and I always wanted to but Caroline—"

"Oh what, Caroline wouldn't let you? Were you *scared* of her?"

Clyde chuckled and Roxy glared at him. There is no way to convey how brokenhearted she felt, and it seemed as if her family didn't care. Though they did, and they felt terribly for her, she couldn't see that. Her eyes were clouded by anger.

"I don't know why, to tell you the truth. I should have and I'm sorry. Things went on and everything became routine. Daisy was off living in different cities, living her life and as the years went on I began to love Caroline. Not like I did your aunt—or—mother, but I did."

"Daddy—" She gave him a snarky laugh, not believing what was coming out of his mouth.

"And we had a great life! Both our families were booming and we—you, me, and Caroline, had a great family. I didn't want to mess any of that up."

"And what's this business with Nick Terry?" Clyde interrupted, curious of what Roxy had found out.

Roxy took a bite of the pie she had received. It was a mouthwatering, aroma heavy, warm apple pie, *one of her favorites.* She sat there, staring out to Central Park for a moment before she calmed down and decided her father was telling the truth and had nothing but love for her, and that the rest of them had only kept his wishes at heart. They weren't trying to lie to her, it was merely something that had to be done.

Roxy began to tell the story—*everything*—down to the last detail. Everything about how it was her friends who helped her find her mother, or now—*aunt*. How, thanks to Dalton, they had an address in hand. They were in shock by the idea of Caroline cheating on Dennis and getting pregnant by Nick. No one could have imagined that. She wasn't the type, or I guess—she wasn't up until she was. People change, right? Dennis was heartbroken, yet he understood. Nick Terry was Caroline's first and true love. Though, she *did* fall in love with the young Elliott back before Roxy. When she found out about Daisy, that love began to wither away. Dennis didn't have any sympathy for what Caroline had done—getting pregnant and leaving her family. However, he couldn't really say much, since he had fallen in love with her own sister while with her. I mean, that *is* the reason their marriage wasn't perfect, even if it appeared to be.

February 23rd, 1925

Dear Diary,

I haven't written in a while, but quite frankly I haven't had the time. Frankie was the perfect gentleman, almost, during our trip to San Francisco. The trip that changed everything. We came back today, and I confronted my dad on what happened and why he never told me that Aunt Daisy was my mother and Caroline my aunt. Grandma and Grandfather were there, along with Aunt Elizabeth and Uncle Clyde, but Tommy was out with his fiancée. I told them everything. Everything about why she left and about Nick Terry. This was all a few hours ago—now I'm at Marie's, telling her and Virginia everything.

I went to one of the guest bedrooms because I felt that I needed to get in a quick diary entry, so I can go back someday and read about how I'm feeling in this very moment. Frankie told the boys what happened, and we are all meeting at the Elliott speakeasy under The Dakota for drinks later. Hopefully I can drown my sorrows in a large glass of champagne, or possibly more than a few martinis with extra gin. We didn't have school today, and we don't tomorrow either. Some staff day, I'm not really sure why but I'm not complaining. Between everything that happened at the Valentine's Dance and the trip to California, I'm not really sure what is to come next.

And she didn't—she hadn't a clue what was to come next.

CHAPTER 10

THE DAY SHE RETURNED

Let's skip to March. March 16th ... to be exact.

March 16th was a special day for Manhattan, and in particular, the Elliott family.

In the past few weeks, little has happened. Roxy and Dean are still together, Claire and Johnny are still an item, and Marie is dating a new boy. Dalton was grounded for two weeks due to drinking; Virginia, her brother, and her mom went to Chicago for a few days to see family; and as for Frankie? He's participated in nothing but trouble, as usual. All has been relatively ordinary lately, considering what events had rolled out since the weekend of February 21st. That was all until March 16th. The year of 1925 has been an interesting one so far, though this is still only the beginning. As I promised you before, it will only build from here and leave you with heartbreak in the end, *so continue to keep that in mind.*

"72nd and Central Park West, please," she said to the taxi driver as they took her and her Louis Vuitton luggage to The Dakota.

"On vacation or coming back home?"

"I'm not sure yet," she said as her eyes looked up at the early morning sunlight shining upon the New York City buildings—how calm and serene the city was before the excitement as the city awoke.

It was Monday morning, March 16th of 1925. The air was crisp and cold, though warmer than it had been in February. Wall Street was ready for another day of financial games, actors were eating breakfast before getting ready to perform later in the day, and schoolchildren were being anxiously woken up by their tired parents, ready for another grueling week.

Dalton was already up finishing the homework he had forgotten to do over the weekend as Frankie and Johnny came over to eat breakfast with him. Marie and Virginia were at Roxy's doing their hair and makeup before school, as they usually did. They all walked down to the main level of the Dakota penthouse to find the Elliott staff serving them a perfect breakfast. The boys rushed as they ate and finished their work and the girls gossiped and laughed while drinking orange juice out of crystal glasses, that was all until a familiar face walked through the tall, heavy wooden double doors of the penthouse. Dennis had fixed his tie as he walked into the living room, which was conveniently located directly across from the foyer—where she had been standing with a bag in each hand, a hat on her head, and of course, a pair of designer leather gloves on both of her perfectly manicured hands.

"It all looks as if nothing's changed."

The air stood still and their voices silent. The laughing of the girls was terminated by the echo of her voice, and every person standing in the Elliott penthouse fell into a striking state of shock as a rather breathtaking woman in the doorway continued to make herself feel at home, though it hadn't been for quite some time now.

"Where's Roxy?" she asked in a soft tone.

Dennis stood still with a blank, inexpressive look on his face. This wasn't a feeling he had imagined he would feel so soon. He wasn't ready yet, even though he had missed her for so long. Dennis looked right into her eyes as she gazed back into his. She was wearing red—red all over. A cherry-red coat with the matching red hat and gloves, along with red lipstick and red heels. This was Roxy's favorite color.

CHAPTER 11

Manhattan's Warm Welcoming

I am sure you are all *very* confused.

March 16th, 1925

Dear Diary,

I was eating breakfast with Marie and Virginia, and everything was grand and perfect. The first time things had truly felt great since my trip to San Francisco, since information so paramount was revealed to me. Sure, I wanted to know the truth, but it took a while for it to sink in and for me to go about the world, adjusting to the new life I would have to live. Everything I knew had changed so suddenly. I never thought she'd return. After finding out everything, I had the smallest bit of confidence in her return. I can't describe the feelings I felt when she walked through that door, and I cannot even begin to imagine what it was like for my father. The entire place stood in silence and shock, immobilized by the woman who had just so confidently walked through the door. Why, why was she back? What prompted her to come back after everything? When I heard the words "Where's Roxy", I dropped my glass full of fresh-squeezed, pulp-free orange juice to the ground and the only sound resonating through The Dakota was the shattering of a tall crystal glass. I was in utter shock myself, though I felt a wave of comfort and elation as I began to take in this cardinal moment. My mother had just walked through the door.

It was as if time had stopped in an instant, as if she had power over every clock in the world, and as if Manhattan itself knew its Brooks girl had come home.

She had finally returned to New York City, and it was glad to have her back. Everyone had missed her while she was gone, and she was nothing but delighted to be back home in the excitement of her old city.

The last time she had seen it, things were quite different, and it was only better now. The family missed her, all of them, and every friend she had jumped at the opportunity for a night back out on the town with our old Brooks girl. But above all, it was our dear Roxy that got the most out of her return; not even Dennis shared the ever-deep emotions Roxy would as she so eagerly stepped into the foyer to greet the woman standing in red.

"It's you," Roxy said as she stood under the grand chandelier.

"Darling," she grinned as a single tear ran down her beautiful face.

"Daisy!" Dennis exclaimed with a smile.

Marie and Virginia shared a look.

"Daisy?" they whispered simultaneously as they got up from their seats and raced to the foyer, as did every one of the Elliott maids and butlers.

"I hope you understand, and I hope you don't blame me. I hope you know that I love you very much and always have, and I truly hope you don't think that giving you up wasn't the hardest thing I've ever had to do. I made a mistake by falling in love with your father who was set to marry Caroline, but love is love and it always prevails—"

Roxy cut her off before she could continue to plead. "I don't blame you for anything, it was all Grandma Ruth who made you do it. I know you had no control, and goodness am I glad you finally returned," she said as she ran to the woman whom she had previously known as Aunt.

"Oh honey," Daisy barely got out, as beautiful tears dripped down her face and onto Roxy's shoulder, and she held her tightly.

Joy. A feeling Roxy was finally greeted by. It had been a while.

This was the first time Daisy had held Roxy as a mother. Every other time she had given her a hug, it was as Caroline's sister, *Aunt Daisy*, and nothing more. This was the first time the little girl looking back at her knew she was her mother, the person in whom she spent nine months being created.

"I have wished for this moment for seventeen years," Daisy said as she pushed Roxy back to get a good look at the beauty she had become.

"I never thought you would return." Roxy continued to smile and cry tears of joy.

"I was eighteen when I had you. I'm a thirty-five-year-old woman now, I am not letting my mother dictate anymore. I don't care if the whole town finds out!"

"Wow, she's so beautiful," Marie whispered again to Virginia.

Virginia replied, "Prettier than the pictures."

"She is truly Roxy's mother!" the maids whispered as they eavesdropped the extraordinary moment.

"Your father has kept me up to date on everything. He rings me once a week, telling me about you and what has happened recently. He has told me about all of your friends and sends me photographs of you every month. You and your adorable friends."

If the boys ever got word of being called "adorable" they'd have a hissy fit.

Roxy looked back to her father. "Is that true?"

"Of course." His eyes began to water. "Daisy, I haven't seen you in—"

"Many years," she smiled softly. A love like that doesn't disappear.

"Your voice is different than over the telephone, seeing you in person is a whole new type of joy. I just, I can't believe it. It's really you."

They all smiled.

Daisy hadn't been sure how this would go down. She had prepared for the worst, for Roxy to refuse her company and Dennis to shame her for returning. Talking to her on the telephone and sending her pictures was a dramatic leap away from her coming back to New York.

There was still one other person she had to convince, however, and that was Ruth Brooks. Her mother had not seen little Daisy since the day of Roxy's birth on November 17th, 1907. Her father, Walter Brooks, had seen her a few times and phoned her every now and then. His and Ruth's views differed from one another when it came to Daisy, though Ruth controlled the house. While Ruth still had a love for her daughter, she could never accept what she had done: foolishly falling in love with her sister's fiancé. Walter kept the connection to his daughter; he couldn't bear to let her go so suddenly, as Ruth did. Daisy knew if she rang her father first, and he was there when Ruth found out the news of her return, she might gain a warmer welcome.

As for the rest of Manhattan, they were happier to see her than they would have been Caroline, though the city missed *both* of our Brooks girls. When Daisy went over to the Brooks townhome on 5th Avenue, her mom greeted her with a shock of emotions and a surprising hug. Daisy had been certain she would go off on her, but her father must have put in a word or two. It had been seventeen years and Ruth's heart had apparently softened since their last gathering. I'm not going to go into detail on what was said, but I am sure you can imagine and paint a pretty picture of the reunion between the old family members.

As for after she left The Dakota? Roxy and the girls went to school and she told Johnny, Dalton, and Frankie everything. After school, they all went for dinner at the Brooks residence and everything seemed to be out-of-a-movie perfect. Straight out of the newest, heartwarming sappy film. That was all until our *other* Brooks girl, our *former* Elliott, arrived.

CHAPTER 12

A NOT SO WARM WELCOMING

It seems as if the pesky silence has taken a steroid and infected all of Manhattan, because here we are again, sitting in utter silence as another one of Manhattan's most glamorous women *once again* graces us with her presence.

This ... was Caroline Elliott.

Dennis practically choked on his champagne as she walked into a dining room full of guests: Ruth, Walter, Daisy, Dennis, Roxy, Marie, Virginia, Dalton, Johnny, Frankie, some of Roxy's cousins, and a few of Daisy's old friends. It was a soirée of guests for a dinner party consisting of duck and escargot—and Caroline had just crashed it.

Hadn't they had enough surprise stories and guests? Apparently not.

"What do you think you're doing here?" Walter let out. By now he had heard of her running off with Nick Terry and her new baby girl, God what a scandal. What is it with the wealthy?

"What happened to you, all your class and decency has gone," Ruth chimed in.

It was almost as if the tables had flipped. It was now Caroline whom Ruth had shunned, and Daisy whom she welcomed with open arms. *And all within an instant.* Doesn't everything seem to always happen "all within an instant"?

"I felt that it was time—"

"It was time? I don't think this was needed—" Dennis added in before Roxy cut him off.

"I think you need to leave, you had no business coming back."

"I had to, you don't understand—"

"I think we damn well do. You have shamed this family and this city more than Daisy ever could have. Cheating on your husband, getting pregnant by Nick and then leaving without a goodbye? Leaving your entire family and your daughter to mourn you as if you had died?"

"I know, Mother, I know what I did was wrong and I cannot begin to describe—"

"Don't go there, Caroline," Dennis said sternly.

"Nick's been in an accident."

A silence fell once again. The arguing and loud voices came to a complete halt as every guest was welcomed by an "aha" moment.

"So this is why you're here? Not to see me again, not to see

132

Dad, not to see your family or the friends you left behind," her once daughter got out before taking a bite of her dessert, as if she couldn't be bothered by Caroline's presence.

She began to weep. "I would have come back sooner, but I was ashamed!"

"Well now's not the time—"

The butlers took away the dirty dishes as Caroline sat down at the only empty seat at the rather large table.

"He's—"

Suddenly the room felt a sorrow for her. Regardless of her mistakes, if something had happened to Nick, they wouldn't completely shut her out like they did Daisy back in 1907. It was a different time and though they were all filled with anger and rage, they weren't going to leave her stranded. She *was* still family after all.

"Nick's been in an automobile accident."

"What?" Dalton said, not realizing he was speaking out loud. This was a man who had been close friends with his mother, and he had met him many times. Nick Terry was a good man. Whether or not he was wrong to sleep with a married woman, it was still heartbreaking.

"He's dead."

There was that silence again, though this time there was a haunted feeling in the air. Everyone in the room bowed their heads, taking in what they had just heard. What an eerie ending to a perfect dinner. This was all so sudden. Three weeks ago, Roxy had come back with news of Caroline's whereabouts, her new child, and her affair with the man who had just been killed. Like I said, he was a good man aside from sleeping with Caroline while she was still married to Dennis. He had made a successful life for himself, built his wealth and was a genuine, kindhearted man. His death was mourned by many. Caroline, in particular.

"Baby Ruth is with a friend of mine, Stella, who lives in Midtown. I thought it would be better to come without her," she said. Ironically, she had shown up the same day as Daisy's return. Who knew the Brooks girls were so alike? "His family knows, they were first to know. The house is going to his sister who lives out in LA. She offered to let me stay until I figure things out, but there was nothing keeping me in San Francisco except for him. Now that he's gone I have no one. I know none of you want me back, I understand that the city is done with me—"

"Don't say that, it isn't true. Only *we* know the real story—" Daisy added in.

"Daisy, I'm so happy to see you."

"Now's not the time, Caroline," said Ruth.

"I want to move back—to New York. Dennis and I will obviously get a divorce—"

"Obviously," he whispered under his breath with a grin and a laugh.

"And I'll raise baby Ruth here in the city, and hopefully you can all someday forgive me, but for now I've just lost the love of my life and the father of my child."

Everyone could sympathize with that.

"You'll move in here, we sure have enough room. You can

stay on the top floor of the townhome until needed. I'm not excusing your behavior, but I'm very sorry for what's happened," Ruth said, with a much calmer tone than she had started with.

March 16th had been quite a day.

It was on the 15th that Nick Terry had been in the awful accident, leaving Caroline and baby Ruth alone on the West Coast. This was the best option for her, and as families do, she was forgiven with time and the city of New York welcomed her back as Caroline Elliott.

As for Daisy?

The rest of the dinner was quite strange, but things lightened up after the adults had consumed more alcohol. Liquor has a way of making awkward situations *much* more tolerable. Frankie and Johnny may have also snuck a bit—or more than a bit—into their glasses, but who am I to snitch?

Caroline and Daisy ended up making amends, and the gang had gotten to know Daisy well that night, as they were looking forward to. Grandma Ruth told Roxy she could have her gang join them for dinner as they were so excited to meet Roxy's real mother, which was why they all attended.

Caroline did as Ruth said and moved into their home on 5th Avenue for the time being, until she bought her own place not far from her good friend Stella in Midtown.

Dennis and Caroline divorced, and he even began to forgive her, *with time of course*. Whether or not that was due to Daisy's return will forever be a mystery. All I know is that Dennis never stopped loving her, and things were due to change between them soon.

She moved into a residence at the Plaza—not far from the Brooks townhome. This is all the information on this specific topic that you need for now, to see where we all stand in the matter, so I guess it's on to the next rather *roaring* story.

CHAPTER 13

APRIL SHOWERS HIT HARD IN 1925

"She's in the room, I locked her up and she won't be able to escape."

"I'll phone Griffin in the morning, telling him to give the message to Dennis. Oh, and I heard Caroline and Daisy are back in town," Kenneth said to his cousin, Daniel Decker.

Daniel smirked. "They'll all fall with this one."

Once upon a time, not long ago, I told you the story of the fall of the Deckers. How their envy and anger got the head Decker, Thomas, killed by the hands of one of the Elliotts—a family who were their *superior*. While many Deckers were left alive, Kenneth was out for revenge on the family for killing his father, though he had it coming. Trying to take down an Elliott was like trying to take captive a wild tiger; you thought you could get close enough to capture it before it attacked, if you had all the right equipment, but instead your ego backfired. Leaving you in the dark with more than just a simple scratch on your face—*if you were lucky enough to be left alive, that is.*

This was how the Deckers went about.

Every time they made an attempt at taking down the Elliott name, they were only left with scratches so deep the recovery time was infinite. Though, they always seemed to think they could outrun and outsmart the tiger.

I may have hinted that their fall would be the last time you heard that name—but it won't be, and this won't either. Kenneth set out a target for the Elliotts, something that could *truly* destroy them. The Deckers were done trying to take their wealth and power, and they were done with their attempts to take control of the speakeasy scene, the bootlegging, and the gambling. All they wanted now was for the Elliott name to bleed, though they didn't realize it only bled with Decker blood.

Kenneth Decker, on April 2nd, proposed to his family a way to take revenge on the untouchable Elliotts, and to hurt them like they'd never hurt before. Kenneth Decker decided the best way to harm the family was to retaliate by taking the thing they cared about most. This wasn't their power, this wasn't their fortune, and it sure wasn't their name in the mafia game. This was the Elliott princess herself, Miss Roxy Elliott.

Despite the fact that she was *supposed* to be off limits, due to her age.

Daniel would be the one to break into the Elliott residence on the night of April 11th. They planned to first kidnap her and take her someplace far away from Manhattan, then send a call out to the Elliotts, telling them she would be killed in twenty-four hours. They weren't planning on bargaining her for a fortune; Kenneth only wanted blood. Having Roxy's blood on his hands was the only way he would feel he had avenged his father's death. If the Elliott family didn't find their Roxy in time, she was to be shot by Kenneth himself.

This isn't quite what happened, however.

Being involved with or meeting an Elliott in general was a blessing and a curse. If you did right by one, it was all good things to come. If you did wrong by one, you wished you had never entered their lives. This was a lesson the Deckers never seemed to learn.

On the night of April 11th, 1925, a girl was taken from the Elliott residence at the top of The Dakota. This girl was Marie Romano, *not* Roxy Elliott. Marie had spent the night after a party at Hazel Flynn's they all attended. Virginia had gone home sick (mixing alcohols is never a good idea) and the boys were off to The Hamptons for the weekend while Marie went home with Roxy. It was three in the morning when the girls finally arrived at home, and exactly fifteen minutes later they were passed out in Roxy's bed. At four, Marie woke up to get a glass of water downstairs from the kitchen. This is when hell broke loose at the Elliott residence.

"Go in, grab the girl, and get out as quick as possible," Kenneth said to Daniel before he managed to bypass all security and enter into the Elliott penthouse.

This was, I will say, *quite* an accomplishment in itself. Every Elliott family member had high security at their residences.

Daniel had never seen or met Roxy, and Marie and Roxy both had short bobs, though he wasn't aware of the difference between Marie's jet-black hair and Roxy's golden brown. She was in the kitchen, half asleep, holding a glass of water in her right hand when Daniel came behind her with a drugged cloth, placing it over her nose and mouth as he caught the glass of water before it fell and shattered all over the black-and-white tile floor. He brought the girl downstairs and exited the building through a back door as Kenneth and a few other family members got ready to lay her in the back of the automobile. The plan had worked out, surprisingly, to a T so far—before Kenneth came to realize he had taken the chief of the NYPD's daughter, Marie Romano. Only, Kenneth realized this *all* too late. The girl had been taken to a house out in Connecticut, in a small suburban town called Southport.

Kenneth was the one driving, and when they had all arrived at the house, he went to unlock the doors as he saw Daniel carrying a rather different face into the Connecticut home. "DANIEL!"

"What?" Daniel was shocked by Kenneth's angry and disappointed tone.

"Are you kidding me?" he said, as everyone stood still in fear of what might come out of Kenneth's mouth next. "You took the wrong girl."

They all began to panic; this was not your usual kidnapping-gone-wrong hiccup, this was not something they had accounted for when going over issues that could possibly come up. Taking Marie Romano instead of Roxy Elliott was an idea that never crossed any of their minds. They were all immobilized in fear of what to do next. How were they supposed to execute their plan of revenge on the Elliott name if they took a Romano girl?

"You're an absolute asinine idiot, you know that?"

"I'm sorry, she was in the picture—I thought this was our girl. The kitchen was dark, she had short hair—I was positive this was our girl—"

"Well dammit, Daniel, it's not!"

"What do we do now? Return her? Go back for Roxy?"

"We can never go back for Roxy—after your screwup the Elliotts are going to make sure this could never happen again. They'll bring us all down this time. Taking a girl from Dennis's place isn't going to make them too happy."

"Well then maybe we can still take our revenge. If we kill her they'll be just as upset—"

"No, they won't. They won't be happy, but it won't hurt 'em like it would with Roxy. Killing this girl will only piss them off—they won't cry about it, they'll just slaughter us and everyone we associate with."

"So then what, what'll we do?"

Meanwhile, morning was creeping up on the island of Manhattan and Roxy was beginning to wake. When she ran to her windows to let the morning sunlight in, she thought nothing of Marie's absence, only assumed that she was in the powder room or downstairs eating whatever one of the chefs had conjured up for her. However, this sadly wasn't the case.

Roxy walked down one of the staircases yelling, "Marie! Marie, where are ya?"

"Good morning Miss Roxy, would you like some coffee?" one of the butlers asked.

"Yes please, leave it for me in the main family room would you?" she responded, as he nodded.

Roxy continued throughout the penthouse, searching for her dearest friend, who was nowhere to be found. She ran into her father's study with her piping-hot cup of black coffee in her right hand.

"Daddy!"

"Good morning, Roxy doll—"

"Marie—she's not here."

"What?"

"We came home last night together from Hazel's party, you know, Hazel Flynn?"

"Yes of course! Her and her brother are fine young kids—"

She cut him off. "Yes, well Marie came home with me last night and when I woke this morning she wasn't here. She's gone."

"Well, it's not like her to leave without a goodbye, or at least a note to say she'd gone home."

"I know that Daddy, why do you think I'm in such a panic?"

They both simultaneously took an anxiety-filled sip of their coffee and sat it down on the wooden desk.

Roxy sat down in the chair across from him. Dennis put down the newspaper he was reading and put his right hand over his mouth. He knew this girl like she was his own daughter. Virginia too—they were like family to the Elliotts. All of Roxy's closest friends were. He *knew* there wasn't an explanation for her absence other than something terribly awful. If she had left early in the morning to return home (which she'd never done and would never do in the first place), she'd at least write Roxy a note and leave it on her nightstand for when she woke, if not wake her up and say goodbye.

"Let's not panic. First, I'll ring her father and see if she's home. You ring Virginia and see if she knows anything."

"Yes, Daddy."

He took her hand and squeezed it tight, relieving some of Roxy's contagious worry. She went back to the main family room and rang Virginia as Dennis rang the Romanos from his study.

They both received the answer they feared—a clear-as-crystal "no, she's not here".

As for the Deckers, they were in fear of what would come next for them. Marie was still out like a light and they knew if they could return her back to New York before she woke, she'd have no idea of what had happened. No memory of anything. The only issue remaining was that the Elliotts were now involved. The Romanos' immediate response was a fear she that had been kidnapped, and the conversation between Marie's father and Roxy's was filled with ideas on who would have done such a thing.

"I'm the chief of the NYPD, Dennis, I've got enemies."

"But one that would go so far as to take Marie? In my home, nonetheless?"

"I don't know Dennis, you got any other ideas?"

He thought for a quick moment. "I do."

"You do?"

"It wasn't Marie who was supposed to be taken, it was my Roxy."

"The Deckers."

"Don't you worry Calvin, I'll have my guys out for Decker blood. We'll find her and end them."

"Dennis, I know you will, but I've got to get *my* guys on this too. Luckily the majority of the NYPD has a liking for your family, despite your family business. I think we should be able to work together, don't you?"

Only this wasn't the complete truth. Sure, the Elliotts had quite a few on the inside of the NYPD, but it was by no means a majority—and we will come back to that later on, when Calvin and Dennis are on very *different* terms.

April 12th, 1925

Dear Diary,

Marie, she's gone. My father and hers are together as I'm writing this, figuring out where she is and what to do with the Deckers when they find her. If it is the Deckers who took her, anyways. Daddy's theory is that they were meant to take me, as revenge for Thomas Decker's overdue death. I rang Virginia and the boys and they are all coming over soon. Frankie, Dalton, and Johnny were in The Hamptons when this all went down, but they left immediately after my call. Virginia has got a violin lesson, but she'll be here shortly after. If anything were to happen to Marie I'd only blame myself. I love her like a sister and it was supposed to be me. And if I'm being completely honest, she isn't the strongest girl out there. She'll only have a panic attack in a situation like this. She won't fight back or defend herself to the best she could. Marie's not like me. She's amazing, oh God I love her, but she doesn't have the strength of an Elliott and I worry. I'll keep praying for her and hope that my family and hers can pull this one off. I don't worry that my family won't take their revenge, I worry that they won't make it to Kenneth in time. If they were willing to kill me, an Elliott, then why wouldn't they do the same to her? Oh Lord … I just heard the door open, Virginia's here. I'll write later, hopefully with damn better news.

The sun was soon to set over Manhattan, and Marie was still nowhere to be found. Calvin, her father, had the NYPD all over the city searching for her. The Elliotts had many family members and associates looking for her as well, and searching for a fight with the family whom they loathed with such great power. The boys had arrived at Roxy's and they all sat in agony wishing there was something they could do to help their friend, but there wasn't. The Deckers had already set in motion their next step to their failed plan. They would return Marie and flee the city, knowing this was their only option if they wished to stay alive.

Kenneth drove them back to New York and they dropped dear old Marie on East 97th and 2nd Avenue, where no Elliott nor NYPD had searched yet. After they let her out of the car and onto the street she began to wake. They drove off before she could see who they were.

When she woke, her vision was blurry and her mind confused. She stood up on her feet and looked to the street sign and realized she was on the Upper East Side, a way away from her Upper West Side home. She walked to and eventually down Park Avenue, then ended up at the Plaza.

Thankfully, she had money in her coat pocket to make a call. When she arrived at the Plaza her hair was far from done up and she looked as if she had stumbled in after a few too many drinks and a night with a boy. She used a phone to ring Roxy first, knowing she'd be home with the others waiting for a call. She wasn't sure if her mother and father would be home or out searching for her, so Roxy was the best bet as she only had enough money in her pocket for one call. Her purse was, of course, in Roxy's bedroom.

"Marie?" said a velvet voice from a few feet away.

Marie, dialing the number to the Elliott residence, stopped and turned around. "Caroline?"

Caroline had been visiting her sister at the Plaza, and was headed to the Romanos' to comfort them as they waited for Marie's hopeful return.

"Oh, baby girl, thank God!" she said as she ran to her and gave her a hug. She had always loved Marie like a daughter and was distraught over the kidnapping.

Marie dropped the telephone. "Caroline, I am okay! I'm here, I'm alright—"

"Oh, everyone is worried sick about you. Dennis has got the whole Elliott family out looking for you and the Deckers, ready to take them all down once and for all. Your father's got the NYPD searching town as well. What happened? How did you escape?"

"I—don't know? I don't remember anything. Last thing I remember I was at Roxy's, getting a glass of water in her kitchen and from there on everything is just—black," she said, extremely confused, before adding, "The Deckers?"

"Odd, they must have drugged you then. Yes, the Deckers. Dennis believes this was an attack on the family, that it was Roxy who was to be taken but you were instead."

"Oh gosh, is Roxy alright? Where is she—"

"They are all fine, waiting for you to return. I've got a car out front waiting for me, ring your parents and we will head straight to them."

"Alright, thank you Caroline."

She gave Marie a smile and waited for her to finish the call before they both left the Plaza with great joy, walking down the red velvet steps and entering the shiny black automobile. When they arrived at the Romanos', the family was more than overjoyed, as you can imagine. Calvin thanked Dennis and Roxy and the gang ended up at Marie's as well. This wasn't the end, however. The Deckers were in deep trouble, but they were also gone. Nowhere to be seen. Dennis and Griffin were ready to take them all out. However, that couldn't happen if they'd fled the city. For now, they would keep their hunt for blood top priority—but nothing of the Deckers came up for months. In fact, we won't officially see the wrath of the Deckers until next summer. So, I guess you'll have to wait until we've reached July of 1926 to find out the true and tragic ending of this feud between the two families. As for this very moment, Marie is safe and Manhattan is free of the envious, rage-filled Decker family. Life seemed to be good.

As for our next story, it will introduce the very two characters who threw the party on April 11th: Hazel and Henry Flynn. They were a fellow uber-wealthy brother and sister duo who were close to our six friends. Not quite a part of their tight-knit group of six, but indeed important to each of them. Let us see what happens in the ever so busy lives of our Manhattan teenagers of the 1920s, and here's to the Flynn family!

CHAPTER 14

HAVE YOU MET THE FLYNN'S?

Hazel and Henry Flynn were twins, of course. Twins who grew up right beside our six tight-knits, though they didn't *quite* make the cut. The Flynns weren't anything less than elite, however, so don't get me wrong. They might not have been as "special" as the others, but no one was. So who can you blame? They were, however, quite uniquely special and the gang was close to them. They all grew up going to the same schools, finding their independence in a rather busy city, and witnessing Manhattan enter the shiny golden era—all with the special six by the Flynns' sides. (I like that, "special six". Let's call them that, it's—roaring!) The Flynns threw incredible parties too, and they were at every party Roxy, Frankie, Marie, or any of the others threw. I wish I could tell you that they will both continue to have the great life they've lived so far, but unfortunately these stories don't exactly have a picture-perfect ending. Because let's face it, all the glamour of the 1920s and the lives of New Yorkers is all but a disguise, keeping the real events hidden from the outside world. It's an illusion, if I may. Especially with those who were intertwined with an Elliott, Romano, Williams, Matthews, James, or Davis. But they certainly weren't the only wealthy families in town, and they weren't the only ones with enemies.

Even more unfortunately, their enemies oftentimes overlapped with some of those of the names above. Let's just say, if the Flynns were to host a yacht party, one that included the parents of our special six (along with their children we love so dearly), this party wouldn't be a smooth sailing down the East River. More like a recipe for disaster, you could say. I mean, if all of your enemies were lined up for you at the same party, on the same night, wouldn't this be your time to strike?

Kill two birds with one—*flaming*—stone, right?

Well, this was the case for another rather *special* family. They weren't the Deckers, they weren't as wealthy, they didn't hold any power in the city, and they certainly weren't associated with any organized crime. They were merely a figment of the past. A girl gone too wild due to the green feeling we all know too well: envy.

You see, all of our families, including the Flynns (we're talking about the older generation: Roxy, Marie, Virginia, Frankie, Dalton, Johnny, and Hazel and Henry's parents), were all close friends growing up. However, they had a friend: Suzy Klein. Suzy was close to them, up until around the eleventh grade, when the rest of them exiled her from their friend group, leaving her with no friends, stripping her from happiness.

The reason, you ask? It's a sad one, I won't lie.

It started with Hazel and Henry's mom—who is quite the angel, so don't get the wrong idea. However, junior year *is* quite the difficult time. She found out that Suzy wasn't on the same financial level as the rest of them. She had always acted like she was wealthy, however, trying to fit in while keeping this terrible secret. Suzy didn't want anyone to know she and her mom lived in a 600-square-foot studio apartment on 108th Street and Columbus. Far from the glamorous, large residences that ran from the upper 60s through 80s on Central Park West.

When the secret came out, everyone turned on her for lying to them, and they didn't exactly come to love the real her.

The *poor* her.

So they exiled her from the group—Mrs. Flynn being the one who initiated it. However, Marie's mom Anne had a large part in shunning Suzy too. As did Dennis, Johnny's mom Lillie, Frankie's mom and dad, Virginia's mother, *and* Dalton's mother. All people who would be on the yacht tonight. *How convenient.*

"Are you going?"

"Am I going?"

"Yeah, are you coming? Tonight, to my parents' party …" Henry asked.

"Ohhh, that," Frankie said as he poured himself three ounces of rather esquisite bourbon into a fine crystal glass.

The boys were all at Johnny's, at The Majestic. It was Johnny (obviously), Frankie, Dalton, Henry, and a few other guys from school. They were drinking and having their own grand old time while Johnny's parents were out of the house.

"Yeah I mean, my mom's sorta forcing me to go."

"Mine too," Johnny added.

"My mom wants me there, but I could probably get out of it. But hey, why miss a chance to see the girls extra dressed up, am I right?" Dalton smirked.

"Yeah," Frankie smiled, imagining escorting Roxy onto the boat. Though if you'd ask him, *he'd deny it.*

"I like how you think Dalton," Henry said, "it should be a good time though. Live jazz, free alcohol, a whole lotta people to keep our parents distracted …" He laughed.

One too many … however. *Little did he know.*

"Imma ring Roxy, see if the girls are going for sure," Johnny said as he left the room, heading to his bedroom telephone.

The phone rang and Roxy picked up. "Hello?"

"Look out your window."

She walked toward the window that faced Johnny's. "Johnny boy!"

"You and the girls going tonight?"

"Funny you should ask, Hazel's over here trying to convince us into going," Roxy said before she sipped the last of her gin.

"What are you drinking?" he asked, distracted.

"What do you think?"

"Gin … *right.*"

"You?"

"Some great bourbon, Frankie brought it over."

"'Course he did. I'm heading over," Roxy smiled, and put

down the phone. "Girls, we're going over to Johnny's!"

They grabbed their handbags, left the doors of The Dakota, walked across the street and were greeted by the doormen of The Majestic. They entered the Davis residence and Roxy went straight for Frankie.

"So where's this great bourbon you're responsible for?" She pulled him around by the arm with her ever so charming sass.

"Hello to you too, Roxy darling—" he seductively smirked.

"The bourbon, Frankie—"

He gave her a kiss on the cheek, then took her hand and walked her over to where the almost empty bottle was, before he poured her, then himself, a glass.

"Well dammit Frankie, this really is great," she said with a smile.

"So you coming tonight?"

"My dad, Daisy, and Uncle Clyde are going. Some of the other family too."

"You didn't quite answer me there, Roxy—"

"Oh but what would I wear!" she laughed, and batted her eyelashes toward the ceiling.

"Right, because your closet is empty," Dalton said as he walked up behind her. "How are you, you smell great."

She gave him a hug, "Chanel Number 5, darling."

"Roxy, are you going or not?" Frankie asked again, this time with his own bit of attitude.

"I guess you'll find out," she said before she downed the last of her bourbon and pushed the glass into his chest, walking over to Johnny, Henry, and Hazel with Dalton by her side.

Roxy looked back and threw Frankie a wink as he rolled his eyes and poured himself another round. The Flynns left Johnny's and went back home, getting ready for the party about to take place. *A party that will result in utter choas.* The girls soon left and went back over to Roxy's.

This party will be one to go down in the books. A *lot* happens.

As the sun began to set with an orange-and-pink sky painted behind it, the guests were beginning to head to the yacht and our special six would soon be on their way.

"You ready to go pick up the girls?" Johnny asked as Frankie was combing his hair—for the seventh time.

"Hold on."

Dalton and Johnny shared a look.

"HEY!" Frankie yelled as Johnny ripped the comb out of his hand, opened the window, and threw it down to the streets of Manhattan.

"That was an expensive comb. I bought it in Italy."

"You are the female version of Roxy, you know that?" Johnny added.

"That's a good one," Dalton laughed, "spot on really."

"Are you ever going to admit it?"

"Admit what Johnny?"

"Oh boy, I am not going through this again. I'll be at the Elliotts'."

"You know you're in love with her, that's why you've combed your hair seven times, trying to get it right."

"You're kidding me, right? That's real funny Johnny, let's go."

"What is it with you two? Both so stubborn."

"She's still dating Dean Andrews, don't forget."

"Frankie, she's not even bringing him to the damn party ..." Johnny said to him.

They were headed over to next door.

"Well hello ladies, look how beautiful you all look," Dalton said as he walked into Roxy's bedroom.

Marie and Virginia hugged him and they all sat on Roxy's bed as she struggled to zip her dress up all the way.

"Should we help her?" Virginia asked.

"It's all jake, she'll get it."

"The cat's meow can't get her zipper to work? Shocking, even sad," Frankie teased as he came up behind her and fixed the zipper, zipping it up to the top. "Maybe I'll unzip it all the way and zip it back up just to be sure it works ..."

Roxy turned around and gave him a gentle slap on the face. "You look nice," she said with her velvet voice. "Johnny! Dalton! My boys are rather fine tonight, aren't they?"

"Only for our girls," Johnny said as he checked his watch.

"Time to go?" Marie asked.

"Yeah, Henry said we should all get there around eight. Plus if we're any later my parents'll kill us. And I'd rather not deal with the wrath of *them*."

"Roxy, you ready?" Virginia walked over to her.

"Hold on," she muttered as she fixed her lip liner, for the fourth time.

Virginia took the red liner from her and sat it down on her vanity. "You're ready," she said as she took her arm and escorted her out of her bedroom. Marie joined them, the three girls linking arms.

Johnny, Frankie, and Dalton had watched the scene happen.

"What did I tell you, they are the opposite-sex versions of each other."

"Can it, Johnny," Frankie said before grabbing his hat off Roxy's bed and following the girls out the room.

They soon all ended up in a car together, squished tight in the most expensive of 1920s automobiles. The car dropped the well-dressed six off at the docks, ready to board the grand, pearly-white yacht.

"Damn," Marie said.

"Damn is right, I forgot how glamorous this ship was," Dalton added.

"Boys, this is gonna be one hell of a night!" Virginia said with a grin. "I can't wait!"

Little did she know, this night was going to be much more of a *hell* than any before. But let's not go there yet, let us first focus on the scene. One of the largest yachts in Manhattan, setting sail on the East River, filled to capacity with the most glamorous New Yorkers of The Roaring. The music was loud and the band was full of energy. Half the guests were dancing while the other half were sipping on the most expensive of alcohol, that came in all forms, biting down on shrimp cocktail and caviar, and mingling with their fellow elites.

This was *quite* the gathering.

Roxy was dancing with Dalton, Marie with Frankie, and Virginia with Johnny before they all switched partners. Hazel came over and stole Dalton away and Roxy began to dance with Henry. They were good friends—they all were, really. Within the hour, our girls were more than tipsy and our boys were singing loud. The night carried on, the ship kept sailing, and the twinkling skyline glimmered behind the excitement of a truly *roaring* party.

It had been a couple hours, it was now half past ten, and Marie was headed down to the bedrooms with a boy she had met only twenty minutes ago. Roxy and Marie had somehow ended up *much* more, let's say … "out of it" than the rest of the group.

Roxy went over to Frankie and started dancing with him before he realized what was going on, why she seemed so *off*. Marie and her new boy entered a cozy bedroom on the lower part of the yacht. It's also important to point out that *he* made the first move on Marie, and that he was *not* drunk, but barely tipsy on champagne. I'm sure you are wise enough to gather how this isn't an ideal situation. The party was still going as hard as it had been an hour ago, if not harder. The music was getting louder and louder, the guests were becoming drunker and drunker, and our Marie was ready to get it on with this new mystery boy. However, not as *on* as he expected. She pulled him into the room and he started kissing her, soon to turn things into a full on make-out sesh. This was as far as Marie meant to take it, which you can imagine was a problem for him.

"FRANKIE! OH darling, oh darling Frankie!" Roxy said before she threw herself into his arms, slurring her words.

"Roxy, baby, you're a bit more than tipsy, aren't you—"

"Frankie, FRANKIE! I feel great—"

"Baby, I think you need to sit down."

Frankie took her to the nearest table and helped her into a chair as Dalton came by.

"Is she okay?"

"I don't know, I know she's been drinking but not enough to be this bad."

"Frankie—"

"Oh boy," Frankie said with a sigh.

"Roxy, who else were you with tonight?"

"Well, a coupla boys came over to Marie and me with a glass of champagne and we danced with them for a bit—" she said as her words began to slow.

"Who were they?" Dalton said, with a stern and worried voice.

"Ohhh, I don't know, but they were handsome!"

"Roxy—" Frankie said before he shared a look with Dalton.

What they soon came to realize was that Roxy and Marie had been drugged. Thankfully for Roxy, she ended up leaving that handsome boy on the dance floor after Marie and her boy made their way downstairs.

"This doesn't sound like Roxy, she doesn't take drinks from boys she doesn't know, she was taught at a young age about being drugged," Frankie said to Dalton.

"Well she's been a bit different lately, I mean with everything that happened with Daisy and Caroline, and I heard her and Dean aren't doing too well."

"Dalton, where's Marie?"

"Marie! Oh she's ..." Roxy began to lose her words. "Oh umm—" she began to say out of confusion.

"Roxy, do you remember where she went? Is she with one of the boys?"

"Frankie, she's having a good time! She—is, downstairs?"

Frankie and Dalton shared another look before Johnny came over.

"Hey, what's the tension for? God, you two look miserable—"

"Johnny you gotta come with me downstairs to find Marie, I think something's gonna happen to her, she's not safe. Dalton, stay with Roxy."

Dalton kept Roxy company, got her some water, and tried to help her as she was slowly beginning to pass out. Johnny and Frankie quickly began to search the rooms in the lower part of the yacht as the party was still going strong. Eventually, Frankie opened up a door to find this mystery boy beginning to undress a very drugged and "out of it" Marie—she could barely keep her eyes open. She was lying on the bed as he was removing her tights, before Johnny took him by the back of the jacket he was wearing and threw him off of her. Frankie went to get Marie and take her upstairs as Johnny gave the boy a roughing up, *to say the least.* He was bruised and bleeding by the time he got off the ship. Frankie brought Marie upstairs and sat her down next to Roxy. They were both so out of it they weren't exactly sure of what was happening. The boat was docked at this point, and Johnny brought the boy upstairs and told him if he didn't watch him get off the ship, he'd let both Mr. Romano and Mr. Elliott know what had happened—and the chief of the NYPD and mob lord Elliott aren't exactly the best people to have issues with, so he ran off before Johnny said anymore.

Roxy, Marie, and the gang ended up leaving soon after, though the party hadn't quite stopped. This had been one hell of a night so far, but it wasn't over yet. After Frankie carried Roxy off the yacht and Johnny did the same with Marie, as the rest made their way back to Roxy's, the party was beginning to die down.

The majority of the guests had left, and only the Romanos, some of the Elliotts, and the Flynns (of course) were left. They were all sitting down at a table, the guys smoking cigars and playing poker and the women smoking cigarettes, drinking their last sips of expensive champagne and gossiping about whatever new scandals of Manhattan had gotten out that week. This was moments before the heat turned up, and the boat went up in flames. Yes, you read that correctly … flames. As in the extremely dangerous, rather hot ones. They quickly fled the scene in a panic as the ship began to resemble hell itself. They were soon all off the ship and Hazel hugged her mother as their eyes reflected the flames in front of them, before Mr. Romano caught Suzy in an escape from the south exit. He yelled out to her and Dennis Elliott followed.

Hazel looked around the small crowd for Henry. "Ma, I don't see him."

"Honey, I think he went home with a friend, he told me he was going to leave early."

Only, this wasn't the case at all. He had decided to stick around after everything happened with Roxy and Marie, and moments before the fire was lit, he went downstairs to grab his coat—where he was then stuck in the, *coincidentally*, same room in which Marie had been almost raped. It was only by chance, only by a mere unfortunate incident, that the doorknob had been stuck, and he was trapped on a burning ship with no way out. There was no window to break and no escape for our dear Henry Flynn.

What happened that night on the Flynns' yacht was chilling: everything from the almost brutal attack on Marie, and what could have happened to Roxy if she hadn't left the other boy to dance with Frankie, to the *very* expensive, and *very* destroyed Flynn yacht, all tied up with the worst of it all, a seventeen-year-old boy's death. Henry was loved and he was a great kid, a great kid who didn't deserve what he got. Suzy set the fire that night; she meant to set it much earlier, but some problems came her way and she figured at the very least she would hurt the Flynns by destroying their beloved yacht.

The fury filled bitch was taken in by Mr. Romano, before receiving a death threat by Mr. Elliott. The hardest part of it all was the fact that Mr. and Mrs. Flynn didn't know their son had burned with the boat until the next morning. They went home, uneasy about what they had witnessed and about how Suzy could go so far with revenge for something that had happened in high school. And the loss of their ship was devastating, but this was all before they telephoned Johnny's, then Frankie's, then Dalton's, followed by every one of Henry's friends to find out where he was. Hazel dropped to the ground when she was made aware of her twin brother's devastating death, and Mr.

and Mrs. Flynn did the same. Mr. Flynn held his wife and daughter in his arms as they all wept, as did a grand portion of Manhattan. When Dennis and Clyde found out about Henry, they sent for someone to pay a special visit to Suzy.

She was dead in her cell an hour later.

As I told you before, this would be one *hell* of a night, and hell is *exactly* what greeted Suzy after her plot of revenge on the Flynns. Envy is an odd and bitter, lonely emotion, and though they say revenge is best served cold, I believe Suzy would *strongly* disagree.

CHAPTER 15

COUSIN VITA

Vita Elliott—I've mentioned her before. She's the daughter of Jeanette Elliott, who is Bruce's daughter, the brother of Griffin who moved to Chicago. Jeanette and her brother Douglas are first cousins to Clyde and Dennis: they are the Chicago Elliotts, remember now? Vita is second cousin to Roxy, and of course Clyde's kids. Vita also has a sister, Jennie, who lives in Chicago but is thinking of moving to Los Angeles (that's irrelevant, but I thought you should know). As for why they go by the Elliott name and not their father's last name? Because no one gives up the damn Elliott name ... and let's just say Bruce made this clear to their father, so naturally, he was fine with it. Long story short, as I said a while back, Roxy and the girls are close to Vita. She visits often and Roxy makes trips out to Chicago to visit family as well. Then there is always the reunion every August in The Hamptons. As for where we are now with our special six, well, after the whole yacht incident, nothing extra "spectacular" happened, as everyone was grieving the loss of both the Flynn yacht and Henry Flynn himself, so I thought I'd move along to May.

May 22nd, 1925

Dear Diary,

It's Friday and the girls and I decided to ditch school today for a shopping spree and tea at the Palm Court.

Things have been slow since the night of the Flynns' yacht party. I am still beyond devastated about Henry's death. He was real cute you know, a real good guy with a kind heart.

The boys have been down too—they were close with him, we all were, but they had a special bond, you know, that "boy bond". The "stealing parents' liquor and smoking cigars while playing poker" kind of bond. I mean, me and my girls do the same, but it's different, you know? They talk about all the guy stuff, about the best broads in New York, while we talk about the best boys and dance to the best records. Without Henry, the boys haven't done any of that. They've been in an odd headspace, lemme tell ya. I almost decided to throw a party this weekend to lighten the mood; I convinced Daddy to close the Dakota speakeasy for the night for my friends and me, but I'm not sure if it's a grand idea, I don't know if it's the right time. However, I guess it's always the right time. I mean, a little party never hurt nobody right? Isn't that the saying?

Roxy was the master of persuading people to do what she wanted, and if they didn't, having the mafia behind her always helped. The person she could convince best was her father, considering she was an only child and "Daddy's little princess". She also managed to do well with convincing herself into things, and that is exactly what she did as she stopped writing and set down her diary on her delicate glass nightstand.

Roxy imagined throwing a grand gathering would cheer everyone up, and it did. This party wasn't any crazier than the majority of the ones she threw, and it surely wasn't the party of the year. Just a great, alcohol-filled, *roaring* party. Spirits were being lifted and the boys came out of their grief-filled slum, and even Hazel had come to drink her sorrows away. Roxy was having a great time doing the usual: making her rounds and sipping either champagne or gin, and dancing with everybody— *especially our Matthews boy.*

Around two in the morning the party began to slow, half of her very intoxicated guests had left and gone home, and the gang was lounging about on one of the round, velvet sofa booths of the Elliott speakeasy. Marie and Virginia were in the middle with Dalton on one side and Johnny on the other, with Frankie next to Johnny and his arm around Roxy. Though, they were all cuddled up with each other in a rather cute image.

She was sinking into his chest while smoking the best of quality cigarette in her long golden cigarette holder. They were talking about the last few weeks, then the conversation switched over to Henry, and Johnny began to cry.

Though, *to him*, they were just "allergy tears".

The boys were strong and sometimes hard-asses—and they sure were tough—but they also had huge hearts and they were truly torn up about Henry. The girls comforted them and figured they'd all just stick together for the night, not leaving the speakeasy till morning. However, when morning came and the sun rose, a surprise was waiting for them. *Specifically* for Roxy. This, my friend, was Vita Elliot.

"Roxy," she said with her Chanel purse in one hand and the other on her hip. "Roxy!"

Virginia woke up first. "Vita?" she said, all groggy.

"Hey V, how are ya doin?"

"I'm good Vita, why are you here?"

"You'll know soon enough. ROXY!"

"I'm up! I'm—Vita?" she said before lifting her head off of Frankie's chest. Funny how they somehow, someway, *always* ended up sleeping together. Yet all without the sex, *of course.*

"Looks like you guys had quite the night. I went up to the penthouse and one of your maids said you hadn't come home, that you'd be down in the speakeasy."

"We had a party," Johnny said as his eyes opened. "Good morning Vita, might I say you look beautiful."

"Vita! Cousin Vita," Frankie joined in.

"Did someone say Vita? Chicago! Why are you here?"

166

Dalton greeted her, excited to see her again after she had been absent for so long.

"Ah it's my girl, good morning babe, how are you?" said the last to wake, Marie.

Vita sat down next to Roxy on the curved booth, put her purse down on the table and took her hat off. "How have you all been? It's been a little while but I always return," she smiled.

Everyone loved Vita—she was the Roxy of Chicago, only a little older and not *quite* as striking or fabulous. Though, any Elliott you met, born or married into the family, was grand and sensational.

Vita was a little bit older than Roxy: she had graduated high school and was in her first year at the University of Chicago. She had visited Roxy because she felt like she needed to escape Chicago, and though she was close to her sister Jennie, she needed Roxy.

Roxy was always the person you could count on and go to for any given reason; she had a way with words and she could always calm you with her charm. She made everyone feel like things were under control, because they felt like the control had been placed into her hands. Vita came for her comfort, but this wasn't the only reason. She came to talk to Dennis as well. He had that same charm he passed on to his daughter—he was very comforting for a rather powerful and dangerous-when-needed man. On top of that, he had a hell of a lot of experience with the Deckers. Like I said before, there were some Deckers in Chicago, but the Chicago Deckers did not present the same problem as those in New York; there weren't as many face-to-face conflicts. That didn't mean, however, that the two families hated each other any less.

It was now noon, the boys had gone across the street to Johnny's, and the girls were up in the Elliott residence, in Roxy's living room. Well, one of them. It was Marie, Virginia, Roxy, and Vita. They were served tea and sandwiches by one of the butlers as they gossiped for hours, before Vita began to open up about the *real* reason she was in New York.

"Now honey, I love you, but why are you really here?" Roxy said to Vita as she set her cup down.

"Ladies, it's a big one."

Marie and Virginia looked over to Roxy as she made eye contact with them.

"What is it, V?" Virginia asked.

She took a pause before saying, "I'm pregnant."

"YOU'RE WHAT?" Roxy yelled as she almost knocked over her teacup.

"Vita, how the hell did this happen?" Marie asked.

"Marie, it's called sex …"

"Okay, enough of the sarcasm Roxy—"

"Girls, can it with the elementary behavior, V is pregnant."

"We heard."

"Vita, darling, what the hell happened?" Roxy said as she moved closer to her cousin.

"It gets worse."

"Don't tell me—it's twins—"

"No no, my goodness."

"He got another girl pregnant too?" Marie added in.

"No no, it's nothing like that."

A silent pause took over the room.

This was at the exact point that Dennis had sat down in the kitchen, sipping his coffee. The girls were in the living room that was situated right by the kitchen, so you could hear every word. Mr. Elliott wasn't sitting there to eavesdrop, so don't get the wrong impression.

He did this every day. He sat in the kitchen and drank his coffee while reading the paper.

"I'm pregnant and it's Paul Decker's kid."

Vita was going to eventually tell Dennis, but not yet, so this wasn't the best timing for him to be practicing his daily ritual. He sat there in shock, then got up, went to his study, and rang his cousin Jeanette who, wonderfully, didn't know about Vita's pregnancy or love affair with the young Decker. Oh, how Romeo and Juliet of them.

"It's what?" Roxy asked angrily as the other girls sat in a state of utter shock.

"We had been secretly dating for about two months and, well, we fell in love and next thing you know I'm losing my virginity to him in this fancy hotel, oh Roxy it was so sweet—"

"Vita, you do realize how terrible this is, right? Are you an absolute idiot?"

"What, because I had sex before you?" she sassed back.

"No, dumbass, for sleeping with the enemy. Do you really think Paul loves you? Are you kidding me right now?"

"He does Roxy, he does."

"Oh my—oh my God. You really got yourself into a

situation, now didn't you? I can understand the pregnant but certainly not with the devil—"

"That's enough. This baby is innocent and so is Paul—"

Vita wasn't greeted with the response she expected from Roxy.

"Vita! Are you absolutely kidding me?"

"Girls, I think we were going to go for now, ring me later Roxy," Marie said as she and Virginia left and went over to Johnny's to tell him about everything.

"Vita, I cannot believe this, how did you even get involved with Paul anyways?"

"It was at a party—me and my friends were there and it was all grand and then I saw Paul, and next thing you know I gave him my telephone number and he rang me that night. We talked for hours and—"

"Did he seek you out or did you him?"

"Why does that matter—"

"Tell me, did you give him a look or a wink, or did he come up to you, telling you just how 'beautiful' you are?"

She took a pause. "He came up to me—"

"Case in point." Roxy rolled her eyes.

"I'm telling you Roxy, it wasn't like that."

"So out of ALL the girls in Chicago, *all of them*, he comes up to an Elliott and tells her she's beautiful?"

"I don't think he knew who I was at first—"

"Dammit Vita, yes he did."

"You know what, this was a mistake. I never should have come. I'm not sure what I was thinking—"

"Neither am I! I'm not sure what you were thinking when you jumped into bed with a Decker! Do you know what this could do to our family? To you? To the child! I mean my God Vita, do you understand how big of a problem this is going to be? An out of wedlock child with a DECKER nonetheless?"

Vita began to shed a tear. "Goodbye Roxy, I'll get my things and I'll leave. I'll go back to Chicago and deal with it myself."

"Yes, please do."

There was a tension between them that they had never expressed before. Roxy wasn't angry with Vita, she wasn't mad at her—she was upset by the situation and worried about the turmoil it would bring for her. She didn't want Vita in a situation like this. Vita, however, didn't understand that. And Roxy wasn't all that great at displaying her feelings well, in situations like such. Though, she *did* always say what was on her mind, even if it didn't come out peach perfect.

While Vita was packing up her things from one of the guest bedrooms and getting ready to head back to Chicago, Dennis was finishing up with Jeanette on the phone. She was devastated, but mostly filled with rage. Rage toward the little lollygagger who got her daughter pregnant. Vita was smart but she was an absolute fool in this situation. She truly did love Paul Decker, but he was only a piece in another attempt to take some sort of revenge on the Elliotts. This wasn't gonna go well for them, however.

Jeanette called her father Bruce and they decided they would take him out, then figure out some cover-up for Vita's pregnancy. *That was a problem for tomorrow.* When Vita got back to Chicago the next day, her parents didn't tell her they knew of the less than delightful news. Instead, they discreetly planned their next move. They had eyes everywhere and knew that this Paul would be at the cinema that night with his friends. What they didn't know was that he had invited his lover, Vita, to the exciting night. *Oh what a night this would be.* He was standing outside the doors of the cinema, alone, waiting for her to show up. It's an interesting thing how time works, how by just leaving your house a minute later, you can change the outcome of a situation drastically. This was the case for our pregnant little Elliott. Bruce was driving the automobile down the street with Jeanette in the passenger seat.

"So, Vita's pregnant."

"Yes."

"Wow, I did not see that coming."

The six were gathered at Katz's, eating and talking about everything they had learned yesterday.

"I cannot believe what she got herself into. Paul Decker?"

"Do you think it's true?" Dalton asked.

"What?"

"That this Paul, that he really does love her."

"No," Roxy said in a confident, stern tone. And she was right.

"I don't know Roxy, she's a smart girl, would she really get involved with a Decker if it weren't true?" Johnny added in.

"Not if she's blinded by a love for him." Which, unfortunately, *was* true.

The car was racing down the street before it began to slow.

Roxy and her friends continued to eat and moved on to a new topic. Dennis was over at Griffin's, where Clyde was as well. They checked the time.

"Jeanette will handle it, she always does. She's an Elliott."

They sipped their drinks and ate a nice meal with their parents.

The car began to slow as Paul was leaning against the wall of the building, about two feet from the corner, and fifteen feet away from the cinema doors. He was smoking a cigarette, waiting for Vita. The car was soon to approach him, with the passenger seat facing Paul. Jeanette didn't see Vita come around the corner. Her eyes were on Paul. Vita, however, saw her mother roll down the window as Paul looked up.

"NO!" Vita yelled as she approached Paul, jumping in front of the boy she loved.

Jeanette pulled the trigger just a sliver of a moment before Vita jumped in front of him; there was no way to stop it, and Jeanette couldn't have prevented this in any way. Vita was fast and her mother couldn't have seen her coming from around the corner—the opposite corner from where her grandfather was driving the automobile that would take her breath away. Jeanette was there to kill Paul, that's what needed to be done. Everyone in the Elliott family, both those in Chicago *and* in New York agreed on this.

The Deckers had ordered Paul to get Vita to fall in love, then to get her pregnant. He was never in love with her, but that's not to say he didn't end up developing an unfortunate and unwanted *care* for her. And as she fell into his arms after the two shots pierced her heavy heart, he was consumed by emotions he had never felt before. Emotions he didn't know he was capable of feeling. But they rushed over him like the heavy waters of Niagra Falls, devouring his every thought.

Jeanette couldn't comprehend what had just happened, and Bruce of course didn't see it happen as his eyes were glued to the road.

"STOP THE CAR!" she yelled as it came to an abrupt stop. She jumped out of the car.

"Oh, oh my." Bruce looked to his right, only to see a heart-wrenching picture of his granddaughter in a white dress, with blood staining it so deeply it looked as if it were out of a film.

He got out of the car and ran to them.

"Vita, oh baby oh baby," Jeanette wept.

Paul was still holding her, and a surprising tear came trickling down his cheek. Bruce was standing over Jeanette as she took Vita into her arms, holding her and crying hysterically.

"Maybe I shouldn't have been too rough with Vita. I mean, we really ended things on a bad mark," Roxy said to the table.

"I mean, you have a right to," Virginia said to her.

"It's just, I haven't heard from her since she left and—I know it's only been a day—but I feel like she'll never forgive me for the way I reacted."

This was not the case at all. As Vita took her last breath, her last thought was of Roxy, and how she was right. How she should have stayed with her and how much she loved her, and how she wished she hadn't stormed off in a fuss.

"Vita, Vita, Vita ..." Jeanette cried as she continued to hold her bloody daughter in her arms.

Bruce began to cry, *an angry cry*. "You did this!" he said in a dangerous tone, "this was all you, Decker!"

"I never meant for this to happen, sir. I promise, Mr. Elliott, this wasn't—"

Two more gunshots—straight to his head. Two dead bodies on the sidewalk in front of a cinema in Chicago, and three Elliotts in a bad situation.

"We gotta go, Jeanette, as hard as this may be—we gotta get these bodies out of here."

Bruce grabbed Paul and threw him in the trunk in true mafia style. Jeanette carried her daughter and placed her carefully in the backseat of the automobile. They drove off before the police showed up to red and gory bloodstains painted on the sidewalk. They made it back to Vita's house and her dad walked out to a distraught Jeanette.

"I don't understand—" he whimpered as his heart sank deep into his chest—just like the two bullets sank deep into his daughter's moments before.

"Oh, it wasn't supposed to be like this, I don't know what happened."

"No, no honey no." He began to cry.

He opened up the backseat door and carried Vita's lifeless body into the house. Three lives were taken that night. Three innocent lives. Though Paul was a Decker, he was doing what he was told to do, and in that he was somewhat innocent in the matter. *Somewhat* innocent. Vita was never meant to be taken, and her unborn child would never see the world. Jennie walked out of her bedroom as she heard voices and crying. She ran to her sister's body, which was now lying on the carpet. The blood, everywhere.

Young Elliotts always seemed to get caught in the crossfire.

They were all weeping over the loss of dear, sweet Vita. Bruce rang Douglas, who came over with his wife and kids. Then he rang all of his brothers, including Griffin.

The phone rang. "Mr. Elliott, you have a phone call," the maid said.

"Who from?" Griffin responded.

"Your brother, Bruce."

Clyde and Dennis looked up from their plates, finishing up their dinner.

Griffin got up and took the phone. "Thank you. Hello?"

"Griffin—"

"Yes, was it taken care of? Did Jeanette take care of him?"

"Griffin, there has been an accident."

"What kind of accident—"

"Vita, she jumped out of nowhere from around the corner, right into the crossfire."

The moment stood still, as if the clocks had stopped in time. Griffin looked back at the dining room, as his wife and two kids looked at his ghost-white face in fear of what might come next.

"She's dead, I've got to tell the rest of our brothers. You all need to come out here tomorrow. The funeral will be in a couple of days. I have to go—love you."

Griffin aggressively hung the telephone on the wall. He

broke the news to the rest of them, as the other Elliotts were learning of the rather morbid events that took place that night. He shed a tear, but kept his sadness inside of himself. Clyde and Dennis were closest to Jeanette and Douglas out of all of their cousins, and they were close to Vita; she was almost like another daughter to both of them. Everyone in the Elliott family was mourning the great loss of the bright young girl. Clyde went back home with Dennis, where he rang his wife and kids and asked them to come over to The Dakota. Roxy arrived soon after them.

"Hi Uncle Clyde, have you seen Daddy?" Roxy said as she entered the double doors of her penthouse with Frankie and Johnny by her side.

Virginia and Marie had decided to go back to Dalton's.

"Roxy—" Clyde said to her as she went toward the nearest telephone.

"How are you doing, Clyde?" Frankie asked.

"Not well, Frankie." He turned to Roxy. "Scarlett—"

"I've got to ring Vita, we left things pretty bad and I want to apologize. She's going through a lot right now—"

Clyde's wife Elizabeth began to break into tears as their son Tommy opened up his arms for her.

Roxy was holding the telephone in her hand. "What's going on?"

Dennis emerged from the south staircase and wiped his tears. "Hi, baby girl—"

"Daddy, what's going on?" she said as her heart dropped. "Has something happened with Grandfather? Grandmother?"

Her immediate thoughts were that something had happened to Griffin or Margret, and that was why her Uncle Clyde and his family were there. Though they came over often, their tears told a very different story.

"There's been an accident," Dennis said with a crack in his voice.

Roxy looked over to Frankie and Johnny.

"With your cousin, Vita."

Roxy continued to look around the foyer where everyone was spread around in grief. "Excuse me?"

"Honey," Dennis said as he walked closer to Roxy.

Roxy was extremely close with Vita and the thought of anything happening to her made her stomach turn inside out.

"Daddy, what's going on?" She began to worry.

"Vita, oh Roxy," he said as he began to lightly cry once again, "she's gone."

Roxy dropped the telephone and placed her hand over her mouth. "Gone?" Her tone was empty and afraid.

"She's dead honey, there was an accident."

"Oh my," she yelled out, and she jumped into her father's arms as they both wept.

Frankie looked over to Johnny and they both shed a tear. They adored Vita; she was so much like Roxy and they all got along so well.

They walked over to Roxy.

Frankie crouched down as Roxy sat on the steps and took her hand. She squeezed it tight. Johnny put his hand on her shoulder and rubbed it back and forth. Dennis had his arm around her, and her head was lying on his chest. All of them distraught, shocked, and in a rather blurry state.

"We are taking the first train out tomorrow morning."

"I'm sick, I am absolutely sick," she said. Her eyes were blurry with tears and her voice barely there.

The night went on with everyone holding each other and crying, mourning the loss of cousin Vita. The next morning, every Elliott in New York was on a train to Chicago. Grand Central Station was filled with those of the Elliott family, devastated. The funeral was beautiful and sad. Roxy gave a speech, and so did the majority of the Elliotts. They all said something. It was a long service that ended in a *lot* of alcohol. This was an awful and unfortunate trial on the Elliott family, but again, it won't be the last. For now, I'll share some happier stories. Not perfect ones, but there won't be any deaths until after summer, I promise. Though, it's the last death that will hurt you the most. Yet again, I'll say once more—let me move on to warmer weather and brighter days. The summer is here once again.

CHAPTER 16

THE SUMMER OF 1925

June 28th, 1925

Dear Diary,

It's been about a month since Vita's death, and no I'm not doing well. But I've got to heal, I've got to get past this. After the funeral, Jeanette and her husband, Jennie, Great Uncle Bruce, Douglas and the family, and every other Elliott in Chicago came back with us to New York for a few weeks. They thought it was a good idea, to clear their heads and be with the rest of the family. Though, submerging them into now yet another mafia war wasn't the best of options. The Deckers have backed off for now. They aren't the only ones who lost a family member. And they know they were the ones who brought it on. The whole situation is still so baffling to me. I'm part devastated and part angry at Vita for ever speaking to Paul in the first place. But I guess I don't really have a right to be angry with her anymore. It's been quite a year so far, first finding out about Daisy, then losing Henry, then Vita? What the absolute hell. We have all gone through so much and I want to leave it all in the past and move on to a roaring summer. We are packing up to go to The Hamptons—our Southampton estate awaits us. Some of the other Elliotts are already in The Hamptons. Clyde and Elizabeth are in East Hampton, but Tommy decided to take a trip to Cape Cod. I guess his fiancée's family lives there and they'll be spending half the summer up there in Massachusetts. The Cape is nice, but I much prefer Martha's Vineyard. However, The Hamptons are superior to both in EVERY way. Anyways, this summer should be good … God knows I'm praying it is. Johnny and his family are already in The Hamptons and Frankie leaves later this afternoon. Marie and Virginia are going to come with me and stay at my place, like they always do, and their families should be heading out to Long Island by the end of the week.

It was truly summer in Manhattan. The wealthy were fleeing off to their waterfront mansions, ready for the scent of the ocean and taste of summer ice cream. Most of their homes were in

Southampton, and as for the Elliott family, they were spread almost equally between Southampton and East Hampton.

They all had their own homes, but the largest of them all was the Elliott estate in Southampton, which was built in 1807 and had been passed down through generations. This is where Dennis and Roxy were staying. Dennis and Caroline had bought their own mansion years back, only a mile from the estate, but hadn't been there since everything went down when she left way back when. Dennis told Caroline she could have it in the divorce, and so naturally, she took it. *Who wouldn't?* Dennis was bound to soon be handed over the estate by Griffin anyways, so it didn't matter much.

The estate was of course welcome to any Elliott when it came to who could stay there, but it was solely owned by only one Elliott at a time. Griffin as of right now, Dennis soon, and someday Roxy. It goes to whoever is the head of the mafia, the boss, the don. The home, however, was big enough to fit every Elliott if needed, and many times Uncle Clyde and Aunt Elizabeth and their son Tommy had come over and stayed for a few weeks here and there. It was 70,000 square feet with twenty-four large bedrooms and bathrooms (some larger than others), *multiple* fireplaces, eight balconies, *multiple* marble staircases, a library, hidden rooms behind bookcases, three full kitchens and two bars, both indoor *and* outdoor pools, a tennis court, and every piece of handmade furniture imported straight from Europe.

The extra company was nice in such a large home filled with more space than was ever needed, and this was also where the annual Elliott reunion was held in August, when every Elliott on the planet meets for a few days of fun. The Chicago Elliotts, the Los Angeles Elliotts, and the Paris Elliotts, all back home in glorious New York. At the estate, Marie and Virginia of course each had their own bedrooms, with Roxy's in the middle, all in the west wing of the home. Each of their rooms looked out directly to the ocean. Roxy always kept her windows open at night so she could fall asleep and wake up to the sound of the ocean. She loved the ocean. So did the other girls. The boys often came over for a few nights at a time as well. The Matthews family had a place two homes down from the Elliott estate and the James family were about four houses from them. The Davises lived two houses away from the estate on the other side, then the Romanos three houses from there. The Williams family mansion was in East Hampton, which was part of the reason why Virginia always stayed with Roxy in the summer; to avoid the hike between Southampton and East Hampton every day to see her friends.

"Are you ready to go?" Roxy asked Marie.

"If she isn't, why don't we just leave her?" Virginia laughed.

"Funny, real funny."

"Miss Elliott, the car is here for you girls," one of the maids came and told Roxy as the other maids grabbed the girls' bags.

"It's going to be a good summer. The summer before our last year in high school, can you believe it?" Virginia said.

"Honestly, I can't. I remember kindergarten like yesterday. Boy how time flies!" Marie said as she fixed her hair and walked out of the doors of The Dakota.

They all began to drive off to Long Island.

"I don't know, I'm real ready for it to be over, and for me to start at Harvard."

"Roxy, that's only if you get in—" Marie teased.

"I think they would be making a grand mistake not letting an Elliott in," said Virginia. "I'm just worried about Columbia. For Marie and me both."

"Hey, speak for yourself, I know I'll get in!" Marie said.

The girls all laughed.

It was Roxy's dream to attend Harvard next fall, and Marie and Virginia had their hearts set on Columbia. Frankie was also set on Harvard—he and Roxy had talked about going to college together for the longest time—while Dalton was torn between Yale and Columbia. Johnny had no idea what he wanted to do; he liked the idea of Harvard or Yale as well, but didn't want to ever leave the city, which means he'll end up at Columbia.

Where someone else out of the group will end up too.

Someone else who loves the city more than anything else— except maybe gin and Paris, of course.

But enough of this college talk, we will get to it soon enough. For now, our six friends and six families are all in The Hamptons, ready for a summer of moving on from the dark and gloomy first five months of 1925, and ready to transition to new ideas and new memories.

I think it's time to introduce you to some of the best memories these six made. There are two birthdays to be celebrated: Dalton's seventeenth on July 13th, and Virginia's on the 22nd. Then we have the introduction of Roxy's new beau,

Marie's, *and* Virginia's as well. Let's call them "two great guys and one summer fling gone bad". Not *too* bad though, don't worry. I promised no more deaths until *after* summer, right?

But it will be one hell of a summer, let's just say that.

CHAPTER 17

The Prelude to One Hell of a Summer

All of our wealthy Manhattanites were soaking up the June sun, bathing on pristine beaches and swimming in the cool Atlantic Ocean, lying beside their grand pools as butlers served them cold, crystal-glass-served drinks. It was all a beautiful picture encompassed by a capacious amount of wealth.

Only a *certain* type was fit for The Hamptons, especially in the 1920s. It was a haven for the affluent to bathe in pure luxury. Some may argue that Martha's Vineyard or the Cape held that status, but no one could beat The Hamptons. Or the opulent clientele that called it their summer home—and that would be due to the fact that no one could, nor will ever, beat the glamour of a New Yorker.

Now that you have a picture of what our scene is, I'd like to introduce some new players into the roaring world: Arthur Casey and Dylan McRyan.

These were two *extremely handsome* fellas Marie and Virginia happened to come across while walking down Main Street with an ice-cream cone in each of their hands.

They both came from wealthy families as well, though this was expected considering they *were* in Southampton in the first place, and they would soon become our two girls' new boyfriends. Both of them were single at the moment, while Roxy was still entangled with Dean—for now.

"But I just don't understand, you know it's the superior flavor—"

"Marie, nothing beats old-fashioned vanilla—" she grinned while licking her cone.

"Virginia, I can't comprehend how wrong you are. Vanilla is bland, while cherry is something magical!" Marie said with a laugh.

"You know what, I may have to agree with that."

The girls turned and looked to their left, where two boys had overheard their voices as they approached them on the sidewalk.

"Hi, I'm Dylan McRyan," one said while putting his right hand out for a shake.

"Well hello," Virginia said with a sexy smirk, "I'm Virginia Williams."

A few moments went by during which Dylan and Virginia glaring longingly into each other's eyes, infatuated by one another's beauty. They were both *quite* beautiful.

"Oh get a room, you two." Marie rolled her eyes before they landed on a certain someone.

"Well, hello. Who might you be?" she said.

"I'm Arthur Casey, Dylan's friend." He gave her a smirk. He was already smitten beyond explanation.

"I'm Marie Romano."

After they introduced each other, they began to chat. The girls had been hoping for a summer fling, and they had found it.

"You girls live in the city?"

"The one and only."

"What part?" Dylan asked.

"I live on the Upper East Side and Marie lives on the West," Virginia stated.

"No kidding," Arthur told Marie, "I live on the West Side too."

The two smiled and began to talk some more.

"So are you dames by chance attending the Elliott party tonight?" Arthur asked.

The girls laughed.

"Well considering we are staying at the Elliott estate and Roxy is our best friend, that would be a yes." Marie gave them some sass.

"You don't say?" Dylan grinned.

"How did you boys get invited to the summer kickoff?"

"Our families always go, but we usually stay in the city an extra week and miss it. This year we decided to drive out with our parents. "

"Why?" Virginia said with a strong tone. "Sorry, I didn't mean to come off that way," she laughed, "I'm just curious."

"Let's just say Arthur may have been grounded and forced into it, and if *he* wasn't staying then I might as well come. All of our other friends are here—"

"Ahh I see ..." Marie glanced over at Arthur. "So what exactly did you do?"

He laughed. "I may or may not have been caught with some bourbon."

The girls shared a look and chuckled over the idea of getting caught drunk. This was something that hadn't happened to them since they were fourteen.

"What, are you girls allowed to drink or something?" Dylan asked.

"Well the Elliotts, they own speakeasies."

"Oh I know."

"And Roxy's father, Dennis Elliott, though he's in charge he rarely ever goes down into the Dakota speakeasy, he's usually elsewhere. I'm not sure why, but I assume it's because that one is right under his building so he's always out looking after the other ones further away," Virginia stated, "but who knows."

"*Therefore*, we never get caught down there. The bartenders don't tell on Roxy or any of her friends, they tend to stay under her 'control'; so we go down there for drinks on the weekends and have our parties there," Marie added.

"And the unlimited supply of alcohol is handy when the boys have their parties. We usually stock up from Roxy's and bring it over."

The boys were shocked by how easy it was for them. Though they drank, as did most privileged Manhattan kids during prohibition, they were always looking over their shoulders.

"Well damn, having her as a friend must be nice," Arthur smiled.

They ended their conversation with the boys and made dates for the party later on. After their rendezvous with these new beaus, they went back home where they found Roxy and Frankie in an unusual situation: making a homemade pizza together. It was especially weird because each of them relied on their personal chefs for food, and each despised cooking. However, the grand brick oven that sat center in their largest kitchen was one that had inspired the two to entangle themselves with dough, sauce, and the finest mozzarella cheese. And, if I'm being completely honest, it was kind of cute ... and Marie and Virginia thought so as well as they came in and interrupted the scene.

"HEY, you're stretching the dough too much—" Frankie exclaimed.

"Darling, this is how you do it!" Roxy shouted back.

She threw the pizza dough into the air before he came around behind her, put his arms under hers and grabbed it before she could catch it.

"Excuse me ..." she sassed, before tossing cheese into his face that he tried to catch with his mouth, resulting in them both sharing a laugh.

"Oh I gotta say, this is one odd scene," Marie said as she and Virginia walked in.

"I can't imagine your maids are going to be too happy with the mess you're leaving them."

"Oh don't you worry, I'll make Frankie clean it up," Roxy said before snatching the dough back.

"Ha ha, very funny, I think you guys pay your maids enough that they won't mind!" Frankie said.

It was noon, about two hours before the mansion would begin its preparation for the summer kickoff party.

June 29th, the day the party was *always* held, regardless of what day of the week it fell on. This year it was a Monday, but that didn't mean any less of a good time.

The party consisted of almost every elite family in The Hamptons, not just those from Southampton, but all over. It was the largest party by volume, but the mansion and its grand lawns could hold the many, many guests with no problem. Roxy really only knew about half the people there.

There were always so many, there was no reason to befriend them *all*.

While Roxy and Frankie attempted to finish the pie and place it in the oven, they almost started a fire in which one of their maids had to put out. Don't ask me how, but knowing them, this wasn't an unlikely thing to happen. Marie and Virginia told them about the boys they had met on Main Street and how their families were on the guest list, while Frankie ended up leaving and joining Dalton and Johnny for lunch downtown— after theirs hadn't quite gone as planned.

"Damn, that was some lunch," Dalton remarked, complimenting the delectable meal they had just enjoyed.

191

"Hey, isn't that Dean Andrews?" Frankie asked, ignoring Dalton's comment.

"It is—who's the dame?" he replied.

Johnny joined them outside the restaurant with a smoke in his hand. "Is that Dean Andrews?"

"Mmhm, with some girl that ain't Roxy," Frankie said before squinting his eyes and lighting his own smoke, trying to get a better glance at who she was.

Dean was standing with a blonde on the other side of the street, directly opposite the sidewalk the boys were on. The pair were speaking to each other, before they began to kiss … and for a rather long time, might I add.

"Oh my God!" Johnny said. He had broken up with Claire a few weeks back.

"We gotta tell Roxy, right?" Dalton asked.

Frankie jumped in. "Definitely. In fact, why don't I also rough him up a little, just to—"

"Frankie no, Roxy wouldn't want that today. It's the day of the party and the Andrews are on the guest list. It'd be too messy. We don't need any added drama tonight." Dalton always seemed to have more of a moral compass than Frankie or Johnny.

"I don't know, he deserves it—" Johnny added on, before being interrupted by Dalton.

"No. Let's just go, we gotta get ready."

As it turns out, Roxy and Dean's entire relationship had been about Claire—*all of it*. He wanted to get back at her after their breakup.

If you have forgotten, Claire and Dean were an item before Roxy began dating him, and before Claire was ever with Johnny.

Long story short, Dean was still in love with the beautiful bitchy blonde we call Miss Reed, and they had rekindled their love about two weeks ago, though he *was* still in a relationship with Roxy.

So yes, he was cheating.

Thankfully, the boys had been there at the right time to catch the lollygagger in the act, and they reported back to Roxy in a jiffy.

She wasn't surprised and had honestly been ready to break up with him anyways.

Though, this did give her an excuse to threaten him, which was fun, though she wasn't *actually* planning on having him roughed up in any way.

She hated the idea that she had been cheated on, but for some reason it didn't bother her that much, even though it was with Claire, whom she despised.

Roxy was in a different mindset; a lot had happened in the past few months and this seemed to be the least of her troubles.

However, this is not the last we will hear of Claire Reed.

Moving on, the day resumed and the Elliott mansion was soon filled with guests and booze and a glamorous night that ended in fireworks, a classic kickoff to a hopeful summer. Marie and Virginia had kicked it off with their dates, and both had rather exciting nights. Virginia actually almost had sex for the first time, but backed out at the last minute. The *very* last minute. I guess you can't spell "Virginia" without "Virgin"!

Anyways, the special six all had a grand time, as usual, though nothing *extra* spectacular happened. That was until Roxy went upstairs to grab a sweater.

"I'm so happy, you know, I've waited for this for so many years," he said to her while holding her hands.

She grabbed him and kissed him for a brief but powerful seven seconds.

"When will we tell Roxy?" she asked.

"Daddy?" It seemed that they would skip that conversation.

"Baby! I thought you were downstairs," he said, startled.

Dennis and Daisy had been caught in the hallway kissing like two teenagers sneaking around. They had been talking about getting back together, now that everything was out in the open, and I guess it had finally happened. They didn't know how Roxy would take it, especially with Caroline being back in the city now with Baby Ruth.

"Is there something you two would like to tell me?" Roxy was sassy with them as she put her sweater on. She was, however, grinning on the inside.

"I think it's pretty self-explanatory," her father answered.

"Dennis ..." Daisy sighed. "Roxy dear, are you okay with this?"

"Are you kidding me?" she said as fireworks went through their veins. "I'm ecstatic!"

Though for so long she had dreamed about Caroline returning and reuniting with her father, this would never be the case. The divorce was final and she was a single woman, and Dennis a single man. Since Daisy had returned to the city Roxy had become close with her—though she still currently referred to her as "Aunt Daisy" instead of "Mom", she sure as hell loved her like one. It was only out of habit that she called her "Aunt". Roxy and Caroline's relationship was still a bit patchy at times, but seemed to have healed since all hell went down. She had fantasized about Daisy and Dennis getting together; they were always meant to be together in the first place, and they *were* her *real* parents after all. Roxy was absolutely in one of the happiest states she had been in since Vita's death. The news had her enthralled with joy. After she had found out, the night was creeping closer to morning and the party was nearing an end as the summer kickoff fireworks went roaring through the skies.

June 30th, 1925

Dear Diary,

Last night was a riot. The party glittered all night long and the fireworks were the best they have ever been! What a proper beginning to an amazing summer. Not to mention, Daddy and Aunt Daisy are together! I have to say, I am rather excited about this. I mean, they are my real parents after all. And Daddy deserved this after what happened with Mom.

Or … Caroline.

I've been debating if I should continue calling her Caroline after all that happened, but to me she still feels like a mom, even though she didn't give birth to me.

But Daisy is feeling more and more like a mom to me too. So, do you see the dilemma? I mean, I guess Caroline will always still be my "mom", and she has made it quite clear how sorry she is and how she wants our relationship to go back to normal, and how she wants me to have a relationship with Baby Ruth. Who's quite adorable, if I do say so myself.

Mom has been showering me in jewelry and shoes, though I told her material items aren't going to make up for all the pain she caused me. Though they do help ... anyways, I don't know. I feel confused at times. I love Caroline just the same and I love Daisy so much now, but I don't want to always call her "Aunt Daisy", now that I know she's my mother and all.

But would I call both Daisy and Caroline "Mom"? Is that weird? I guess not. Oh we'll just have to see, nothing about this is jake. But it'll get better, I think.

Marie and Virginia apparently have new boys now, and I've been cheated on by Dean Andrews. He was apparently involved with that bitch blonde Claire Reed the whole time he was with me! I care, but at the same time I don't. Not sure why, but I guess he wasn't ever the one for me anyways. I'll find a new boy this summer as well. For now, the gang and I are getting ready to plan Dalton's birthday. It's on July 13th, which is unfortunately a Monday, so we'll be having the party on the 11th at his place.

It's been a couple weeks since the kickoff party, and the summer has gone well so far for our special six.

Marie and Arthur are *officially* an item, as are Virginia and Dylan. They've all been basking in the sun, spending every day lying on the beach and swimming in their large pools, walking around downtown Southampton, and shopping *way* too often.

Roxy and Johnny had been working on Dalton's birthday party, *a surprise one*, of course. Dalton had told Johnny he wasn't really up for a huge party this year, after everything that happened with Henry Flynn, but the group decided that a birthday celebration was *exactly* what he needed.

They'd tone it down a *bit* however, make it more of a medium-sized party rather than such a grand one.

All of his friends would be there of course, and luckily his parents had decided to go back to the city for the weekend, promising to return the morning of his birthday. It was perfect, a grand home *all* to himself *all* weekend—except for the many guests he'd be sharing it with on Saturday, of course. Although, knowing him, he secretly wanted it filled with all of his favorite people, partying with him in celebration of a new age. A new age that would bring new problems, drama, and tragic events.

Oh, aren't you excited? We've got some more clichés and Manhattan scandals to be uncovered. Buckle up, we're in for another ride.

CHAPTER 18

OUR FRIEND DALTON JAMES

It was almost time, and Virginia was heading back to the house with Dalton by her side, ready to see his big reaction when he walked in and heard the voices of forty of his closest friends scream "SURPRISE!" simultaneously, followed by many "Happy Birthdays" of course.

He was—in fact—surprised.

Johnny had done a pretty good job at making Dalton believe they weren't planning a party for him, after he gave them strict orders not to. Dalton was taken aback in that moment, but he was then filled with joy and an array of happy emotions. His friends were right when they thought a smallish birthday party would serve him well and do justice to a celebration. It wasn't anything too crazy, though there were still forty guests. Normally, there would have been close to sixty or seventy, but

Marie had suggested a guest list of forty and they all figured that was a good amount. Enough to fill the ballroom but not too many to overwhelm Dalton in his "down days". He had been closer to Henry than the rest of the group, even though they all truly considered him a dear friend. Dalton and Henry had been more like brothers, and his death sent Dalton into a deep state of depression.

Hazel was there at the party; the Flynns had almost taken the summer and escaped to the French Riviera, but Hazel had convinced her parents that they needed to try and get back to life as normal as possible, and that included spending the summer in Southampton, just like they had done every year since she and Henry were two years old. So, they did. Dalton spent a good majority of his party with her. They had always had a little "thing". He had always found her to be one of the most beautiful girls in school, *next to Roxy*, and knew her well because of his close friendship with her brother. Talking to each other all night was comforting for the both of them, and they had never really gotten into such a deep conversation before, even though they were always pretty good friends. It was different this time.

"I don't know, it's just, all so hard," he said to her, "I can't imagine what you're going through. I think about how much of a dark place I'm in, but it must not compare to you."

"You have no idea." She looked into his eyes and grabbed his hand. "I find ways to cope, and so will you."

He smiled. "Can I get you another glass of champagne?"

What he didn't know was how she had been coping. Let's just say her allowance had been useful to fuel her new addiction:

opioids. However, we aren't going to get into that just yet. For now, it was Dalton's birthday celebration, and in just a couple of days he would be seventeen years old. *Finally.* He and Virginia truly were the babies of the group, even though they didn't act like it. They were all pretty mature for their age.

"Hey, where's the birthday boy?" Roxy asked Marie.

"I don't know, I haven't seen him in quite some time."

"I'll go ask Johnny."

Dalton had taken a little excursion to his bedroom—*with Hazel.*

"Have you seen Dalton?"

Johnny sipped his bourbon and put the glass down on a table. "I saw him go upstairs a while ago, maybe check his room?"

"Upstairs? Why would he be up there?"

They gave each other a look; they knew exactly what the other was thinking.

"Do you think?"

"Nah … well?" Johnny said.

"Well, we have to go upstairs and see … don't we?"

"Definitely."

Roxy and Johnny made their way upstairs, where the music was significantly quieter. Sure enough, they opened his door to find him on top of Hazel.

"Attaboy," Johnny smiled.

"Johnny! My God." Roxy slapped his arm.

"Oh my God," Hazel said as she pushed Dalton off of her, suddenly aware of the two new guests in his bedroom.

200

"Hazel?" Roxy asked.

"Huh, wow," Johnny said.

"Hello? Get out!" Dalton gently yelled, annoyed with them interrupting what seemed to be Hazel losing her virginity to Dalton.

"Sorry!" they said simultaneously, laughing, before turning around and bumping into Frankie.

"What's going on in there?" he said before they closed the door.

"Hazel and Dalton …" Roxy said with another hint of laughter.

"NO WAY!" he said before peeking his head through the door. "Attaboy," he smiled.

"That's what I said!" Johnny laughed before Dalton threw a pillow at the door and Frankie closed it.

"Oh you two, what am I going to do with you two idiots?" Roxy said before grabbing both of them by the arm and taking them back downstairs.

"When did they become a thing?" Frankie asked.

"I think he's always kind of had the hots for her," Johnny replied.

"He has, I just didn't know *she* was smitten by *him*. She never told me."

"Interesting," both boys said.

It got later and later and eventually the two new lovebirds came out of Dalton's room, with significantly messier hair, and made their way downstairs. Everyone sang "Happy Birthday" to Dalton as seventeen candles burned and dripped little bits of wax onto his cake. Around one in the morning the party began to die down and about fifteen guests remained, the closer close friends. Our special six all included, of course. Everyone was a little bit more than intoxicated by the enormous amounts of giggle water they had all indulged in. Dalton's house was right on the beach, so Roxy and Frankie decided they'd go out for a little late-night swim.

"Bet you can't catch me!" she yelled as she made her way across the sand, running toward the dark ocean.

"That's a bet you'll lose, Roxy darling," Frankie yelled back as he removed his shoes and followed her out of the house.

They kept running, sand now in between their feet and wind running through both Roxy's short, curly hair and Frankie's semi-messy black hair. He eventually caught up with her, and when he did he grabbed her gently but quickly by the waist and lifted her up, spinning her in the air before letting her down, grabbing her hand, and leading her closer to the small waves in the calm Atlantic Ocean that night.

"Are we going in or what?" she challenged him as she pulled him closer and closer.

"You bet we are," he smiled before she responded with a grin and a laugh.

With hands still interlocked they ran gracefully into the darkened sea. He splashed some of the ice-cold water on her before she did the same.

"It's cold, Matthews!" she squealed.

"Well this was your idea!" he laughed before they both ran back out of the water they had been so keen to get into.

"Oh God, I'm freezing—" she said, shivering as they made their way back onto the sand.

"Do you wanna go back inside?"

"Hell no!" she protested.

He came behind her and bear-hugged her tight to make her warmer. He was cold too, but wouldn't admit it.

"Isn't it such a beautiful night?" she said with a sigh.

He almost told her, "Not as beautiful as you," but instead just responded with a simple, "Yes love."

"Do you remember what the sunset was like before it got so dark? Oh boy, it was just the best I have ever seen. The sky was painted with a mixture of dusty pink and midnight blue. I miss it, but there's nothing like the dark night either."

"The stars?"

"Yes," she took a pause, "the stars."

He still had his perfect arms around her, and she was holding onto them with loving force. They were both drunk, but not so drunk that they wouldn't remember this moment in the morning. *Though, they wouldn't speak of it.* Roxy turned her head around to look back at the boy that was holding her so tightly. They were soon gazing longingly into each other's eyes. His blue eyes interlocked with her brown, before their heartbeats became one. Suddenly it felt as if the waves had come to a standstill and there was no movement around them. It was just them. Roxy Elliott and Frankie Matthews. They looked at each other's lips before returning to their eyes, before both leaned in for a kiss. A kiss that came so close to happening, before a very drunk Johnny joined their party.

"Roxy! Frankie! My good friends!" he yelled as he made his way down the sand. Or should I say, *stumbled*, down the sand.

They quickly separated once he approached, and their almost kiss ceased to happen. The moment was gone. Johnny came in—between the two, putting his arm around each of them. Him in the middle and all three looking out into the vast, dark ocean.

"It was a good party wasn't it?" he said.

"It really was. We did good," Roxy answered.

"You wanna know something?" he asked, almost out of it.

"Yes Johnny …" Frankie said.

"I love you guys. I love you guys so much," Johnny said with a slightly slurred speech, before giving them each a kiss on the cheek.

"We love you too Johnny," Frankie and Roxy responded, looking at each other and laughing at how drunk he was. *He* would not remember the second half of Dalton's party. He wouldn't remember the girl he slept with either.

It was now 2:30 and everyone had left, leaving the six and only six of them. They all ended up on the beach, sitting down on the sand, all drunk and gazing out into the sea. It was Frankie, Johnny, then Roxy, Marie, Dalton, and then Virginia, all lying right beside each other in a line on the soft sand. Roxy and Frankie continued to replay their ever so intimate moment in their minds before they all ended up asleep on the beach. By the time the sun rose and the birds began to chirp, every single one of them was greeted by a massive headache. Johnny and Frankie worse than the others. They made their way off the beach and back into Dalton's house, where they all made breakfast together. Dalton's maids had taken the weekend off as well, considering his parents weren't there. They thought he was capable of taking care of himself for two days. All seemed good: the party had been a nice gesture for Dalton and he was feeling happier about his life. Hazel was on his mind all morning. That was, of course, until a guest arrived.

"Dalton, are you going to get that?" Virginia asked.

There was someone knocking at the door, but it was hard to hear as the group's loud voices drowned out the noise. When Virginia brought it to Dalton's attention, he then of course went to see who could be there. It was someone unfamiliar to him, but someone he was a lot closer to than he had ever known.

"Hello sir, I am looking for a Dalton James."

Dalton looked him up and down. "I'm Dalton James, who might you be?"

The mystery guy smiled back, but this wasn't your average "nice to meet you smile". It was something a bit more sinister, full of some type of mischief, a secret agenda. "I'm your long-lost brother."

CHAPTER 19

MR. DAWSON

Dear Diary,

Last night we had a party for Dalton's birthday, and I think it went rather well. He looked dapper and seemed to enjoy the rather beautiful Hazel Flynn. Oh yes, I mean ENJOY ... they had sex. Johnny and I actually walked in on them, and then Frankie joined us and we all had a laugh. They would make a nice couple, the cat's meow really.

The party was a nice turn out, nothing huge, we didn't want to overwhelm the rather depressed Dalton, but enough for a grand old time. The gin was perfect, and so was the *champagne. A little too perfect really. Frankie and I, in our rather spifflicated state, decided it was a marvelous idea to take a dip in the cold Atlantic Ocean at one in the morning. It was fun however, as it always is with him.*

It was after the quick swim when it got weird.

The running down the sand and looking back at him chasing me wasn't the problem. The splashing each other with ice-cold water wasn't an issue either, it was when he held me. He came behind me, holding me because I was so cold, and I of course looked back at him and for a moment we just gazed into each other's eyes and for a few brief seconds, it felt like we were going to kiss. Not on the cheek like all of us do, but kiss kiss. A kiss on the lips, his on mine and mine on his. Crashing into each other like the passionate waves of the Atlantic ocean.

Then Johnny came stumbling down the sand and it was over in an instant. Just like that. We were both drunk but not too drunk to remember.

I know he remembers, but we haven't spoken a word to each other about it. I suppose it should stay that way, I mean, it's Frankie after all.

And that's exactly what happened. They didn't speak of it. At least not for a long time. *Don't you just wanna slap them across the face sometimes?* I sure do.

Anyways, on to the more pressing matter: Dalton's long-lost

brother. This was *quite* a surprise to everyone. It seemed that Mrs. James had given birth about five years before marrying and having Dalton. Two years before meeting Mr. James. This child was out of wedlock, of course, and not the product of Dalton's father. Naturally, Frances decided to give the child up. Then she fell in love with Dalton's father and married, eventually getting pregnant with Dalton. She decided she would keep her first child a secret, and Dalton and his father would never find out.

That was until now, of course.

So here we are again with yet another scandal of the past, secrets buried underneath the wealth of an elite New York family, once again, coming out for all the world to see.

You see, that's the thing with secrets and scandals, they always seem to have a way of showing up at unexpected times. Taking you by surprise. No matter how deep they get buried, somehow, they are revealed, and they always stir up problems. That was certainly the case with Roxy, and the secret that was supposed to never get out.

So here we are *again*—what was with our special six's parents in their younger years anyways? Always getting into some type of trouble.

As for the long-lost brother himself, his name was Gene Dawson, and he was adopted by a nice and somewhat boring Chicago family.

We have all seen this happen many times, the story of an adopted kid wanting to find his birth mother and birth family; we all know it *too* well. It's the classic cliché.

This, however, wasn't that story.

It seemed to all connect back to the Elliotts, which so many things conviently tend to do. I wonder why that is?

"Dalton, we're all going to eat on the sand, are you coming?" Roxy yelled to him.

"Just one minute, go and I'll be out there soon," he answered back, still in shock at what had just been said to him by the mystery man at the door.

"I know this must be a lot for you—"

"What do you mean you're my brother?"

"Well, just that. Half-brother, technically."

"You know what, I think this is nonsense, you should beat it," Dalton said as he began to close the door.

"Wait!" Gene responded, putting his hand against the door to stop it from shutting. "Please, I'm telling you the truth."

Dalton was confused, as most seventeen-year-old boys would be if a guy showed up claiming to be their long-lost brother. This wasn't some common thing to happen, and certainly wasn't the birthday present Dalton was expecting. He didn't know how exactly to react—who would?

"My name is Gene Dawson, and Frances, your mom, she's mine too," he said with the door close to shut in between them. "I was adopted, obviously, and I just—"

"Let me stop you right there, if you've come to seek out family because you need some dough or something, you're not going to get it—"

"Hey there's no need to get in a lather, that's not why I'm here. I just want to meet her. I believe I deserve at least a brief moment. Is that so wrong?"

Dalton took a pause, pondering and trying to understand the life-changing information he had just been given.

"She's not here."

"Well, where is she?"

"She's back in the city, she'll be home tomorrow. Listen, I've got my friends out there on the beach waiting for me, you need to leave. You can come back on Tuesday." He was blunt.

"Why not tomorrow?"

"Because tomorrow is my birthday and I don't need any nonsense drama to mess it up. Come back on Tuesday and you can speak to her. But just remember, I don't believe a word you're saying. If my mom had another son out there, she woulda told me," Dalton said as he shut the door, leaving Gene alone on the other side.

Gene wasn't expecting some warm welcome. In fact, it went better than he had pictured in his mind. Dalton went out and joined the others on the beach for breakfast but kept what had just happened to himself. He wasn't going to start all this excitement until he knew for sure that the man at the door was really his brother. He didn't want to think about it either, about the idea that his mother had hidden this from him for seventeen years. Although, it *was* of course the only thing on his mind. For now, however, let's steer in another direction, because Gene won't be back until Tuesday, so there's no point in telling you his agenda right now.

After breakfast, the girls decided to head downtown for a little shopping, while the boys spent their day smoking cigars and talking about girls and cars, as they did so often. Dalton's mind was nonstop spinning with all of his new and not so wonderful thoughts; he didn't know how to comprehend what he had just been told, and as bad as he wished to ignore it, it was a thought that would infiltrate his entire day. So maybe I *should* just skip to Tuesday and tell you how it went …

"There is someone at the door, Mrs. James," the maid said to Dalton's mother.

"I'll be right there!" she responded.

As she walked toward the door, there was nothing she could have done to prepare for the moment she was about to experience. The moment she would once again see her first son, the son that she had given up for adoption. The son that had mysteriously decided to place himself back into Dalton's family, who are coincidentally quite so close to the Elliotts.

"Hello, how do you do?" she said to the young man standing on the porch.

He smiled; this was the first time he had ever met his birth mom. Other than the day of his birth, of course.

"Hello, are you Frances James?"

"Yes, yes I am."

There was a pause, on both ends. Frances had this feeling in the pit of her stomach, I guess you could call it a woman's intuition … or a mother's. She knew, deep down, that this young man standing on her doorstep on that hot Southampton day, was someone important. On the other hand, Gene felt a sense of nervousness. He knew why he was there and what he was meant to do, but he couldn't help feeling the emotions that ran throughout his entire body. Seeing his birth mother for the very first time, in person, not just a lousy photograph. She was standing there, in full color, the woman who carried him for nine months before giving him up to some random and wealthy Chicago family.

He knew what he was there to do, but it didn't mean a part of him didn't wish it could have maybe been just a bit different.

His agenda was bigger than this moment, more important to him, yet for a second while he stood there taking in what he was experiencing, he briefly wished that the James family didn't know the Elliotts, that they *weren't* associated with the oh so powerful, wealth-intoxicated, mob-loving crime family. But that wasn't the case now was it—*oh no.* He was on a mission, one that meant more to him than his birth family.

"My name is Gene, Gene Dawson."

"Nice to meet you, Gene," Frances said, not knowing who he was yet. *It hadn't clicked.*

"Mrs. James, do you know who I am?"

There was yet another pause before her eyebrows raised, along with every hair on her body. "Oh, oh Gene. Gene Dawson!" Tears began to slide down her face.

"So you do?" he smiled.

"I never in a million years imagined I would see you," she said before grabbing him, hugging him tight. "You're so grown up! Look at you, so handsome," she spoke softly as she examined him. "Please, come in."

She led him to the great room; no one was around. They talked for an hour about an array of different things.

This was quite an emotional day, for both of them, but

more so for Mrs. James. Imagine if the secret son you had given up for adoption showed up on your doorstep one day, out of nowhere. It would evoke some emotions you hadn't felt before, wouldn't it?

Imagine what would be going through your head. A myriad of thoughts both in the mind and the heart.

They were still sitting on one of the couches in the great room, looking out to the ocean, sipping bourbon in heavy crystal glasses imported from Europe, as Dalton walked in.

"Gene," he said, startled. He hadn't expected him to be sitting right there with his mother, laughing and talking up a storm.

Thankfully, Mr. James was out playing golf at the club with friends, one of them being Dennis Elliott.

"Dalton! I thought you were with your father?" Frances said, also startled.

"I decided to leave early, it's rather hot outside. I see that you've met your son." There was a hint of attitude and sarcasm in his voice.

She didn't know what to say. What *would* you say in that situation?

"Dalton, please—"

"No, please, carry on. Don't stop on my account. I'll head over to Frankie's," he said before storming off, lighting a cigarette.

"Will you please excuse me?" she said to Gene with a soft, endearing voice before chasing after Dalton.

"Honey, I always wanted to tell you but—"

"No I see, scandals are always best kept a secret. I mean, we saw that with Daisy and Caroline didn't we? It's best to keep them hidden."

"Dalton!" she yelled as he headed toward the front door.

He turned back before opening it. "It's fine. I'm not mad I've got this sudden long-lost half-brother. I'm mad you never told me. Please, catch up with him. I'll make my way back later, to get to know him. For now, I'm leaving—"

"Dalton, please—"

"Stop it, would you! I said I am not ready yet!" And he left.

He went over to Frankie's. The entire gang was there. He told them everything. Everything about how Gene had showed up the morning after his party and how he hadn't been ready to tell everyone until he had confirmation it was true. That his mother had been lying to him for all these years. That she had another son.

They were in shock, but not utter shock, as scandals seemed to present themselves quite often in the roaring world they lived in.

"Why do you think he decided to show up so sudden? Does he want money?" Roxy said, curiously concerned.

"I have no idea. By the way he dresses, it doesn't seem like it."

"Maybe there *is* no agenda. Maybe he just wants to meet his birth mom and family," Virginia chimed in.

"That's not likely," Frankie came back at her.

"Oh my God Frankie, you don't know that," Marie responded.

"No, he's right. It's *not* likely. Not when it comes to us, to a family like ours. Wealthy and all, I don't believe that after so many years he would decide to search for his birth mom. Why not when he was eighteen, or nineteen? Why at age twenty-two? Most of the time, when you're curious about where you came from, it's during your adolescent years that you take it upon yourself to journey off and seek your birth family. Not once you're in your twenties," Dalton said.

They discussed possible reasons, possible agendas that this Gene Dawson may have had. Why he was there, why he showed up at their Southampton home. How he was even able to find them so easily. Though, none of their reasons or ideas were anything close to the truth (sadly). If they *had* been, it could have saved them future trouble. A dark cloud was truly heading the Elliott way, once again.

The day had passed and Frances fessed up to her husband, telling him everything. He took it quite well. Mr. James was a good man, an understanding one. It wasn't like she had cheated on him or anything. She had the baby before she ever met and married Dalton's father. He was surprised and not happy with the fact that she hadn't ever told him, but he understood. *God, what a guy.* He took it a hell of a lot better than Dalton did, and better than most husbands would have. They decided that they would invite him for dinner the following night. Gene would have a chance to get to know his brother and Mr. James, and they would get the chance to know him. The dinner went well, for the most part. Mr. James took a liking to the kid and Dalton took a while to warm up to him. By dessert, he actually seemed to have retired his crazy agenda idea, soon believing that this Gene Dawson was genuine, that he had wanted to find them for years and finally took the steps to do so. Dalton was beginning to feel some excitement toward the idea of a long-lost brother.

"So, tell me about your friends."

"Oh they're great. All of them. My closest friends are Frankie, Johnny, Marie, Virginia, and Roxy. Maybe you can meet them, there's a little party happening tomorrow," Dalton said, "they'll all be there. You should come!"

When was there ever *not* a party?

"I'd love to!" Gene was delighted by the invitation, but the information to come next was even better. "Where is it?"

"It's going to be at Roxy's. You'll love her, she's a roar. One beautiful dame, I'll tell you that."

"Roxy?"

"Yes, Scarlett Roxy."

"As in, Roxy Elliott?" He was interested now.

"Oh yes. You'll get to see the Elliott mansion, their famous summer estate. It's grand."

"Wow, what an honor! I've heard it's the biggest on Long Island."

Dalton chuckled. "It sure is. The Elliotts only accept the best."

"So I've heard," Gene said, almost in a sinister, conniving way. "So, will Dennis Elliott be there? I've heard so much about him back in Chicago, you know, the 'favorite' Elliott."

Dalton laughed again. "Oh yes, he's quite great isn't he? Dennis sure lives up to the Elliott reputation, the name and all."

"Will he be there, I asked," Gene said, this time with a hardness to his voice.

Dalton was taken aback.

"I'm sorry, that came off a little strong!" Gene said, attempting to clear the air from the tense energy.

"No no, no need to be sorry. And uh—yes. He'll be there." Dalton gave him an awkward, forced smile.

Gene smiled back.

This was nearing the end of the night. Frances told Gene he was welcome to stay there, in their home, but he insisted he had somewhere to stay and thanked them for the wonderful dinner. He gave his mother a kiss on the cheek and told her he'd see them all at the Elliotts' tomorrow, before walking out the front door and back to wherever he was staying. Dalton had wondered why he didn't take Frances up on her offer. If he was so eager to get close to his birth mother, and spend time with her, why not stay in her home?

Where *exactly* was he staying?

Well, I can tell you that it wasn't anywhere Dalton could have imagined. Let's just say there was a family out there, still quite angry and a rival to the Elliotts. One who hadn't yet gotten proper revenge. One that had failed at every attempt, and one who would continue to fail until next summer.

Do you remember Kenneth Decker? The son of Thomas Decker, father to Helen Decker?

Yeah, of course you do. Last time we saw him was after he and his cousin Daniel had kidnapped Marie, which was supposed to be Roxy, then were forced to return her. Remember that? Oh yes, well he wasn't exactly done with his path of revenge.

There were Deckers in Chicago, as I told you long ago, and they knew of the revenge Kenneth wanted for Thomas. They were on the same page as him, wanting revenge against the Elliotts for their family member's death. Though, Thomas *did* bring it upon himself in the first place. They, however, didn't see it that way. Oh, isn't it funny how things seem to work out sometimes? Well, maybe not, but it sure as hell is interesting. Let's just say that this Gene Dawson had taken upon the path of joining the mob.

As we know, the Deckers and the Elliotts are both mafia families, and Gene had decided to join the wrong one. With both in Chicago, it's sad he sold his soul to the Deckers rather than joining the more powerful family, but he wasn't the brightest to begin with. Many young men had dreams of joining the mob, and you didn't just have to be a family member in order to do so. The majority of the Decker mob was Decker blood, as was the Elliott, but there were many non-blood mafia members who were a part of each clan. Gene was one of them. Though, it wasn't exactly easy to join, or to pledge your loyalty, shall I say.

Gene Dawson sought out the Deckers in Chicago, and they did their digging on him of course, and to their benefit found out that he was the biological son of Frances James. A family extremely close to the Elliotts. *How convenient.* Well, long story short, his first task was in order to pledge his loyalty to the family before he officially became a part of their mob. This task was exactly what you are probably thinking. A hit on the Elliotts.

He was assigned to carry out the revenge they all wanted. To hit the Elliotts where it would hurt most. *Maximum damage.* An attack on the family, specifically on Dennis Elliott, the cream of the crop.

Now, he could have been assigned to whack Tommy Elliott, Uncle Clyde's son, considering he was the one who pulled the trigger on Thomas, but it sent a bigger message to take out Dennis. He was the most in control, after Griffin of course, and to kill him was more important. Plus, Tommy was still a kid, and they weren't *that* evil. He still had years of Elliott-ing to do before he deserved a bullet in the head.

Though, don't worry, he doesn't.

Anyways, this is why Gene was there in Southampton. Why he decided to come home to his biological mommy and pretend he was there to create some type of relationship. Upon seeing her, he began to rethink everything, but all in all, being a part of the mob was something he wanted more. And so he would do what was requested of him. He would pledge his loyalty to the not so great Decker family so that he could return back to Chicago as an official member of the mafia. The Decker mafia.

Let's jump to the next day, the little not-so-little gathering at the Elliott mansion.

They all arrived together: Dalton, Gene, and Mr. and Mrs. James. They entered through the double doors and made their way toward the grand backyard. Beautiful, expensive landscapes accompanied by multiple brilliant pools, a glimmering champagne tower and tall tables filled with fancy food. Everyone was once again in awe of the Elliott name. Even

Gene admired the glamour of the Elliotts, but he was there on one mission and one mission only: *kill Dennis Elliott.*

Time went on and Gene hadn't yet done the deed. He couldn't just shoot him point blank in the middle of the party, with everyone around. He would have been shot dead and dragged over to the Deckers immediately with every Elliott accompanying him. He had to get him alone, shoot him, and leave as soon as it was done. Before any other family member could catch him or hear the sound of the bullet flying from the barrel and into Dennis's chest. He had a plan.

"Nice, ain't it?" Dalton asked as he grabbed a chilled shrimp cocktail off of a tray one of the butlers was carrying.

"Sure is, so where's the famed Roxy? I'd love to meet her."

"She's right over there, come on, I'll introduce you," Dalton responded.

He took him over to where Roxy, Marie, and Frankie were standing, smoking and drinking of course. They were delighted to meet him, he seemed like a stand-up fella. The truth, however, was a slightly darker reality.

"So Roxy, your family, they put on a good party don't they?"

"Oh yes, this was all my mother and father. They do a grand job!"

"And your home, it's—"

"Marvelous, yes," she smiled.

"So, your father, where is he exactly? I'd love to thank him and compliment his grand style."

"Oh, I'm not sure," she responded.

"Actually, about ten minutes ago he told me he was heading

upstairs to find some special cigars? I believe?" Frankie said, somewhat confident in his whereabouts.

Thanks Frankie, couldn't have just kept your mouth shut.

"I see," Gene said, there again with that sinister smile, and his gun in his jacket, loaded, ready for fire.

"You are of course welcome to go find him, though it may be difficult. It's not exactly a small home," Roxy chuckled, "but if he's looking for his 'special' cigars, he'll be in his office. It's in the west wing, on the third floor, the door at the very end of the longest hall." She gave him exactly what he needed to carry out the hit on her father.

"Wonderful, I guess I may as well try."

"And while you're at it I'm sure you'll find time to admire some of the art on the walls. The Elliotts are quite the collectors," Dalton said.

"Sure will!" Gene responded.

Sure won't was more like it.

So there he went, with clear directions given by the Elliott daughter herself.

Gene walked inside, took the first staircase he saw and made his way up to the third floor and down the longest hallway of the west wing, just as Roxy said, ignoring the rather expensive artwork on the walls. He found the room, at the very end, the door slightly cracked open. Dennis was just as he was said to be, looking through his cigar collection to find the "special" box.

Gene was nervous—he had never killed anyone before, he really didn't even know how to, or what it would feel like after. Knowing he had taken a life, a life that shouldn't have been taken. Dennis had never hurt him in any way, had never done anything to his family. He may have been a member of the most powerful mob family in America, but he wasn't an evil guy.

Sure, he had taken many lives, but only the ones worth taking. Never any innocent ones. He may have been a criminal, but really his crimes only benefited other people. His speakeasies brought joy to anyone who ever entered them, among some other crimes he had committed.

He didn't deserve to die; he didn't deserve a bullet to the chest. And surely, most of all, Roxy didn't deserve to lose her beloved father.

He was a fantastic father; Dennis was always there for Roxy, raising her up right. He'd do anything for her at the drop of a dime, he'd give his own life for hers if she was ever in danger. Dennis wanted the best for her, the best life she could ever have. He loved her so much, as he would have loved her grandchildren someday. She was his only child, his little princess. She couldn't handle losing him like this, on a hot July day in Southampton, at a summer party. The entire family didn't deserve this. Dennis was fearless, strong, and stubborn, much like Roxy in that department—he always put family first, he cared about so many people, and so many cared about him. He had the biggest heart out of all the Elliotts, besides Roxy. This wasn't his time. It wasn't his time …

"It's been a few huh, have you seen Gene?" Dalton asked Frankie.

"Well I know he was eager to meet Mr. Elliott, maybe he's still with him."

"I don't know, I guess. I want to introduce him to some other people though, before it gets too late."

"Well you heard Roxy—west wing, third floor, longest hallway, last door," Frankie said with a smirk.

"Guess I'll go find him," Dalton said.

"I'll come with," Frankie responded, to Dalton's surprise, "there's something I want to talk with Mr. Elliott about anyways."

"Alright," he said, and they made their way toward Dennis.

Gene carefully opened the door wider, nervous for what was to come. He was a twenty-two-year-old kid after all, and he hadn't even officially joined the mob. Though, this was the only way he was going to be able to. So he got it together, he took his right hand and reached into his blazer, grabbing the gun he had hidden, pulling it out. Locked and loaded to go. He began to enter the room; Dennis was facing the shelf which contained a myriad of cigars, all imported, and all in expensive cases. He was sorting through them and Gene began to approach him, slowly and softly with the gun now out in the open, in his right hand, dangling. Dennis was unarmed at that moment.

The perfect target.

Gene's palms were beginning to sweat, not enough for the gun to fall out of his hand, but just enough so that it was ever so slightly slipping. He was in the room now, just past the door, with tunnel vision on his mission. Frankie and Dalton were heading down the hallway, almost approaching the door, just as Gene began to raise his arm up, getting his gun in position to shoot Dennis … in the back, might I add. *How classy.* Maybe it was easier this way, he wouldn't have to see his face as he took his life. Though, it is rather awful. Just as his arm was approaching the appropriate height, they appeared at the doorway.

"MR. ELLIOTT LOOK OUT!" shouted a very, *very* frantic Frankie.

Just as he said it, Dennis quickly spun around, and the shot was fired.

Oh don't fret, Dennis isn't dead. Frankie saved his life. Our Matthews boy came behind the sinister Gene, grabbing him and his arm, pushing it away from Roxy's father. Though, he did this just as the gunshot was being fired, so it still went off. Only, it went off into a bookshelf rather than into Mr. Elliott's heart. Dalton came around and took the gun from Gene and held it up to his head.

"Are you a Decker, or a soon-to-be one?" Dennis said to an extremely, *extremely* nervous Gene. This was a different type of nervous, however. He was now nervous for his life. There was *no* getting out of this.

Dennis was rather calm, considering he had been a millisecond away from being shot dead in his office.

"What the hell, Gene!" said Dalton.

"You know him?" Dennis asked.

"He's my half-brother."

Dennis chuckled. "I see."

"Or are you? Are you even my brother?" Dalton was angry, clearly.

"I am, and I'm sorry. But this wasn't about you, or our mother, it never was."

"I don't think I understand," Dalton said.

"I do—he wants in on the Deckers, to join the mob. Now, are you from New York or Chicago?" Dennis said.

"Excuse me?" Dalton asked.

"Chicago," Frankie told Dennis.

"I see," Dennis said, before lighting a cigar, "and this was your task wasn't it, your proof of loyalty. To take me out?"

Gene was sweating, and Dennis walked over to the bookshelf (which was now decorated by a nice little bullet) and leaned up against it.

"How could you?" Dalton said; he was upset. He had let Gene in, he had been excited about having a new half-brother, and this is what happens? Yikes.

"I told you, it wasn't about you."

"I don't get it, if you wanted into the mafia, why didn't you try and join the Chicago Elliotts?" Frankie asked before he and Dennis shared a laugh.

Gene knew this was going one of three ways. Either Dalton himself would pull the trigger, resulting in his death, or Dennis would, also resulting in his death and shipment back to the Chicago Deckers. Or, he was leaving in handcuffs. That, however, wasn't necessarily the best option. The Elliotts have friends at the NYPD, *lots of them*. One being the chief of police himself. Mr. Romano, Marie's father.

"So, you really are Frances's son?"

He stood there, in terror, silent.

"I asked you a question," Dennis said, this time with a more aggressive voice.

"Yes," he answered, softly.

Dalton was still standing there with the gun pointed at his head, Dennis smoking and leaning up against the bookshelf. Powerful yet nonchalant and unafraid, he didn't seem to be at all worked up over the event, his almost-death. Frankie was standing next to him, arms crossed, staring Gene down.

"Well, that's wonderful. Now I can't kill you," Dennis said sarcastically with a grin, and Frankie chuckled. They seemed to be somewhat enjoying this; meanwhile Dalton was quite the opposite.

And it was true, he couldn't kill his friend's son, whether she had raised him or not. It was wrong and he wouldn't do it. He *could*, however, have him arrested and sent away for a *very* long time. Along with a note back to the top Decker in Chicago, signed with "Love, Dennis Elliott" at the bottom.

How *Elliott* of him.

Dennis told Dalton to hand the gun over—it was all too much for him, he needed to go outside and catch some air. He told him to relax and have some scotch, to clear his head and be with his friends. Frankie, however, he kept by his side. He handed the gun over to Frankie and sat Gene down on a chair, this time with Frankie holding the gun pointed at his head. Dennis made a telephone call to downstairs. There was a maid that remained near the telephone by the front door, and when she picked up he told her to find Mr. Romano and send him up to his west wing study. While they were waiting for him to arrive, however, Roxy decided to make an appearance.

"What the absolute hell!"

"Roxy, baby!" Frankie said, startled by her.

"What are you doing? That's Dalton's brother," she said, ready to slap Frankie across the face.

"Hi honey," Dennis said.

"Daddy, what's going on?"

"Long story short, this little fella is working for the Deckers. He's got some mob dream and he was ordered to take out your father," Frankie responded.

Suddenly Roxy had a different tone in her voice. "Oh my," she said.

"It's true, Frankie saved my life," Dennis said.

"I did." Frankie grinned at Roxy.

"Gee, thanks Matthews," she said to Frankie; she was extremely grateful but *of course* couldn't let Frankie think that. You know, the pride thing?

Mr. Romano made his way up to a rather interesting scene, and that was how it ended. He took the bastard away in cuffs and down to the station, then had him put away for a long time. Dennis wrote the Deckers a rather nice note and sent it off, and that was it for now. That was once again the last we will see or hear of the Deckers trying to take down the Elliotts.

For a while, at least.

CHAPTER 20

A Rather Handsome Ending to a Rather Lousy Lunch

Oh, what a party, they all seem to have their own unique charm to them, don't they?

Well, it was coming to an end.

Nobody but the Elliotts, the Romanos, and those close to them knew of what went down in Dennis's study, and life around went on as if it never happened.

As it was coming to an end, Roxy was greeted by a much greater way to end the night. She met a rather handsome new boy. One she hadn't seen before. One who caught her eye immediately. One she knew she *had* to meet.

When Roxy is determined to do something, she does it, and she *always* ends up getting what she wants. I guess it was the Elliott in her.

July 16th, 1925

Dear Diary,

Oh what a damn party! First of all, the most important part, Dalton's long-lost brother was a Decker wannabe and attempted a hit on my father, only for Frankie, of all people, to save him. He's been put away though, of course.

It was an interesting scene, I'll tell you that much.

And Frankie doesn't look half bad with a gun in his hand.

Anyways, after the excitement of all that, I met a boy. A rather handsome one, might I add. His name is Warner Davenport, what a name!

Davenport … I've heard of the Davenports. I haven't ever met any of them myself, as they come from Boston, but I guess they just moved to the far better East Coast city. We all know Boston is nice, but it's no New York.

They also bought a summer home here in Southampton and are neighbors to Frankie. My father knows Warner's father and invited him to our lunch soirée so he and his family could become acquainted with some other families in our circle, rather than just having one friend in town: my father.

I guess a few of my relatives in Boston know the Davenports as well, though they didn't all move. Just him, his mother and father, and his sister. She's nine, and adorable.

After all hell went down, Dalton became somewhat of an

*ossified wet blanket, which is understandable, and left. I had
settled by the pool with a glass of champagne and Marie and
Virginia by my side, when I caught a glimpse of him. He's
tall, about six feet and two inches. He's got dark brown hair,
almost black, and beautiful brown eyes. He's quite dreamy,
really. So I kept glancing at him ever so slightly, while sipping
my champagne and lighting a cigarette. I guess the Matthewses
know the Davenports as well, which makes sense considering
Frankie's grandfather is originally from Boston, and he's still
got family there. Frankie had met him quite a few times, so
I'm told, whenever they were in Boston visiting family. They
weren't the best of friends, but they were friends. He went over
and began to talk to him by one of the tables, sipping scotch and
smoking up a storm ...*

"What's this?" he said, picking up a luxe cigarette holder. "A cigarette holder, is it?"

Frankie nicely took it from Warner's hand. "Oh yeah, it's Roxy's, she must have left it."

"Roxy? An Elliott, right? Dennis's daughter?"

"You got it."

"She must be one hell of a girl to own a white-golden cigarette holder—covered in—"

"Diamonds, yes, you have no idea," Frankie responded, laughing and taking another sip.

"With diamonds!" he laughed. "Who the hell would need

something like that?" Warner asked.

"Well, you haven't met Roxy," he laughed again. "She *is* an Elliott after all."

"Yeah my father knows hers, and we know a few Elliotts back in Boston. Never thought I'd come across Roxy though."

"Well now that you've made the move, you'll have to meet her. She's roaring, you'll love her," Frankie said, looking over at the pool where she was.

"I can imagine any girl with a white-gold and diamond cigarette holder would be!" Warner chuckled. He had never seen anything like it. Who *would* need that? I guess our Roxy Elliott.

They continued to talk and smoke and drink, and Frankie began to introduce his old distant friend to others, acquainting him with the New Yorker lifestyle. He wanted to "break the Boston out of him", or so he said. Roxy and the girls eventually got out of the pool and headed inside. A lot of the guests had left, but the party wasn't over—there were now just fewer guests. The "even more elite" of the crowd, as lunch was so clearly over and the afternoon was creeping closer and closer to evening.

"He's beautiful, isn't he?" Roxy said while changing out of her swimming suit and into a dress.

"Darling, he's gorgeous," Marie responded.

"Who are we talking about?" Virginia asked.

"The boy who was standing next to Frankie."

"Ohhhhh, he was," Virginia laughed.

The girls changed into an evening outfit and made their way back downstairs, hair made up and lipstick freshly applied.

Frankie was still with Warner, but they had retired to the ballroom where a lot of the guests were. Many were still outside, swimming, but the ballroom was filled with the majority, listening to music and conversing about whatever the wealthy found as an interesting topic.

It was a serene scene, beautiful really.

Not wild or roaring, but beautiful. People lounging on couches, people standing, leaning up against a wall. All sipping some fancy drink, smoking, laughing, and living out the summer like they always did. Frankie and Warner were leaned up against a wall, still with scotch in hand. Roxy entered the room, stunning, in a long light-golden dress embroidered with beautiful beads and fringe from just above the knees all the way down to the shiny floor. A feather in her hair and red, *daring* lipstick of course. All accompanied by a fresh spritz of Chanel No. 5.

"I'm going to make my move," Roxy smiled.

"Go get 'em, gorgeous," Marie said before she wandered off somewhere with Virginia, ready to spy on Roxy and Warner. Well, Roxy, Warner, *and* Frankie.

As Roxy was walking toward them, Frankie spotted her out of the corner of his eye. She approached them and they both smiled.

"You're rather stunning, Miss Elliott," he said with a half-grin.

"And *you're* rather dapper, Mr. Matthews." She gave him a half-grin back.

"So this is the famous Roxy Elliott?" Warner said, with a

full smile, admiring all that she was.

"That's my name," she said before walking closer to Frankie, giving him a kiss on the cheek, her lipstick leaving a mark. "Who's your friend?" she asked him.

"Warner Davenport," Warner responded.

"Oh," Roxy said, her eyebrows raised, "you're a Davenport boy? I believe I have some family in—"

"Boston," he gently cut her off, "yes, that's where I'm from. I just moved here. Well, I'll be living here in Southampton only in the summer, then officially moving to Manhattan in the fall."

"Very nice, but next time … don't cut me off," she sassed him.

"I told you, she's not like other girls," Frankie laughed and took a sip.

"You're right, I won't do it again," smiled Warner. He was infatuated by her, everything about her.

Frankie pulled the cigarette holder out of his pocket. "Darling, you found it!" Roxy exclaimed.

"So please, enlighten me, why is it exactly that a girl would need such a … luxe … cigarette holder?" Warner asked.

She glared at him, dead straight in the eye, waiting exactly seven seconds before responding with, "Because I like it." She put a cigarette in, placed it in her mouth, and Frankie lit it.

Warner was taken back by her ability to say things just the way she wanted, never sugarcoating the truth or holding back her attitude and sass, her character and charm.

She turned her back and walked away with her white-golden diamond cigarette holder in her hand, lifting her arm up high as her bracelets dropped down her arm closer to her elbow, waving beautifully back at them.

"Goodbye boys," she said as she waved, making her way out of the ballroom where Marie and Virginia then followed.

"Wow, she sure is something," Warner said.

"She really is, my golden diamond," Frankie answered. "You truly have no idea."

"Oh, oh I didn't realize. Are you two a couple?"

Frankie hesitated. "Oh, no no, just real great friends."

"So, she's free?"

"Well she's not dating anyone at the moment, no." Frankie found it hard to get those words out of his mouth. He didn't exactly expect their introduction to go this way. He wanted Warner to *meet* Roxy, not *date* her.

"Not yet at least," Warner said, grabbing Frankie's shoulder. "I'll see ya."

Frankie gave him a worrisome smile. "See ya."

... After meeting him, I decided to leave him wanting more. So I exited the room and told Marie and Virginia everything.

He's so dreamy!

As night fell, mostly everyone cleared out, leaving to go home for dinner. Before the Davenports left, I had Marie go and talk to him, so she could tell me if she approved.

She did, of course.

Then they left and well, that was it ... for now at least. I know I'll be seeing him around, I just hope it's soon.

CHAPTER 21

THE FIRST DATE

Oh to be young and in love—well, *almost* in love. I've introduced the rather dreamy Davenport boy whom Roxy has been fawning over, and I can tell you this much: he *is* rather dreamy. One of those very put-together, has-his-life-in-order type of guys. He also dresses nicely, as did all of the boys Roxy knew, but considering he was an out-of-towner, this was a pleasant positive.

After they met, Warner couldn't find Roxy, but while he was speaking with Marie he asked for Roxy's telephone number. Marie didn't know it, of course, but I guess we can't blame her. It was the summer home telephone number after all, where she only lives three months out of the year. If it means anything, she *did* however know the number to the Elliott residence at The Dakota. Though, that wasn't going to help. So she gave Warner her own number, telling him to phone her later that night where she could look up Roxy's and give it to him so he could ring her.

If you ask me, it would have been easier for him to spend a few extra minutes looking for Roxy rather than going through all that, but I guess he was already on his way out the door.

It was the next morning. "Hello?" Marie answered with a chirp in her voice. "This is Marie."

"Marie! It's Warner. Warner Davenport," he said with excitement.

"Good morning Warner! How are you?"

"Oh I'm just fine. I was just calling to ask if you had Roxy Elliott's telephone number now."

"Oh yes! That's right! I forgot." That was a lie, she remembered *exactly* why he was calling, but wanted to play it cool, for Roxy's sake. "Are you planning on ringing her now?"

"I was, yes," he responded.

"Oh, you might want to wait an hour or two. She's never up this early."

"Seven in the morning? That's early?"

"Oh yes, I myself just barely woke up."

Warner laughed—he came from a family of early risers. "Alright, well I'll phone her at nine, will she be up by then?"

"It's likely," Marie laughed. "Here's her telephone number," she said before giving it to him.

He was eager to speak to Roxy again and would spend the next two hours planning out what he would say and how he would say it; the way he would ask her out to dinner. Frankie had mentioned to him that Tavern on the Green was her favorite restaurant, so he thought he'd take her into the city and have dinner there. What Frankie failed to mention, however, was how it was "their place".

"Are you planning on asking her out on a date?" Marie asked Warner.

"Yes, I'd like to take her out tonight. I was thinking Tavern on the Green."

"My my, that's just her favorite! However, *Warner*, you can't take her there."

"Excuse me?" He was confused.

"Well, you see, it's sort of her and someone else's thing," she said, referring to her and Frankie.

"Her and someone else's thing?" Warner said, not wanting to hear that about the girl he had spent all night thinking about.

"Yes, it is. So, don't ask her there. Ask her to … Delmonico's! It's downtown," she said, reassuring Warner that he should still continue with his plan of asking her out.

"Yes, I've been. I love Delmonico's!" he said, still wondering who the other person was, who made Tavern on the Green off-limits.

"Then it's settled, you'll take my darling best friend to Delmonico's!" she said before they ended their conversation.

Later on he rang Roxy, and her eyes lit up and her heart raced as she heard his voice over the telephone. She said yes to dinner without a doubt in her mind, and without a hesitation of any kind. After the phone call ended, she rang Marie and then Virginia, telling them everything before they both came over (Virginia was with her parents and Marie had decided to spend a few nights back at her family's summer home, which is why they weren't already at Roxy's).

The girls went shopping with Roxy, trying to find the most perfect outfit for her to wear on her date with Mr. Davenport—although it's not like she didn't already have closets full of unworn dresses and shoes. Being Roxy, however, she felt the need to shop for something *new*.

After Roxy had spent nearly the entire day searching for something similar to a dress she already owned, Marie and Virginia made their way back to the Elliott mansion with her, and helped her get ready. The boys came over as well, smoking cigars and drinking out by the pool, before Roxy came down one of the marble staircases, ready for Warner to arrive and take her into the city for dinner.

"Hello boys, how do I look?" she said as Johnny, Dalton, and Frankie gazed at her in awe. Eyes wide, infatuated by her beauty. "Do I look alright?"

"Oh, yes," Johnny said, looking her up and down.

"Yeah, I agree with him," Dalton added.

"Wow," Frankie said, at a loss for words.

Marie and Virginia made their way down the stairs.

"Stunning best friend!" Marie yelled.

"The cat's meow! He won't be able to get his eyes off of you!" Virginia added.

"Or his hands ..." Marie laughed.

Frankie didn't like the sound of that.

"Why thank you." Roxy smiled and did a twirl. "Warner is in for a surprise," she giggled.

"He sure is! You better ring me and tell me all about it the second you get home. In fact, Virginia and I'll stay here and you can tell us in person," Marie said, giving Roxy a hug as she started at the door. Frankie had remembered where exactly she was going: her date with Warner. His smile disappeared and his happiness faded away.

Johnny looked over at him. "You okay?"

"I'm fine, why wouldn't I be?" he said, bothered.

"I think you know the answer to that."

"You don't know what you're talking 'bout, Davis." He got up and walked away.

Dalton went over to Johnny. "He won't ever admit it, he wouldn't want to lose her."

"He wouldn't lose her, I know she feels the same way."

"Well he doesn't believe that."

"I know, and I don't know why," Johnny told him and he walked over to Roxy, catching her on her way out. He whispered into her ear, "Have a good time doll, but not too good."

"And what is that supposed to mean?" She smiled and laughed.

"Frankie isn't as excited about your date with Warner as you are."

"And?" she said, suddenly with a slightly different tone.

"Don't act like you're not in love with him. Go and have fun, but just not too much." He walked away, leaving Roxy with confusion painted across her face.

Warner knocked on the door and Roxy had one of the maids wait thirty seconds before answering it; she didn't want to seem like she had been standing at the door for five minutes, waiting for this moment.

"Hello Mr. Davenport, ready for our date?" she said as the door opened to the well-dressed Warner.

"My, you look stunning."

"Why thank you," she said as he took her hand and gave it a kiss.

"Have fun!" they all yelled as their friend walked out the door—all but one of them.

On the way into the city, Roxy pondered about what Johnny said. He always gave little hints about Frankie, but had never flat-out said the word *love*.

"I'm taking you somewhere you'll love, Roxy," Warner said to her. She was looking down and clutching her purse tightly. "Roxy?"

She looked up; she had been distracted by her thoughts. "Oh yes! I am so excited, darling," she smiled.

As they began to approach the city, she forgot all about her and Johnny's little "talk". Warner took her for a nice dinner, then a romantic walk after, and she began to fall for him. Though she *was* cluelessly in love with Frankie, she would come to develop deep feelings for this Davenport boy.

A love, if you will.

Just, not a *true love*.

CHAPTER 22

Oh What a Night

Oh, what a night.

July 17th, 1925

Dear Diary,

Warner Davenport, what a boy. Oh he was such a gentleman, took me to Delmonico's for an exquisite dinner, and after we went for a rather long and romantic walk where we held hands and continued intelligent conversations on various topics. He also drives quite the automobile, I'm not even sure what it was, but it was absolutely gorgeously stunning. Navy blue with white leather, and completely open. The air driving back from the city felt so great, flying through my hair as we drove through Long Island in not only style but speed.

When we arrived home, he walked me to the door and that's when he kissed me. Waited until the very end of the night. And boy, was it a kiss! He kisses softly, but at the same time it was rather electric!

After he kissed me, he asked me out on another date, to which I answered with a kiss.

After he left, I told Marie and Virginia all about it— they are downstairs searching for the right champagne at the moment. We're having a girls' night.

I have to say, I'm real taken with this boy. Especially after Dean and I ended things, I wasn't sure if I would find someone so soon, someone I truly felt that way about. But with Warner, oh it's just, it's special. I know I hardly know him, it's been all of one date, but I feel like we've got this real connection. You know? It sounds goofy, but I feel like I could end up loving this boy. I think he might even be worthy of losing my virginity to.

I promised myself that I wouldn't have sex until I was in love. I mean sure, I'm supposed to wait until marriage, but that's really not the flapper way. And if I want to embrace my true flapper self, I sure won't be abiding by tradition. Anyways, I'm not saying I'm in love with this Davenport boy, all I'm saying is that he could end up being my first time. That this summer could end up being a rather special one. He's got this *fantastic personality, he's funny and entertaining and smart, but he's not some wise guy, he's soft and unassuming. I like that about him. He's different than anyone I've met before. He doesn't know he's all that, he's unaware of how great he is, unlike SOME boys I know (Frankie). I learned all about him tonight too, his family, what his aspirations are.*

Oh, and did I mention? I'm going to lunch with him tomorrow! Anyways—I think I just heard the opening of a bottle.

When Roxy says she's smitten with a boy, she's sure not kidding. This Davenport boy has her mind running wild (and Frankie's too). While she was out in the city having a night she would always remember, Frankie, Johnny, and Dalton made their way back to Frankie's mansion, in which he spent the entire night indirectly talking about how upset he was that Warner had asked her out. Even though, if I must say, he didn't *exactly* make it clear to Warner that he didn't want him going out with her, and that's because he still won't say it out loud.

Frankie, despite the encouragement, seems to find himself stuck when it comes to his mafia princess.

He knows he's mad about her, head over heels, but at the same time he doesn't. He'll sit around and drink and pout all night about the thought of her with someone else. This was always so baffling to me, because this wasn't how Frankie was. He was confident, sexy, he knew what he wanted and how to get it, and he always went for what he wanted. He was never afraid, especially with girls, and for good reason. Frankie could have any one of them he wanted. Though, with Roxy, it was different. He cared for her so deeply, he respected her, and for some reason this meant he couldn't use his usual tactics.

Also, subconsciously, he knew that there was always some jeopardy when it came to the thought of them as an item. If, for some reason, she didn't feel the same way, things would never be the same between them, and he couldn't bear the thought of losing her, of losing what they had. They had been the best of friends since kindergarten. She was his favorite person. Though, I feel that I've told you all this before, haven't I … well, that night he decided that he needed a new girl, and so he found one.

However, it's not one *any* of us are fond of.

Remember Dean Andrews? Roxy's now ex-boyfriend who cheated on her with the infamous Claire Reed, who used to date Johnny?

Well, within a week of the Roxy–Dean breakup, he ended up moving all the way to Texas due to his father's work.

Yes … Texas. *Scary, I know.*

Anyhow, Dean and Claire, who had rekindled their love, knew the long distance would never work and ultimately broke up. *The irony.* Well, though this wasn't all that long ago, and Claire recovered rather quickly from him, which brings us here: it's now the end of July, Warner and Roxy have been dating for a couple of weeks, Marie and Virginia are still happy with their boyfriends, Dalton and Hazel have become rather serious, and as for Johnny, he found himself with a few different girls.

(I don't keep track unless he's stayed with one for longer than two weeks.)

Frankie, meanwhile, has also been with a few girls in these past couple of weeks, but mostly just dates and steamy make-outs—nothing serious and no one of girlfriend material. Although, the girl he decides *is* girlfriend material isn't exactly what I'd call worthy either ... and yes, that is one Miss Claire Reed.

The bitch Roxy can't stand—isn't that ever so convenient?

It is rather scary that she was completely over Dean Andrews so quickly, after calling him her "one true love" and sleeping with him while he was still with Roxy. Claire was always green with envy when it came to Roxy, *always* jealous of her. Her beauty, her wealth, her family and their power, despite the fact that Claire herself was a beauty and came from a long line of wealth. Still, no one could beat out our lovely Miss Elliott. Have I told you that before? Oh well. So long story short, this brings us to today, where this not-so-lovely Claire happened to cross paths with our very lovely Frankie Matthews.

"Oh! So sorry," she said after bumping into him.

"It's alright," he responded with a half-smile before attempting to walk away.

"Wait! I—uh, how are you Frankie?" she said, wanting to make conversation.

He turned around slowly. "I'm alright Claire, and how are you?"

"Doing alright. I've been a little bored this summer though, since Dean left for Texas."

"Ahh that's right, how ironic," he smirked.

"But I'm alright, I've gotten over it completely. In fact, I'm ready to find myself a new boy."

"Are you now?" Frankie knew this was a bad idea, but considering how fed up he was with Roxy and her newfound love for his old friend Warner, he didn't care all that much. "Well, how 'bout that," he smiled.

"So, Frankie, are you dating anyone as of now?"

"Not really, no," Frankie said, ready to do something he knew not only Roxy but the entire gang would hate him for, "how 'bout you come out to dinner with me tonight, say, eight?"

"I'd love to," Claire responded with a smile. Mission accomplished.

You see, there were a few variables here that added up to a major problem. One being that Roxy despised Claire Reed—she hated her from the beginning, then gave her a chance because she was dating her dear friend Johnny, but after she found out that she had been sleeping with her boyfriend, knowing that he was taken, Roxy knew she was right all along. The other issue with Frankie taking Claire out on a date was the fact that his best friend, our Johnny Davis, had dated her.

This made things rather complicated for the two of them.

Frankie wasn't in the best place, however, and he had never been directly hurt by her, and therefore he didn't give a damn. So he took her out that night and found that he grew fond of her over the four hours they spent together. He saw in her what Johnny and Dean had, a different side of her. Not the side Roxy ever saw. They ended the night with a long and romantic kiss, before he dropped her back at her summer home and pondered how he would tell his friends he was going out with Claire Reed.

August 1st, 1925

Dear Diary,

I think I'm falling in love.

Warner is just absolutely amazing, I don't think there's anything about him I don't like! He's dreamy as the day is long, he's respectful, and I really do think I may be falling in love with him.

Sure, it's only been two weeks but this boy is the absolute bee's knees. I think I may be ready, as in, ready to lose my virginity.

I thought I maybe would with Dean, but it never felt right. With Warner it's completely different, I feel like we've got this connection that's just undeniable. And I feel so safe with him.

On another note, I found out some rather disturbing news. Frankie, my dear old Frankie, has decided that it was a grand idea to date the bitch Claire Reed, as in Johnny's ex and Dean's once so-called "one true love". Well, Dean moved to Texas, which is scary, and now she's "completely over him". Within what, like, a few weeks? Honestly, I thought that Frankie was spifflicated when telling us he had already taken her on one date and planned to take her on another, but he wasn't. He says that she's different with him, and that for some rather insane reason he likes her.

CLAIRE REED. My goodness!

He is absolutely out of his damn mind. Johnny isn't too happy about it either, but he's a lot calmer than I would imagine he'd be about it. The rest of the gang doesn't really like the idea of them as an item either, but I guess it's "his life". Although, if he thinks that I'll let that lollygagger in any of the Elliott speakeasies, he's terribly mistaken. And if she causes us any problems at all, or hurts Frankie, I'll have my father deal with the bitch Elliott style.

It's pretty clear that Roxy was the most upset by Frankie's brilliant idea to begin dating Claire Reed, but in time she would get used to the idea. She didn't really have a choice in the matter, so there was no reason to dwell on it.

As for her and Warner, she was serious about doing the deed with him, and this Frankie and Claire relationship made her all the more serious.

"I'm serious, I think I am really beginning to love him."

"Roxy … it's been what, two weeks?" Virginia asked with concern.

"Almost three," Roxy said with a stern voice.

"I just, I thought you wanted to wait. Until you were sure, until you were ready," Marie said.

"That's just it, I am ready!"

"Ready for what?" Frankie asked as he and Dalton entered her bedroom.

"Nothing," said Marie.

"No no, you gotta tell us," Dalton said.

"It's nothing!" Virginia assured.

Frankie walked over to Roxy and laid down on her bed, with his hands behind his head, making himself comfortable. "You gotta …" He batted his eyes at Roxy, giving her a mischievous grin.

"I just, I think I'm ready. Tonight—"

"Ready for what?"

"Well, Warner and I are going into the city tonight, and— we're going to get a room at the Plaza and—"

"Whoah whoah whoah," he jumped up suddenly, "you're getting a room at the Plaza?"

"That's what she wants," Marie answered unhappily.

"What would you do that for? Why would you—"

"Frankie, let it go—" Dalton chimed in.

"No! What the hell Roxy, what you're gonna—" He started to get worried.

He knew where this was going, and he didn't like it. The thought of her having sex, for the first time, *with Warner*, made him sick. Even though he rebuked the thought when it crossed his mind, a part of him always imagined they'd lose their virginities to each other. And yes, Frankie was still a virgin, for this very reason. That small sliver of a part of him was saving himself for his darling Roxy Elliott. How romantic.

"Frankie, enough—"

"No, not enough. What you're gonna—you're gonna sleep with him?" he said, with a crack of sadness and a loss of hope in his voice.

The room went silent.

"Yeah, Frankie, I think I am," she said fiercely.

He looked at her straight in the eyes; she could feel his distraught and shock, and the disappointment he was radiating.

"Fine then," he said before grabbing his hat off her bed, heading toward the door, "but you're making a mistake."

"I don't think I am." Her voice was stern.

Marie and Virginia looked at each other, and Dalton glanced over at Roxy before making his way toward Frankie.

"I think we should go," Dalton said.

"You've barely been dating him what, two weeks? You always said how sex was special, how it meant a lot to you, and you give it away to some boy you barely know? You're too good for him Roxy, you know he doesn't deserve you, how could you be so reckless all of a sudden."

"RECKLESS?"

"Yeah!"

"Are you kidding, Frankie? It's not like you didn't lose it to some dumb broad back in freshman year—"

"I haven't lost it yet either Roxy, and you know that."

A silence fell over the room once again. That was quite a shocking statement. It's not like Frankie didn't have the chance about a million times to do it. He had gone pretty far with a girl, starting back in the ninth grade, but he had never gone all the way.

"I'm waiting for the right one, just like I thought you were," he said before storming off.

"Bastard," she whispered to herself.

Roxy fell onto her bed, thinking about what had just gone down and how angry Frankie was over such a trivial subject. Only, it wasn't really so trivial after all.

The day went by and Warner picked Roxy up and took her into the city, once again for a beautiful, romantic dinner. This time they went to Keens Steakhouse, then for a horse and carriage ride that led them to the steps of the elegant and world-renowned Plaza Hotel.

They held hands tightly as they walked up the wide steps and entered the opulent lobby, the smell of fresh flowers permeating the entire hotel, and the crystal chandeliers hanging high above their heads, arousing decadent emotions among anyone who stood happily on the shiny marble floors.

He walked up to the desk, gave his name "Davenport", and the well-dressed lady on the other side handed him a key to the suite. He turned around and Roxy gave him a half-smile as a bellboy carried their leather bags, following them into the elevator. As they made their way up, the sexual tension only grew. Roxy knew she felt deeply for Warner, but also knew she was taking a big step that night. Frankie's words "You're too good for him Roxy" were ringing loud in her mind as they approached the top floor of the Plaza.

"Miss," the bellboy said, extending his arm out, signaling for Roxy to exit the elevator first—because "ladies first", of course.

She smiled and exited, as did Warner, and then the bellboy followed suit with their bags. One bag for each of them, as it was only a one-night stay after all.

The bellboy opened up the double doors to the grand and rather spacious suite, and Roxy's eyes immediately spotted the chilled bottle of Dom sitting proudly on the table by the window, with two tall glasses right beside. Then her eyes went in a different direction, to the long-stem bouquet of red roses, which she loved—however, her *favorite* were white roses. Though, she still smiled at the sight of them, because red roses *are* quite stunning, even if they aren't your favorite.

The bellboy dropped their bags down gently and exited the room as Warner walked over to the radio and turned it on. Smooth 1920s jazz began playing idly in the background.

He removed his jacket and placed it over a chair.

"Shall we?" he said with a smile as he picked up the bottle of champagne.

"We shall," she answered, thinking about how great of a bottle he had chosen.

Dom Pérignon is, in fact, quite wonderful.

Meanwhile, the boys back in Southampton were consoling the rather agitated Frankie. He was in a state of shock. He never in a million years thought Roxy would throw away her very first time having sex like this.

"I mean, she's making a huge mistake, isn't she?"

"I don't know Frankie, he seems like an okay fella."

"Sure, sure he is. But she doesn't belong with an 'okay fella', Johnny," he answered back with a bit of attitude.

"Gee Matthews, I didn't say that," he responded before lighting a cigarette.

They were at Johnny's place, sitting out in the backyard watching the waves crash.

"Frankie, I think he may be good for her. They seem to have a good relationship. Especially after the whole Dean thing, I think he's good for her. And who are you to talk, dating Claire Reed and all—" Dalton exclaimed.

"First, we aren't talking about me and second, oh come on, Warner Davenport? He's a—he's a—"

"Frankie, I think I sense some jealousy here," Johnny laughed and looked over at Dalton.

"Are you kiddin' me? Jealous?" Frankie laughed nervously.

"Yeah Matthews, jealous. Jealous because you're the one who wants to get into bed with her."

"Oh shut it Johnny, it ain't like that."

"I guess so, I mean—every guy wants to get into bed with her—"

"Dammit Johnny!" Frankie said angrily. "I mean it, that's damn disrespectful."

"And talking bad about her boyfriend, who happens to be your friend, isn't?" Dalton said.

Frankie took a pause as he poured himself a glass of bourbon. "He's not good enough for her and both of you know it," he said before placing his glass down, picking up the bottle and storming out of the house with it in his right hand.

"I don't know what's gonna get him to fess up to the truth."

"That poor bastard has been in love with her since the day

he met her. Yet, instead of telling her, he does this. Has a damn hissy fit. I've never seen him so—"

"Lousy?" Johnny responded.

"Exactly. He's the most good-looking, most confident guy in our school, yet when it comes to letting himself feel it with her, admit that he loves her, I just—don't get it. What's he so afraid of?"

"Her not feeling the same."

"Bullshit, we know she does! We all know it. She's the same as him, in love but refuses to admit it. What damn fools."

"He doesn't know it though. Or at least, doesn't believe it."

"Should we go after him?"

"No, we gotta let him get it out of his system. What did he think, that she wasn't gonna eventually sleep with Warner?"

"But if he gets caught walking down Main Street with a bottle of bourbon he'll get arrested."

"I don't know, I highly doubt it's gonna be much of an issue for him, being a Matthews and all. Nothing ever is. The perks of being wealthy, I guess. God, we sure have it good."

They both laughed and looked out onto the water.

"You got that right."

Roxy and Warner were on their last glass of champagne, talking and laughing and having a good time. Warner put down his glass and took her hand,

"Wanna dance?"

"Always," she smiled.

They stood up and held each other close as "Everybody Loves My Baby" by Aileen Stanley began playing on the radio.

They danced for the entire song, before he pulled her close and their lips touched. Butterflies in her stomach as his hands moved through her hair.

All the while, Frankie was walking the streets with a once-full bottle of bourbon in his right hand, now almost empty thanks to his foolery. He could barely walk straight, *clearly*, as sirens began roaring behind him, louder and louder as they approached the rather drunk Matthews boy.

Roxy and Warner continued kissing, more and more passionately, more and more aggressively. Their lips brushing up against each other as the temperature of the room rose. She began unbuttoning his shirt before taking it off of him completely. Next to go was his belt. She turned around and he began unzipping her dress.

Frankie turned around, his eyes blinded by the red-and-blue lights; he put his left hand up to block out the lights, trying to make out what was happening. Two officers got out of the car.

"What are you holding there, boy?" the first one yelled.

Frankie stood there for a second, attempting to sober himself up so he could think of a plan to escape what was happening (although that's just not how it works). So instead, him being Frankie and all, he dropped the bottle onto the ground, the glass shattered into a million broken pieces, and then he ran. He ran from the cops as they ran after him.

"STOP! STOP RIGHT THERE, YOU LITTLE BASTARD!" they yelled before the second officer caught up to him.

I guess Frankie wasn't as fast when intoxicated. Figures.

The officer tackled him to the ground and cuffed him, then brought him over to the automobile before throwing him in the back. Frankie laughed. Somehow all of this was amusing to him. Being caught with liquor, running from the cops, all while thinking about whether Roxy had done it yet or not. They took him to the station and gave him a telephone call. He rang Marie. Then she rang Johnny, and he made his way over to her place.

Roxy's dress fell to the ground and she kicked her shoes off, turned back around to Warner and continued kissing him, all right before being interrupted by a hard knock on the door.

"Miss Elliott, Miss Elliott!" the man on the other side of the door said.

Roxy turned her head back and looked at the door. "Did you hear that?"

She was almost happy that they were interrupted.

The entire time she had been thinking about someone else—her mind wasn't on Warner, it wasn't on the fact that she was about to make love to him, it was rambling on with the words Frankie had said earlier that day. About how she valued sex so much, about how he did too. About how he still, *shockingly*, hadn't lost his virginity yet. That he was waiting for the right person. It made her question if Warner was *truly* the right person, and she had come to a conclusion moments before she heard the voice on the other side of the door, thankfully at the right time.

Five minutes later and who knows, she may have gone through with it.

Just kidding, she wasn't going to go through with it. But the man's voice on the other side of the door sure as hell made it easier for her, rather than her telling Warner at the last moment that she "wasn't ready". I'm sure he would have loved that, being half naked and all.

"I don't know, maybe?" Warner answered.

"Miss Elliott!" the man said again, only louder this time.

Roxy put her dress back on and headed for the door, opening it up to the hotel manager.

"Hello Miss Elliott, sorry to disturb you, but you have a telephone call down in the lobby."

Roxy was confused but intrigued. Warner was standing in the background in his underwear, *also very confused.*

"Hello Mr. Davenport, hope you are well," the man said.

"I'm sorry Warner, I have to take it," Roxy said before exiting the suite and heading back down to the lobby.

"Hello?"

"Roxy! Roxy baby——"

"Johnny? What's going on?"

"You gotta come home."

"Excuse me?" she said.

"It's Frankie."

Her heart dropped. Johnny's tone made it seem as if something was terribly wrong. And that made her stomach curl.

"Frankie? What's the matter with Frankie, is he okay?" she said with worry in her voice.

"He's been arrested," Marie said, taking the phone.

Roxy sighed, then giggled. "Hi darling, he's been what?"

"Arrested."

"What for?"

Johnny took the phone back. "Well it started with a bottle of bourbon, then it turned into him running from the cops."

"My God," Roxy said, grinning, "well damn Johnny, this is absolutely hilarious."

"He's requesting you."

Of course he was.

"What?"

"He's extremely intoxicated, and he's requesting you come get him. Being an Elliott and all, all you'd have to do is walk in and they'll let him go."

"He's a Matthews, he doesn't need me."

"They're being a bit of a hard-ass and won't let him out till morning. And he doesn't want his dad knowing, but if you go in—"

"Alright, alright, I'm coming," she said before hanging up the phone.

She headed toward the elevators as one opened up and Warner walked out.

"So, is everything okay?" he asked.

She told him everything and that she had to go back to The Hamptons. He offered to drive her back but she told him to stay, to enjoy the room. That she'd get a car to take her there, and so she did. She arrived at the Southampton police station a few hours later.

Frankie was sobering up but still not quite all there.

"Hello darling, I have a friend here, Frankie Matthews?"

"Hello Miss Elliott, yes of course, I'll go get him," the officer at the front told Roxy before releasing Frankie.

"What'sa matter with you, Matthews!" she said as Frankie made his way toward her. Then she slapped him.

"Roxy!" he said, "my GOD that was hard!" He held his cheek.

"You idiot—you dumbass. What the hell were you thinking?" she said before taking his arm with force and putting him into the car. The car ride home was interesting; he laid his head in her lap as she continued to berate him for his foolish actions. She brought him back to her place, where the rest of the gang was awaiting their arrival.

"Nice going Matthews," Virginia said as they entered the mansion.

"Alright alright, I get it, I screwed up."

"Go get yourself a glass of water. You can stay here tonight," Roxy said. Her father and Daisy were away in Chicago for the weekend.

So, the night went on, Roxy managed to get Frankie completely sober, and the rest of the gang eventually left.

Frankie stayed over but slept on the floor of her bedroom. She told him to go stay in one of the guest bedrooms, considering there were many to choose from. *So many.* But he of course made his argument: that the mansion was so big and Dennis and Daisy were gone, and that though the maids were in the house, they were in their own rooms on the first floor. Roxy's room was on the third. He said that it was "safer" for the two of them to be in the same bedroom. Despite the fact that crime wasn't exactly all that prevalent in The Hamptons, and no one would dare to break into the lush Elliott mansion. Nonetheless, he made his case—all only because he wanted to be with her all night, of course.

"Fine! Fine—will it shut you up?" she said, annoyed.

"Yes, yes it will," he smiled.

She rolled her eyes. "But you're sleeping on the floor," Roxy said as she threw a pillow aggressively to his chest.

She laid down on her bed and got cozy as he made himself comfortable next to her on the floor.

"So," Frankie said as Roxy turned off the lamps on her bedside tables.

"So? So what?" she responded, confused.

"So you wanna talk?"

"Frankie, it's four in the morning."

"Oh what, you know you're a night owl—"

"Frankie, go to bed before I kick you out," she giggled as she threw him another pillow.

He stayed quiet for a solid two and a half minutes before he couldn't resist anymore, rolling his eyes back and saying, "How was it?"

She took a pause before responding, "It wasn't."

"It wasn't what?"

"It wasn't, Frankie. It didn't happen."

He grinned and his eyes lit up, "Ahh I see, was he nervous? Couldn't quite get there could he?" he laughed.

"My God, stop!" She giggled again. "No ... *you* happened."

"Me?"

"Yes Frankie, Johnny called. I got a knock on the door of our suite before it happened."

He took a pause. "Oh. I see, so it was going to happen. I ruined it for you," he said. "Sorry."

He wasn't sorry.

He was thrilled.

"No."

"No?"

"No Frankie, I wasn't going to end up going through with it," she said quietly, "it's not the right time."

"Oh!" Frankie said with a perk in his voice.

A steady silence fell over the room.

"Was that the only reason?" Fankie asked.

She took a moment as she stared up at the canopy above her, the one that lay royal-like over her bed. "He wasn't the right one."

"I see."

Another silence fell steadily over the grand room.

"Good night, Frankie."

"Good night, darling."

They both smiled in the dark as their eyelids fell gently over their beautiful eyes.

He slept soud that night, knowing that his beloved Roxy hadn't given her virginity to the Davenport boy. *Who aparently wasn't the right one.* Knowing that someday it could be him that she'd lose it to.

CHAPTER 23

Breakups, Overdoses, and Vogue Paris

The next morning, Frankie took it upon himself to make Roxy pancakes, telling the kitchen maids to "take the morning off" as if he had the authority. They didn't listen to him, but still allowed him to make a mess in the kitchen. After they had breakfast, Frankie left to go golfing with his parents, and Dalton and Virginia came over to Roxy's.

"Oh come on. Frankie and I could never be a couple, he's a bad boy. He's reckless, he's been arrested—"

"Yes, for drinking in the streets," Dalton cut her off.

"Exactly!"

"On the night you decided to make it known that you and Warner were ready to take things to the next level," Virginia chimed in.

"Coincidence? Sorry doll, but it's true," Dalton said.

"Oh, you two. He may have been concerned that I was ready so soon but that didn't cause him to finish off a bottle of bourbon by himself. He wasn't *that* upset about me losing my virginity to Warner."

"Is she serious?" Dalton asked Virginia.

"Roxy come on, we all know that's why he hasn't had sex yet. If you didn't exist he would have lost his virginity years ago, deep down he's waiting for you—"

Roxy laughed nervously. "Oh goodness that's ridiculous! Frankie doesn't want to have sex with me."

"My God, you two. Both of ya, so stubborn and in your heads. Won't ever admit it. How long are you both going to be so utterly clueless?" Dalton said bluntly.

He was tired of having the same conversation with Frankie, Roxy, and the rest of the gang. Tired of constantly talking about why Frankie was the way he was, the reason behind him refusing to fess up on his true feelings.

"And if you think you want to lose it to anyone else but him, you're really out of your mind," Virginia said.

"Oh what, you think I wanna sleep with Frankie?" Roxy answered with an eye roll. "I'm going to pour myself a drink," she said as she walked over to the cocktail cart, grabbing the most expensive scotch and pouring a large sum of it into a crystal glass.

"Whatever Roxy, believe what you want to. Someday it will be too late and you will have lost him."

Remember those words.

Dalton and Roxy decided to head to town for lunch, and

Virginia left to go surprise her boyfriend. She knew he'd be at the club and decided to show up unannounced. They had been doing well this summer. Dylan was a good guy from a good family, as was Marie's boyfriend Arthur.

"Hey baby!" she said as she walked up to him playing golf.

"Virginia!" he said nervously. "What a surprise!"

"Well, I thought I could surprise you, maybe steal you away for lunch?" she smiled.

"Baby, I'm kind of in the middle of something here."

Dylan and Virginia *had* been doing alright, but lately things were taking a turn for the worse. Virginia and Dalton's girl Hazel Flynn had begun a new little hobby, one that no one knew about but Dylan, and when he found out … it changed things between them. For the past two weeks, they had been seeing each other less than usual, and he had become more distant. There was a clear rift in the relationship and Virginia was desperately trying hard to fix it.

"Dylan, we've hardly been seeing each other lately. I think you can find time for me, can't you?"

"Virginia, you know I really like you, and want the best for you, but—"

"But what?" she responded with a stern voice.

"Can we go inside and talk for a bit?"

Virginia wasn't happy about this; she knew where it was going.

"Sure."

He took her inside to a private area. "I just—I'm not sure this is working out."

"Excuse me?" Virginia had already fallen for Dylan—even if she had never said the words "I love you" to his face, she scribbled it in her diary every night. Yes, Virginia was *that* kind of girl.

"I know."

"You know?"

"I know. About you and Hazel, and I thought I could be with someone like that, but I just can't, okay? I'm sorry, Virginia. You're a beautiful girl and all, and really sweet and funny, but I think we should end things."

Virginia's heart sank; she hadn't been aware that anyone knew about her and Hazel's new hobby.

She turned around and left the club before the tears began to rush down her red face. Virginia had her driver take her straight to Hazel's where she told her about what Dylan had said, about how he knew, but clearly hadn't told anyone. *Which was actually quite terrible of him.* In return, Hazel helped her get over him through the one and only thing she knew would help: medication. Yes, Hazel and Virginia's new hobby was in fact the ever so daring opioid.

"I don't—I don't think this is even going to help me this time, Hazel," Virginia cried.

"I promise it will. And I've—uhh, got something else too, some new stuff. You can try both! I swear Virginia, you're gonna feel so much better," Hazel assured her.

While Virginia was over at Hazel's doing drugs in the middle of the day, Roxy had finished lunch with Dalton, and he had to meet his father for some type of "business" (who knows), so Johnny met Roxy for ice cream in town. How very *summer* of them.

"Let me have some of yours," Johnny said as he reached over her in an attempt to take hold of her cone.

"You have your own!" she responded, not letting him get the chance.

"Yeah but it's a different flavor!" he chuckled. "Please?"

Roxy smiled. "Oh fine, one bite!" she said as they both laughed.

"So I was thinking of throwing a party tomorrow night, my mom and dad are going to visit their friends in Martha's Vineyard—" Johnny began saying as Roxy's eyes widened, and she stood still. "What? What are you looking at?" he responded.

"Oh my God," she said, stunned at the sight before her eyes.

It was none other than our Davenport boy, on the corner with someone else. *Kissing* that someone else. What is it with these boys? Don't they know better than to cheat out in public? Johnny saw. "Oh my God."

A simple tear ran down Roxy's cheek. She had thought he was different from Dean, yet he had now proven otherwise.

"I'll go teach him a lesson—"

"No—I'll take care of it myself," Roxy said in a stern voice before turning around and walking the other way.

"Whoah whoah whoah, you're gonna let him stand there and french the girl on the street?" Johnny said, taken back by Roxy's response.

They couldn't get a good look at who he was kissing, but I think you'll be shocked by who exactly it was.

"I'll deal with him later. Privately."

And that she did.

What a day for breakups. First Virginia and then Roxy? Two happy couples accompanied by a stark ending rather soon. Virginia was still with her new pal Hazel, and she was surely feeling better about the Dylan situation, though not feeling so great about herself. The pills were stronger this time, Hazel was right on that, but this didn't mean they were right for her to take.

When is medicating your sorrows away *ever* right?

Though, I think it's safe to say that while the rest of our special six may not do drugs (besides the occasional hash the boys enjoyed), they all took upon moonshine to tie up their troubles. Yet again, Virginia's situation was very different. Champagne and gin only do so much harm; a foreign drug being taken by a seventeen-year-old girl for purposes only to make her feel better is a *whole* different story.

Both Virginia and Hazel had been addicted to opium for quite some time now, and, though this was not a good thing, they *had* been alright. Today was a different story, all thanks to Hazel's "new stuff" she thought Virginia would take delight in trying. And what exactly was that new stuff Hazel thought it was a good idea to mix with opium? None other than the wonderful white powder we like to call cocaine. Or should I say *not so wonderful*, because in fact it's quite the opposite. Our pure, virgin, somewhat good-girl Virginia was high on opium and suddenly snorting cocaine.

How did this even happen? If you'd guessed anyone out of

the group would have ended up on drugs, it sure as hell wouldn't have been her. Actually, it wasn't very likely that any of them would! They may have enjoyed their drunken nights at roaring parties but becoming an addict to a drug was beyond them. They knew better. They chose life. They were smart enough to know not to ever dare try it. (Again, despite the occasional hash in the case of the boys, but that's quite different from opium and cocaine.)

Anyways, Virginia was quite out of it and managed to get Hazel's driver to take her to Frankie's. She was still very, *very* much drugged when she arrived at his grand Hamptons home. Hazel didn't want her to leave but Virginia suddenly became paranoid and wanted to be with someone who wasn't in the same drugged-out state she was in; so she arrived at Frankie's. While all this was happening, Roxy made a telephone call to the Davenports' new estate, telling one of the maids that she requested Warner in the parlor of her home immediately; and so he came.

"Are you mad?" Warner said as he put his hand on Roxy's shoulder. She was sitting in a beautiful velvet chair, looking out to the ocean.

She looked at him, smiled, and took his hand off her shoulder. As she stood up and walked away, she said to him in a rather passive tone, "Oh darling, I'm not mad!"

"You look angry," he said as he made his way closer to her.

"I am not, *angry*," she said with a smile (an angry smile).

"You aren't?" He was confused. He had suspected Roxy had spotted him kissing that *other person* on that empty corner off of Main Street. "Well—well that's just wonderful!"

"I'm not angry, I just—well I now know that we can't be together!" She gave him a wide grin.

"I don't understand, you said you weren't angry—"

"I'm not angry. I'm only done," Roxy said as she looked down at her cup of tea, swirling the spoon to mix in the sugar cube, "done with you, Warner Davenport. Did you really think that you could cheat on Roxy Elliott and still have her? Oh honey, I don't work like that." She laughed and picked up her cup of tea, still hot from the kettle, took a sip, and poured the steaming cup of Earl Grey directly over Mr. Davenport's head. *She was clearly angry.*

"ROXY!" he screamed as the tea poured over him. There was nothing much to say. Roxy, being the Elliott she was, continued with a smile on her face, knowing she had won this battle he began. Warner *did* in fact deserve what he got.

She looked him right in the eye, for the first time during their short and passive conversation. "Goodbye, Mr. Davenport. I hope you enjoyed your tea. Earl Grey happens to be my favorite, I don't think I ever told you that." She showed yet another smirk and said, "I mean really, you must be the biggest idiot on Long Island. To kiss someone out in the open like that? As if I wouldn't learn about it, let alone see it happen?" She laughed. "Absolutely the dumbest thing I've ever seen! To cross an Elliott like that, one who loved you. One who gave you her heart? You told me you loved me, Warner. How could this be? How could you be so careless! All you had to do was tell me you didn't love me anymore, that you didn't want to be with me, and you could have had her. Whoever she was. I couldn't even see the bitch, but now I'm rather curious, who was it? Who was it that you deemed better than me, *Roxy Elliott*—"

He cut her off. "It's not like that, Roxy—"

"Then what is it like? Because I could have you roughed up so bad you'd wish you had never met me. You know who I am, who my family is, and you choose to cheat on me? I'll get my cousin Tommy over here in a second, hell—I'll even have my father or Uncle Clyde show you a good time."

"Roxy please, let me explain myself—"

"Fine! Explain! I'd LOVE to hear this."

He sat down. "You really don't understand. I did love you, I do love you, it's just—"

Roxy rolled her eyes. "It's just what? You also wanted someone else while loving me? Sure, Davenport—"

"It's that I just don't love you like that."

And a silence fell over the room.

"What do you mean, Warner?"

"You know what I mean—"

"No, quite frankly I don't."

"It's true, I was kissing someone else, there off of the corner of Main Street, but it wasn't another broad."

Roxy's eyes widened; suddenly she wasn't so mad anymore, just confused and in shock. "You were what?"

"I know it was a mistake, a big one, especially out in public—"

"My God Warner, you're a homosexual?"

"Roxy, I—"

"You really are even dumber than I imagined. A guy kissing another guy out in public? WARNER!"

"There was no one there! It was an empty street and it only lasted a few seconds, and we were on our way. We rarely get to see each other, so we looked around and didn't think anyone would see."

"Warner, I am thinking so many things right now but one of them is how much of an idiot you were to do something like that. You could have been arrested."

So there it was—Warner batted for the other team, though he sure gave one hell of an acting job playing straight. In fact, he was quite the ladies' man, yet it was all a show. The thing was, in the 1920s, him being gay wasn't really an option. Especially coming from a family like the Davenports; so dating a girl of a high social status ensured that no one would ever blink an eye about his true identity or sexuality. Dating Roxy Elliott, a girl of the *highest* social status, fit the plan well. He wasn't allowed to be his true self, and though Roxy was angry, a part of her understood and felt bad for the way he was forced into hiding his real identity. She was angry at him for not telling her, and angry that he had clearly been using her to hide his true self, but she was *most* angry that he took the chance of kissing another guy out in broad daylight. This was a big mistake, and thankfully no one else had seen.

"I just—can't believe you never told me, that you used me—"

"I didn't mean to use you. I really have grown to love you, but *telling* you was a risk. I needed everyone to believe in us, especially my parents. They had already been making some speculations, but when we began dating that all disappeared. They were so thrilled that I had somehow gotten you, Roxy Elliott, the most desired girl out there, that their assumptions about my sexuality were gone. I didn't know how you'd take it, if you would shame me and tell the whole town, forcing me to give up the life I have—"

"I would never do that, Warner. God, you should know that. I may be a bitch but I'm a good person—"

"I'm not saying you aren't dear, it's just that most people don't exactly accept people like me."

She let a pause sweep over the room before responding with, "I won't tell anyone, Warner. I promise. But we can't be friends. Because if we are friends then I am forced to keep your secret from all of my friends on a daily basis. If we all hang out and go to the same parties it just makes it harder. Do you understand that? Especially with Frankie, you being friends with him and all. If we're all together, there's going to be this tension and I don't want to have to deal with that. I won't tell them for your sake but at the same time I can't be forced to live with your lie at every major event. Make sense? And I certainly cannot date someone who I know will never truly love me the way I want to be loved."

"I understand."

"I'm sorry, Warner—"

"No, I'm sorry. I put you through a lot and you didn't deserve that."

"Well I'm sorry we live in a world where you can't be

yourself," she said as she gave him a hug, wishing he didn't have to hide his true self.

"I do love you Roxy, like a sister I never had, and I hope you know that. Thank you for not selling me out or freaking out over the news. I know I'll be seeing you around, but I'll try to keep my distance. And I won't be attending any of your friends' parties—"

"Oh honey, you won't be invited. As far as they know, you were cheating on me with some gorgeous but sleazy broad, and therefore they're gonna hate you for that, so you don't have to worry about dodging parties," she laughed.

"I guess that's a good thing then."

"I guess so," she smiled. "I'll walk you out."

Warner left and Roxy sat down on the steps for a few minutes pondering the conversation she had just had, thinking about how hard Warner had it. She was also sad about the situation, thinking about how deeply she had fallen for this boy—yet at the same time she felt a sense of relief, despite not quite knowing where it was coming from.

I, however, know exactly where it was coming from.

Roxy was thankful she hadn't had sex with him that night at the Plaza, that she hadn't lost her virginity to a boy she never actually had a real connection with. Wouldn't that have been tragic? So there she sat, reliving every moment with him, wondering if there had been any clues. There were a few, but they were so subtle that no one would have known. Maybe Warner should move to California and give himself a shot at Hollywood, because he was sure one hell of an actor.

"Miss Elliott, I have the telephone for you!" one of the maids yelled across the room.

"Thank you!" she responded as she got up in a hurry and took the phone. "Hello, this is Roxy speak—"

"Roxy!"

"Frankie?"

"You gotta get over here now, it's an emergency, it's Virginia—"

"My God!" she said as her heart sank. "I'll be right there."

Roxy ran over to Frankie's, considering he lived only a few houses down from hers, and entered a situation in which one would in fact be quite worried. Johnny and Marie showed up shortly after, and then followed Dalton.

"WHAT THE HELL, FRANKIE—" Roxy shouted as she entered his grand home. Frankie was on his knees holding a very unconscious Virginia in his arms.

"She came over a little while ago, out of it. Completely out of it, then all of a sudden—"

"Frankie, what's going on—"

"I think she overdosed. She won't wake," Frankie said with a crack in his voice and a worrisome tone.

Roxy's eyes got bigger and her thoughts louder; her heart felt heavy and her stomach sick. "Overdosed?" she said with a sliver of a cry.

"That's what it looks like."

"But—Virginia doesn't do drugs, Frankie—"

"Well maybe she does, or did, I don't know! I don't know what to do! I'm here all alone so I thought I'd ring you, then I rang Johnny and he's coming with Marie, and Dalton should be here too—"

"We have to get her to a hospital now, Frankie."

"Well I'm waiting for Johnny, he's driving here himself. All of our cars are gone because my parents decided they wanted them all to have a new paint job, and the only other one is back in the city where they are—"

"God Frankie, why didn't you say that over the telephone? I would have driven one over—"

"Roxy, darling, I am not exactly thinking straight here!"

"Oh my God, is she okay?" Johnny said as he busted through the door.

"Virginia!" Marie yelled.

"We have to get her into the car—now!" Roxy said with a worried and stern voice.

Frankie carried the unconscious Virginia into Johnny's backseat as Dalton pulled up and jumped out of the car.

"Oh God—"

"I'll ride with you Dalton, follow Johnny to the hospital," Marie said as she hopped in the passenger side of Dalton's car.

And there they were, Johnny driving, Roxy beside him, and Frankie in the back with Virginia. Dalton and Marie following swiftly behind. All frantic and filled with worry, not knowing where this would go or what exactly had happened. None of them knew of her most recent hobby, and therefore had no idea something like this could ever happen. Especially to a girl like Virginia. For her to overdose? You gotta be kidding me.

"WE NEED A DOCTOR!" Johnny yelled as he chaotically

pulled in front of the hospital, jumping out of his car and into the waiting room.

Doctors rushed out with a gurney and Frankie placed Virginia gently on it. Dalton and Marie joined them seconds later, standing in a line side by side, terrified for their dear friend as she was rushed away by doctors who told them they were prohibited from staying with her. That they had to wait there until further notice, which is *not* something you want to hear when you have an unconscious friend who looks half dead.

Roxy turned to Frankie and he held her in his arms, as a tear ran down his face simultaneously with the tears running down hers. He was standing on the end, with Roxy on his left, then Johnny right beside her, grabbing Roxy's hand and holding it tight, then putting his left arm around Marie, as she grabbed Dalton's hand. They stood together, the five of them, with one of their special six sadly missing. They stood there in terror but in pride, banding together, praying for the recovery of their friend. No one knew what would happen. None of them had ever dealt with or seen anything like this before. They all individually wondered what could have drawn their sweet Virginia Williams to drugs, and to such an elaborate dosage. What could it have been that drove her to indulge in so much that she would overdose?

It wasn't anything in particular—I mean, it was more Hazel than anything. Hazel was still, of course, mourning the loss of her brother Henry, and therefore had a clear reason that drove her to drugs. *Not that it makes it okay.* For Virginia, it was more of a "why not" approach when Hazel had confided in her about her new hobby. This time, however, she had a clear motive. *Her breakup*. Although, it is quite odd that an average boy caused her to plummet deep into this situation. She knew she was taking a chance when combining opium with cocaine. It still shocks me, the idea of *her* doing drugs, but she had, and she went deep into them.

Hours went by and our special six were idly waiting for a doctor to come quickly through the doors, telling them their friend was alright and how they could come see her—but yet, the night continued to go by and there was no such event.

"What if she's dead?"

"Oh my God, Marie!" Roxy said as she slapped her arm.

"I'm just saying. What if—what if they couldn't save her?"

"We can't think like that—"

"Roxy, they haven't come out yet and it's been hours!"

"My God, stop you two! Roxy's right, we can't think like that," Dalton chimed in.

"Why not? Clearly something's wrong or they would have come out by now," Frankie said with a stern voice, keeping his arms crossed and his eyes on the floor.

"I can't imagine losing her—" Johnny said before being cut off by Roxy.

"God, why don't you shut up. I'm serious you guys, what the hell? Talking about how she's dead before we even know anything? Assuming the worst? I'm done with all of you," she said angrily before standing up and walking outside to light a cigarette.

Frankie followed her.

"I'm sorry. She's going to be fine," Frankie said with remorse.

"And what if she's not?"

"Hey, I thought it was you that just said we need to stop with that kind of talk?"

"But what if you're right? What if something really is wrong? What if they can't bring her back—"

"Stop it Roxy, stop it! We shouldn't have been talking like that in there. She's going to be fine. She's a tough broad, and so are you, so stop this," he said before grabbing her sweetly and hugging her tightly.

They were both scared for Virginia, but knew they needed to keep their minds positive or they'd all lose it. Every single one of them.

They shared a cigarette out there, right outside the hospital doors. Standing there together for twenty minutes looking out at the stars and talking about various topics unrelated to Virginia, trying to keep each other's minds off of the overdose situation.

"I think the doctor might be coming out soon," Johnny said as he told the two to come inside.

They put out the cigarette and ran back inside. The doctor came out with a harsh look on his face, which was not one they wanted to see. All of their hearts sank simultaneously as they braced themselves for what they were about to hear. By now of course, everyone was at the hospital: Virginia's family, Dennis and Daisy, and Marie's parents. Dalton's mom also joined them. Frankie and Johnny's parents were still in the city, but if they had been in The Hamptons, they would have been there as well. These six families were all close, so if one had an issue, it became everyone's issue. Each parent treated the rest of the gang like their own.

"I have some news about patient Virginia Williams," the doctor said bluntly as everyone stood up.

And so there it was: he reported to them the news they had all awaited so anxiously all night.

"So she's—" Virginia's mom began to say with a cry.

"She is in recovery and you can now visit her," the doctor responded.

Everyone rejoiced and cried gentle, happy tears as they all rushed through those doors, making their way to Virginia's room. There were about fifteen to twenty of them, I lost count. Grandparents and aunts of Virginia's were also there. Her father, however, was back in Chicago of course.

"Oh baby," Mrs. Williams cried as she sat by Virginia's side.

"Hi Mother," Virginia responded, hugging her gently.

Virginia apologized to her mom and everyone else for putting them through such a harsh ordeal. Though, they weren't exactly concerned with a punishment for her new drug habit and less-than-ideal actions at the moment. They were all so happy with her recovery. None of them had any idea if she would be alive by the next morning—if she had gone too far. Although that *was* almost the case, I did promise you no deaths this summer, didn't I?

It was around seven in the morning and Virginia was now doing well. Mrs. Williams and her sister, Virginia's aunt, remained by her side at the hospital, as did Dalton and Marie.

The rest had left. Johnny and Frankie left to grab some decent food to bring back, and Dennis and Daisy took Roxy to grab Virginia a present. Nothing made Roxy feel better than shopping, and she knew that a shiny new handbag was just what Virginia needed. It was the perfect thing to cheer Virginia up as she was lying in the ever so uncomfortable hospital bed. She also ran back home to grab some nice pillows and silk blankets for her —she needed them, as the hospital wasn't exactly a five-star hotel. After Roxy had got Virginia's present and pillows and blankets, and before she headed back out the door to the car which would take her back to the hospital, Daisy stopped her at the door.

"Roxy, I need to talk to you real quick," she said.

"Daisy," Roxy still referred to her birth mom as Daisy, for the time being, "I need to get back to Virginia. Johnny and Frankie are already there with the food."

"I know honey, just give me a minute," she pleaded.

The maids took everything to the car and Roxy made her way over to Daisy. "What is it?"

"Well you know how I lived in Paris for a little while, and made quite a few good friends?"

"Why yes of course, what about them? Are they visiting?"

"Not exactly. One of them visits Southampton for a few weeks every summer, and we had lunch the other day. She returns back to Paris in a few days."

"Daisy, I don't exactly see your point here—"

"Darling, let me get there … anyways, she works for Vogue, Vogue Paris."

You see, Roxy had many dreams and aspirations in life, and one of them was to work for Vogue.

"My goodness, that's just amazing!" Suddenly her eyes lit up and a dancing smile was painted across her face.

"Well, I told her that you had dreams of someday working for Vogue, and she told me that she needed an assistant—she's pretty high up over there in Paris and deals with a lot. She needs someone to help her out. Someone who could work with her, someone who she could teach and train to someday be someone big at Vogue."

"What exactly are you saying?" Roxy asked.

"I'm saying that she wants you. She wants you to go back to France with her and work with her. You can live with one of your cousins out there in Paris, the one that's got the flat near the Louvre?"

"Oh God I love that flat." Roxy sat down.

"I know darling, what do you think?"

"What do I think? I *think* that Paris is my favorite city next to New York and I'd be a fool not to take up an opportunity with French Vogue!" she smiled.

"I agree," Daisy laughed.

"When would I leave?"

"When she does. Her name is Meredith, by the way."

Meredith Hunter was from New York but had been living in Paris since she was nineteen years old.

"So, that means I'd be leaving—"

"In three days."

"Oh, oh my." Roxy stood up. This was a lot to take in.

"Three days?"

The two continued to talk about details for a few minutes before Roxy headed back to the hospital.

As for the rest of the day, the five friends stayed with Virginia until the doctor released her that night. She had almost fully recovered by then, and they all went over to Marie's before sitting out on the beach, have one of those late-night talks they all loved so much. This was when Roxy decided to break the news. Roxy had spent the entire day thinking about what Daisy told her, about this ever so grand opportunity. Who would pass up such a thing?

"I need to tell you all something," Roxy said as she stood up from the sand.

"What is it?" Marie asked.

She began to tell them everything, about how she could stay with her cousin in her rather luxurious Paris flat (which had a sparkling view of the Eiffel Tower, might I add). Roxy told them about how lucky she was that Meredith had even offered her such a great opportunity.

"When would you leave?" Dalton asked.

"August 5th."

"IN TWO DAYS?" Virginia responded.

"I know it's kind of soon, but it's not like I get a choice in the matter. It's leave with her now or she'll give the job to someone else."

"Well how long are you going for? How long will you be in Paris, when does the job end?"

"Frankie, it's not like that."

"What do you mean?" he said as he stood up, and the rest followed.

"It's not like an end of summer job or anything it's—a job. I'd be working for Meredith, *with* Meredith, at Vogue Paris."

"What exactly does that mean, Roxy?"

"It means that I—"

"Wouldn't be coming back?" Frankie said, now with a much louder tone.

"Well yes I'd be back to visit, and write often—"

"I can't believe this," Dalton chimed in.

"Oh you guys."

The air went silent for what felt like minutes, though it lasted but ten seconds.

"I'd be moving there, okay? I would be moving to Paris for however long it ends up being that I stay."

"And what about school?" Johnny asked.

"My parents would hire a tutor for me out there and I'd learn at home, just the same. Then I'd be able to work and study."

"Wow, so you're really thinking about this," Frankie said with a hurt and slightly angry voice.

They all went on the rest of the night arguing with Roxy, telling her how she'd be missing out on her senior year, how though it may be a great opportunity, she could always try and get a job at Vogue in New York. Roxy told them how, though Vogue in New York was where she always imagined she would be someday, Paris is where the job was at right then. Not to mention the chance she would have at running into Coco

Chanel at Angelina on Rue de Rivoli, where many French designers liked to frequent the tearoom.

Roxy was obsessed with fashion, hence the love for Vogue, Chanel, and Paris. She imagined herself working at Vogue, and then maybe someday becoming a fashion designer herself, or even both. Would it be possible to become editor in chief at Vogue *and* have her own fashion empire? If not, she always had it in her to be an actress, she loved that too—the idea of being in a motion picture, though she had no desire to permanently leave her glittering Manhattan for Hollywood. Regardless, this was not the focus right now. It was on her friends and their lack of support for her. All of them wanted her to succeed but loved her too dearly to have her ditch them and move across the Atlantic.

August 4th, 1925

Dear Diary,

I don't get it. I mean, I do, but I don't.

I have this grand opportunity to go to PARIS of all cities, and work for Daisy's friend Meredith at French Vogue. What a life!

I'd wake up each morning in my cousin's flat, open up the curtains to the Eiffel Tower, get ready and grab myself coffee and a croissant at the nearest local café, then I'd head to Vogue Paris for a dream job. I'd lunch somewhere cute, dining on the best of all cuisines: French. Then at night I would head out on the town and dance and drink and listen to jazz, in PARIS!

I would also of course also find time to study, but that's not important ... oh, and did I mention that my chances of running into Coco Chanel would skyrocket? I hear she frequents Angelina, which also happens to be one of my favorite places. (Hot chocolate to die for.)

Oh what a wonderful life.

But there's one downfall there, and that is the lack of my friends and family. Sure I've got some family in Paris, but it's not my father or Daisy, not my mom, Uncle Clyde, Tommy, my grandparents, none of the important ones! And most of all I wouldn't have Marie, or Virginia, no Johnny, no Dalton, and of course no Frankie. How would I live on without them? God, that would be quite an adjustment.

Oh, did I mention that Warner Davenport and I broke up? Turns out he's a homosexual, which I have no problem with, but sadly the world does. Oh it's such a long story. And then of course Virginia had a little drug problem none of us knew about. She hid it quite well, just like Warner hid his love for boys. Anyways, she's okay now but did in fact overdose, and we all went into a frenzy over the thought of losing her. Alright, back to Paris. I don't get it, none of my friends are supportive of me going. I mean, I guess I do get it, I'm going to miss them so much, but I just don't think I can afford to not take this opportunity. And I'll visit! And they'll visit! Oh God, what do I do?

Well, August 5th came, and so did her decision. A decision that became hard to make, but ultimately I believe to be the one worth making.

So, there she was, August 5th and her bags packed up and ready to go. She chose to leave, to move to Paris.

Everyone said their goodbyes, and hard ones they were. Tears were shed by many. Frankie hid it well, but when he got home he cried at the thought of her going away to Paris, just like that, out of nowhere, in the blink of an eye.

That's sure as hell how it seemed.

No one had time to process this idea, not even Roxy. It came out of left field. But that's life. Opportunities like that seem to always come faster than we expect, quicker than we have time to process, and that's exactly how this was.

Roxy didn't want to go, she didn't want to leave her friends and her family, or Frankie, and certainly not her New York, but she knew she had to. That this was the right decision to make, and she couldn't let it slip away.

If I'm being honest, it *was* a hell of an opportunity. Boy, I think we've overused that word haven't we: opportunity. Yet here we are, saying goodbye to her, so she can live out a dream.

After she left, Frankie went home, alone, and spent the rest of the day thinking about Roxy and what he'd do without her. What his life would be like with her all the way in France. How the group would feel with her absence. What it would be like walking into the Dakota Speakeasy knowing she wasn't there. Not knowing when she'd ever return. Or if she *would* even return. This was when he realized that maybe *just* maybe he had some *other* feelings for her. *Other* feelings, such as romantic ones. I mean, if he was going to finally wake up and smell the roses, this *would* be the way it would happen, once he had lost her. Especially so suddenly.

Roxy made her way across the Atlantic and found herself in the French city of Paris. A city of lights, love, fashion, art, history, and so much more (God, I sound like an advertisement there, don't I?). It was *after all* the city she was born in, remember that? She made her way to her cousin's, unpacking for her new life that awaited her.

CHAPTER 24

City of Lights

August 21st, 1925

Dear Diary,

I've been here in Paris now for a little over two weeks, and every damn moment of it has been incredible. Meredith is amazing and has taught me so much about Vogue, and the job is better than I could have even imagined. My cousin Nelly and I have been having such a great time living together, she's quite the roar herself. I don't usually see her that often considering she's a second cousin and lives across the Atlantic, so it's nice being able to spend so much quality time with her. She's not a part of the whole Elliott mafia deal, she likes to stay out of it and work on her art, which I really admire about her. Although, I don't understand why you can't have both a career and actively be a part of the family business. It's what I'll do! Anyways, Paris is amazing, though I miss everyone so much. School back in New York starts in a few weeks, on September 9th I believe, right after Labor Day. It's going to be quite odd not being there on the first day of school with all of my friends, let alone the rest of the year. I've actually not been doing too well with the whole idea of not having a usual senior year. But I've got to get over it, I'm here in Paris for heaven's sake! Oh, and not to mention, I did in fact spot Coco Chanel on the street the other day—however, I was much too scared to say hello. I have heard that she knows a few Elliotts though, but the distant ones who live here in Paris who I'm not all that close to. I may, however, end up getting closer to them …

I mean, it would be in my best interest. It's not like I don't like them or anything, they are just a little bit more distant in the Elliott family tree and therefore us New York Elliotts aren't as close to them, that's all. Also, I'm thinking about going shopping later with this new friend of mine I made at Vogue. Probably at Chanel's boutique on Rue Cambon, then maybe Louis Vuitton and a few cute clothing boutiques. God I love Parisian fashion.

Roxy had been doing well over in Paris, despite every night lying in bed, not being able to sleep because she couldn't help but think of her friends and family whom she missed so dearly. Though, every morning as she woke up to the Eiffel Tower, the thoughts seemed to disappear from her mind like a train rushing away from a station, off to its next (and greater) destination.

Vogue Paris had welcomed Roxy quite quickly, and she became the youngest employee there. Though she wasn't quite 'Roxy Elliott, Editor In Chief' yet, she was certainly making a name for herself with the magazine.

As for everything back in Southampton, the gang missed Roxy just as she missed them, but they'd continue to live the rest of their summer out to the fullest.

Johnny threw quite the roaring party, something Roxy was upset to miss, and Dalton helped Hazel get rid of her drug problem before she ended up overdosing like Virginia. Marie and her boyfriend Arthur had been taking things to the next level and Marie wrote Roxy a letter telling her how she had lost her virginity to him while his parents were away, giving her every juicy detail. Roxy was happy for her, although she *was* extremely competitive and wanted to lose it first. Virginia couldn't really have cared either way, and she did end up being the last person of the group to have sex. It was Frankie (surprisingly), Roxy (also surprisingly), and Virginia who were the virgins left in the group.

Frankie was still dating Claire, and since Roxy had left it looked like their relationship had actually been doing well. Claire became less of a crazy neurotic bitch now with Roxy out of the picture (jealousy does that to you sometimes), and therefore Frankie had begun to use her to get over Roxy. Like I told you before, Frankie had finally started accepting the fact that he was *just maybe* in love with the young Elliott, now that she was conveniently gone of course. Claire served as a grand distraction for him, taking away the pain of Roxy's departure. However, Johnny and Dalton always seemed to know when to bring it right back.

"So, are we going to talk about this or what?" Dalton said to Frankie as he held up a letter he had written to Roxy, though never planned on *actually* sending.

"Dammit Dalton, how'd you get that?" he said in response, ripping the letter out of his hand.

"You had it out in the open on your desk idiot, I glanced over and saw and well——"

"Don't you think that's an invasion of privacy?"

"Not with us, come on Frankie, we share everything!" Johnny laughed.

"Oh what, so you guys had a little party with it? Is that it?"

"Actually yes, it served as *quite* the entertainment for the night," Johnny laughed again as Dalton joined him.

"Oh go to hell, you two."

"Frankie, whether or not you wanna talk, we are talking."

"I think my favorite line in the letter was 'I don't know how I never let myself feel it before, but now that you're gone it's like every bone in my body is aching in heartbreak'," Dalton chuckled as he ripped the letter back out of Frankie's hands and into his.

"Mine was 'You know I love you, you know I do, but it's different now. I'm in love with you, Roxy darling'—"

"Stop it, Johnny!" Frankie responded.

"'—in love with every single part of you'," Johnny continued.

"That's enough, Johnny."

"So here it is, right here! You finally fessing up after all of these years."

"Yeah, so?"

Dalton and Johnny shared a look. "Yeah so, will you finally admit we were all right all along. I mean God you denied it for the longest time, then she leaves and *that's* when you decide to tell her?" Dalton said.

"I'm not going to tell her."

Dalton and Johnny shared yet another look. "What do you mean you're not going to tell her?" Johnny said.

"I mean I was never going to send that letter. I just wrote it, I don't know why, but I did, okay?"

"Oh, you have got to be kidding me," Johnny sighed.

"What? It's not like it's going to matter! She's not going to read it and drop everything in Paris for me, and I wouldn't want her to anyway. As much as I want her here, Paris is where she needs to be right now, and I'd never take that away from her."

"But shouldn't you at least give her the truth? Roxy deserves that and you know it—" Dalton began to say.

"No, actually she doesn't. Because, let's say she has the same feelings for me, even though I don't think she does … let's just imagine. If I were to tell her, then she would have a tough decision to make and I don't want to put her into a place where she second-guesses her living in Paris. If she decides on her own that she wants to come home, then so be it. But I'm not gonna be the one to sway that, okay?"

"So what about Claire?" Dalton asked.

"What about her?"

"You're dating her …" Johnny said.

"You don't say."

"God Frankie, I mean are you going to tell her?" Johnny responded.

"Hell no. Why would I do that?"

"Oh my God," Dalton said.

"Listen, Roxy is in Paris, okay? For as long as she decides to stay there, or until she can eventually get a job at Vogue here in New York. That means I need to get over her, and Claire serves as a perfect distraction."

"Well, all I'm saying is that if Claire finds this unsent letter of yours, she's gonna go wild."

"Well I'm not going to let that happen, Dalton."

"Alright alright, and what if Roxy moves back, huh? Then what?" Johnny asked.

"Then I'll be forced to deal with that. But from her letters going on and on about how much she loves it there, it doesn't seem likely. So will you just let me live my life and move on from this?"

"Whatever, Matthews."

"And I gotta go, I'm picking Claire up and heading into town for the night," Frankie said as he took the letter back into his possession and put it in one of his drawers.

This was *not* a good idea, however.

Dalton and Johnny spent the rest of the day at the club while Frankie had a grand night with Claire back in the city. Marie and Virginia ended up meeting up with the boys later on that evening to discuss Frankie and everything that had gone down when they confronted him about his feelings for Roxy.

They all talked about how *they* should maybe tell Roxy themselves, but they could never betray Frankie like that. If he wanted her to know, he'd tell her; and someday he would.

"Hey baby, do you want some tea?" Frankie said to Claire as they returned to Southampton.

"I'd love some! I'm just going to head up to
your bedroom, bring it to me there?" she said as he nodded.

Claire walked up one of the beautiful staircases and down the wide hall, turned right and entered Frankie's bedroom. She took her purse and threw it down on his desk, then wandered around his room for a bit until she spotted one of his drawers open.

The drawer to his nightstand …

She made her way closer before spotting a letter placed perfectly in it. Claire saw that the letter was addressed to one Miss Scarlett Roxy Elliott, and to an address in Paris. Immediately, without hesitation, she picked up the envelope and removed the letter inside.

Dear my beautiful Roxy,

How are you, darling? I hope Paris is treating you well, though I have no doubt in my mind that it is. The city sparkles with almost as much charm as you have. We miss you over here in New York. All of us feel as if something is wrong in the group, and it is. You're not here. Other than your absence, things have been alright. Hazel is doing well now, and her and Dalton have really grown closer. As you know, Marie and Arthur took things to the next level. Virginia and Johnny are pretty good too. I really hope you're good, but at the same time I hope you're miserable so you come home. But I know that won't happen. There's something else too, something I've got to tell you. Something you have to know. I don't know how I never let myself feel it before, but now that you're gone it's like every bone in my body is aching in heartbreak. You know I love you, you know I do, but it's different now. I'm in love with you, Roxy darling, every single part of you. I guess a part of me always knew, but I never let myself go there, I was too afraid of losing you. But now I've already lost you. I've lost you to Paris. So I figured, what the hell, might as well tell you.

I know what you're thinking ... well I don't ... but I imagine it's something along the lines of "what the hell Frankie", wondering why I didn't just take the chance and tell you before. That I should have known I wouldn't lose you. It just ... wasn't that simple, darling. And you always had a boyfriend, and I sure wasn't gonna take away your happiness. Anyways, I'm sure you're probably wondering what I am gonna do about Claire. Well, to be honest, she's sure no you, but she's a good distraction. And a distraction is exactly what I need. Having someone else to take my mind off of you. Off of hugging you, kissing you, making love to you, taking you on our first date at Tavern on the Green. I can't think about those things or it'll tear me apart. So she's there. And if I'm being honest, I think our relationship is doing alright. It has to be, because I have to get over you.

Love,
Your Matthews boy

Claire stood there in utter rage. Her entire body felt hot, as if her blood was boiling, burning her from the inside out. Her eyes were fixated on the ending, the part where Frankie had stated that she was only his distraction.

Jealousy is quite the feeling.

She wanted revenge, and she was set out to destroy Roxy, even if she was never coming home. However, Claire knew she didn't want Frankie knowing she had read the letter. So, as she heard his steps coming down the hallway, she quickly folded the letter back up and put it in its envelope, placing it exactly where she had found it. The night went on and they drank tea and made out, while both of their minds were on Roxy. Frankie wishing Claire *was* Roxy, and Claire thinking about how she'd destroy her. What a lovely night. What a romantic scene.

As for our Roxy herself, it was now morning in Paris and she awoke to her cousin handing her a letter. A letter from Virginia, telling her once again how much she and the rest of the gang missed her. She read it as those heavy emotions continued to stir up in her heart. That was when she got dressed and headed out onto the streets of Paris, where she would grab herself an espresso at the nearest café, along with a croissant, then head to Pont Alexandre III, one of the most beautiful bridges in Paris.

She stood proudly on the bridge with her coffee and croissant, looking out over the Seine, facing the Eiffel Tower as the morning sun lay gently on it.

Roxy was in pure heaven, but at the same time missed her city more and more each day, along with the friends and family she cherished more than anything else.

In a perfect moment, she turned her head to the left as a rather stunning woman was crossing the bridge, walking just her way.

"Mademoiselle!" she gasped as the woman smiled.

"Bonjour," the woman responded.

"It's you," Roxy said as her eyes continued to widen and she stood there in utter disbelief.

"Why it is. And who might you be?" the woman asked.

"I'm—I'm Roxy. Roxy Elliott."

"An Elliott? I know a few, any relation?"

"Oh yes, I've got some distant family members here in Paris.

The other ones back in the States, and then the most in New York of course," she said, trembling in shock and joy.

"Well, your family's speakeasies are divine. I frequent them often."

"Wow, how marvelous. If you are ever in New York, stop by one of ours at The Dakota. It's the best one."

"I'll keep that in mind."

There she was. Roxy standing with her idol, the one and only Coco Chanel.

Coco had been visiting her friend and had decided to walk back over to her boutique on Rue Cambon. It was a beautiful morning and she wanted to take advantage of such a nice walk, early in the day before the city began to crowd.

"Real quick, could I just ask you a question? Just one?"

"Of course."

"How did you do it?" Roxy said.

"What exactly do you mean?"

"How did you become what you became? I want to be a designer someday, along with dealing with the family business. And I'd like to have some part at Vogue. I know that sounds like a lot, but regardless, the designing part, it's difficult and some days I just feel like I'm not made out for it."

"Nonsense," the young Chanel said, "by the way you dress, you must have good style, but if you give up you won't ever be a designer. I never gave up, I did everything I had to in order to get where I am today."

"Of course," Roxy smiled.

"Any other questions before I go?"

"One, yes. It's about Paris. Do you believe this is the only city where one can become a designer?"

She laughed. "This city is my everything, and while I believe it is one of the best cities to become a designer, New York and Milan would also be on the list. Most importantly, you have to be in the city that is *your* everything."

Roxy nodded and Chanel continued along the bridge, walking past her as Roxy's eyes followed in awe. Roxy then continued to stand there on the bridge, though this time with her mind going off in a *much* different direction.

CHAPTER 25

SENIOR YEAR

September, *what a month.* Fall is just beginning and school is returning. *Among other things.* It was September 7th, Labor Day. The Hamptons were full of wealthy New Yorkers wrapping up their last day of summer before returning to the city. Parties were held all over Long Island. Big ones, little ones, sad ones, happy ones. Everything from fancy soirées to wild and roaring raves. It was a day that America celebrated the American Labor Movement and paid tribute to workers and their achievements.

Every year since our six families first met each other, which was long, long ago, they would throw a Labor Day party together.

As you know, and as I'm pretty sure I told you before, the Elliott family, The Matthews family, the Davis family, the

Williams family, the James family, and the Romano family have been connected for generations.

It's not just our special six, but their parents and their parents' parents that have been close-knit, which is how our specific group of friends met each other in the first place.

They were all from New York, and had been there for years. Except for Mr. and Mrs. Williams, who moved to Chicago after marrying, but then moved back to New York when Virginia was young.

Anyways, that's irrelevant.

This year, 1925, was the Davis family's turn to host. So in the grand tradition of our fancy families, they threw quite the end-of-summer gathering, which about a hundred guests attended. The entire gang was there of course, with the exception of Roxy. Lillie and Allen (Johnny's parents) put on quite the party that year. There were about fifteen champagne towers, food and desserts catered from only the best and most expensive places, multiple bands playing in multiple areas of the mansion with jazz music blaring so loud you couldn't help but dance, and of course, the best-dressed guests. It was a roar. What a beautiful way to end the summer, am I right?

After the party, and all the guests had left, the gang decided they'd stay over at Johnny's, making the most of their last summer night. Around one in the morning, the five of them decided they'd go out onto the sand and watch the waves while they talked about various things, including how excited they were for their senior year: their last year in high school. God, time really goes by fast, doesn't it? It feels like 1921 was yesterday, and they had just started as young, short, and not as eccentric freshmen. However, once they started high school, their innocence began to fade into a past distance and their wild sides truly blossomed.

"Are you guys scared?" Virginia asked.

"Scared? Why the hell would we be scared?" Frankie responded.

"Of growing up," Virginia said.

"Virginia, growing up isn't scary. It's exciting!" Marie added.

"She has a point though, I mean, this is our last year of high school. It's all going to be over soon," Dalton said.

"Oh shut up, none of it's gonna be over. We're gonna be in college but that doesn't matter. I mean, most of us wanna stay in New York anyways. And at worst, we'd be spread between New York, Connecticut, and Massachusetts. It's not like we're going far away," Johnny said.

A little time went on as they assured each other this wouldn't be their last year together, and that their friendships would never fade. *And they wouldn't.* I mean, look at their parents, they're all still extremely close with each other.

As the night went on and conversations shifted, they were greeted by someone in a rather sudden manner.

"Did you miss me?"

There was that velvet voice once again.

They were all startled. No one was on Cooper's Beach but them, not to mention it was two in the morning and their portion of the sand was private.

302

Frankie was first to speak. "ROXY!" he said with bright eyes, and a full heart he tried desperately to hide.

"Hi darling," she smiled.

He jumped up faster than lightning and ran to her, grabbing her as tight as he could, lifting her feet up off the sand and into the air—and she embraced him back.

"What the hell! How long are you here for? Why'd you not tell us?" Johnny exclaimed before he hugged her.

"Oh because," she said.

"How long are you staying?" Marie asked before hugging her.

"You see, that's the thing."

Dalton and Virginia stood up, ready for their hug.

"What do you mean?" Dalton said.

"Don't tell me you're only here for a coupla days," Frankie added.

"No no, it's not a couple. It's a bit longer than that."

"How long?" Virginia said.

"A little longer," Roxy responded with a sly smirk.

That was just it, she had made up her mind. There, on a bridge over the Seine. While the Vogue job was perfect, and living in Paris was amazing, Roxy didn't *need* to be in France to carry out her dreams. She could work hard and eventually get herself a job at Vogue in New York. Especially considering she was an Elliott. After her run-in with *the* Coco Chanel, she knew that as much as she loved the city of Paris, New York was her everything, and for many reasons. Her family and her friends were in New York, as were most of her fondest memories, her favorite places—the majority of her inspiration stemmed from the sparkling city. So she came back, and to stay. Everyone was overjoyed, and no one saw it coming. Every telephone call and letter had made it seem as if she was happy as day there, and she had been—she had given no indication she would be returning. Especially not this soon. She had spent the month there and learned a lot, but the biggest thing she had learned was how Manhattan would always be hers, and she wanted it back.

As for the Frankie situation, he sure as hell didn't see it coming. What was he supposed to do now? He had finally made it clear to the others that he was, in fact, in love with Roxy. Yet, he was still in a relationship with Claire. A relationship that grew closer and closer every day. He *was* moderately happy with her and didn't intend to break it off with her and pour out his heart to Roxy. It was different when she was away. He could feel like that and not have to deal with it, but now that she was back it made things extra difficult. Johnny told him to tell her, that she'd want him too, but he wouldn't. It wasn't the "right time". So, for now at least, the five of them kept the secret, and he continued to date Claire.

September 8th, 1925

Dear Diary,

I can't believe how fast time has gone by. Tomorrow is the first day of senior year, and I couldn't be more excited. I'm so happy being home. God, I've sure missed it. Do I miss Paris?

Of course ... but I made the right decision coming home, and I don't regret it one bit. I couldn't imagine not being here for my last year at Manhattan West.

I didn't tell anyone I was coming home. Not even my dad, who was extremely happy for me to be home. He was always supportive but wasn't exactly happy that I had decided to pack up my bags and leave home so suddenly. He actually cried when I left, but regardless, I'm back now and I couldn't be happier. Marie, Virginia, and I went shopping today, getting everything we need for our senior year. I plan on it being my best-dressed year, though that's going to be difficult considering I've always had great fashion. This year, however, I have quite a few new dresses from Paris. Oh French fashion, it never disappoints. One thing has been a little bit weird lately, however. It feels as if everyone is hiding something from me, especially Frankie. And he's sure not one to hide something. He tells me EVERYTHING, well, we all do really. It's just a tad bit odd.

What Roxy had been referring to, of course, was Frankie's newfound love for her. It was quite the secret.

September 9th came and all of New York was up bright and early for their first day of school. The only day where you actually *enjoy* waking up and going to school, of course. The gang was ready and all ended up at Roxy's before school, since her and Johnny's apartments were in the closest proximity to the high school. Johnny came over first, then Marie and Dalton arrived together, then followed Frankie, and finally Virginia. They stepped out of the doors of The Dakota and made their way to school, walking a few blocks uptown. Their school was on West 78th Street, right in between Central Park West and Columbus Avenue. They walked up the steps to the school in style and entered the doors as seniors. What a feeling.

CHAPTER 26

THE WRATH OF CLAIRE REED

Oh Claire Reed, we really love her, don't we?

Well … we don't.

However, I'd say everyone deserves a good second chance, and if once again they've failed you, that's when you cut them out for good.

"Oh come on Roxy, give her a chance," Frankie said as they entered the Dakota speakeasy after school. "I mean—you kinda started to before you left for Paris—"

"No Frankie, I really didn't. And I'm not—"

"All I'm asking for—"

"Okay, you interrupt me one more time—"

"Is a second chance. That's all," he said while batting his eyes.

The bartender made them each a Manhattan and Frankie continued to plead with Roxy, hoping she would make an attempt at accepting Claire into her life. At this point in time, she wasn't even allowing her into any of her family's speakeasies.

"She's my girlfriend, Roxy."

Roxy put her glass down and looked straight into his icy blue eyes. "The fact that you think I give a damn is laughable."

"I really care about her. She's not so bad once you get to know her better. She's got a gentle soul, like a flower."

Roxy rolled her eyes. "All roses have thorns, don't forget."

"Oh God Roxy, just—have a drink with her, please?"

"I'm not letting that psycho rat into my family's speakeasies," she responded.

"Then go to one of the Deckers'," Frankie laughed.

"Real funny."

As the day went on and they worked on their school project together, he got her to cave in by making a deal. If she gave Claire another chance, and once again Claire proved to be the bitch Roxy saw her as, Frankie would break up with her. Now, if Claire had truly changed and Roxy began to like her, she owed him an apology—which was something he knew she'd hate doing. So it was settled: Roxy wouldn't avoid Claire at all costs or exclude her from events. Instead, she'd make somewhat of a small effort to get to know her better.

Now, as I said before, *despite her return*, Frankie had vowed to get over his feelings for Roxy, or at least keep them hidden, and even a month into Roxy's return, he continued to date Claire as the group held the secret tight. And they did a decent job at it.

Though, they truly hated it.

Frankie had phoned Claire that night, asking her to invite Roxy out so they could get closer. Claire was all for the idea (with Frankie in the dark on her true feelings over the situation, of course). All Claire had wanted to do since Roxy's sudden return was get close to her, close enough so she could hurt her. But Roxy wouldn't budge. Now that Frankie had persuaded her into giving Claire a second chance, Miss Reed would be able to enact her revenge plan.

The next morning at school, Claire ran up to Roxy at her locker. "Hey!" she said, a little too enthusiastically.

"Good morning, Claire," Roxy said in a monotone voice.

"Frankie, he's real great you know."

"Sure is."

"I mean—just—lousy with sweetness, you know?"

Roxy turned to her, closing her locker in a rather loud manner, then said with a fake grin, "Absolutely lousy."

Claire laughed. "Well, he had this grand idea, for us to get to know each other better. I know we aren't exactly the best of friends—"

"You don't say?" she said. It was going to take a little while for Roxy to get used to the idea of being nice to Claire.

"He just, he thinks it would be a good idea for us to maybe get a drink sometime. I told him why get a drink—"

"Yes, why, we really don't have to! We can even tell him we did and he'll never have to know!"

"Oh Roxy, that's not what I meant."

"Then what exactly *did* you mean?"

"You should come over this Friday night!"

Roxy's eyes widened as she took a pause. "As in, to your place of *living*?" she said, nauseous at the thought.

"Yes!"

Roxy nervously laughed. "Why don't we just start with a drink at Ear Inn?"

"On Spring Street?"

"That's the one."

"That's silly, why go all the way down there when your family has multiple speakeasies much closer?"

Roxy paused and took a sigh. "I get bored, that's why!"

"Oh no no, I think it would be much better if you just came over. You can even teach me how to make a drink? A martini, maybe?"

Roxy knew it wasn't worth fighting this one, so she kept her deal with Frankie and gave Claire another chance. "Sure."

"Great! Come over on Friday, around seven maybe?"

"Will do," Roxy responded with a half-smile.

Frankie had applauded her for actually agreeing to Claire's wishes in having her come over, versus just meeting her for a quick drink. He was even surprised, and to be honest, I was too. All week Roxy had dreaded the ever so close Friday evening when she was expected to attend. She knew there was no backing out after she had already agreed. On Friday afternoon, Claire asked Frankie to come over for a little while before Roxy came, and he of course did, thinking nothing of it. She had told him she wanted to spend some time with him, and that he could leave around six-thirty so she could get ready for Roxy. When he came over, they did what most couples in high school did: made out endlessly until they decided they'd take a break and eat. Claire asked Frankie if he wanted some tea and biscuits, to which he answered yes, and she went downstairs to get it. What Frankie *didn't* know was that his answer should have been a strong and confident *no*.

"I'll be right back!" she said, making her way down to the kitchen.

It was around five-thirty when Claire returned upstairs, and Frankie questioned if he should get going soon. She told him that Roxy wouldn't be there until at least seven and that he was fine, that he could wait a little while before leaving. They sat on her bed and drank tea. Two different types of teas. Frankie liked Earl Grey, just as Roxy did, but Claire's favorite was oolong. Because of this, Claire made two small pots and brought them upstairs on a silver tray. The clock continued to run and suddenly Frankie became tired, thinking it was probably a good idea to get home.

"Claire—it's almost six-thirty, I should go," he said in a slow voice.

"No, Roxy's coming later, it's fine!"

Claire knew there was one perfect way to get back at Roxy, the only way she could think of. The only revenge plan she could truly carry out successfully.

As Roxy was getting ready to head out, Virginia and Marie were with her in her bedroom.

"I think it's really nice you're going over there," Virginia said.

"Yeah, I mean, lately I've spent a little time with her and she's really not a bitch anymore," Marie laughed.

"Yeah well, we'll see. We've never liked each other, not since we were little. She's always had it out for me, I swear," Roxy said with a strong doubt that Claire truly had changed.

"Oh I think you're just paranoid. We're seniors now, we've all matured," Virginia said.

"Again, we'll see!" Roxy said as she grabbed her lace gloves and put them on. "Aright, here goes nothing."

"Bye babe," Marie said.

"Love you!" followed Virginia.

Roxy made her way over to Claire's townhome, for a night she didn't quite expect.

While Roxy was walking over, Claire knew she would be getting close. This "plan" Claire had come up with was for Roxy to believe Frankie had slept with her. This was something that would truly, truly hurt Roxy. Just as the idea of Roxy having sex with Warner had hurt Frankie. Claire knew that Frankie was waiting for Roxy, even if for now he was keeping his love for her a secret. Claire hated this. Not only was she extremely jealous of Roxy in other ways, but now having read the letter *her* boyfriend wrote Roxy, Claire had nothing but pure envy and rage flowing through her veins. While seven o'clock came close, Claire lit a few candles around her bedroom, put her radio on low, and dimmed the lights. Frankie was still there, and beginning to lose sight of what was really happening. He was becoming woozy, and slightly hallucinating. He felt detached from reality and completely out of it.

Have you ever heard of the drug ketamine?

"Claire—I don't, I don't—"

"Shhh, you're fine, lie down," she said, helping him lie back on her bed.

Claire unbuttoned Frankie's shirt, eventually taking it off of him completely and throwing it onto the floor a few feet away from her bed. Then she removed his belt and pants, dropping them closer to the edge of her bed. As she heard the front door shut (it was a loud door), she removed her dress and headpiece, leaving only her undergarments on.

"Go upstairs, turn left, and Claire's room is down the hallway. Second to last room on the right," the maid said as Roxy entered the Reed residence.

Claire then made her way on top of the very out-of-it Frankie, kissing him, making it look like they were finally doing the deed. Roxy made her way down the hallway, then found Claire's door on the right.

Roxy opened the door, and her eyes couldn't believe what she was seeing. Her heart dropped and her stomach felt sick. Claire looked back and gave her an evil grin, then turned back around and continued to do what looked like making love to Frankie. There was no way Roxy could see Frankie's face, and realise that he had no idea what was going on. She believed she had walked in on Frankie and Claire having sex (because that's exactly what it looked like from her angle). She shut the door and stood there for a long three seconds, unable to process what she had just witnessed. Then she looked over at a table on the other side of the hall. On top of the table were a lamp, a telephone, and a box of matches. She started toward the box of matches as though she were going to use them (she wasn't, however, because she isn't the psycho bitch Claire is).

Roxy then quickly ran down the hall, as one of her gloves fell off of her soft hand, landing beside the table. The gloves were slightly big on Roxy, so it made sense that they'd easily slip off as she was making a quick attempt to escape the gates of hell she had just entered. Roxy continued out of the townhome, shutting the front door loudly, making her way out into the fresh Manhattan air, then down the street. The harsh shutting of the heavy door rattled the whole place, making it clear that Roxy had left. This was when Frankie was beginning to come round. The effects of ketamine last for about one to two hours, and he was thankfully coming out of it on the one-hour side.

"What's going on?" he said, extremely confused.

"Frankie!" Claire said, startled, not thinking he'd come to so quickly.

"Claire, what is this? What are you doing?" he said louder, pushing her off him.

"It's not what it looks like—"

"Are you insane? What—what happened?"

"Frankie, you don't understand, I wasn't going to do anything to you! I just needed to make it look like it so—"

"Did you drug me?" he said angrily as he got up.

"Frankie, baby, I just had to make it look like we were having sex, so that Roxy would back off. I found the letter, I know you love her, but I love you!" she pleaded, as if what she had done was okay.

"Oh my God, Roxy was right."

"Frankie, how could you say that?" Claire said, turning her emotions once again toward rage.

"Roxy, where is she—"

Claire stood still.

"CLAIRE!" he yelled.

Claire's face reddened. "She's gone—she just left."

"Get out—"

"It's my bedroom—"

"I said GET OUT!" Frankie wanted her out so he could get dressed, then escape the gates of hell Roxy had so swiftly left.

Claire left her bedroom, closing the door so Frankie had privacy, as angry tears fell down her red face. Her mind was running wild with jealousy.

Her plan had failed.

After Roxy had seen the two together in bed, Claire had planned to return Frankie's clothes back to his body, then wait for him to awaken from his rather unconscious, woozy state, hoping he wouldn't really remember much of anything. Or at least only enough so that she could twist the truth into something he'd believe. She'd tell him that he got really tired, then decided to lie down for a few minutes before Roxy came over, but that Roxy no-showed so she let him sleep. She knew that Roxy wouldn't confront him on the matter, at least not for a while, so she knew there'd be no room for failure.

Roxy wanted Frankie to be happy, and she wasn't going to go and ruin that after promising not to. Claire knew Roxy would tell Frankie that she forgot about their little get-together, and that she didn't care anymore that he was dating Claire. I mean, if he was happy enough with her that he'd lose his virginity to her, then she knew it'd be wrong to mess with that. So there was Claire's revenge. To hurt her in a way she hadn't been hurt before, to mess with her emotions so deeply that she wouldn't even mention them.

As Frankie was dressing, there stood Claire outside her room, looking out to the hallway just as Roxy had. She saw Roxy's glove by the table and there an idea entered her mind.

She really was crazy.

Claire stared at the matchbox, walking over to them with young yet rheumy eyes. She picked up the box, and in a rather wicked scene, pulled out one of the matches, then lit it quickly. She stood there for a second as the light of the fire burning off of the match reflected into her watery eyes, then made her way over to the window at the end of the hallway. This was a tall, beautiful window accompanied by tall, beautiful Victorian curtains. The Reed family *did* have quite fine taste, if I do say so myself. They just didn't have very fine children.

Roxy, realizing she had left her glove, started back toward Claire's, thinking she had probably dropped it outside her front door.

Claire gazed into the elegant design of the curtains as she lit the very bottom of them, then watched as they went up in flames as she dropped the match. She stood there for a long four seconds before walking away, picking up Roxy's glove on her way down the hall. She walked down her stairs and grabbed the keys to her front door. Frankie felt the heat of the fire as he

316

opened up her bedroom door, in shock at the flames. He quickly darted out her door. This was as Roxy walked up to Claire's, where flames were clearly burning from the inside.

"FRANKIE!" she yelled as she ran into the burning townhome.

Roxy opened the front door to see Claire.

"Where is he?" she demanded.

"Upstairs," Claire said, lacking emotion.

Roxy didn't hesitate to continue inside as Claire took a large vase and hit Roxy upside the head, knocking her out from behind. Then she walked out her front door and onto the street as she watched her home go up in flames. The maid had already left for the night and her parents were in London for the weekend, so it was only Roxy and Frankie inside. As Frankie made his way downstairs, Roxy was behind a wall, in a position where he couldn't see her. He ran out of Claire's and onto the street, then Claire made her way up the five stairs to the front door.

"What are you doing?" Frankie yelled. "Can't you see the place is on fire!"

"Locking the door."

"Why the hell would you do that?" he yelled, once again.

Claire was now standing beside him. "So you can't get to Roxy."

Frankie's eyes bugged out, his heart sank deep into his chest, and he felt sick.

After Claire locked the door, she tossed the keys up into one of the windows above. It was an impressive throw, as the window wasn't too close to the ground; it was far enough up that someone wouldn't be able to climb to it.

As this happened, Frankie didn't know what to do.

He at first made an attempt to break in the door, but he was unsuccessful. Then he looked around for something he could use to break the first-floor window. There were two big windows right beside the front door. The Reeds had two plants on each side of each window, and he grabbed one from the left, throwing it into the window, causing it to shatter (it was quite a large and heavy vase, the type you have outside).

He entered through the window and found Roxy as the flames got closer and closer. He picked up his unconscious love and opened the front door, carrying her out as the firemen pulled up.

Her face was black with smoke, and he could hardly hear her breathing.

"SHE NEEDS HELP!" he said as he handed her over to a fireman, who had to perform CPR.

Police also showed up, and when they did Claire was the first to speak with them, as Frankie was too focused on bringing Roxy back.

"Can you tell us what happened, how the fire started?" the police officer asked as the other firemen were making their way into the burning townhome.

"Yes, that girl right there. She's in love with my boyfriend, and she's jealous we are together. She came over knowing Frankie was here, that's my boyfriend, and came inside. After witnessing us together I believe she lit the fire. Frankie and I escaped, but she must have stayed to commit suicide. I think she might be mentally unstable."

"And you know that for sure?"

"She even left her glove right by the matches, I have it here—see," she said in a believable tone.

"Alright, you stay right here with my partner," the policeman said as he walked over to Roxy, Frankie, and the fireman.

"That's not true, none of it! If anything, she did it, Claire. She lit the fire," Frankie said, vouching for the truth. "This is Roxy Elliott, you've got the whole story backwards."

"Roxy Elliot? As in of the Elliott family?"

Frankie nodded.

The fireman was still with our young Elliott, giving her CPR and praying she would wake.

He knew her, he knew she was an Elliott. Therefore, not only did he want her to wake because he wanted to save a human life, but also because he knew if he couldn't save her, the family would have him taken out in a heartbeat.

I mean, that is how the mafia did things, so are you surprised?

And finally, there it was, her first breath after much too long without one. Roxy, there, still black from smoke, was coughing heavily—but also breathing lightly. Frankie went to her and held her.

"Are you okay?" he said.

She coughed and slowly said with a raspy voice, "Do I look okay?"

He laughed. "I would say so."

She coughed again. "So do you choose to be a fool or does it just happen?"

"I'm pretty sure it's assigned to us at birth," Frankie responded as the policeman went to the now conscious Elliott.

"Is it true that Claire lit the fire?"

"Then knocked me out, yes," Roxy responded.

What a day … so much for second chances.

I think it's safe to say Claire Reed did in fact fail again, and it's time to cut her loose for real this time. Which is exactly what happened. When the police heard both Frankie *and* Roxy's side of the story, they knew it was the truth. Especially with her being Roxy *Elliott* and all. Roxy was ready to take out Claire, but knew that wasn't the right way. *Though the bitch did attempt to kill Roxy.* Anyway, instead of having her killed, or even doing the deed herself, both the Elliotts and the Reeds came to an agreement: lock up Claire for a *very* long time. So, there Claire went, upstate to a rather scary-looking place: a mental asylum for the criminally insane. Doesn't that just have a nice ring to it? I sure think so.

A couple days after the fire, Marie and Johnny were over at Roxy's and they continued to talk about it, and about Frankie.

"I think you do," Johnny said.

"No, you two, I don't."

"Roxy, you literally went into a burning building to save him," Marie added.

"That doesn't mean I'm in love with him. I do love him, but there's a difference. Of course I'd go in to save him. You all would. Just as he did for me," Roxy said.

They were pushing her to fess up, hoping that now since Claire was out of the picture, Frankie would think about telling Roxy how he felt, if only they could work on her a little bit beforehand. However, she refused at all cost to say a thing.

October 2nd, 1925

Dear Diary,

It's been a week since the fire at Claire's. God, what a hell of a day.

How did that even happen? I mean, sure, I always called her a psycho bitch, but I sure as hell didn't mean a LITERAL fire-starting psycho bitch.

Wow. I mean, at the very least, I was right about her all along. More right than I even knew.

And then there's the drugging Frankie to make it look like they were sleeping together … wow. I mean, at the very least, I must say that it was creative. There is one thing though, one thing I must write down before I absolutely go insane. When I saw them together, or, thought I did, I just … I felt sick. All I could think about was how that awful broad had somehow gotten Frankie to sleep with her. I mean, he told me he was waiting until he was ready, until he found the right one, and then he was going to sleep with HER, as if SHE was the right one? I mean, he didn't, but it's what went through my mind as I saw her on top of him. It stirred up some feelings I didn't know I had, and, ugh! Now I'm just—I'm all disoriented. I don't know. Nothing's jake anymore. Everything feels off. Then I've got the whole crew (Frankie excluded) asking me if I'm in love with him all the time. I mean, they've always been this way, but it's different now. I'm starting to, oh God, I don't know … feel different? Have I always felt this way? Did I just not know it before? But think about it, Frankie and I would not be a good couple. I mean we'd be the greatest-looking couple, one of the wealthiest, most exciting couples. We'd sure be one hell of a team, but we'd be terrible together!

There are times when I really don't understand a word of what Roxy means, do you?

Well, for now, things would stay in the rather interesting state they were at. Frankie having realized and confessed his true emotions to the gang (except for Roxy herself, of course), and Roxy having just now begun to let herself feel something *romantic*, something *passionate*, something *sexual* for Frankie. Something she hadn't quite let herself feel before, and it was utterly consuming. For now, I think we'll move on and I'll tell you yet another one of our ever so wild stories.

CHAPTER 27

An Unexpected Turn of Events

I told you I'd eventually explain the Elliott crime family in greater detail, and that time has finally come. I don't believe I've given you the key information yet, and if I have, well cheers to hearing it twice. In order for me to tell you what was next to come for Roxy and her ever so close best friends, I'll need you to know what *exactly* the Elliotts have a hand in when it comes to the mafia—and why it's important. Especially considering the current circumstances with them nearing a takedown by the NYPD (we'll get to that later).

Let's start with the never-ending fancy parties, fancy clothes, fancy houses, and fancy people. After reading everything I've written, I would hope you have a clear understanding about how truly opulent their lives were. It may be all parties and pearls, lipstick and lavish cars—but remember, behind the facade are lies, secrets, and scandals. Each of their homes hold history. The most precious people have the most daunting problems.

Bootlegging is not the only crime committed by the Elliotts; the bootlegging is but a portion of the other crimes committed. They will do anything to protect their name and their family, and that's why they are who they are. They are of the highest of all classes and everyone knows *not* to deal badly with them. The Elliotts do things right—they commit their crimes the "right" way.

The Elliotts are a crime family, part of the mafia, but nonetheless a family who protects and loves (I know that can be hard to understand, as people aren't *usually* inclined to *sympathize* with the mafia). Dennis Elliott is not only some big-time bloodthirsty mobster—he's a family man. A family mobster, *so to speak*. He doesn't go around killing innocent people or harm just anybody in any *random* situation. The Elliotts don't go around taking things or collecting money from people without reason.

That doesn't mean that people aren't in debt with them, because they are. But the Elliotts don't go around killing everyone who owes them something. If they did, they would never get what they were owed—makes sense, right? A mistake *many* mafia families make, but the Elliotts always knew better. They only kill when needed, as in to protect their family. Such as when a person is a threat to others or has committed a wrongdoing against their family or close friends. An example would be the Deckers, when Tommy Elliott had to kill Thomas Decker after he had tried to take down the family for the *hundredth* time. (Now don't get me wrong, I'm not advocating for murder, I am simply trying to explain how the Elliotts don't spill innocent blood. The lives they have each taken have all been far from anything that resembles innocence.)

The Elliotts commit crimes that involve money, alcohol, and tobacco. They operate one of the biggest tobacco and cigarette companies in the word, supplying everyone with a smoke. But it's the way they do it that's illegal: trading money, illegal transactions, hiding money, and bootlegging. The bootlegging is the root of the other crimes. They trade money for alcohol, then alcohol for tobacco. They trade tobacco for alcohol, then alcohol for money (it's one hell of a crime circle, and it's rather confusing if you ask me). The Dakota is one of many fronts for their speakeasies, and the speakeasies are fronts for alcohol and illegal tobacco trade (or trafficking, if that makes more sense). The Elliotts have the most speakeasies in America. Speakeasies owned by the family range from New York City, Boston, Philadelphia, Chicago, and Los Angeles, which I've mentioned before. Not to mention their part in Las Vegas gambling, but that's a much longer explanation—so if you don't know how gambling works, I suggest you look it up.

Marie's father had just come home from a long day at work. If you didn't remember, he was the chief of the NYPD. More recently, he was appointed the New York City Police Commissioner by the mayor. Though the Elliotts had connections with the NYPD and handled their family business well, the mayor was set out to take down New York City's five families, the Elliotts being one of them. The mayor knew of Mr. Romano's close connection with the Elliott family and figured he was the perfect person to conduct an investigation. When Mr. Romano was called into the mayor's office a couple months back, the mayor made it clear that he wanted Mr. Romano to be in charge of this takedown. Marie's father hated this, as Dennis was a close friend to him, but knew it was either take the mayor's orders or he'd be blackmailed in that town.

Something I should also mention, and don't believe I have before, is that Marie's family's wealth comes from her mom's side, not her father's. He's paid well, but it's nothing compared to the annual salaries of our other families. Her mother, however, came from a long line of old money and this is how they lived in such a lavish residence, able to do whatever they pleased at any given moment.

Her father came from a middle-class family and had dreams of entering law enforcement since a young child, and eventually became a cop. After years of hard work he was promoted time and time again, and now he was the head of the NYPD. It's all he knew how to do, and he didn't want to give it up. It was his livelihood, and though theoretically they could all live off of Marie's mother's wealth, Mr. Romano had a bit too much ego and pride to do that. He wanted (needed, even) a career. So, when told he'd have to take down a family he was close to, he was heartbroken. Dennis was his friend; the Elliotts had always been close to the Romanos. This would tarnish their friendship for good, whether or not the takedown was successful or failed. Mr. Romano had a decision he knew he had to make, and unfortunately, that was taking the mayor's orders. This was about two months ago or so. Now, in present day, it was time for him to tell Marie the inner workings of what was soon to happen to her friend's (and his) dear family.

"Honey, I've—I need to speak with you, dear," he said nervously.

"I can't Daddy, I'm busy right now!" Marie responded, finishing an essay on Shakespeare's *Hamlet*.

"Marie, it's important—come downstairs now please."

She left her typewriter and made her way downstairs, annoyed by her father's demands. "What is it?" she said with a harsh tone.

"It's about my job. You know it's a demanding job, Marie, right?"

"Well yes of course, what about it?"

"Sometimes we are—assigned investigations. Ones that we don't like—"

"Where are you going with this, Daddy?" she interrupted him.

"Honey, sit down please," he pleaded.

He told her everything, explaining in great detail how he couldn't risk his career over a friend, even if it killed him to do so. She was furious at first, filled with rage and agony. The Elliotts were like a second family to her; Dennis like a second father, Griffin and Margret like a third set of grandparents. This turn of events was not something she'd *ever* expected from her father. They sat there at the dining table, talking for over an hour about everything and why he had to do it, him trying to talk his way into making it seem necessary.

"But honey, you know, regardless if they are our friends

... they *are* a part of the mafia. They are a crime family, they have murdered. Even if they aren't as violent as the other five families, they are the mafia, Marie, and justice has to be served," he said, though he didn't quite believe himself. Sure, in the grand scheme of things they *technically* did deserve justice; however, that doesn't mean Mr. Romano enjoyed serving it to them.

After their conversation, Marie felt inclined to phone Roxy, explaining in detail what her father had just told her. Roxy didn't believe it. She genuinely assumed Marie was kidding, that she was playing some type of prank on her. But that wasn't the case at all. Roxy and Marie's telephone call was one of heartbreak and pain, though, at the same time, one of intense anger toward the Romano family.

October 23rd, 1925

Dear Diary,

I've just got off of a phone call with Marie ... and learned some rather disturbing news. News that I will run and tell my father as soon as I finish this entry. I've got to write it now, I couldn't wait.

Marie, she ... her father, he's out to get our family. He's been ordered by the mayor to take them down. All of the five families. All of the mob families of New York are at risk as of this very moment. Especially ours. I don't know what to do, but

I'll be going to see Marie in a little bit, to warn her for what's to come.

After Roxy finished writing, she was greeted by Marie once again. This time, however, in person. When Roxy had learned that Marie was in fact telling the truth, and that her family was at risk of a takedown, she went off on Marie. That was when Marie's own thoughts began to change. It seemed as if she had been brainwashed by the conversation with her father—the one where Mr. Romano made an attempt at convincing Marie that the Elliotts deserved the justice they were soon to be served. So now, she brought it upon herself to greet Roxy with a few brash words.

"Oh come on Marie, you know we are more of a refined mafia family—"

"There is no such thing Roxy, the *mafia* is the *mafia*—"

"What the hell is wrong with you, Marie?"

"What, all I'm saying is maybe your family needs to pay."

"Needs to pay? Where is this coming from, Marie?"

"Oh come on, I know you have killed."

"Me? I have not, and you know that—"

"Not yet, but you will."

"And? When I do, it'll be only when necessary—"

All her life, since she learned of the family business, Roxy battled the idea of her family being the mafia. Of her family being gangsters, criminals, *killers*. She didn't know if she'd ever for *sure* go into the dark family business. If she'd become one of them. But here she found herself defending them the best she

329

could. *And she liked it.* Something had changed. This was who she would become, and she knew that.

"Stop saying that Roxy, trying to justify murder."

"You know we have only taken a life when the life was worth taking."

"Roxy—"

"Marie, you need to stop. Whatever this newfound hatred is for our family needs to come to an end. You need to tell your father to call it all off—"

"That's just not going to happen," Marie responded with a raise in her voice.

Roxy went silent as she looked out the window for a solid minute, glancing down at the busy street below her and onto the orange, yellow, and red trees that filled Central Park this time of the year. She thought about what she'd say next, but knew this conversation wasn't going anywhere too pretty.

"Well then Marie, I don't know what to tell you, because the minute you leave here I'll be warning my father and he'll stop it—"

"Roxy that's just it—there *is* no stopping it—"

"You're wrong and you'll see. He'll stop it, they all will."

"It's happening tomorrow. They have all the evidence ready to go, and they're going after every one of the five families tomorrow."

Roxy took another ill moment of silence, then turned back around so she was facing Marie. "Get out—"

"Roxy, please—"

"I said get out!"

As Marie left, Roxy ran to her father's study to warn him. Of course, he already knew, and he was not going to take it upon himself to put out a hit on Mr. Romano, but other members of the Elliott family were. And so were the other four families. Dennis told Roxy he would never directly hurt Mr. Romano because of Marie and his friendship with him, but that he wouldn't stop it either. He couldn't stop what everyone else planned to do. Dennis told her everything the families were planning.

It was one of the other five families that first got word of what was to go down on October 24th of 1925: a mafia takedown. They had only got word of it that morning, and they all came together to devise a plan that would guarantee them freedom. A plan that would ensure all evidence was destroyed. When Dennis told Roxy everything, she ran upstairs to ring Marie, warning her. She told Marie to find her way to the police station where the evidence was held. To take her father's set of keys and make her way into the room where it was all stored. To take every piece of it and burn it. If she did this, the families wouldn't need to carry out their plan, and nobody would need to get hurt. Roxy begged her.

She said no.

"You're making a big mistake."

"The only mistake made was by you when you chose to side with your family over me. You know in your heart this is what needs to be done."

"You're wrong."

"No, you're wrong! Stop and wake up Roxy—you try and

pretend you aren't from the family you are, that they aren't all criminals. You hide behind the lie of 'well they aren't as bad as the other crime families', but the truth is, they may not have killed as many people as the other four, but they have ruined just as many lives, if not more. They are a mafia family, Roxy—*you* are a part of a mafia family, whether you choose to agree with that or not. Every single person in your family has committed some kind of crime, whether it be anything from the nonviolent act of bootlegging to murder. Your mother has killed, your father, your uncles, your aunts. It goes back generations Roxy, they are a crime family, the Elliotts. Everyone knows it. You say that they only kill when it's completely necessary—well honey, that doesn't make it any better. They may not be as violent as the other crime families, but they still have blood on their hands and it's time they are brought to justice. There's nothing I can do—"

"You know what Marie, just stop. And yeah, maybe in the past I tried to make it seem like I didn't come from the violence I do but I'm proud of my family. I'm proud of who we are. We are the most powerful family in New York and I'm sure as hell not ashamed. I'm giving you a way to stop what they're all planning to do, but you're refusing. You're going to regret this. You are the *only* person who could convince your dad to put this to an end, you're the only one who could persuade him, but you wouldn't. So I gave you another way—to destroy the evidence and save us all."

"Save us? You mean save your family?"

"I mean save your father, Marie. I love you but it's out of

my hands, my family and the rest know what he's planning tomorrow and they will take him out if you don't stop it."

"They won't be able to."

"Oh they will, and you know it. If my dad doesn't find out by five tonight that it's been taken care of, then he will be taken care of. And neither of us wants that."

"You're a big talker, you know that Roxy?"

"Marie, this is not the time to go against me, you're one of my closest friends—don't do this."

"It's not me doing it—it's my father, and it's what's right. But I guess you could never understand something like that. But I guess I can't blame you, you're an Elliott," Marie concluded, before hanging up the telephone.

"Marie!" Roxy yelled. "Marie!"

Oh dear.

Roxy knew there was no way Marie was changing her mind after that conversation, but also knew if she went to her in person and pleaded, that maybe she could at least still save her father. Mr. Romano was at the station, but Marie remained at home.

After their phone call ended, Roxy ran out of the Dakota doors and into a car that awaited her. She ended up at Marie's in just a few short minutes.

"Hello Miss Elliott, how are you?" the maid greeted Roxy as she walked through the door.

"Where's Marie?" she asked.

"Oh she just left! I believe she mentioned something about Matthews?"

I guess Marie had a change in thought and decided she'd go over to Frankie's.

She had her own plan.

Marie thought it was a good idea to plead with Frankie; to get him to understand why she couldn't destroy the evidence nor ask her father to call it all off. She assumed that if she could get to Frankie, that he could then be the one to convince Roxy it was the right thing to do, and with that Roxy would then be able to put some kind of hold on whatever the Elliotts and the other four families were planning on doing that brisk October night.

What she didn't know, however, was how there was no chance in hell that was going to happen, for one of two reasons. One being that Frankie would never believe it was the right thing to do—he had loved the mafia scene since he was a child. He'd never agree with a takedown.

The second reason?

Well, this is something I haven't told you yet, but should probably mention. About two weeks before, Dennis had called Frankie into his study while Roxy was out for dinner with Dalton and Marie. He had brought him in, poured him some scotch, and asked him if he wanted to join the Elliott crime family. Frankie, elated and proud, took the offer and within two weeks began to work for the Elliotts.

Roxy didn't know this yet, as Dennis had told Frankie not to tell her for a couple weeks, all to make sure he was mob material (which he was). Now, fast-forward to today, and Marie going over to his place to get him to convince Roxy that a hit on the five families was a good idea—*yeah, that was just not going to happen.*

"Marie! Hey baby—"

"I need to talk to you about something—and it's urgent."

"Yeah, sure, what is it?" he said, worried that something was wrong. "Are you alright? Is everything jake?"

"Actually Frankie, no, I'm not alright. You see, my father, he and the NYPD are planning a takedown on the five families—"

"Yes, I'm aware," answered Frankie. Dennis had told him this earlier that day, telling him to stay put and not to worry— that it was all being taken care of.

"Well are you aware that they are planning some type of retaliation? How the five families are going to do something tonight—something bad. Something I'm worried about. Roxy begged me to have my father call it off, then when I refused, she asked me to destroy the evidence. But ... I can't do that, Frankie. As much as I love Roxy and her family, they are criminals. They are the mafia—"

"Marie, why are you telling me this? What is it that you want me to do?"

"I want you to convince Roxy that this needs to happen. That, regardless if they are her family, they are the mafia and they deserve this."

Frankie stood silent for a quick minute, thinking about his next move. What he should say to her. Obviously he didn't agree with the statement she had just made. Sure, they were criminals, but he was a part of it now and he loved it. Every little bit of it. He didn't care, along with Roxy and just about everyone else in the mafia. They didn't care that they broke the law. In their minds, laws were meant to be broken by people who were sly enough to break them and get away with it. It wasn't just a game; it was a lifestyle. One they all loved.

"Marie, I don't—Marie, it's just not that easy—"

"What's not that easy?"

"Baby, you just don't get it—"

"What Frankie, what do I not get—"

"I'm a part of it now! Okay? Dennis didn't want me talking about it yet but he recruited me a coupla weeks ago. He asked me if I wanted a part in the Elliott family business. I told him yes, of course yes. I always have. And I'm not sorry either. I don't care if it makes you suddenly hate me—I don't give a damn because I love it and I'm good at it. And honestly, I don't understand where any of this is coming from. The Elliotts have always been like a second family to you and now you turn your back on them? For your father? Because he said so? What the hell Marie," he said as his front door slammed shut.

Roxy was standing there, angered, right up against the door. "My father did what?" she said.

"Roxy! Darling, I—"

"He offered you a place in the mafia? And you didn't tell me?"

"He asked me not to. Just in the beginning—"

"I don't give a damn! My God Frankie, how could you not tell me—" she said, angered with both her father and Frankie for keeping this secret from her. Of course she loved the idea of him in the family business, but the not telling her made Roxy furious.

"Wow, I genuinely cannot believe you two. So proud to be

a part of something so evil—" Marie said, interrupting Roxy.

"Evil? Are you kidding me right now, Marie?"

"Yes, Roxy, *evil*. But you don't care do you, because all you care about is the glamorous lifestyle it brings you. The wealth, the power, that's all you care about. You don't give a damn that your entire life is built on crime and—"

The night was creeping closer as the sky darkened. Roxy was running out of time to save Marie's father. "Marie, I suggest you quit it with this sudden spark of morality and listen to me. They're taking him down, okay? And it's happening soon—"

"What's happening—what are they really going to do?"

"They've all decided on taking the station. All of the five families, with the Elliotts included. It's happening tonight, and it's happening soon. They're going to do it before anyone leaves, before their shifts are over. And that includes your father."

"For the record—I don't actually know what's happening. Dennis just told me it would be 'taken care of' so Marie, don't go yelling at me," Frankie made them aware.

"Marie, are you listening?" Roxy said, ignoring Frankie's comment. "Everyone's going to die. If your dad doesn't burn the evidence right now, it'll be burned—"

"What do you mean?" she cut Roxy off.

"They're lighting the place up in flames. They have people that are going soon to set little fires all over the building. It's going to be terrible, Marie—just *terrible*."

"Roxy, you can't," Marie said.

"What do you mean 'you'? I'm not in control of it. I can't stop it, are you kidding me?"

"It's your family."

"It's not just my family, it's all five families. Are you even listening to me?" she began to yell.

Frankie sat down and continued to listen to everything going on before making a call himself. A call to the don of the Elliott family, Mr. Dennis himself.

"You know, when we were kids and I found out about your family, you promised me they weren't like the other four. You said that they didn't harm the innocent. Somehow I believed it. What a fool I was," said Marie.

"Marie—"

"Roxy Elliott, the spawn of a mother with secrets and a father born into the mafia—"

"That's enough Marie, I'm trying to help YOU—"

"A family of crime, murder, and scandals—"

"Marie, all I can say is I hope your father ends up in heaven. You are clearly not going to take this into your own lousy hands so I'd phone him and tell him to get out of the building. And if not, I'd tell him you love him—"

"Go to hell," Marie said with a sinister tone, as she grabbed her handbag and walked out the door.

She could have made the call from one of Frankie's telephones, telling her father to get out of the building, but she knew deep down if she told him, that he'd still stay. That he wouldn't abandon his officers, and it would take too long to get everyone in the building aware of the threat and out of harm's way. That fact hurt her, but it was the truth. And if she had made up some lousy story on why he needed to come home immediately, he'd never buy it. Marie was a terrible liar and her father was a master at spotting a lie—so that was just not going to happen, and she was out of options.

Marie left Frankie's as the sky went from a midnight blue to an eerie black. A sky so dark that the smoke was hard to see. Yet there it was, a station on fire. Another building up in flames. What is it with all these fires so suddenly? The five families also made sure that the fire trucks wouldn't be able to make it to the station in time to salvage anything. They needed to be certain that all evidence was burned to the ground. And sadly, along with that, came many innocent lives. None that had connections to the mob, however—they were all warned and taken care of. I mean, where would the mafia be without corrupt cops anyways? The fire was made to look like an accident, so that there would be no trace back to anyone. And boy were they successful.

Marie made it home in a panic. "Where's dad?" she asked her mom.

"I don't know, he should be home soon," Mrs. Romano responded. She hadn't gotten word of the fire yet.

Earlier, when Marie and Roxy were having their little argument in Frankie's living room, he made a call to Dennis. He told Dennis that Roxy would be unsuccessful and if he didn't do anything, Mr. Romano would burn in the fire along with the evidence and the rest of the cops set out to take down the five families. As angry as Dennis himself was with his old friend, he wasn't going to let him die. Before the fires were set, he had someone handle him.

What do I mean by that exactly?

Well, Dennis couldn't ring Mr. Romano and tell him what they were planning and to get out of there. That would have compromised the whole mission. So, instead, he sent someone to snag him when he was alone, drug him, and get him out of there. And they were successful. With *everything*.

Mr. Romano lived and the station burned and burned until all evidence was lost in a fiery abyss. The five families were no longer in the red and Roxy and Marie would eventually make up and become best friends again. However, it did take a while for them to return to normalcy. After everything Marie had said to Roxy about her and her family, Roxy was ready to drop her. How could you be friends with someone who suddenly thought so ill of your family and their way of living?

In time (around three weeks), however, they made up.

Marie came to her senses and took back everything she had said. She apologized for turning on Roxy and the Elliotts and blamed it on what her father had said about them. Marie told Roxy that she didn't want to go on like that, and how she needed her dear best friend back in her life. She told her that she loved the Elliotts and that she'd never betray them again.

Oh, don't you just love a good best friend makeup? Because let's face it, best friend breakups are the worst. Marie and Roxy had been the best of friends since age four, and to end something like that would be devistating.

You can always find a new lover, but best friends aren't as easily replaced.

CHAPTER 28

THE SCANDALS NEVER END

When I told you there'd be scandal, I really wasn't lying.

"Hey, Elliott, I'd watch your back from now on—" Raymond Decker said to Roxy in the hall.

Oh, *I'm sorry*, I haven't introduced him yet … have I?

Raymond Decker, also known as Ray, is another member of the wonderful Decker family. One who is in the same class as Roxy and her friends.

They've always hated each other, deeply, and often make snarky remarks in the hallways during school. Lately, the Elliott–Decker feud has been growing in tension, and therefore the arguments and brash comments between Roxy and Ray have done the same.

"Decker, if you think for one minute that you'd ever be able to take aim at me, you're sadly mistaken," Roxy responded with utter confidence.

Ray Decker is the grandson of the now dead Thomas Decker. Thomas, of course, is the father of Kenneth Decker—but he had a few other kids as well. His other kid's names were Lawrence, Nancy, and Marshall. Raymond was the son of Marshall and Regina Decker. Helen and Julia Decker are the children of Nancy, though they took their mother's maiden name of Decker. Which of course made Ray cousins with Julia and Helen, and the nephew of Kenneth. I haven't brought Thomas Decker's other children up because they weren't vital to the story I was telling at the time. Just like I don't tell you every detail about every one of the Elliott family members. Let's just say this … both families are large, and if I were to give you a rundown of each and every member and their spouses, we'd never get to the stories themselves.

"Honey, you don't even know what we're planning, alright? And you won't know till it's too late—"

"Hey hey hey, what's going on over here?" Frankie said as he joined the conversation.

"Oh look, it's Matthews coming to the rescue—"

"I don't need rescuing, Ray," Roxy responded with heat.

"All I'm saying is that you guys are going to be in real trouble soon, so I'd be extra careful."

"I really don't think you ought to be talking. The Deckers have never been successful against the Elliotts—" Frankie began to say.

Roxy continued, "And you never will be."

Ray took a moment, staring down Roxy as she stared back, before glancing over at Frankie, responding with, "You know, Frankie, I find it kind of funny you've joined the Elliott crime family. You've got a lot more in common with me than them—"

"Excuse me?" Frankie said.

"Both you and Johnny, actually."

"What's this nonsense about?" Frankie said as he stepped closer to Ray, now up close in his face.

"Why don't you ask your mom," Ray responded with a smirk. "Goodbye Roxy. Have a *wonderful* day," he said before the bell rang and he made his way to class.

"What was that all about?" Roxy asked.

"I've got no idea. Let's just get to class," Frankie said as he took Roxy's books out of her locker before she closed it, then carried them for her as they made their way to seventh period.

Frankie sat right next to Johnny in the back of the class.

"Why so tense?" Johnny whispered to him as they were taking a test on the Revolutionary War. "Test too hard?" he asked.

"No, nothing like that," Frankie responded.

"What then?"

"It's nothing, I said—" Frankie answered before being interrupted by the teacher.

"Boys, is there something you'd like to share with the class?" she said.

"No, Mrs. Nelson," they said simultaneously as Roxy looked over to Frankie and gave him a confused look.

After school Frankie went home alone, pondering about

what Ray Decker had said to him. What did he mean by "you've got a lot more in common with me than them"? What *exactly* did that mean? He had an idea, of course, as I'm sure you do as well. However, could that *really* be the case? I mean, not *another* case of lying parents ... right? It's quite the never-ending cliché, isn't it?

While Frankie was figuring out how he'd approach his mother on the topic, Roxy told her father about what Ray had said to them in the hallway. About how the Deckers were once again planning something, and about his comment toward Frankie and Johnny. Dennis didn't know anything about it (surprisingly) but knew he'd better find out soon before it ended in yet another colossal Manhattan scandal.

CHAPTER 29

A DECKER FAMILY REUNION

Tensions continued to rise between the Deckers and the Elliotts. Dennis was trying to find a way to figure out what exactly the Deckers had planned this time, and if it was something he needed to worry about.

As for Frankie, he had been cold and drunk the past few days, trying to hide the fact that his emotions had decided to ride a rollercoaster of angst and sorrow; a quite interesting combination.

He knew what Ray meant, but he wasn't going to accept it yet. He didn't want to imagine a world where his mother had been lying to him his whole life. Kind of like how Roxy didn't want to accept the fact that she had been lied to either. But in time, both would learn to navigate their new identities. It's not like they had a choice in the matter.

A few days after the Raymond Decker situation, Frankie's father (Clayton Matthews) left for Boston on a business trip. Frankie decided this was the best time to approach his mother on the subject. He knew that if his father was around, all hell would break loose. I haven't ever really gone into much detail on it, but Frankie's father was abusive. Not to his mother, *but to him.*

On the outside, they looked like the perfect Matthews family New York knew them as, but once they entered the Matthews townhome walls, Clayton was quite the different man. He himself had self-esteem issues and an ego too large for him to handle. Because of that, he always had a weird jealousy over his son, and therefore he wanted to make him suffer like he had when he was a child. Clayton Matthews's father had been abusive, and as many times it goes, the apple didn't fall far from the tree. However, don't worry, Frankie would never grow up to be abusive like his father and grandfather were. Anyways, Clayton Matthews was hard on Frankie both emotionally *and* physically. Though, he never usually hit the face or anywhere that could publicly be seen. Whenever Clayton felt the need to hit Frankie, it was usually a hard and nauseous punch in the stomach. He knew he could never give Frankie a black eye, because if he did, everyone would begin to speculate and that would ruin their facade.

Frankie's father also had a slight tendency to veer toward the alcoholic side of life. He wasn't one of those terrible drunk-all-the-time fathers, but when he was drunk, he was certainly harder to handle. Frankie always kept this to himself, however.

Absolutely no one knew of what went down at home. Not even his closest friends, not even Roxy. Which was surprising, considering our special six usually shared *everything* with each other. But Frankie never wanted to seem as if he had "daddy issues", so to speak; he didn't want anyone to know that his father was far from kind, that he dealt with this evil on a daily basis. He couldn't let anyone know this, because if they did, they would have something over him (or at least that's the way he thought). He was seen as this perfect bad boy. The best-looking guy in school, he was careless and free and did whatever he wanted, because he could. Frankie couldn't let word get out that he wasn't so perfect after all. He'd no longer be from the pristine Matthews family.

From the outside, everyone saw Frankie, his mother, and his father as *wealth* and pure *perfection*. And, while they sure as hell had the wealth, they were miles away from perfect.

People always assumed that his parents had this perfect and soulmate-style marriage—yet the truth was quite the opposite. While Clayton never hit his wife, they fought all the time. Frankie's mother was a strong woman, and anytime Clayton abused Frankie (both emotionally and physically) it of course stirred up tensions between the not so happy couple.

Why didn't Frankie's mother leave his father, you may ask? Well, it's simple: she didn't want to. Even if he was awful to Frankie, she still had some type of love for the man. And Frankie had a love for his father too.

Another reason for her staying, that is *quite* important, is that a divorce screams "trouble in paradise", and she didn't want to be known as the Upper West Side divorcée. She wanted to keep up the perfect family she had created. She didn't want the rumors going around like they always did when an elite Manhattan marriage broke up. Anyways, now you have a little more information on Frankie's background. I could have told you this sooner, but it wasn't ever necessary to the stories I was telling. So, there you go. Now you know the other side to the Matthews family. *The dark side.*

Frankie's mother was out with a friend for cocktails at the Cotton Club when he took it upon himself to do some research. He went into his mother's closet, searching for whatever he could find that would get him answers. As he stepped over a certain sensitive spot, he realized that the floorboard was a bit different, so he got down to inspect it and discovered it was an open floorboard.

You know, the kind you have when you want to hide something? Something vitally important that if found could lead to catastrophic emotions and events?

Yes, well, it seems as if Mrs. Matthews had one of those hidden in her closet—a place where only she ever went.

Frankie opened it up and found an old white box that had taken quite the beating over the years. He opened the frayed box and found a few of his mother's old diaries.

Now, most of the time, children aren't exactly interested in reading their parents' diaries—it's usually the other way around—but in this instance Frankie knew it had to be done.

He opened up the diary labeled 1907, the year he was born.

Oh, and by the way, he had turned eighteen a few weeks

ago on October 15th, and as per usual they had a grand party and a great time, but nothing extra special happened so I didn't bother to bring it up.

Anyways, Frankie opened up his mother's diary and searched for answers under the "January" entries, and sure enough, it was all there. The answer he had been searching for these past few days. An answer he never wanted to know, but couldn't abandon now.

He teared up a little, which wasn't like Frankie at all … but this was quite the situation. He then tore the page out of the diary and placed it in his pocket before returning the journal back to the box, then the box back under the floorboard just as it was before. He shut off the light and left his parents' bedroom before phoning Dennis.

"Hello, this is the Elliott residence," one of the Russian butlers said as he picked up the phone.

"This is Frankie, Frankie Matthews, and I need to speak to Dennis," he responded frantically.

"Hello Mr. Matthews. Dennis is not here."

"Well where is he?"

"I believe he said something about heading to the club."

"Which one? Is he down in the Dakota speakeasy?"

"No, I believe he is at the Elliott club on East 57th between Madison and Park," he said.

"Perfect, thank you."

"Of course, Mr. Matthews. Have a fine day."

"You as well," he said before hanging up the phone, grabbing his hat and coat and heading out the door.

He hailed a taxicab, as his driver was sick that day, and headed to one of the other Elliott speakeasies, the one on East 57th between Madison and Park.

This one was slightly smaller than the one they had underneath The Dakota, but it was just as opulent.

When he arrived at the laundromat he signaled the guy behind the desk, who let him through the door in the back, then down the dark stairs. Frankie arrived at a shiny black door where a man on the other side slid open a tiny window, saw that it was a Matthews boy, and let him in. It was the middle of the day and there wasn't a lot of action going on. A few Wall Street sharks taking a break from the craziness downtown, a few paid-off police officers, and of course, many mobsters.

Frankie looked around for Mr. Elliott but he couldn't find him. He walked over to the bar, sat his hat down, and asked for an Old Fashioned. After receiving his drink, he took it with him to the private room where many poker games were held. He figured that if Dennis was still there at the club, he'd probably be in there with his fellow gangsters. The door was guarded by two men decorated with guns, but they of course let him in. He *was* officially a member of the Elliott crime family, after all.

"Frankie! What brings you here?" Dennis asked as Frankie entered the private room.

"I need to speak with you sir, now," he said.

Dennis nodded off the other guys and they cleared the room, leaving only Dennis and Frankie. Ready for a rather heavy conversation.

"Did you know?" Frankie asked.

"Did I know what?"

"About me," he responded with a concerned face.

Dennis took a moment to pause before saying, "A few days ago, Roxy came home telling me what Raymond Decker had said to you, and of course I then assumed. But I didn't know. And I never knew before that. These past few days I've been trying to get answers myself, but always came up empty—"

Frankie interrupted him. "Here, read this," he said as he pulled the paper out of his pocket and handed it over to Dennis, before lighting a cigarette and lying back deep into his velvet chair.

Dennis read it, then read it again, and then again for the third time before looking up at Frankie. "Alright then. Well, that's that," he said to Frankie's surprise.

"That's that? What do you mean 'that's that'?"

"I mean exactly that. It doesn't change anything, alright?"

"I'm a Decker and you don't care?"

"Frankie, listen here," he said as he finished off his bourbon, "this is disturbing news, I'm not gonna lie, but while you may be a Decker by blood, you are certainly *not* a Decker. Your mother's indiscretions are a surprise to me, but they don't change things between you and me, or you and the family. You are a Matthews, and you'll always be one. And you are one of us now, and that you'll always be as well."

Frankie took a moment to comprehend what had just been said to him. He had assumed that Dennis would flip, that he'd be banned from the family. That he'd no longer be in service to them. He was utterly shocked.

"Mr. Elliott, sir, are you sure?"

Dennis laughed. "Are you kidding me? Frankie, does your mother know you took this?"

"No, she's out with a friend at the Cotton Club. I found this in one of her diaries in—"

"The floorboard of her closet, in a white box?"

"How ... how did you know?"

"Well don't forget Frankie, your mother and I have been good friends for a while now. She told Caroline and I about it years ago," Dennis said.

"And why didn't you just look there then? Why not send a few of your men to retrieve them in order to find out?"

"I would never do such a thing. As much as I wanted to know, I'd never invade her privacy."

Frankie smiled. "Of course not."

"But I'm glad you did," Dennis laughed. "Are you going to approach her?"

"I'm not sure yet. Also, would you do me a favor?" he asked.

"That depends on the favor."

"Would you not tell Roxy? Please? I'll tell her, I promise, but just not yet."

"Of course."

Frankie drank the last of his cocktail while he and Dennis continued to talk about the new and sudden news, before he left the club. It was Saturday, November 7th, and Frankie knew before Monday at school that he'd have to tell Roxy. He couldn't lie to her face, but if he avoided her all weekend, he wouldn't need to tell her.

After leaving the club, he met Johnny in the park. He told him everything. How his mother had lied to him his whole life. How, only weeks before her marriage to Clayton Matthews, she was secretly in love with one Lawrence Decker. So yes, Frankie is *actually* a Decker by blood. **Yet again, how Romeo and Juliet;** Roxy being an Elliott and Frankie now a Decker. Although, their ending won't be *quite* the same. Anyways, Frankie's mother knew she couldn't be in love with a Decker, or ever be seen with him publicly. She knew that, because of her close friendship with the Elliott family, there was no way in hell she could marry the young Decker.

While she was secretly with Lawrence, she had been dating Clayton Matthews, another good friend of the Elliotts. After finding out she was pregnant, and knowing it was by Lawrence and not Clayton, she cut all ties with him and married Clayton, lying to the world about the truth behind Frankie's real father. Clayton never knew, and he never thought for a second that Frankie wasn't his. Both Clayton and Lawrence had similar features, so there wasn't ever any reason for doubt.

Frankie's mom had been living this lie now for eighteen years, something that weighed down on her every single day.

However, there was still one other question floating in the air: Raymond Decker mentioned that both Frankie *and* Johnny had something in common with him.

How could that be? Well, it seems that way back in 1907 when Lawrence had been involved with Frankie's mom, he was also secretly involved with another one of the Elliott family's close friends: Lillian. Yes, Lillie … as in Johnny's mom. And their situation was quite the same as that of Lawrence and Frankie's mom.

Lillie knew that she couldn't be with a Decker due to her ties with the Elliott family, so she ended it and married Allen Davis, despite getting pregnant by Lawrence (how the hell did they both manage to get themselves into such a scandal?). Lawrence knew of the pregnancies and knew both Frankie and Johnny were his, but didn't do much about it because—frankly—he didn't care. He had been sleeping with two women around the same time, getting them pregnant just for both of them to cut their secret ties with him. If the world found out, it wouldn't just make for a grand scandal for the Matthews, Davis, and Elliott families—it would also be one for the Decker family, and they didn't want that. The majority of the Deckers found out about the scandal years after it all went down, but again, kept it a secret. This whole situation is quite the doozy, making Johnny *Decker blood* as well. Meaning that Frankie and Johnny are half-brothers, and first cousins to Raymond Decker. Guess Ray was right, they *do* have more in common with him than the Elliotts.

However, don't fret—Johnny didn't care one bit about being a Decker. It didn't change a thing for him and once he found out from his mother, they never really spoke of it again. Also, his father never found out. He was a good man and this would most likely ruin him. He wouldn't want to leave Lillie because he loved her so deeply, yet at the same time, their marriage would never be the same. I mean, how could it?

So, while Johnny, the Deckers, and all of his close friends knew—it wouldn't become public scandal. As for Frankie, he hated the fact that he was a Decker—for now at least, and his father hadn't found out yet. He told Roxy after school on Monday, then the rest of the crew that night at Johnny's, when they both fessed up.

In the days that followed, tensions continued to rise and rise. On Tuesday, Johnny, Frankie, and Raymond had a little conversation about everything, where they made Raymond promise to not spread the news to the rest of the school.

"Don't you think if I was gonna tell everyone, I already would've? Jeez, you're not that special. And also, the Deckers don't need a scandal either, alright?" Raymond said as Frankie held him up against the wall by his shirt.

Frankie let him down.

"Alright then. We're done here," Johnny said before walking away.

Frankie began to follow before Raymond whispered, "Hey, hold on."

"What do you want, Ray?" he responded.

"We need to talk, just us," Ray said.

Johnny looked back at Frankie. "It's alright, I'll catch you later," Frankie said.

"What do you want Ray, seriously?" Frankie protested.

"Oh come on cousin, just to talk," he said. "Whether or not you accept it, you're a Decker. Yet you're working for the Elliotts—"

"And?"

"And ... come on! You're on the wrong side—"

"No Ray, I don't believe I am."

"I'm just saying, think about it. You could join us, be a part of us. Your blood. My uncle Lawrence, your father, he'd be for it. The world doesn't have to know you're our blood, all they'll think is that you crossed over to a different crime family. That's all. We think you'd fit well in our family."

"You're crazy."

"Just think about it. Here," Raymond said as he wrote down his telephone number, "when you're ready, ring this number. We'll be waiting for you."

Frankie took the number and put it in his pocket before leaving their little talk. He went home and rang Dennis, having a long and quite interesting conversation with him.

Friday came and Frankie had made his decision: *to join his true family.*

Shocking, you may say? I thought so too, but bear with me through this rather odd time.

"Frankie, get over here," Johnny said as he passed Frankie in the hallway before lunch.

"Yeah?"

"We need to talk—"

"Alright alright, I know what you're thinking, but it ain't that bad really—"

"It ain't that bad? You kiddin' me? I'm just as much Decker as you Frankie, and you don't see me selling out my soul to them."

"Johnny, it's really not like that—"

"What are the others gonna say? What's Roxy gonna say? How do you think Dennis and Griffin are gonna take this?"

"Just give me a few weeks and you'll understand why I did it—"

"No, Frankie, I won't. None of us will. This is an act of betrayal, and when the others find out about it, they're gonna want nothing to do with you."

"Excuse me?"

"Don't bother coming to lunch with us today, alright? Go sit with Ray and his little possie."

"Johnny—" Frankie pleaded.

"I'm done, Frankie," Johnny said in a disappointed tone.

Johnny walked away with anger in his heart as he headed toward the rest of the gang. They all decided they'd go out for lunch.

"Where's Frankie?" Virginia asked.

"He uh, he told me he didn't wanna go out," Johnny responded. "Roxy, I need to speak to you for a second."

"What's so important that you can't tell the rest of us?" Marie asked, confused. They never kept secrets from each other (besides the one about Frankie being in love with Roxy, of course) and they never stole each other away for private conversations.

"It's not—okay, fine. Do you all know about Frankie?"

"What about him?" Dalton said.

"About the offer ..."

They all looked a bit confused.

"The offer from the Deckers, asking him to leave the Elliott crime family and join theirs? Since he's now their blood and all? Well, us both, but yeah."

"Well of course, but never in a million years would he even consider it," Roxy said with confidence.

Johnny stood silent for a second before saying, "That's not exactly true."

Roxy's eyes bulged out of her head and her face went pale, almost lifeless. "What are you talking about, Johnny?" she said, concerned.

After lunch, Roxy didn't return to school that day.

She went straight home, hoping to find her father, but he was over at his brother Clyde's. She then made her way there, barging her way into Uncle Clyde's study where she found him, her Aunt Elizabeth, Tommy, Griffin, Margret, and of course, her father.

"Baby! Why aren't you in school? Did they let you out early?" he asked.

"No Daddy, I left," Roxy said as her cousin Tommy laughed.

"As in, ditched?" Tommy said.

"I had to. I need to speak to you. All of you."

"Yes, honey?" Grandma Margret said.

"It's about Frankie. I heard from Johnny that he took the offer. That he left us and joined the Deckers. It's got to be a joke, a complete lie. There's no way in hell he'd ever do that. Johnny must be a damn fool, right?"

They all shared a look. "No, Roxy, I'm afraid it's true," Aunt Elizabeth said.

Roxy's heart sank so deep into her chest it felt as if a 3,000-pound weight had just hit her.

"I know you feel betrayed, we do too, but just—" Dennis

began to say, before being cut off by his heartbroken Roxy.

"Just what? Look past it? How could you ever say that?"

"I mean just give it time—"

"How could you possibly say that? He betrayed not only you but the whole damn family. You should be furious," Roxy said with utter rage as she stormed out of the study and back out onto the streets of New York. She had one of her handguns strapped to her leg. She had taken it after leaving school. Roxy didn't usually travel with a gun, but this was a unique situation, and with Ray acting like they were planning something against the Elliotts, she needed protection. As for the majority of the other family members, they of course always carried a gun (or two or three) with them at all times. Roxy had first learned how to shoot at ten years old. Her father wanted her to know how to protect herself, but now, at almost eighteen, and given growing tensions with the Decker family … it was time to strap that baby to the inside of her leg.

The day went on and the night grew near. It was Friday, November 13th. As the sky went from a light blue to a mix of purple and mauve, Roxy was headed toward Frankie's for a talk. She was walking the streets in rage when she spotted Frankie and Raymond out of the corner of her eye. They were on West 70th between Central Park West and Columbus Avenue.

"Frankie!" Roxy yelled as he turned around.

Stunned, Frankie responded with, "Roxy! Hello, darling."

"We need to talk," Roxy said in a stern and concerning voice.

"Walk away Elliott, he's one of us now," Ray said.

"Come back. It'll be fine, we'll forgive you. My father, everyone, we'll all forgive you. Just come back Frankie, walk away. Come with me," she said, ignoring Ray's comment.

"Roxy, baby, I—I just can't do that," he responded.

"Told ya. Like I said, he's with us, he's one of us now. He's found his home—" the smiling Ray began to say, testing Roxy, hoping to pull a reaction.

Roxy pulled out the gun and pointed it at the unarmed young Decker. "Shut your mouth Decker, this doesn't concern you."

"Roxy!" Frankie said. "Put the gun down, okay? I think you should put it down."

"I don't give a damn what you think."

"It's just not a good idea, alright? Take my advice, you won't want to kill him."

Roxy glared back at the boy who had betrayed her. "I don't take advice from men. Or should I say boys? Because you're nothing close to a man."

"Roxy, I know you're angry—" Frankie said.

"No, she's got a point. We're not quite men yet. But we will be. Frankie certainly will be soon. I mean, he's got his first task tonight to prove his allegiance to the Deckers. He'll be taking out Harold Wright," Ray said.

"Excuse me?" Roxy said to Frankie.

"I told you, he's one of us now—"

"Ray, I said shut it—"

"Or what? You'll pull the trigger? Little Miss Princess Elliott—"

"Raymond," Frankie said in a stern and masculine voice, unhappy with the way Ray was speaking to Roxy.

"What? She won't do it," he said, "or will you? Come on then, show those true Elliott colors. Pull the trigger, let the bullet fly into my chest," he laughed. "You'd never kill me."

"You're right, I wouldn't kill you. Not yet at least," she said to Ray before looking back over at Frankie. "Come on, let's go. Come with me," she pleaded.

"He's not coming, God don't you listen?" Ray said.

Two shots fired out of her pistol.

"MY GOD ROXY!" yelled Ray as he dropped to the ground.

"Roxy!" Frankie said, both shocked and impressed by what Roxy had done.

"I said I wouldn't kill you. I never said I wouldn't *wound* you," she said as she looked away from the two bullets in his leg and back at Frankie. "Goodbye Frankie."

"Wait, wait!" Frankie said as she was walking away.

"Frankie, you gotta help me," said a whimpering Ray as the blood continued to seep through his white pants, dripping all down his leg.

Frankie took one last glance at Roxy as she faded into the street before turning back and helping his cousin up. Later on that evening, Frankie did as Ray said he would, and made his first kill. He hadn't even killed for the Elliotts yet, but there he was. Late at night in some back alley, throwing a somewhat innocent man into a trunk, later to put a bullet through his head.

Blood on his hands. *Decker blood.*

CHAPTER 30

A BLOODY BETRAYAL

Saturday morning came and Frankie didn't know what to do. He knew he needed to speak with Roxy, to plead with her not to let him go, but he didn't know how to go about it. He didn't even know if she'd ever speak to him again. I mean, he *had* decided to join the crime family of their rival, after all. Being related to them wasn't ever going to be an issue. No one cared about that. Just as Johnny was related to them. The difference is—Johnny rebuked the thought of ever being a part of anything they were involved with. He wanted no ties to them whatsoever. Frankie, on the other hand, chose to go about the darker side—and how shocking that was. I mean, I sure as hell wouldn't have ever imagined the new Elliott mob member turning away from the family he loved so dearly in such an act of true betrayal. The Deckers? He joined them?

Frankie *really* pledged allegiance to them? Trust me, I'm in just as much disbelief as you.

Roxy knew that she needed to talk to Frankie alone, so she decided she'd go over to his place while it seemed empty, hoping he'd be there.

He was.

She knocked on his door and he answered it immediately, pleasantly surprised to see her. Frankie hadn't expected her to come over, or to ever see him again. This was a good sign.

"We need to talk," she said, gruff.

"I know," he responded.

They began the conversation, and it was just as you would have imagined it.

It started off in a heated manner with Roxy yelling at Frankie and condemning him for what he had done, expressing the sad but furious emotions she had for him. This went on for a solid twenty minutes. He didn't really get much in during that time; it was mostly her going off on him, all before things began to take a turn.

"Please—don't say goodbye to me forever," he begged.

"I already have." And after staring him in the eye for a few seconds, then looking him up and down, she walked away. She was no longer crying—she had wiped away the tears from her damp face, though he had been holding back tears for a while.

As she walked away from him, he began to lose it. "Don't walk away. Elliott!" he yelled as she made her way toward the door. "Scarlett!" he said under his breath.

He couldn't lose her—he felt broken without her. She was

the brightest light in his life, and when that light went out, he felt as if he had nothing to live for.

She turned around, realizing that there was more to say before she officially said goodbye.

"You know what this family is to us. It's not just some stupid rivalry over business or mob deals, they've shed our family's blood just as we have shed theirs. They've killed our own, Frankie, and you go and become a part of that?"

"They are my family."

"We were your family. You betrayed the family Frankie, you betrayed me—"

"Stop, Roxy, please—"

"You went too far Frankie, and I'm done. Goodbye Matthews. Or should I start referring to you as Decker?"

"Roxy … Roxy!" he exclaimed with agony. "Roxy, I love you. I love you Roxy, don't go, you can't go—"

"Don't do this," she said.

"You know it's true. You know I love you. You know that I'm in love with you. You're all I've ever wanted, love, please—"

"Stop it I said!" She slapped him across the face with force.

He took a pause, then responded with, "I realized it when you left for Paris. I was heartbroken, burying my pain into my relationship with Claire."

"I've had enough, Frankie—"

"Just give me a few days Roxy, that's all I ask for. You know I love you, I—"

"Frankie, STOP," she said, still withholding a cry. "I don't care."

"You don't mean that," he said, tears falling out of his ocean blue eyes.

"I do actually."

"Roxy, you know we are perfect for each other. You know just as well as I do that in the end it's always going to be us."

"No Frankie, I don't. I love you, but I don't want you."

"Don't say that. Roxy I love you, and that isn't easy for me to say to a girl, and you know that. I love every single part of you, so much so that you have no idea what all of this is doing to me. Seeing you so upset with me. You are always on my mind, love. Twenty-four hours a day, seven days a week, 365 days a year. Please Roxy, let me in. Just tell me you love me."

She paused in a still and miserable moment, searching her heart. *Trying*, to search her heart.

"We'd be a terrible couple. We'd fight all the time. And you'd be a terrible boyfriend, a terrible lover."

"You don't mean that."

"I do. I don't love you like that, Frankie. I don't."

"Roxy—"

"I love you, I love you dearly," she was tearing up again, "but I don't love you romantically. I never did. I care about our friendship but I don't ever want a relationship. It's not what I want with you, it's not what we are meant to be. But if I'm being honest Frankie, none of that matters now."

That was a lie.

"Roxy, please—"

"Because I don't want anything with you anymore. I don't want a friendship, I don't want to love you. I don't want to ever hear the betrayal in your voice or see the lies upon your face," she said as she turned around, walking toward the door once again.

They were both shattered souls guarded by secrets and scandal, their hearts full of love but afraid of being broken again and again. Yet, in this moment, Frankie knew he had nothing to lose. He was already as broken as he could be.

His heart was shattered. Torn up and shredded to pieces.

He ran after her, beating her to the door, placing his back up against it, grabbing her arm gently. "You know you don't mean that."

She took his hand off of her with force. "You can only have so many mansions, so many maids and butlers, chandeliers and fancy furniture, cars, so much alcohol, so many dresses and jewelry, pearls and diamonds, shoes, you can only have so many *things* before it all washes away as meaningless vanity. People seem to think it all brings colossal joy, but only the fools of the world are the ones who think that. It's the intelligent that know true happiness only comes from love. And not the love of material, but the love of people, and the love by people. I love a lot of people in the world, but I don't believe as many love me. Sure, my family and my close friends love me, but the rest of Manhattan? They only love the idea of me, they love my wealth and my family's power. They love my glamour and the allure that comes from the pearls that dangle down from my neck. They don't love the person I am or the way I talk, they don't love my compassion. Now, the thing that tears your joy away the deepest is when you lose this love, when you can no longer love that person. Or when they no longer love you. Why am I telling you this, Frankie? Well, because the joy I get from you is colossal. The way I love you and you love me back, you're one of the few people that I love the most. Though I've been hurt, real terribly, by my mother the most—today you beat her. You stripped my joy away like no other."

He stood there—silent—with no words to explain himself.

"You have no idea how much I love you," he said, staring deeply into her golden eyes.

"And you have no idea how much I love *you*, Frankie. But you've taken that all away. You've ruined it. Goodbye Frankie," she concluded, before moving him away from the door, leaving the broken Frankie behind.

That day was one they would always look back on. A day where both of them felt empty, alone, and brokenhearted.

Frankie had kept the diary page in his pocket all week, but decided to take it out and place it on his desk in his room.

He left and went over to Johnny's, but Johnny wanted nothing to do with him for the time being. Then he went over to Dalton's, but received the same. He then tried Marie and then Virginia, but every single one of his once great friends had abandoned him. He had crossed a line he knew he'd never recover from.

At least … not yet, anyway.

After a long day of abandonment and sorrow, Frankie made it back home, where his father was waiting for him with a fist of fury. His mother was out with a friend, and it was around seven at night.

"Boy, you better get in here," Clayton Matthews said to his son as he walked through the door.

Frankie walked into the living room, where he found his father with a piece of paper in his hand. A very important piece of paper. Clayton had found it after going into Frankie's room, looking for him, asking what he wanted for dinner since his mom was out and wouldn't be cooking that night. He saw it on the desk, and of course, read it.

What is it with Frankie leaving important documents out for the world to find?

Frankie's heart sank deep into his chest. "Dad—"

"What is this?"

"Father please, don't get mad, it's—"

"You're a Decker? A filthy little Decker? You aren't even Matthews blood? How long have you known, son?"

"I only found out this week, but please, don't be angry with Mom."

What Frankie didn't know is, while Clayton was of course angry with Frankie's mom, he would take it out on Frankie. It was still his son that was the product of his wife and a Decker's love affair.

"Get over here."

"Father, please—"

"I SAID GET OVER HERE SON!" Clayton Matthews yelled.

That's when the hitting began. Clayton was full of rage. To think that his son was never really his? He was infuriated and wanted to take it all out on Frankie, as if it were his fault.

It became quite an awful night. Mr. Matthews beat Frankie like he had never beaten him before. He didn't care about avoiding his face anymore, he went for everything. The stomach, the gut, the legs, the face ... all of it. All of it until Frankie was left bloody and bruised. And Frankie could have hit back, he could have escaped, but he didn't. He felt that he deserved it, and he was too deep into an emotional state to even care. Frankie had lost everything, he was broken. He fell prey to his father's hands and let him hit him, all until his mother arrived home to a rather disturbingly graphic scene. When she opened up the door to her husband beating her young son, she yelled and begged him to stop, but he wouldn't. He continued, and to a point that could have resulted in Frankie's death. Frankie's mom knew there was no stopping him, no way other than the most permanent way; so she opened up the cabinet and grabbed the pistol, turned around and shot one fierce bullet into his head.

Clayton Matthews: age 42, death by a frantic wife.

CHAPTER 31

A MOMENT OF REDEMPTION

November 14th, 1925

Dear Diary,

I am immobilized with grief and heartbroken by a rather foolish soul.

Frankie, Frankie Matthews.

The Matthews boy that was once my best friend has now pledged his soul to the Decker family. I sit here still in disbelief, on my bed, wondering how this is even real. How and why this could have ever happened. I cannot describe how confusing all of this is. I know Frankie, I know him best. He'd never do such a thing ... Decker blood or not. It wouldn't matter to him that he's related to the bastard family, none of this makes any sense! All I know now is that he and I will never be what I once thought we would. I know I always denied it, but I won't any longer. I love him, and not just the love I have for my other best friends, but rather, I'm in love with him. I have been since the day I met him and forced him into friendship with the sassy little kindergartener I was. And he's in love with me too. Oh God what a love story we'd be. But a love story that will forever remain unwritten. His betrayal is unforgivable. I tried to bring him back, but we've all lost him.

The night kept creeping into twilight, leaving only the eccentric New Yorkers awake. The types who stay up all night drinking themselves into a roaring oblivion at speakeasies all over the city. The types who spend their Saturday nights out on the town, unless they were unusually depressed and uninterested in their traditional weekend affairs.

Frankie stood still after the gunshot went into his father's red and raging body. His eyes wide and on the brink of tears. Tears that would run down his beaten-up and bloody face. His mother looked to him before she dropped the pistol and hugged her broken boy ever so tightly. He burst into tears, water gushing from his wounded eyes. His long black eyelashes soon became wet as his icy blue eyes were filled with a pain they hadn't quite seen before. She told him to go, to get out of the apartment. That she'd handle it—and that she did. She called upon Daisy to help her, and within the night it was all settled and cleaned up. The dead body gone, the gun destroyed, and the bloody carpet cleaned to perfection. Nobody would truly miss Clayton Matthews anyways. Everyone would buy the story given to them: that he had run off with his mistress, who may or may not have existed. As for Frankie, he ran out of the apartment on that crisp November night and ran to the place he felt the safest: The Dakota.

He lived on Broadway between West 79th and 80th, a few streets up and over from Roxy's. He found a taxi and jumped in, telling the driver to take him to The Dakota. He arrived in a distraught state. Completely broken, both inside and out.

"Matthews—I'm here for Roxy Elliott," he told the front-desk man.

He traveled up to the penthouse and arrived.

"Mr. Matthews, I'm sorry, I was told not to let you in," Theresa, one of the maids, told Frankie as she opened up the door to him.

"By who?"

She gave him a sorry smile. "Roxy," she said gently.

"But you know the truth, so you have to let me in, please."

She sighed. "Yes, I do, but regardless—I must follow her orders—"

"Theresa please, I need to speak with her."

She looked him up and down and let him in.

He ran up the main marble staircase, took a right turn to the second staircase, then a left turn down the hallway which led to the mafia princess's bedroom. She was on her bed, lying on her left side, looking out the window toward The Majestic, waiting to see if Johnny would open his blinds, simply just to notice how upset she was—so that he'd call, giving her an excuse to discuss the Frankie situation.

Her bedroom door felt a knock, a knock that first went unnoticed. Then another one, a slightly heavier one. This is when she got up. She was wearing a short silk and lace nightgown, one that was bought in Paris. It was baby pink with white lace details, and quite revealing for the era, in true flapper style. She opened up her door, and there he was. Frankie Matthews, beaten up and bruised, eyes wet and sad. She stared at him with no emotion. She herself was broken, just as broken as he.

"Roxy," he said, softly, his eyes connected to her soul.

"I told Theresa not to let you in, how'd you get here—"

"Please—"

"Leave, now," she responded in a strong tone, ready to slam the door in his face.

"I have to talk to you, give me two minutes, please Roxy."

She contemplated her next move carefully. Although she wanted him out of her penthouse, and certainly away from her bedroom, she was curious as to where the bruising had come from. Was it a Decker hit gone bad? What had happened?

"Two minutes," she said.

She moved back and let him in, closing the door behind him. He walked over to one of her windows, looking out to the park. His eyes fixated on the dark trees, as he searched for the words his heart wanted to say.

"All of it is a lie, Roxy, you have to understand that—"

"All of what?" she quickly responded.

"I wasn't supposed to tell you," he said, turning around to look at Roxy, "he told me not to. No one else knew but him, Griffin, and a few of your maids—"

"Knew what? You make no sense, Frankie—what the hell is going on?"

"The truth—no one else knew the truth."

Her eyes focused in on his. "Knew what?"

"I would never do such a thing, you know me, you know it's true. I'd never want any part in the Decker family, not even after finding out I am one. When your father found out, he knew it was a perfect way in. I could be a Trojan horse."

She took a pause. "Excuse me?"

"Once Ray offered me a spot in the Decker crime family, I phoned your father. He told me to accept, that I could join them as an undercover Elliott soldier. That I could find out exactly what they were planning against the family, then we could work to take them down. But I wasn't supposed to tell anyone, he forced me not to. The more people who knew, the less likely it was that I'd succeed. I hated lying to you, seeing the way you looked at me. The hurt in your eyes. I hated it Roxy, I did. But I had to, can you understand that?"

Her eyebrows raised and her mind rambled on with many thoughts. She was happy, angry, and frustrated—but in the very end, relieved. So much so that she could finally think clearly, and maybe get a good night's rest.

"You're not working for the Decker family?"

"No, not really, no."

"You're with us?"

"Yes."

"You're working undercover … for us?"

"Yes, darling."

She smiled and her eyes lit up once again. "Oh, oh that's just wonderful!" she said as she jumped into his arms, holding him ever so aggressively. Finally, Roxy let go of him. "Where the hell did all of this come from?" she asked, referring to his face.

Oh boy, here we go.

Frankie sat down on her bed and she followed.

He went through the whole night, the whole story, and gave her a full rundown on the wild events that had taken place. Everything from his father finding out about his true identity to the beating that followed, eventually making it to the grand finale where his mother had murdered him to save her son.

God. How tragic.

"Frankie," she gasped, grabbing his cheek as he held it there with his hand. "I—I don't know what to say."

"My mom said she was calling Daisy to help with the cleanup."

"Well, she is rather good with that," Roxy laughed as Frankie smiled. "Why have you never shared this with me? How he's hurt you in the past—"

"Because, Roxy, I can't be like that."

"Be like what?"

"Weak. Imperfect."

"Dammit Frankie, you're none of those things. Being abused

doesn't make you any different in anyone's eyes. Certainly not mine."

"Really, Roxy? How can you say that? I never fought him back, not once. That makes me weak—"

"No, Frankie, it makes you broken."

That was true—he wasn't weak, he was far from it. He was, however, *broken*. Frankie's refusal to defend himself against his father's fists wasn't out of weakness, but out of a broken spirit. He couldn't hit his father. He could hit just about anyone else, but not his father.

"I guess you're right."

"I always am," she smiled.

He laughed. "I guess you are."

Their smiles lasted a few seconds before the serious tone once again took over. "Are you alright?" Roxy asked.

He looked at her right in the eyes. "No. I'm not. I mean, he almost beat me to death as I lay there and let him, yet, my heart still hurts at the idea that he's dead. He was still my father and regardless, I loved him. I don't know why, and I hate that about me. But I loved him. I loved my father. And now he's dead."

The sad thing is, most abused children *do* tend to love their abusive parent. Interesting how that works, but nonetheless, quite sad.

"I understand," she said softly before his slow tears began to run down his cheeks once again. *Which he hated.* He *hated* crying in front of people.

Roxy didn't see this side of Frankie often. He kept his emotions bottled up, not wanting to show the world his broken spirit, assuming it would change their perception of him.

"I'll miss him, even though he's done such harm, I'll still miss him," he said as Roxy wrapped her arms around him.

"I love you," she whispered into his ears with her velvet voice.

She kept her arms wrapped around his neck but backed away so they were face to face. Their eyes looked deep into each other's souls.

"I love you too," he said with his whole heart.

"I'm sorry I was so fast to turn away from you. I know I hurt you—"

"Darling, don't apologize. I hurt you too. You gave me the reaction I expected. And yeah, it hurt, but I prepared myself."

Her eyes continued to peer deeply into his soul. "I heard what you said, and no, I haven't forgotten."

"What do you mean?"

He knew exactly what she meant.

A silence fell over the room as they continued to look ever so lovingly into each other's eyes—and then she did it.

Roxy removed her eyes from his and focused them onto his lips, before hers met his. She felt the taste of him for the very first time, and it was exhilarating—and he felt the same way about her.

She kissed him with force and with passion, but then fell into a romantic, slow, dancing type of kiss. His lips and hers, finally touching as sparks erupted in each of their bodies.

The butterflies were like no other, and the feeling was glorious.

They kissed and they kissed, before she backed away. She told him that she loved him, and that she wanted him, but that it wasn't the right time.

What—*the literal*—hell.

She was conflicted, confused, and troubled with a mind that told her not to be with him, even though her heart wanted it. He was so confused. Why had she kissed him, then? Was it the heat and emotion of the moment? Was it to tease him? Why? The real reason was simple: she wanted to. She wanted him and she wanted to feel his lips up against hers for the first time. And when she did, she loved it. She loved the taste of him, the feeling that he was entirely hers. Every second of it, but she knew that it wasn't the time.

When *is* the right time?

There was nothing he could do but pretend to understand, which he did. He knew deep down that it wasn't what she wanted, that they belonged together. But he also knew that someday they'd be together. *For real.* Not just in a fleeting moment of passion, but as a real Manhattan love story. And for the rest of the night, they lay together on her bed, dreaming about each other, falling asleep in each other's warm arms. And as the darkness faded into light, they faded into each other.

The next morning was interesting, as Roxy went on as if the kiss never happened. She told no one and neither did he. They kept the kiss hidden in their hearts. They kept it as their own unspoken moment, their own erotic secret.

As the weekend went on, the rest of the gang found out about Frankie's little undercover mission, and things went back to normal. Frankie continued to stay undercover with the Deckers, until he realized that there was no plan. Raymond had been full of absolute shit. They weren't plotting revenge on the Elliotts—they could barely keep drama out of their own family, let alone create more with the Elliotts. The tensions may have remained high but it was all without action. After about a month, Dennis told Frankie to pull out. The Deckers found out about his little operation after he went back (publicly) to the Elliott crime family. Were they enraged? Yes. Did they do anything about it? Not quite … but eventually the two families would face off once again.

As for the rest of 1925, the special six continued to live fabulously, but nothing extra-special went on.

December came and Christmas was white, then they all rang in 1926 in their habitual roaring way. January greeted them once again and Roxy's annual soirée was a hit. Even better than last year's, which *was* quite hard to beat. Frankie and Roxy continued to keep the kiss a secret, and each eventually began to date again. Roxy briefly dated a boy from The Dalton School in December, but broke it off as the new year hit, then dated a Columbia boy until April. Frankie had a few girls before getting somewhat serious with one in February. Marie continued to date Arthur, and Dalton with Hazel. Johnny continued on his playboy way before finding a dame who kept his company between January and May, before she moved to Philadelphia with her mom (her parents divorced). As for Virginia, she stayed single, but only because she wanted to. After the cheating incident with Dylan back in the summer, she swore off boys until college. High-school boys were too immature for her, and considering they were graduating soon, there was no point in getting into a serious relationship. Dennis and Daisy were still strong, and the family continued to boom unlike it had ever before. Dennis and his little Wall Street "career" continued to prove worthy as well, all increasing the grand net worth of the Elliott family.

I could tell you in detail everything that went down between December of 1925 and May of 1926, but I'd rather just skip to the end of our special six's senior year. That's when things get real interesting. So sit down and get ready, because you're in for a ride.

CHAPTER 32

GRADUATION

May 22nd, 1926

Dear Diary,

Graduation is in two weeks. How is that even possible? We actually made it ... to graduation. And somehow Johnny managed to graduate. I still don't know where I'm going to college yet. I was supposed to have figured that out a few weeks back, but I just can't decide, and the colleges aren't going to argue with an Elliott on not making deadlines, so I still have some time. Dalton turned down Yale for Columbia as he couldn't bear to leave New York. But I mean, who can blame him? Marie and Johnny are all set for Columbia as well, and

Virginia is all ready to begin at Barnard. I'm torn between Harvard and Columbia. If I go to Harvard, I'll be at the school of my dreams, and I'll be with Frankie ... and his girlfriend Cecily who will also be attending. However, I'll then have to leave my city. My beautiful Manhattan. I can't imagine leaving, I love this city too damn much. Boston? Sure, it's nice, but it doesn't compare. And Harvard isn't even in Boston, it's in Cambridge. It's a real doozy, I'll tell you that.

"So?" Frankie asked.

"No, Frankie, I don't take advice from men."

Roxy and Frankie were enjoying a drink at one of the Elliott speakeasies down in the Village when he made an attempt at giving her proper advice in regard to where she should go to school next fall. He was hoping she'd of course go to Harvard, as they had planned since they were kids, but she was straying further and further away from the idea.

"Come on, you've wanted to go since we were kids."

"Yes but—I don't want to leave New York, you know that."

"You sound like Dalton."

"Well he's got a good point—"

"Roxy, you have to do what's best," he said, grabbing her hand. "What makes you happiest?"

She looked away from her drink and straight into his eyes. "Not you," she smiled and threw his hand off of hers.

"Darling, you have to make a decision—"

"Don't you think I know that?"

"And it needs to be now—"

"But it's hard."

"What's hard?"

"The name."

"I don't understand—"

"Roxy Elliott, the name everyone knows. Being Roxy Elliott … it's hard."

"Yes but it's glamorous, Roxy. It's arguably the best name a person could have in Manhattan—"

"Sure, but there's glamour in everything, you just have to find it. However, there are also hardships in everything, and being Roxy Elliott is one of them."

"And what does this have to do with choosing a college?"

"Well, darling, everything! I'm Roxy Elliott, a name everybody knows, and it's an expectation. One I have to live up to *every single day*."

"A grand expectation."

She looked over with a sparkling grin and uneasy eyes, and said, "It quite is, darling. And part of that means that, well, Harvard is looked at as the best school in this country. I mean, Columbia is just as great, being an Ivy and all, but Harvard is Harvard. The problem is that … I'm not sure if I want Harvard anymore. As much as I love crimson red, that Columbia blue is really speaking to me."

He took a brief pause and sighed. "Then forget about the expectation and go to Columbia. Roxy, I want you to be your happiest, and it looks like you won't be at Harvard. Leaving this city—"

"Won't do me well."

The two continued to rant on about college as Roxy came to her final decision.

"Hey, get over here," Johnny said to Dalton.

"Yeah?"

"Roxy just rang me from the club. She's going to Columbia."

"How is it that we all ended up there?"

Johnny set down the phone. "All except Frankie."

"Are we sure about that?"

"How do you mean?" Johnny questioned Dalton.

"Well I mean, with Roxy making the decision to stay in the city, do we really think Frankie will actually go through with Harvard?"

"Dalton, it's been his dream for years—"

"Yeah but I mean, you really think he's just gonna leave? Leave all of us? I mean, especially now that I've decided against Yale. We are all staying in Manhattan, and *he's* going to be the one to leave?"

Johnny took a pause, thinking about it, "Honesty, if he wasn't with Cecily, he'd probably stay."

"But it's not like he's even all that crazy for her. She's just another distraction from Roxy."

"Exactly. If he stays here, he's gotta deal with being madly in love with her despite her not wanting to be with him. If he leaves with Cecily, he can escape it all at Harvard."

Johnny had a point, and he was right.

Cecily was a fine girl: she was pretty, smart, and athletic. Yet, despite being all of these things, she was *no* Roxy. No girl could *ever* be Roxy. Regardless, she was his girlfriend and she was doing a great job at taking his mind off of wanting to grab and kiss Roxy at every given moment. He had replayed their November kiss in his mind like a great song on repeat. Except, it never got old ... not once. He wanted more, but he knew he couldn't have it, so Cecily entered the picture. Frankie had been debating if he really wanted to go to Harvard after all, if he wanted to leave his beloved city and all of his friends behind, but his blonde broad convinced him that leaving was the right choice.

Two weeks went by and graduation was approaching. A day where parents shower their kids with flowers and "congratulations" all while secretly in pain over the fact that they grew up so damn fast. It's a day where kids finally feel as if they have entered the real world and left high school behind, ready to begin their adult lives. Is this really true? *No*—because eighteen-year-olds don't know anything about the real world or adult life. I mean, in all honesty, does anyone?

"Roxy ... it's the rule. You can't break it," Marie said to Roxy as the girls got ready for the big day.

"I don't break the rules—I simply set my own."

"Not wearing your robe isn't 'setting your own rules', okay? It's a tradition and you'll look absolutely ridiculous if you don't wear it—" Virginia schooled her.

"Untrue—in fact, it's just the opposite. I'm going to look utterly ridiculous if I *do* wear it—"

"Oh my goodness, this is nonsense! You're wearing it Roxy, end of discussion," Marie stated in a frustrated tone.

Roxy was a girl of fashion, and graduation gowns don't exactly scream "chic", if you know what I mean. Nonetheless, she ended up wearing it, matching her peers and walking across the stage just as everyone else did. Their graduation was a beautiful ceremony. It took place in the courtyard of their Upper West Side school with a graduating class size of 150 students. It wasn't a large school, but large enough that everyone didn't know *everyone's* business. They did, however, know our special six's business, as they were the most popular crew in school. A crew that was now moving on to their next chapter in life, closing out the childhood they knew so well, and diving into something brand new. The class of 1926—*what a class.*

Cue the band: Pomp and Circumstance playing loud in the background as the graduates proudly made their way to their seats wearing navy blue gowns with matching navy blue caps, decorated by white tassels with a silver "1926".

"Congratulations class of 1926!" the British principal yelled, as the students screamed with joy and threw their caps into the sunny June 5th air.

What a *special* class they were.

CHAPTER 33

A HEARTFELT GOODBYE

"Life's a ROAR!" Roxy yelled over the live and eccentric jazz music that roared heavily over the party, and danced on the bar counter while drinking Dom straight from the bottle.

After graduation, Roxy and her friends threw quite the roaring party. They held it in one of the grand ballrooms at the Plaza, where almost their entire graduating class attended. There were champagne towers everywhere, crystal chandeliers, bands playing in all corners, shrimp cocktail and caviar, and an open bar filled with only the highest end of liquors. Everyone was dressed to the nines and celebrating the fact that they had finally escaped the hellhole commonly known as *high school*. Around half of the students would be attending a top-ten school, with a third of them attending Ivies. This was one of their last moments, one of their last nights together before they would all be heading their separate ways. Though they were pleased by the idea of never having to set foot in those wooden halls again, they'd all miss each other dearly. Roxy loved the majority of her class, and knowing that she wouldn't be with them again, all together, in a rather roaring situation, absolutely tormented her. But in the end, it would be alright, because she'd still have the most important of her friends with her in New York. Well, all except for Frankie, of course.

"What time does your train leave tomorrow?" Dalton asked Frankie by the bar.

"I believe around ten?"

"You don't know, do you?"

"Why should I? Cecily knows, she'll make sure I make it on time," Frankie laughed as the two boys took a sip of their bourbon.

The party went on and each of the 120 adolescents grew deep into a drunken oblivion. Frankie, Johnny, and Dalton had their driver take them to Johnny's where the girls would eventually meet them after. The six of them spent one last night all together, laughing and making a memory they would learn to keep close to their hearts. They all ended up fast asleep on the floor of Johnny's bedroom at around four in the morning. By seven, Cecily had made her way over and took Frankie away, reminding him that they would leave for Cambridge in two hours.

Time went by slowly in the following two hours, but not slowly enough. When the time finally came, they all made their way to Grand Central Terminal, walking toward the train tracks, ready to say goodbye to their dear friend.

"If you don't visit me, I swear, I'll kill you," Johnny said with a straight face before grabbing Frankie and hugging him tight.

"Are those tears?" Frankie asked with a laugh.

"No dammit, I've got something in my eye," Johnny protested as he walked away from Frankie, not wanting to face the fact that the was *actually* leaving.

"I love you man," Frankie said with watery eyes.

"Right back at ya," he responded before walking away in an attempt at stopping himself from having a full-blown meltdown.

"Oh Frankie, what the hell. Why do you have to do this? Why?" Marie said, already crying.

"I promise I'll be back for Christmas."

"That's months away!" she said before throwing her arms around him.

"I love you Marie, watch out for Roxy, okay?"

"Honey, she doesn't need 'watching out'."

Frankie laughed. "I guess you're right on that one."

"Hey, I love you too. Be safe, okay?" Marie finished, before Virginia made her way toward him for a goodbye.

"You are really doing this, you are really leaving."

"Virginia, don't cry baby," Frankie said, trying to hold back his own tears.

"How are we supposed to be the same without you? It will never be the same," she cried, and hugged him tightly as they shared an "I love you" and made a path for Dalton's turn.

"You're not gonna be happy there," Dalton said to him.

"You're probably right."

"Then why are you going?"

Frankie took a pause. "I need a change. Something new in my life."

"And you couldn't have gotten that at Columbia?" Dalton laughed.

"Harvard has always been my dream, you know that."

"Yeah, your dream with Roxy—"

"Shhhh! Cecily is right over there, she'll hear you," Frankie whispered.

"Frankie, I don't give a damn," Dalton began to say as Frankie rolled his eyes, "but hey, I know there's nothing I can do to persuade you into staying here, so I guess this is goodbye."

They shared a hug. "I love you, Dalton."

"Love you too, man," he responded with a crack in his voice.

They had all said their goodbyes, all except for one special girl.

She walked toward him slowly. "Hey stranger," she said in a soft voice.

"I would really rather not do this—" Frankie said before being cut off by Roxy. He didn't want to go through the process of saying goodbye to her, it was too painful.

"Well you don't have a choice," she said before grabbing him and hugging him tight, both of them with tears running gently down their beautiful faces.

"I'll be phoning often, okay? And I'll write—"

"And you'll visit."

"And I'll visit."

She took a pause. "I love you," she said, straight into his soul.

"I know you do," he chuckled. "God Roxy, I love you too," he said before giving her one final hug.

June 6th, 1926

Dear Diary,

When is it that we are granted the pleasure of knowing our true heart's emotions for the man we secretly love. The boy we desire.

Is it after we've already lost them?

As I walked in, he took a glance at me. A look that lasted but five seconds.

Frankie has a way of making the heart of any girl race as he looks at her. When our eyes met, not only was my heart racing a mile a minute, but the butterflies in my stomach were fluttering just as fast. This specific time, this specific day, this specific glance, this was the moment my mind finally let me, finally allowed me to feel what I knew I already did. I am in love with Frankie, and I've known for a while, but I've made excuses. Telling myself that it wasn't the right time, or that we shouldn't be together. The Matthews boy, the boy I had known all my life. With whom I was the best of friends and extremely close. I was cluelessly in love.

Now it's clear, there will never be a "right time". That doesn't exist. Frankie and I have been in love since the day we met, and I wanted to deny it.

Johnny would mention to me that I needed to stop trying to find the perfect boyfriend, that Dean was great but the real reason it never worked out with him was because of Frankie. That all my failed relationships were because my heart belonged to someone else.

As I looked back through my diary, reading everything I had to say about Frankie, I realized that I should have let myself love him.

Today when he looked at me, today when our eyes met, his ocean blue and mine copper brown, it was the look of love, and my heart knew. The hurt I felt this morning was like no other. My heart aches, my stomach is empty, and my mind ill. Witnessing him step on that train with some other dame—what have I done? I could have stopped this, he would have stayed. Dalton and Virginia were standing beside me waving goodbye to our dear old friend, with tears in their eyes. Marie was walking back from the restroom as she saw the train whistle down the tracks; she stopped and stared at one of her best friends depart from the roaring life we created. Johnny was looking in our direction as the train left and saw the way I gazed into Frankie's eyes with tears running down my cheeks, mouthing the words "I love you". Johnny came behind me and put his hands on my shoulders, then whispered into my ear, and when he did my hopelessness went away.

There they were, all five of them, staring woefully out at a dear friend leaving them behind on a train set to transport souls to a new life. Frankie, leaning up against the window, wondering if he had made the right choice as the train quickly left behind his old life: the life he knew, the city he loved, and the people he cared about so dearly.

The day went on and the gang found their way to their Hamptons homes. They were already packed up before graduation, and after Frankie left, there was no reason to stay in the city. So each of them hopped into their luxurious cars and their drivers drove them out to Long Island, where they'd spend the rest of the summer before returning in the fall for Columbia. Roxy got settled in her room at the Elliott estate in Southampton as Marie and Virginia spent their first night at their own Hamptons homes with their family. The next day, however, they planned to do as they always did and move in with Roxy for the summer.

After Roxy's maids finished unpacking her things, they left and she lounged on her red velvet sofa and ate a box of Mallomars, drowning her sorrows in the rather tasty cookie. This was right before things took a turn for the worse. Daisy walked in on her depressed daughter looking out to the garden as she listened to "Nobody Knows You When You're Down and Out" by Bessie Smith.

"Scarlett Roxy, baby, I need to tell you something."

"Yes Daisy?" Roxy said, concerned by the ghostly look on her mother's face. "Well, is it bad? What is it about?"

"Honey, it's about Frankie—"

"What about Frankie? I don't want to hear it—I don't care about Frankie, he left and now I've forgotten him. Go away, just go away!" she said as she began crying. Roxy turned her back against her mother, looking out the window at the dark ocean. She missed him terribly and attempted to keep his name off her mind.

"Roxy, I need to tell you something—"

Roxy wiped her tears and turned to her mother. "Mother, I said get out. I'm in no mood to talk. Especially about Frankie," she said as she stopped crying, Roxy was not one to show her pain in front of anyone. She didn't cry in front of people unless it was necessary—only tears of joy. Roxy especially did not want to worry Daisy with her tears.

"Scarlett, there was an accident," Daisy blurted out with no hesitation.

Roxy looked at her mother as a fear entered her eyes. "What—how do you mean?"

"The train Frankie was on, it went off the path and crashed at Providence station, Mr. Matthews just phoned me and told me everything. They said they can't find Frankie, he hasn't called and they don't know where he is. The people at the station took count of everyone who survived the accident, they are identifying the people who didn't as we speak. Frankie was not on the list of survivors, Roxy."

She was stunned, in shock. Couldn't move. She was

immobilized with fear and with grief. She got off her bed and walked to one of her windows, looking out the other window to the mansion's beautiful garden and pools.

Roxy walked back to her bed and sat down. "I'm sure there's an explanation, Mother, my goodness!" she said, staring at the floor. "Oh it's alright, they will find him," she said with an emotionless voice.

"Oh darling," Daisy began to weep, "they think he was one of them who didn't survive."

Roxy cut her off and started to yell, "NO! No no, he's fine, it's all alright! It's all alright."

They say denial is the first stage of grief.

"Roxy, they think he's dead," Daisy said sternly, wanting to get through to Roxy.

"No, this can't be. This can't be Frankie!" Roxy said as she began to sob. She was bawling her eyes out. She took off her earrings and threw them forcefully to the ground, then ripped her pearls off her neck and threw them against the wall. Suddenly it felt as if the room was closing in on her and as if her body were burning from the inside out. She felt hot and short of breath. Roxy fell into Daisy's arms, breathing heavily, and began to hyperventilate. Daisy shed tears with her as they fell to the ground, lying up against a wardrobe by the window. Roxy had felt like her heart was broken into a thousand pieces when she watched Frankie leave on that train with Cecily, but at the very moment when she was told Frankie was dead, she realized her heart was now not broken into a thousand pieces— but shattered into a million.

The sun was falling fast out of the sky while Daisy told the sad tale to Roxy; the blue was darkening at a lightning speed. Clouds filled by pouring rain were approaching fast and near. Thunder came, blocking the sound of Roxy's screams of terror and grief. Next to know, after his family, were the rest of the gang. Their reactions were all similar to Roxy's: first came denial, then anger, then utter heartbreak and a dark cast of misery. This was Frankie Matthews, our dear, handsome, bad-boy Frankie. Dead.

What a heartbreaking goodbye.

CHAPTER 34

A SHOCK AND A HALF

Empty: a word of which we all know the definition. An adjective which precisely depicts the way every single person who knew and loved Frankie Matthews felt. Absolutely *empty*.

The night of June 6th brought horror, terror, and emptiness to many. Roxy felt ill the entire night, as did the rest of the gang. None of them really slept.

I mean, how could you?

Henry Flynn's death had brought a heavy sorrow to the group, and they weren't even *that* close to him. You can imagine the effect Frankie's death had.

I myself felt a sense of emptiness, that pit in the center of my stomach, imagining what the rest of The Roaring would look like without him. There isn't a word I can think of to describe such a thing. Terrible. Awful. Horrendous. None of these words come close to what it would really be like.

June 6th, 1926

Dear Diary,

    I feel sick.

After the dark and stormy night that followed the news of Frankie and the train situation, Johnny came over to Roxy's to talk.

Marie, Virginia, and Dalton all planned to come over later in the day, but were spending it grieving alone for the time being. And by grieving alone, I mean finally sleeping, as their night had consisted of approximately two and a half hours of combined rest.

When learning of such news, sleep isn't exactly the easiest thing to come by.

"I don't know how to cope. I don't know what to feel. All I feel is sick to my stomach. This can't be true," Johnny said as he lay down on Roxy's bed, next to the sleep-deprived Elliott.

"I couldn't sleep last night."

"Neither could I. I was just waiting for another call, his mother, telling us that he's fine and it was only a mistake."

"I'm afraid that's not going to happen, Johnny," Roxy said as they both began to shed misery-filled tears again. Their faces wet and their eyes red, they knew they needed to get their minds off of Frankie. At least for the time being. "My father, he said there was a shipment coming in from France."

"A shipment? Of booze?"

"And other things. Do you wanna head down to the docks? Get our minds off of it? Then maybe get a bite to eat with cousin Tommy?"

"Sounds better than lying here in our sorrows," he responded.

"Thought so."

They got up and out of bed, then made their way to Johnny's Rolls-Royce. They drove down to the docks, where the ships brought in goods for the Elliotts. They arrived to an unfamiliar scene, however. Instead of a plethora of Elliotts accepting and inspecting the goods that arrived off of the ship, then their associates taking them to where they were needed, there seemed to be a rather sinister scene.

"What's going on out there? Are those—" Johnny began to say as they pulled up.

She looked to him, worry in her eyes. "The Deckers. You know they want to take over."

"Of course, we all know that."

"Yes well, lately they've been extra assholes and they're threatening to rat out all of our speakeasies to the cops if we don't hand them over."

"What?"

"Well in these past few months they've been doing real bad. They ended up losing and closing all of their clubs, so they've got nothing to lose now. But don't worry, we won't be giving up our speakeasies that easily. Our family has something on them, something much worse than bootlegging,"

"And what exactly is that?"

"Honestly, I'm not quite sure. My dad wouldn't tell me, let's go find out."

"Roxy, I don't think that's a good idea, it's getting real heated out there—"

"Johnny, I'm an Elliott, I can handle myself. And I've got a pistol strapped to my leg."

"Roxy please, what if something happens, I can't lose you too."

"I said I'll be fine!" Roxy raised her voice as her father looked back at her, confused as to why she was there.

That was when the first gunshot went off. His attention was on her, instead of the man standing in front of him: Marshall Decker.

Roxy's eyes widened as she ran toward him in a panic. "DADDY!" she yelled as her voice cracked.

Two more gunshots, making a total of three. The first one went into his arm, the second and third straight into his heart.

"DADDY!" she screamed at the top of her lungs, continuing to run toward him as the gunshots continued to roar.

This had taken quite the turn, and rather quickly. It went from a plea, to an argument, right into a mob war. One like the two families hadn't seen before. A war started by the Deckers and ended at the hands of the Elliotts. After the three shots went off into Dennis, the bloodshed began. The Elliotts (the twenty that were there) began to fire back at the Deckers (the twelve who showed up). The Deckers were outnumbered and outgunned. Did they *really* think after *all* of this time that they'd come out on top?

As the Elliotts fired back, Roxy continued to run to her father.

"ROXY, GET OUT OF THE WAY!" yelled a concerned Johnny from his car.

And there it was, **another shot** from Marshall Decker's gun. A bullet flying through the summer air and into our mafia princess. A bullet to the chest, rather close to the heart. Marshall hadn't meant to hit her; she ran toward her father and was caught in the crossfire. Regardless, *he had still hit her.*

"ROXY!" Daisy, Johnny, Tommy, and Uncle Clyde simultaneously cried out as they witnessed the life taken out of her.

When the Deckers saw what had happened, they halted their shooting. Though they were ready for a bloodbath with the Elliotts, Roxy was always off the table. She may have been eighteen, but that was still far too young. She hadn't even begun to take on the family business yet. Just as Raymond was off-limits for the Elliotts, she was for the Deckers. Everyone was stunned. The rest of the Elliott family members stopped shooting. All focus was on Roxy, and Dennis of course, but there would be no saving Dennis. The two shots into his heart had killed him instantly, and that's when they were out to kill every single one of the twelve Deckers there. When Roxy was shot, however, they didn't yet know how badly. The Deckers stood there in a moment of fear for what Marshall had just done, then quickly cleared the docks, leaving only the Elliotts. Each Elliott family member dropped their gun and made their way toward Roxy as Johnny ran from his car out toward the docks.

The bullet had penetrated her deeply, and the blood began to decorate the white dress she was in, seeping out and through as she bled red. She stood there in shock, the breath taken out of her and her eyes wide. Roxy looked down at her chest before taking her right hand and placing it over her wound.

They say a broken heart by love is the hardest to fix, but a broken heart by bullet is near to impossible.

Her life flashed before her eyes, and in the flash were all of her favorite memories. Memories with the whole gang and many of Frankie, and of course, what *could* have been.

Going off to college with the boy she loved. A romantic proposal with a sparkling ring. And a wedding—a wedding filled with passion and warmth, yet set in December and therefore accompanied by falling fluffy snowflakes. A Central Park wedding with all of her friends and family. She imagined trees topped with soft white snow, an ice sculpture of a dove, and herself in an ivory princess dress holding a bouquet of red and white roses. Her father walking her down the aisle, and the man she adored so beautifully standing underneath a shimmering silver arch. A man wearing a tuxedo and a smile as wide as a mile. She imagined what would come after the ceremony of love: a honeymoon in the south of France, two pregnancies, one girl and one boy, and a life of growing old with her one true love. A stunningly delightful portrayal of what *would* have been. An image only to be taken away by the slow shutting of her eyes. An image gone black as the blood seeped through her dress. She took a step back, and then another, before falling into Johnny's arms as he came behind and caught her.

"Roxy no," he said, "no, Roxy." He began to cry. The tears blurred his vision as he held the bleeding young Elliott.

Daisy, Caroline, Tommy, Uncle Clyde, Aunt Elizabeth, Griffin, Margret, and twelve of the other Elliott family members and associates crowded her. Caroline and Daisy fell to the ground next to Johnny.

"My baby," Daisy wept.

Roxy looked up at the family surrounding her as a single tear trickled down her right cheek. Her arm fell to her side, no longer holding her wound, as her eyes began to gently close.

"Stay with me, Roxy—don't do this, don't do this I said, Roxy!" Johnny cried.

If only she had stayed in bed.

June 6th would always be remembered as a day of sorrows, a day that couldn't be beat.

That was only until June 7th arrived: a day of pure and utter agony. A weekend of loss and heartache. How could this happen? Well, if I'm remembering correctly, I told you long ago that we weren't done with the Deckers yet. That something else would happen. And it was something quite sinister. Both Dennis and his beautiful daughter, stricken down by bullets, all at the hand of Marshall Decker.

Don't fret, however—he was sure to get a visit. The Elliotts paid him one well, if I must say.

I'm sure you are upset by our ending, *as you should be*, but do remember that The Roaring wasn't made up solely of glamour, elegance, extravagance, allure, and charm; it also consisted of scandal, misfortune, heartbreak, and many rather cataclysmic events. Our special six went through all of this during their time in The Roaring, and I hope I was able to share this with you to the best of your understanding.

The End

Just Kidding

I would never end there.

CHAPTER 35

Divine Intervention

The funeral took place later in the week on Friday, June 11th, 1926.

It was a beautiful service, and a rather large one. Everyone showed up. Every single Elliott alive attended, along with every other mafia family in the Tri-state area (excluding the Deckers, of course), and every other man, woman, and child that knew the Elliotts or had any type of personal connection to them. And boy, there were a lot.

The service took place at St. Patrick's Cathedral on 5th Avenue. There was a large photograph of Roxy and Dennis for everyone to see as they entered the church, then a second one up where the podium was. The photograph was taken back when Roxy was seven years old. It was a lovely picture, Roxy sitting on her father's lap at a Christmas dinner. What a beautiful scene.

There were many speeches. One from Daisy, one from Caroline (yes, even after the scandal, they eventually made up and therefore this was necessary), one from Griffin and Margret, Clyde and Elizabeth, Tommy, and last but certainly not least, one from his very own daughter, our wounded Roxy Elliott.

Confused? I'm sure you are, but you will be delighted to know that Roxy *didn't* die on that eerie June 7th. She was shot rather close to her heart, yes, but she survived (thankfully). Leave it to an Elliott to pull through something like that.

Let me take you back so you can understand exactly what happened.

It was violently raining that night. Roxy was lying in the hospital bed, no longer with a bullet in her chest, but she was unconscious. The surgery had been done, but she had not awoken from her near-death slumber.

All of her friends were in the room, along with her family. The hospital room was not big enough to hold everyone who was there for her, so the rest of the Elliott mob stood nervously in the hallways. Everyone had come out when they heard Roxy was shot, and they would need to be there anyways for Dennis's funeral later that week. Elliotts from Chicago, Boston, Philly, LA, and even the ones in Italy and in Paris. They all came and they were all in disbelief watching the eighteen-year-old Elliott princess lying down with her eyes glued shut and lifeless. They bowed their heads, praying, and all thinking the same thought. It was silent, so silent you could hear the person next to you breathing. It was silent until a finger started to move, just one. That's when everyone shared a hopeful gasp. What followed was two fingers, then three, and eventually all of them. A long second went by and Roxy began to move her hand as everyone looked up at once, all in sync, and all relieved.

"Roxy!" they yelled, hoping she would say something. She opened her eyes and everyone's hearts began to warm. Smiles spread across faces, and there were many thanks to God. The nurses and doctors were all scared for Roxy—they were sure she wouldn't make it. And they knew if she didn't, an Elliott would be paying each and every one of them a rather gory visit. As Roxy opened her eyes, Marie took one hand and Johnny took the other. Dalton came behind Marie, and Virginia behind Johnny. Roxy's family gathered around all and watched her eyelids slowly open. Seeing her long dark lashes move was one of the greatest feelings they had ever felt—revealing her copper brown eyes, wide and open, signifying that she had pulled through.

Three words came out of her mouth. "Who are you?" she said with her doe eyes. Everyone's heart sank so deep into their chest, their stomachs felt sick, and their hearts ill. "Where am I? Who are you all?"

A panic came upon them.

"What do you mean who are we? Roxy, we are your family," Johnny loudly said with terror.

"I'm sorry, I don't—"

"Roxy!" Marie began to cry.

"HA! I'm only kidding, did you think I'd forget my favorite people?" Roxy said as she sat up, no longer lying down in a lifeless pose. They all began to laugh, as did she.

"If you hadn't been shot, I'd totally kill you for that," Virginia smiled.

"Don't ever … *ever* do that to us, sugar," Johnny exclaimed.

Daisy and Caroline came over and grabbed her arm, crying. Her Uncle Clyde and his wife were standing at the foot of her bed ready to hand her flowers. All of her cousins came and hugged her. Everyone was there, everyone except for her father, of course. After the cheers and the thanks subsided, she asked for her diary (which Caroline had brought to the hospital, knowing that if she woke, she'd want it) and she began to write.

June 9th, 1926

Dear Diary,

When it felt as if my heart was pouring out blood, I thought of many things.

I thought of Marie and Johnny, Dalton and Virginia. My mom, my dad, my real mom. My aunts and uncles. All of my family and all of my friends. All the parties and adventures, the experiences and the memories I've had.

I remember thinking about that night, that night we all got together. All six of us, plus my mom and Caroline. That night back when we were little and all crammed into a car for Mr. Williams's wedding (to his second wife at the time). I remember as we entered the grand ballroom, Frankie grabbed my hand and squeezed it ever so tightly. We were just eight years old then, but my heart raced. I remember every moment of that night.

I was shot just the day after he left, after I finally realized I truly wanted to be with Frankie. That it was the right time. It was the day after I found out that Frankie was dead. I remember thinking as I hit the ground after being shot, that if I died, I would be with him. With him forever, and that's the only thing that calmed me down. It was the only thing that comforted me as the sounds of my family's screams of fear and anger roared, as Johnny and Daisy ran over to me in tears. As my name was being yelled, "ROXY, ROXY!", as I was lying there, a bullet in my chest and my heart filled with love.

Now you know the details of her survival, and I would hope are a little less confused. This brings us back to where we are now: the funeral—her *father's* funeral.

After the ceremony at the church, they all made their way to bury the Don. The man that took the Elliott empire and grew its power. After the burial, the reception took place at the Dakota speakeasy, which made perfect sense. It was Dennis's favorite out of all the Elliott clubs.

"I just—it's all my fault. All of it. You don't understand." Roxy began to weep.

"Roxy, calm down, what's your fault?" Virginia asked her.

The five of them were all gathered together, leaning up against the bar, sipping bourbon out of heavy crystal glasses.

"All of it. Vita's death. My father's death. Frankie's death. Each one of them—"

"Roxy, don't be silly," Johnny said.

"That's ridiculous," Dalton chimed in.

"It's the truth. If I hadn't driven Vita away with my judgement, she would have been in New York when they took the hit out on Paul Decker, and she wouldn't have been caught in the crossfire—"

"Roxy, don't be ridiculous, it's not your fault. She chose to leave."

"It is my fault!" Roxy said in pain. She missed all of them so deeply, because she loved all of them so deeply. She wasn't only dealing with the grief of their passing, but also with the guilt on her shoulders. She felt as if she was the cause of each one of their deaths. She wasn't … but it sure as hell felt like it. "And my father, if I hadn't been so keen on distracting myself from Frankie's death, I wouldn't have ever asked Johnny to take me to the docks. And if I hadn't been there, he wouldn't have ever been distracted—"

"Roxy—" Marie said.

"He looked back at me, and when he did, Marshall pulled the trigger. If I hadn't been there, he wouldn't have looked away from Marshall, and he would have stopped himself from being killed!" Roxy cried.

"Roxy, I think it's time we all go upstairs. We'll all spend the night in your room, we'll—"

"And Frankie, don't even get me started. I practically drove him to his death."

"What do you mean?" Johnny asked.

"I'm the reason he was on that train. I'm the reason he's gone," Roxy said with a shattered voice.

Let's flash back to the morning of June 6th. Roxy had gone back to her place to get ready for the day, not long before she was to meet Frankie at Grand Central Station to say her goodbyes as he boarded the train with Cecily.

She was sitting at her desk, quickly writing in her diary, as she heard her bedroom door open.

"Can we talk?" Frankie asked, standing in the doorway.

Roxy closed her diary, pen still in the book, and turned around. "Sure," she said, standing up and walking toward him.

He closed the door and made his way to her. "Tell me not to go."

"What?" she said, confused.

"Say it. I know you want to——"

"Don't be ridiculous——"

"Say it, Roxy. Tell me not to go and I won't go——"

"You're being ridiculous, Frankie."

"Tell me to stay and I'll stay——"

"Dammit Frankie, what are you doing——"

"You know what I'm doing! Roxy—I'm in love with you. You know that and you've known for a long time——"

"Frankie, why are we doing this again, you have a train to catch. I was about to leave for Grand Central——"

"Roxy—darling, please. You know you love me too——"

"Sure! I've always loved you——"

"That's not what I mean."

She took a pause as her shoulders sank into her chest. "Then what."

"Tell me to stay. Tell me that you're in love with me too. Not just that you love me, but that you're in love with me. That you want to be together. You know it's true, Roxy."

"Frankie, that's not true—"

"You know it is—" he said as he took a step closer to her.

She stepped closer to him. "I love you, Frankie! I love you, but I'm not *in love* with you. And you have to go, you have to go to Harvard."

Frankie took yet another step closer, this time landing right up against her, grabbing her soft, manicured hands. "I don't have to go," he said while making an attempt to hide a tear. Roxy looked down as he said this. She didn't want to see the hurt in his eyes.

She looked back up, her eyes now filled with water. "You do," she nodded in heartbreak, "it's your dream. I can't hold you back from that, Frankie. I won't."

I think we both know what she really wanted. That she didn't want him leaving, that she was in love with him. Yet, she didn't tell him. She didn't want him to give up on his dream of going to Harvard, even if it was with Cecily. What she *didn't* know was that it wasn't his dream anymore. Harvard was no longer his dream ... *she* was. He didn't care where he went. Columbia, NYU. He didn't care! He just wanted her, but he needed confirmation that it was what she wanted too. He wasn't going to stay not knowing if she'd ever let herself have him. Frankie knew deep down that she wanted him, that she was in love with him. I mean, back in November was when he'd got that confirmation. Except, back then the excuse was "it isn't the right time". On June 6th, it turned into "I'm not in love with you".

Roxy told this to her friends. Every last detail. She felt as if it was completely on her. That Frankie's death was one hundred percent her fault. That she was responsible.

"If I had been truthful, if I had just said yes, then he'd still be here. But I couldn't stop him from going to Harvard. He's always wanted it," Roxy told her friends, "he deserved to be there. He's smart and he (surprisingly) worked hard to get there. I couldn't take that away from him. But I should have, because if I had, then he'd be alive——"

"No Roxy, you can't blame yourself. Sure, in theory, if you had told him to stay, then maybe he'd be alive. But you couldn't do that, and for good reasons. That doesn't make it your fault that he's dead. He still chose to go, and regardless, you can't blame yourself," Virginia said.

"I love you guys," she said before she made her way over to Daisy and Caroline.

"She's a ticking time bomb," Johnny said to the others.

When the reception came to an end, the five of them made their way upstairs to one of her great rooms, where they drank tea and reminisced. Straying away from the alcohol for once. They talked for a while about Dennis before the conversation led once again to Frankie.

"I feel like my world is falling apart. Breaking into pieces. All of it. It was all so wonderful. School ending, graduation. It was beautiful. A sunny day, all of us in cap and gowns. That is until the clouds came in and the rain washed all the happiness away. The sound of the train leaving its tracks as Frankie awaited his death. The sound of the thunder that next morning as I was shot, and so was my father. Everything, everyone, all of it was surrounded by joy. Now everyone's in misery. We've all shed so many tears within so little time," she said as her eyes stared into an oblivion. "Two people I loved, dearly, taken away from me. Ripped out of my heart." She looked over to the gang. "I don't know what I'm supposed to do. What are we all going to do?"

Johnny began to shed tears, something he had done only eight times in his life. "Roxy, we are all going to be alright, we have each other."

"But my father is gone, and Frankie's gone. We aren't the six of us without our Frankie," she said as they all began to share tears rushing down their cheeks. "What are we supposed to do?" she cried.

"My goodness," Marie wept into Dalton's arms.

Roxy grabbed Johnny and Virginia as they all cried.

Johnny wiped the tears away from their faces and looked to Dalton. "Frankie left us to deal with these drama queens, how rude," he laughed. The girls showed a smile.

"Now it's three girls against two boys," Virginia added. They all shared a slight grin before they returned to crying.

"Do you think he's looking down on us, watching us?" Marie said.

"More like looking up," Dalton laughed.

Let's hope he's not looking up. I've heard hell is a scary

place to go—would not recommend.

"Hmm, I'm not sure," Virginia said, laughing.

"No, I'm sure he somehow talked his way into heaven," Johnny said.

"You're not wrong," Roxy laughed. "Thank God he had a good heart, because we all know he didn't exactly follow the rules."

"Yeah, he definitely wasn't one to follow 'em," Dalton agreed.

"Why don't you say that in your speech?" Virginia said.

"What speech?"

"Well, won't you be giving a speech at his service?"

Roxy's eyes opened wide—she hadn't thought about speaking at his funeral. It hadn't quite seemed real until now, when Virginia brought it to her attention. Her heart sank and she felt ill.

"His service," she said, heartbreak and sorrow resonating deep in her voice. Roxy said it with little breath, and it was soft. "I didn't think of that, his service. It's tomorrow."

"Roxy, I'm sorry, I didn't mean to—"

"No, you have nothing to be sorry about," she said, looking down, searching for a cigarette.

"Hey, it's—" Johnny began to speak, as he was cut off.

"It's what? It's alright? It's all fine? What are you going to say, Johnny, that everything is jake?"

"Roxy, baby, I didn't mean—"

"What? I know, he's gone. He's dead and we have to have a funeral for him. I get it. I guess I'll go write up the speech I'll say before we pretend to bury him, since we don't even have his body. I understand it. In fact, I'll go to Saks and get myself a black dress and hat. Would that be alright? Would that be fine?" she said before getting up quickly, leaving the room.

Roxy did *not* take grief well. She went into the kitchen and cried, lying on the floor, smoking up a storm.

"I don't know what to say," Virginia said to the group.

"It's okay, this isn't your fault," Marie said.

"I upset her."

"No, Virginia, it's okay. She is just in grief, we all are."

Johnny went over and tried to comfort her; Virginia felt as if she had hurt Roxy by bringing up Frankie's service, even though she needed to face the reality that it was tomorrow. *The day after her father's, yikes.* Roxy didn't want to think about it. She put it off every time it entered her mind, as if it wasn't going to happen. Frankie's body hadn't even been found; they were still finding bodies in the remains of the train. The train car he had been in was one of the few unlucky cars that caught fire. They hadn't recovered those bodies yet, and once they did, they would be unrecognizable. Frankie's was presumed one among those. Cecily would have been as well, but she got up to use the restroom which was a few train cars away. This was about ten minutes before the crash. It took a while, as there was a line she had to wait in. She was walking back as it happened and was far enough away from the explosion of their car that she wasn't hurt by it. Frankie, however, was snug in his window seat, staring out to the full green trees as she left him for the restroom. There was one stop before the train crashed, while she was in the bathroom. If only they had *both* gotten off there.

Later that night, after everyone left, Roxy sat by her telephone and rang Johnny, opening up the window so she could see into his room as they talked.

"The 1920s Johnny, what a roaring life."

"Ain't that true."

"But I'm thankful for my life. Are you?"

"I am indeed."

"I wonder if Frankie was—maybe he wasn't. I mean I walked into a mob war and was shot in the chest and I lived. All he did was board a lousy train and he was killed. Maybe he wasn't thankful for his life, maybe he didn't like it. Maybe that's why he's gone." She tried to justify the reason for his death, trying to understand how this could have ever happened, hoping for an answer.

"I think you should get some sleep, Roxy baby. You should be well rested for tomorrow."

"Alright Johnny."

"I love you."

"Love you, goodnight," she said as she hung up the phone and they both went to bed.

The next day was gloomy once again. It seemed as if everyone showed up for Frankie's funeral. Just about *everyone*. Each of the special *five* gave heartfelt speeches. Ones that contained both sadness and laughter. For the rest of the day, after the burial of an empty coffin, the gang went to Keens and spent hours looking at old photographs, reminiscing on past memories, sharing their favorite stories with Frankie, our heavily missed Matthews boy. After a long day of grief and sorrow, Roxy made it back to The Dakota where she carried herself up to her bedroom with a heavy heart.

Roxy began to undress as she heard someone opening up her door …

She turned around quickly and there he was, once again, standing in her doorway.

"Frankie!" she yelled at the top of her lungs. She was in shock. "Frankie, Frankie oh my God! We thought you were dead!" she said with happy tears coming down her face.

"Dead?" he asked, confused.

She ran to him and jumped into his arms. "I'm so sorry, Frankie. I'm sorry that I lied to you. I'm in love with you and that's all that matters," she said before kissing him passionately.

Oh wait, *that was a dream.*

Roxy woke up in a panic, confused for a moment before she gathered her surroundings and realized what had just happened.

None of it was real—Frankie hadn't walked through her door, and she hadn't told him she was in love with him.

It was all a dream and he was still gone.

She sat there on her bed for a few moments, staring at herself in the mirror of her vanity before she got up and began to write in her diary.

June 12th, 1926

Dear Diary,

Some nights I lie awake, staring up at the top of my canopy for hours and hours, thinking about the endless thoughts gifted by my father and Frankie's deaths. And others I fall asleep and dream for hours, hours interrupted, and in my slumber I dream.

I dream about what it was like when they were still here, when I was young and everything seemed so lovely. The innocence of life when you are a young five-year-old playing in the snow. I also dream of if they were here. If they were to come back, and what it would be like.

Then I wake up and I am reminded of the events that have happened in the year I will always remember as the worst of my life: 1926. I lie in my bed, awake, but tormented by the thoughts I have. Knowing they are gone and I have to spend the rest of my life without them. Knowing that I will never get to see my father again and hug him. I'll never have him yelling at me for my dress being too short or my lipstick too bold. Telling the boys I go out with that if they hurt me, he'd kill them.

Then I think about how I will never get to see Frankie again and tell him I love him. Not that I love him how I love Johnny and Dalton, but that I am in love with him. Truly, and ready to be WITH him. I will never get to kiss him or share my love with him. I will never get to marry him and have kids with him. I won't ever get to see Frankie on his knees with a diamond ring, and he will never get to put it on my finger. I won't get to go to new places with him or walk our kids to school. There will be no wedding to him, I will never get to put on a big white princess dress and walk down the aisle to Frankie, in a perfect suit, standing at the altar with a smile painted across his face, ready to say "I do" to the woman he loves. We won't get to share our lives together or grow old together because his life is over. Just like that, within the blink of an eye. My father and my Frankie, gone.

The thing is, no one knew what really happened to Frankie. It's all very odd. He was gone, yet a part of him would always remain with the five of them. With or without his actual presence.

He was on the train, and the train drove off the tracks, and he was gone.

Gone into thin air like the words he once spoke.

Frankie was on the list of non-survivors, but they hadn't found his body. He was on the train, Frankie Matthews was on the train, but nobody knew what had happened to him or which burned body was his.

Well, not yet at least. Not quite yet.

After writing in her diary, Roxy walked back over to her bed and began looking at the photographs placed nicely on her bedside table, as tears began to rush down her soft cheeks. She then went downstairs for a glass of water, and eventually switched to gin before walking into her father's study for the first time since his death a few days before.

While making her way into the study she began to let out a heavy cry, and flashbacks of him and her entered her mind like a movie. Ones of them when she was little. When she was five and he told her how much her Aunt Daisy loved her. When she was seven and was told she couldn't play with the Deckers and her father had to explain to her why.

All the memories, the great ones, the bad ones when they argued, when he held her in his arms after her mom left. They all rushed back into her mind for the first time since his death. Roxy fell to the floor before getting up, grabbing items from his desk, throwing them against the wall, against the window, and down at the floor. Breaking them in an anger and rage like she had never felt before.

She then paused as her eyes met with a small safe.

Roxy gently shut her eyelids, trying to remember the story behind it, then flashed back to when she was a little girl, asking her father what was in there. He said it was something special and she asked him what it was. He smiled and laughed and told her it was a very, *very* special bottle of scotch that he was saving for a *very* special day. The young Roxy asked what day that was, and he said that someday she'd find out. Then she asked why it was locked and he told her that she would find out someday. Then she asked where the key was and he told her it was in one of his drawers, but not to go looking because he'd know and then she'd get grounded. After Roxy had relived this memory of hers, she opened up her eyes and looked around, opening one of his drawers, where she found a red box with a black tie. She opened the box to a folded-up letter and a key. The letter read,

My baby girl,

This is to you on your wedding day. I told you when you were young that this was a very special bottle of scotch for a very special day. And that day has come. I'm most positive it's to Frankie—you two were meant to be together from the moment you met as tiny kids, oh how adorable you were. If it isn't to Frankie, then I'll have to re-write this letter. Though I couldn't imagine you marrying anyone else, or him for that matter. You are two special people, and I know he'll always treat you right. I can see it in his eyes, even though you are only six years old at the moment. He loves you already, though he doesn't yet know what love is. And you too. But I have no doubt in my mind that you made it to each other, and that the wedding will be grand. I can't wait to walk you down the aisle, though by the time you're reading this I will have already done so. I love you my precious darling daughter. Savor this bottle, there aren't many like it in the world.

Love,
Your one and only father

After reading the letter, Roxy ripped it into pieces and threw it to the ground, then made her way to the safe where she unlocked this "special" bottle of scotch. She opened it up and took a sip before walking into the kitchen.

Theresa, one of the maids, came out of her bedroom on the main floor after hearing Roxy. "Honey, what's wrong?" she said, worried. "Is there anything I can do for you? Something I can make for you? Someone you'd like me to phone?"

"Nothing's wrong, Theresa. I'm so tired of people asking me what's wrong and if I'm okay and if they can do anything. I'm sick and tired of all of it, of every 'Miss Elliott are you alright, is there something I can do Miss Elliot?', every 'I'm so sorry for your loss Roxy', every 'I'm terribly sorry, Scarlett.' I'm tired of it! Sick and tired of all of it!"

"Honey, I think you've had a few too many sips of that bottle, why don't I make you some coffee and you can rest—"

"Too many sips? I'm not drunk, Theresa, I'm angry! I'm furious, I'm mad, I'm full of rage, okay? I'm sad and I'm heartbroken. Heartbroken, Theresa, completely heartbroken. I've just lost two of the most precious people to me. My father is dead. My *daddy* is dead and gone forever. Oh God Theresa, why?" Roxy began to sob. "I loved him so much. I miss him so much and—and it's not even been a week! And I know he loved me so much. He was going to start training me for the family business after I graduated high school. He was going to teach me everything so I would someday be head of the family. The boss of the family business. The head Elliott. He was going to show me the ropes so I could someday run this town. He told me that I'd someday be the most powerful person in New York. The most powerful in the mafia. You know, I once asked him if he was upset that I wasn't a boy, considering that most fathers want their firstborn to be a boy. He told me that Caroline asked him if they should try for a baby again, try for a boy, but he said no. That he couldn't be happier. That when he first held me, he knew I would grow up to be a strong, fierce woman. That I'd grow up to run the family, regardless that I was a girl and not a boy. That it didn't matter, that he was so happy and loved me so much that it didn't matter. He said that he was gonna teach me and that I'd grow up and be the first female mob boss. The first female at the top of the mafia. That I'd become a female don and that I'd be more powerful than any of the male ones. Especially coming from the most powerful family in New York. That no, he didn't want to try again for a boy. That I was his everything," Roxy said, looking out the window to the buildings, taking notice of which apartments were lit and which weren't at this time of the night. "And I never got to say goodbye."

"I know it all, honey. I asked him the same thing when they brought you home for the first time. He couldn't stop smiling. *I* even asked if he was upset that you were a girl and not a boy. He said absolutely not. Not even a little."

Roxy took a pause before turning around. She told Theresa about the letter she had found, and asked her if she had known about it, to which she replied with a yes.

"Your father had me read it before putting it in the box. He wrote it when you were about six years old. He knew back then that—"

"That I'd marry Frankie."

"I'm sorry, honey."

Roxy took another sip of the scotch, straight out of the bottle. "Well would you look at them now. Both dead, and never coming back! And no matter how many times someone tells me they are sorry or asks me if they can do anything, it's not going to bring them back."

Roxy was broken, completely heartbroken. She didn't need anything from anyone. The only thing she needed was a cure to her broken heart, that unfortunately, didn't exist.

After Roxy and Theresa's kitchen conversation, Roxy grabbed her shoes and her purse and she made her way to the foyer. She wanted to get out of the house, to go for a walk alone.

A walk at three in the morning …

"It's you—" she said with the utmost shock in her voice.

CHAPTER 36

THE RETURN OF HAPPINESS

"It's you—" **she said** with the utmost shock in her voice. Her eyes were as wide as they could be, and her heart was becoming one again. She glared into his piercing eyes. She began to once again cry, as he was doing the same. He had a cute grin on his face. She then gave him a look of confusion, then took her right hand and slapped him across the face. It left a red mark.

"Not the reaction I was going for, but yeah, it's me—"

"You're real." She was in shock. "But—but how?" She fell into a smile as he took his hand and wiped her tears off her cheek.

Then she jumped into his arms.

They squeezed each other tighter than ever before. "Frankie, we thought you were dead!"

He hadn't heard of anything. He didn't know what had happened to the train, he only knew that he had got off the stop before the crash and begun to make his way back. As he was waiting for the cab to arrive, his bags and all of his cash were stolen, which is why he couldn't get a cab or a train back. So he had to hitchhike, which is why it took him so long.

That's all he knew. He didn't know of the tragic events that took place.

"God, just because I didn't ring you doesn't mean I'm dead."

"What?" She was confused. "What do you mean, the accident—"

"The accident?"

"We all thought you were dead Frankie, they are still searching for your body."

Once he had made it back to Manhattan from Massachusetts his first thoughts were to go straight to The Dakota to see her. To explain the real reason why he had turned around.

"Roxy, I know you never quite make sense but right now you really—"

"Frankie, you don't know?" she said as he gave her a blank stare. She took his hand and brought him inside before shutting the door. "The train, there was an accident. It was going so fast it slid off the tracks. A bunch died, Cecily said she got up to use the restroom and was walking back as it happened. That you were asleep the last time she saw you. Next thing she knew people were screaming and her car was thirty seconds away from lying on its side. It was utter chaos, a tragedy. They are still recovering some bodies and you were presumed dead. We held a funeral earlier."

"Is Cecily alright?"

"She's fine. Frankie, what the hell happened?"

"Oh my God, that's insane. I bet you guys really missed me or something. Is that why you were crying?" He smiled and hugged her again. She pushed him off of her. This time it hurt her; he held her so tightly that it pressed against her wound.

"Ouch Frankie!"

"What! What? I didn't know a hug could hurt—" he said sarcastically.

"No no it's not that, something else happened." She lifted up her silk slip and removed it from her body. Then she pulled the top part of her brassiere down, revealing the wound that was ever so close to her heart.

His eyes widened as he put his large hands on her shoulders.

"Oh my God, Roxy!" A tear came down his face. He looked into her eyes. "What the hell, Roxy?" He was in shock too—he knew it was a gunshot wound. And so close to her heart? Yikes. "What happened, are you okay? You could have died, oh my God." He turned away and put one hand on his forehead and one on his hip before coming back to her. Hugging her gently this time.

She put her slip back on and they walked over to the west wing staircase and sat down.

Roxy one step higher than him. She told him everything. Down to her father's death and everything she had been going through. She asked him what had happened and how he was there, standing in the doorway to her penthouse, *alive.*

The real story? Well ... after Cecily got up to use the restroom, Frankie woke up and realized that it didn't matter if Roxy wouldn't admit it, that he knew she loved him and he couldn't give up on her. In that moment, he knew what he wanted and it was crystal clear.

Frankie wrote Cecily a note (which burned in the fire when the train crashed), telling her everything, and left it on her seat. He got off at the next stop (the stop before the crash), where things then got *real* interesting. While waiting at the station, trying to get a ticket back to New York, his bags were stolen.

Every single one of them.

Unluckily for him, his wallet was in one of them, which meant he was left with no cash.

Through the days that followed, he tried to make it back to the city without any money.

This took a while ... which brings us to today. Frankie Matthews, alive and not so well, standing in the door of the Elliott penthouse.

She brought Frankie upstairs to her bedroom. "You can stay here tonight," she said as he smiled.

She watched him remove his shoes and begin unbuttoning his vest, removing it.

She looked over. "I still don't get it. If you were planning on coming back anyways, why did you leave in the first place?"

"I wasn't."

"Then what made you come back?"

"I told you, Roxy. *You.*"

"But if I was enough in the first place, why not just tell me you didn't want to go, that you were staying?"

"Because I needed to ask you, I needed to know how you felt."

"That's absurd!"

"When you told me, I was heartbroken. But on the train when I woke up, I realized that I didn't care, I was coming back regardless. I knew you had to be mistaken—"

"Mistaken?"

"Yeah, you were lying to me."

"Oh was I now?"

"Yeah Roxy, yeah you were. I don't know why, but I can assume from knowing you that it's because you wanted me to go to Harvard, because I've wanted it for so long. In reality, Roxy, I only wanted to go there because of you. It was our dream, *together*. Since we were kids. And then you decided to stay and I thought that I still wanted it, I thought that Harvard was my dream but I was wrong. My dream was you, but you didn't know that," he rambled on as she looked into his eyes. "So yeah, you're lying when you say you don't love me and that we shouldn't be together—"

"I do love you, I told you that—"

"You know what I mean. Not like Johnny, not like Dalton. Tell me Roxy. Say it. Say it for real, without the 'but' or without the—"

"Frankie, I've been through hell—"

"Say it, Roxy. Say it for real." He held back a mischievous smile.

They were walking closer toward each other at this point, the heat between them rising like a pot of boiling water on the stove.

"Why don't YOU say it Frankie!"

"I already did!"

They continued to stare deeply into each other's eyes.

"I LOVE YOU!" he shouted. "I love you, Roxy."

"That's not what I mean."

"I'm in love with you. I'm mad for you, Roxy, I'm head over heels in love with you dammit. With all of you. Every part of you. Not just your beauty on the outside but on the inside. Even the bad parts, the stubbornness and the need to be right one hundred percent of the time. Every damn part of it. And I've been in love with you since the day we met and I hate it, but I am. My heart belongs to you. And you know that—"

"Oh yeah?"

"Yeah."

"Then why didn't you do anything about it?"

He took a pause. "I—I don't know."

And he truly didn't.

"Well." Her eyes narrowed, as if she was interrogating his emotions.

"Well?" he said.

"Well dammit it Frankie, FINE—I'm in love with you, Frankie. There, you happy? Is that what you wanted to hear?"

"Yeah it is," he said with a wide grin as he got closer.

They gazed deeply into each other's beautiful eyes. They were hungry for each other in the most intimate way.

"Oh is it?"

They smiled and shared a laugh. This was the first time she had laughed since Friday. The first time she had truly felt happy. Her heart was glowing.

"It is, my love."

"Oh Matthews." She turned around and walked to the window.

He stood there, looking at her reflection. One of her curtains was open, looking out to the dark Central Park.

"You are so beautiful," he whispered, astonished by her beauty and the moment.

Frankie walked up right behind her, and she could feel his hot breath on her neck. She turned around and grabbed him, and in that moment, for the second time ever, their lips touched and fireworks went off. It was the most passionate kiss, the kiss of a lifetime. It was strong and exciting yet soft and full of love. It lasted seven seconds before they pulled away, their eyes met again and they smiled.

"Well that was something," rolled off of Roxy's now love-kissed lips.

He tilted his head to her left ear. "Darling, that was only the beginning."

She smiled and bit her lip.

She started unbuttoning his shirt, then lifted it up and back, removing it from his toned torso, throwing it against her window. He slowly made his way closer to the bottom of her slip, before he took his hands and brought it up. Her arms lifted up into the air in consent and he removed it from her body.

He pressed his warm lips up against hers, and she kissed him back with the utmost happiness she had ever felt.

"Are you sure?" he said, looking hungrily into her eyes.

"More sure than I've ever been," she grinned as she unbuckled his belt.

They smiled and laughed a little.

It was finally happening. All of it.

Pieces of clothing began to fly off their bodies faster and faster before she aggressively pushed his chest onto her bed, before climbing on top of him, kissing him over and over again, taking his hands above his head, pushing them down against hers, kissing his neck passionately, all before he dominantly rolled over and began kissing all over her body. He was on top of her, and they made the most passionate love that night. Kissing, smiling, staring deep into each other's eyes. They had waited for this moment. Both of them. Both could have lost their virginity years before, but waited, because they wanted that moment right there, and deep down they knew they were waiting for each other. Waiting for it to happen. And for two virgins, they were surprisingly good.

Although, are we really that surprised?

They continued their carnival of love all night before the sun began to rise. She fell asleep in his arms, her head on his chest listening to his heartbeat, his arm wrapped around her.

What a night.

The warm summer sun came up. The entire gang walked in, shocked, *and for many reasons*, but happy.

"So the first thing he does when he comes back to life is

439

get with her, instead of making a trip next door to his dear old friend," Johnny scoffed as their eyes began to open.

"So it finally happened," Marie grinned.

"He's alive!" Virginia said as her voice cracked.

"I think we've established that," Johnny said in a sarcastic voice. They were all whispering to each other, standing at the edge of her bed waiting for them to wake. Some would say this was an invasion of privacy, but again, they were an especially *close* group of friends. *The special six.* They finally woke. Roxy was startled, and in her shock and confusion, threw a very bare Frankie off the bed.

"Hey look, it's naked Frankie!" Johnny exclaimed.

"What the hell!" he quickly said as he grabbed his underwear and put it on.

Roxy lay there grinning, sharing a look with the girls, her body covered by the sheet.

"We'll be downstairs," Dalton said as they all walked out the room laughing and giggling. Roxy and Frankie got dressed and went downstairs for the big reunion.

"We came to check up on you, Roxy, but it looks like you're doing quite fine."

"Surely doing something," Virginia laughed.

"So it finally happened," Marie said once again.

"So, what now—Frankie is alive and these two slept together, do we plan a wedding?" Dalton said before Johnny elaborated on the more obvious element.

"FRANKIE'S ALIVE!" Johnny yelled as he ran to him, finally, and hugged him almost as tight as Roxy had the night before. "God Frankie, what the hell?" Tears came down his face before Dalton interrupted.

"Ah man, we thought you were dead." He hugged him just as tight as Johnny had, also crying.

"Frankie!" Marie went over and grabbed him. By now everyone was sharing tears.

"How are you here, Frankie?" Virginia said before her hug came around.

"It's a long story, guys."

"We've got time," Johnny said. They were overjoyed, feeling happier than they had in so long. They weren't the special six without him. Every single one of them was equally close to each other (well, Roxy and Frankie were a different type of close, but you get my point). They couldn't contain their joy. They all sat down in one of the great rooms. He told them the story and it all made sense.

"We gotta celebrate," Dalton said.

"Celebrate Frankie's return or the lovebirds themselves?" Virginia laughed.

"Both," Johnny added.

"I'll grab the champagne!"

"It's 9 am," Marie added.

"And?" Roxy laughed.

"I'll grab the glasses," Johnny said.

"I'll—what should I do?" Frankie laughed.

They all celebrated in joy. I mean, who would have thought? After a few hours, Frankie went home to his parents of course, then later that day went over to Johnny's.

"So it takes you dying and coming back to life to finally make a move on Roxy?" Johnny smirked.

"Real funny."

"I mean, I'm not wrong."

"I don't know man, it's not as easy as it seems."

"How so? Who the hell waits on a girl like that?" Dalton asked.

"It wasn't—the right time."

"It never is," Johnny answered.

"Alright alright, enough about Roxy."

Dalton and Johnny shared a look.

Johnny asked, "So tell us, how was it?"

Frankie had the biggest grin he had ever given. "It was better than you could ever imagine."

The boys laughed.

"Oh I can imagine," Johnny said.

"I mean, I had fantasized about us together so many times, but the real deal was—"

"Better?"

"So much better, I can't even put it into words."

"Damn."

"I mean it was so good we did it three times. And each time was better than the last. And I didn't think that was possible. God, I *really* didn't think that was possible."

"Damn, Frankie!"

"Frankie!" Johnny said as he hit him on the shoulder.

"What can I say, you put two incredibly good-looking people into bed—" Frankie said with a laugh.

"Funny," Johnny cut him off.

"Anyways. You guys really missed me, didn't you?"

"Yeah, I mean, whatever," Johnny responded.

"You guys cried, didn't you?"

They looked at each other.

"You guys cried over me! So it takes me dying to make you guys cry—"

"Of course we cried, Frankie!" Johnny said, aggravated. "We thought we had lost you. We were all distraught. And you know what, I'm not ashamed of it."

Dalton added in, "He's right."

Frankie laughed. "You shouldn't be. A real man cries."

"Amen to that," Dalton said.

Frankie laughed again. "I wish l could have seen it though—"

"Oh just stop it." They all laughed.

Marie and Virginia had been at Roxy's all day, and of course their first conversation had to be on the topic of sex with Frankie.

"So it takes Frankie dying and coming back to life for you to sleep with him—"

"Oh my God, Marie—" Virginia said.

"It's true!"

"That it is—my God, it's all just ... rather insane."

"Why didn't it happen earlier? I just don't understand. You've been in love with him for forever."

"I really don't know. I guess I didn't let myself go there. I just, I felt like it wasn't the right time. I guess I was, in a way, scared."

"How the hell—"

"You don't get it. Frankie and I have been best friends our entire lives, all of us have. And so, because of that, I guess, well," she stumbled over her words, "every relationship I've ever been in I've gotten hurt. And they've obviously never worked out. So subconsciously I think I probably believed that if I went there, and we didn't work out, that I'd get hurt and I'd lose him forever. And believing I wasn't in love with him was the easier way. It ensured I'd never lose him. That he'd be in my life forever."

"Sure," Marie said as she rolled her eyes.

They still didn't know about Roxy and Frankie's very first kiss.

They'd find out eventually, however.

"That actually makes sense. The mind is powerful."

"Thank you, Virginia."

"Alright alright, so, how was it?"

Roxy blushed and grinned. "Oh my goodness girls, it was amazing. More than amazing. Better than I ever imagined."

They laughed. "He must have been good."

"Oh he was. It was just, I can't explain. I mean, I guess that's what happens when you put two extremely good-looking people into bed—"

"Oh please," Virginia said. They all laughed.

"So does this mean you guys are officially together?"

"I guess so? I mean, we didn't actually—"

"Oh my God, you haven't officially become boyfriend and girlfriend?"

"Well Virginia, I think that was kind of implied when we told each other we were in love and then had sex all night."

"All night?" Marie asked.

"All night," Roxy grinned.

"Girls, focus. You have to talk about this."

"We will. I mean, like I said, it was implied."

"No, I agree with Virginia on this one—even though you are, I would still say it to make it clear."

"I don't think it's necessary."

"I think it is."

"I'm sure he's going to officially ask her to be his girlfriend," Marie said.

And don't worry, *he does.*

Later that night he rang her, asking her on their first official date at Tavern on the Green (of course), where he picked her up with a bouquet of white roses and dressed better than he ever had been before, which was a hard thing to do considering he *was* the best-dressed young man in all of Manhattan.

Both of them were encompassed by emotions deeper than they had ever fantasized. Bound by the love they shared.

They had quite the date: Tavern on the Green, a horse and carriage ride, a romantic walk, and of course, *plenty* of sex. I mean, that is what two people in love do, right?

CHAPTER 37

THIS IS WHERE I SAY GOODBYE

And as for the rest? Well, as they say, *it's history.*

Our special six certainly *were* rather special, and their lives were quite unique (weren't they?).

Some may even call them *roaring.*

Big city, big lives, and big lies. In the 1920s, in New York City, the truth wasn't always told. If you understood this, then you were prepared to take on Manhattan. If you weren't, it was like diving headfirst into deep and dark waters with the biggest sharks you had ever seen.

The Roaring in New York was an era not to be forgotten, and the souls that filled the island of Manhattan were equipped for its sensational waters. Our special six certainly were. They had their good times, and they had their bad, but whenever scandal and lies, heartbreak and misery struck, they were prepared and met it with a tenacity that not everyone shared. The stories of the roaring girls in the Roaring Twenties don't end here, even though my writing may. Their legacy would live on infinitely.

I've spent some time now telling you a few of their stories, sharing with you the events they encountered, the extravagance of their style, the scandals they witnessed (and were many times a part of), and the misfortune that met them. Now you know the names **Roxy Elliott, Marie Romano, Virginia Williams, Johnny Davis, Dalton James, and Frankie Matthews.** And I hope you'll never forget them.

I only gave you a sliver of their lives. I only shared with you what occurred between 1925 and 1926. I'm sure you can imagine how the rest of The Roaring looked for them, let alone the rest of their lives.

Marie Romano grew up to marry Arthur Casey, with whom she had three kids: two girls and one boy. They had a happy marriage, one that lasted. He became a Wall Street shark, as did many, after graduating from NYU. Marie became a nurse, which was something she absolutely loved. They ended up buying a large place in Chelsea and lived there until their kids were grown; that's when they bought a penthouse in midtown and lived the rest of their lives there.

Dalton James became an extremely successful writer and married a beautiful and sweet girl named Lucille Mae. They had two boys together but divorced after four years of marriage. I guess Lucille wasn't as sweet as Dalton thought—considering she cheated on him with her own stepbrother (I know, *wild*).

Dalton was hurt for a while, but eventually got over it when he realized who he was truly meant to be with.

Virginia Williams put off marriage until her late twenties, age twenty-nine to be exact, when she met and married an attorney named Jack Jones. They had one child, a daughter, and eventually divorced when she was nine. Virginia then moved into her own apartment in the West Village where she would begin painting and eventually open up her own gallery. She did this until she was seventy-five years old, and then retired to East Hampton. But before that, however, she married Dalton at the age of forty, and they had a beautiful and loving marriage (I know, crazy, right?). After years of being best friends, they realized that they wanted to become more than that, and I have to say, they made a *damn* nice couple.

Johnny Davis—where do I even begin? He was sort of all over the place. After college he became a Wall Street boy, which fit him well, and continued to grow his wealth to new extremes. He bought himself a pad downtown before he had a mini crisis and decided to enlist in the army. Johnny fought in World War II, but don't worry, he was one of the very lucky ones that survived. When he came home, he finally decided to end his playboy days and marry a woman named Elsie Adams, who owned her own dress shop in Midtown. They had two kids: two little girls, to whom they were incredible parents. Their marriage was a happy one, and they spent their days in a townhome on the Upper East Side until their girls were grown and they moved back downtown.

Now, as for our darling **Roxy Elliott** and our bad boy

Frankie Matthews? Well, they had quite the life. They broke up a few times in between, and dated quite a few different people, but eventually married at age twenty-six, and had two kids. One boy and one girl, whom they loved dearly. Frankie continued to be a part of the Elliott family business, while also working with Johnny on Wall Street where he too became extremely successful. Roxy became the first female mafia boss at age twenty-seven, which was quite the accomplishment— and don't worry, she killed Marshall Decker two weeks after he killed her father. She also ended up writing a few books on female empowerment, all while working her way to the top of Vogue, where she was titled editor in chief at age fifty. Not to mention the fashion empire she created with her own brand, "R". She made quite the designer. Roxy and Frankie ended up moving into the penthouse at the Plaza, while keeping the Elliott penthouse at The Dakota a family apartment, where anyone a part of the family could stay, like their own secret family club. Later in life, they moved to a penthouse on 5th Avenue between East 74th and 75th. Everyone in Manhattan envied them. They were the hottest couple to ever walk the streets of New York, and though they had their many arguments, they were also the strongest and most powerful. Not to mention the wealthiest. They always did things with style and charm, and their kids were just about the cutest damn kids you'd ever lay your eyes on. They were also the best-dressed children in all of New York. But what could you expect, they were the children of Roxy and Frankie!

Want to know the best part of it all? Each and every one

of them continued on their roaring lives, and they all stayed best friends until the very end. They also never left New York. Sure, they were all constantly traveling all over the world, but their homes stayed in the city. The special six always got together for Thanksgiving, Christmas dinner, and of course, they always threw a grand New Year's Eve party. And Roxy continued her annual January soirée. They also continued to spend most summers in The Hamptons, when they weren't vacationing in Europe, California, or on some exotic Caribbean Island. Each of their lives were lived in absolute glamour and opulence, wealth and power, and most importantly, *love*. Their friendships with each other would always be one of their most treasured parts of life. They were constantly throwing parties, even when there was no occasion, and they would always be seen as Manhattan's best. And it all started with the lives they created for themselves in the Roaring Twenties.

Now, as for me, I know I said these stories were to be told through the narration of an outsider, but I'm no outsider at all. But who *am* I exactly? I'm sure you're rather curious.

Well—that's just it. I'm The Roaring itself.

The Roaring Twenties.

Now, once upon a time, not long ago, I began to tell you these stories of Roxy Elliott and her closest friends. The events and affairs that took place between the years 1925 and 1926. We dove headfirst into their busy and eventful lives. I've given you a summary of what their lives after The Roaring were like, but I'm sure you can imagine what the rest of the 1920s endured. Picturing and fantasizing about what went on through the rest of The Roaring. This is where I stop writing, however—where I leave the rest a mystery.

This, my friend, has been—

The Roaring.

The *Actual* End

EPILOGUE

September 1st, 1926

Dear Diary,

When is it that we are aware we have made a grave mistake? When is it that we are aware we have crossed the blurry line of morals?

Morally righteous ... or morally evil.

When is it that we come to realize we like the darker side, and are drawn to it.

Is it before or after we've already crossed that daring line. And what happens to the person we leave behind? Do we forget them? Do we forget they ever existed?

About

Ever since Tasi was a child, she loved to create. She thrived off of inventing new worlds and fictional universes that would remain in her mind and heart. Storytelling was always something Tasi had a passion for, and that passion grew as she got older. Her Nana was a beautiful writer, mostly writing poetry, and was someone Tasi looked up to. Tasi herself would often write poetry as a kid and short stories set in those fictional worlds she loved to dearly.

When she was fifteen, almost sixteen, she sparked the idea for The Roaring after watching Baz Luhrmann's The Great Gatsby. This was also around the same time she was watching Gossip Girl for the first time. Tasi imagined a world in which both of these universes collided and made what is now The Roaring; something along the lines of Gossip Girl meets The Great Gatsby. At sixteen, she began to write the novel after envisioning it first as a television show. Tasi began to develop the world of The Roaring and eventually completed it after graduating high school in 2020, when she had a lot more time on her hands to finish and publish the book herself.

While researching and learning how to bring The Roaring to print through the indie publishing route, she started her own publishing company Stormy House Press, and is excited to develop not only more of her own works, but someday bring along new, bright eyed and passionate young writers like herself. As for her cover design, Tasi knew she wanted an illustrator that would understand her vision and bring to life the design she had pictured in her mind, and that's when she brought on eighteen-year-old Jorden Salzmann, a fellow young and passionate creator who illustrated exactly what Tasi had envisioned.

Something that Tasi has always been passionate about is the idea that if you want something, you have to go and get it, regardless of your age or inexperience. It's not exactly common for a girl in high school to write a novel, then publish it soon after graduation, but that doesn't mean it's impossible; and it surely doesn't mean you shouldn't do it. Age is merely a number, and it should never hold you back from your dreams.